MY NAME IS JALAV!

I am woman and warrior, Chosen One of the goddess Mida, and leader of the fearless Midanna warriors.

Males I have conquered, both body and soul. Yet now must I join my army with theirs by the will of the goddess. And together we must best an unknown foe whom none alone can conquer, an enemy from beyond the stars, an enemy who can challenge even the power of the gods!

Jalav, Amazon Warrior: V

TO BATTLE
THE GODS

A NOVEL BY
SHARON GREEN

DAW BOOKS, INC.
DONALD A. WOLLHEIM, PUBLISHER

1633 Broadway, New York, NY 10019

First Printing, May 1986

1 2 3 4 5 6 7 8 9

PRINTED IN THE U.S.A.

CONTENTS

1.

An arrival— and a decision disputed

Mida's light touched me strongly where I sat upon my kan, not so strongly as it had in the lands of Midanna, yet sufficiently warming in what was, in truth, the land of males. The skies were bright and clear of clouds, the land all about us open and green, and beyond the rise of ground we had halted behind lay the city of Bellinard. I had returned at last to the place where my sister clans awaited me, warriors who would follow me into battle against the coming strangers, and I would have rejoiced at my return—had my humor not been so foul.

"Now comes Ennat," said Chaldrin from where he sat his own kan nearby; the rumble of his words did not intrude upon my thoughts. "As Wedin and Dotil accompany her, the wenches are likely all in their assigned places."

"More quickly than the legions of Sigurr," said S'Heernoh, amused, as he often was. The male who was called Walker sat his kan somewhat behind, his observation exceedingly soft, yet not so soft that I was unable to hear it. Few others would have had the courage to jest in my hearing just then, yet S'Heernoh always faced my displeasure with little more than innocent curiosity.

"Though the Sigurri are warriors, still they are no more than males," said Ilvin to S'Heernoh, amused herself. "Midanna are true warriors, and take the field of battle more swiftly and with greater eagerness."

"Not to speak of the fact that there are more than twice the number of Sigurri than Midanna," said Chaldrin calmly. "The Sword will see them properly deployed, and then he and Aysayn will join us as agreed. They undoubtedly give thanks, as do we, that this journey is done at last."

7

That this journey is done at last. Chaldrin's words caused me to consider the journey just completed and the manner in which it had begun. I, Jalav, once war leader of the Hosta clan of Midanna, had set out with my Hosta warriors to retrieve the Crystal of our goddess, stolen from us by northern males. First had there been the city of Bellinard, ruled then by males, a place where I and a small number of my warriors had been enslaved. It was there that Ceralt and Telion had bought me, two males with unspoken purposes of their own; we all ended at last in the city of Ranistard. After much struggle, the lives of my warriors lost at the time of the theft of the Crystal had been avenged, yet had our Crystal, and the one which should have been guarded by the Silla clan, and a previously unknown third, all been irretrievably lost to the males of Ranistard. They had placed the Crystals within a device of evil, a device supposedly of the Ancients, and the device could not again be made to release them.

I sighed at the memory of that doing, for the males had thought to use the device to speak with the gods, yet they reached beings they had not envisioned. Strangers were they, who claimed kinship with us, who then spoke of coming to "civilize" us in a manner unspecified, yet one which disturbed all who listened. The males had retired to discuss the matter, paying no mind to the Midanna warriors who were about, for the Hosta had been taken as captives by them, to be held and used as mere city slave-women.

And yet Jalav had shown that she was not one to be dismissed! Despite the agony of a lashing, I had escaped over the wall of Ranistard with the burning need to bring others to help free the sister Hosta, had survived, with the aid of the goddess Mida, wounds which should well have been crippling or fatal, had withstood, with great difficulty, the capture of Ceralt and his Belsayah riders, only to be at last brought before the goddess Mida to learn that the Hosta might not be freed. Jalav was meant to be war leader to all nine of the other clans of sister Midanna, and could succeed only if the Hosta remained captives, leaving Jalav as one who would not favor any clan above the others.

I shivered with the memory of my time with Mida. I had been brought to her by Ceralt, High Rider to those village males called Belsayah, he who had attempted to claim and hold me as his own, and had not known he moved to the will of the goddess. Ceralt thought to seek the aid of Sigurr, dark god of males, against the coming strangers, and therefore we had all journeyed to Sigurr's Peak and the altar which lay in the heart of it. Indeed we succeeded in finding the dark god, but his realm and Mida's lay side by side, and both god and goddess wished me to lead their warriors against the coming strangers.

With heavy heart yet fierce determination, I had led the nine clans of sister Midanna against Bellinard and had taken the city, then had I ridden to the land of the Sigurri, those male warriors who worshipped Sigurr as Midanna did Mida. In Bellinard I freed four Sigurri captives, for I had been told by Sigurr and Mida, they might lead me to their city so that I might raise their host to ride and fight beside Mida's. One of the four had been Mehrayn, a red-haired male of great strength and odd humor, who had proven to be a Prince of the Blood among the Sigurri, called Sigurr's Sword for he led the dark god's legions into battle. Again there had been difficulty, as well as capture and enslavement, during which Chaldrin had proven himself a true brother to me, yet we succeeded in returning Aysayn, the rightful Sigurr's Shadow, to his proper place where he had gladly obeyed Sigurr's will and pledged the city's legions to stand against the coming strangers.

It was then that I had learned that all of Mida's terms had not been met, that there was one additonal task I must attend to before I might return to my own. I had often called myself war leader to all Midanna, but at the time, that was simply not so. Without the Silla, who lay in capture to the males of Ranistard along with the Hosta, the clans of enemy Midanna also numbered nine. It became my task to assume the leader-ship of these Midanna as well, yet I could not ride toward their lands alone as I had wished to do. Each time I had turned about I had found another in my path, among them Mehrayn and Chaldrin and S'Heernoh. Mehrayn desired me as Ceralt had, Chaldrin had pledged himself to stand beside me in battle, and S'Heernoh—S'Heernoh had appeared from out of the forests, had joined our traveling set, and had given more assistance than he, unarmed, should have been able to do. Also was S'Heernoh a Walker, one who was able to reach the White Land and walk the Snows of what-shall-occur, and therefore had been able to aid those of the then-enemy clans as well. At last I had accomplished the will of the goddess and had become war leader to those who were no longer enemies, and then had they and I and the Sigurri legions and the males who led them, all made the journey to Bellinard, where the balance of my warriors waited.

The journey had now been completed, though we could not have anticipated it.

"Had this journey continued for many feyd more, the numbers to reach this place would have been considerably fewer," said Ilvin. "Never had I envisioned such difficulty as that which arose when Midanna and Sigurri attempted to ride beside one another. They are males, I know, and therefore as strange as all males, yet I had not expected their strangeness to engulf warriors as well."

"It could not have occurred otherwise," said S'Heernoh, with a sigh. "The wenches, never having had men in such numbers available to them, happily sought to avail themselves of the bounty, seeking all about for those who would please them most. The men, eager themselves for the taste of wenches who were also warriors, vied for their attention as though they were boys just become aware of their manhood. That two or more men would come to hard words over a single wench was inevitable, as inevitable as some men's belief that they might take what wench they wished. That no more than two score were wounded or killed because of those hard words is truly the thing to be wondered at, for I would surely have expected more. What number were lost in attempts to use force, I have no idea."

"Nearly two hands of males and four warriors," said I in a growl. "All save three of the males were seen to by the warriors they considered no more than city slave-women; the rest ended by Mehrayn and Aysayn when they learned of the harm given the young warrior who was made to serve them. Three of the warriors who attempted to force the use of Sigurri were ended by those Sigurri, the fourth I saw to myself when I saw the deep humiliation and fury of the male, and the laughter of the warrior who cared naught that he

could not bring himself to raise weapon to her even in
vengeance. No other stood with her in her arrogance though
she called upon them as sisters, and her efforts to keep my
point from her flesh were equally unsuccessful. Go and see
what those about the city do now, Ilvin.''

"They do as they have done for the past hin," came the
voice of Ennat as she drew rein beside me, as calm as
Chaldrin. Large was this Ennat, brown-haired and brown-
eyed and newly come to the position of Keeper of the clans
which had so lately been enemies to those whom I led. That I
rode in Mida's name was clear to her, as clear as her gladness
that her clans now did the same. Her Keeper's covering,
ankle-length as befitted her station and of all the colors of her
clans, hiked up high upon her thighs to allow her a seat upon
the kan she rode. Always impatient, Ennat the Keeper did not
indulge in the niceties of her new office; rather than allowing
herself to be carried about upon a Keeper's seat, she straddled
a kan and rode where she willed.

"Are we not yet prepared to ride forth and brace those who
lay siege to the city?" asked Ennat, sounding more like a
warrior than a Keeper. "For what reason do we delay?"

"We must await the arrival of Aysayn and Mehrayn," said
I, calming the dancing of my kan with a stroking hand to his
neck. "To advance unnecessarily before all of one's forces
are properly placed would be foolish. I will not be delayed in
reaching the city because of fearful attack from those we will
ride toward."

"The males remain encamped, Jalav," said Ilvin, for she
had crept to the crest of the hill to observe those about the
city. Her long, pale hair was cinched by war leather, as was
mine and each Midanna who rode with us including Ennat,
and the blue of her clan colors about her hips was sharp
against the green of the grass she lay upon. Her Hitta blue
was somewhat different than the Summa blue upon Wedin
and Dotil, but clan differences were forgotten in the face of
the unity Midanna now enjoyed.

"A knot of the males seem prepared to approach more
closely to the walls of the city," said Ilvin, her light eyes
keen. "Should they be foolish enough to attack, they will
learn that those within have little need of the force which

rides with us. I see forms upon the walls, clearly Midanna,
yet can't make out their clan.''

"We will learn soon," said S'Heernoh, his words drawing
my eyes to his tall, lean, gray-haired form. "The Prince of
Sigurr's Sword and Sigurr's Shadow now approach.''

His words were truth, for beyond him, to our left, I was
able to see Mehrayn and Aysayn riding calmly toward us.
The two Sigurri, the first red-haired and green-eyed, the
second light-haired and brown-eyed, both large and well-
made, rode leisurely, which annoyed me. Behind them were
the two Sigurri warriors, Gidain and Rinain, who had ridden
with my set from their city, all four seeming to ride just to
pass the hind of an otherwise idle fey. I was tempted to berate
the males, but that would only have delayed us further.
Though the males had earned the right to be named brother to
me, supreme war leader, still were they, above all else, male.

"Our legions will not show themselves save at our signal," said Aysayn as he and the others joined our set, his
dark eyes filled with satisfaction. "And, as I see by the
presence of Ennat, Wedin and Dotil that the wenches have
also been deployed, there is little reason for us to remain
behind the shoulder of this rise. Let us advance now, and
learn for what reason those men besiege the city and the
wenches within it.''

"Their reasons may well relate to the coming strangers,"
said I, frowning thoughtfully. "Yet how knowledge came to
them concerning the place the strangers would appear I know
not, for Mida spoke directly to me. Much do I doubt that
Mida would have spoken to them in the same manner.''

"Indeed, your goddess Mida speaks to few beyond her
own Midanna," said Mehrayn, seeming amused. "Little does
she give others, save perhaps an occasional boon.''

My annoyance flared at his amusement, an amusement I
had had far too much of in the previous feyd. My humor had
grown so foul during the journey just past that I would have
welcomed battle of any sort, even beyond a Midanna's ever-
present eagerness for it. Had the male been raised properly as
a Midanna warrior, he would not have refused my need to
bare blades considering even my vow that no more than first
blood would be spilled. His refusal had remained adamant

and his amusement undiminished, and no other had there been among Midanna and Sigurri who might reasonably have faced me with a skill near to my own, save for Aysayn and Chaldrin. Aysayn, he who was called Sigurr's Shadow, might well have been convinced to join what he termed sport, yet had Mehrayn spoken a refusal for him, and he had abided by the wishes of his brother. Chaldrin, unlike the others, truly a brother to me, would have faced me had I asked it of him, yet I refrained from asking. Despite his undeniable skill I felt I had already taken the measure of Chaldrin, and to do so again would have brought little pleasure.

"They most certainly could not have learned of the thing from the Snows," said S'Heernoh, sounding sour at the thought of the efforts he and I had wasted in attempting to reach the White Land. "Once again does that damnable fog cover the paths of that-which-is-coming-to-be, barring all from looking upon it. I dislike this, lady war leader, for I feel it greatly unwise to continue on in so bold a manner while we are blinded and bound. Perhaps it would be best if we were to bide our time, observing these others unseen the while, and then consider. . . ."

"We ride now," said I, not dissuaded, my eyes fixed only on the path which would take me forward and on toward the meeting with the strangers. This, the coming battle, was the last of the duty demanded of me by the gods, the last I would consider attempting. Were I to survive the battle, no longer would I be chosen, no longer would there be so great a number of others looking to me for leadership. Jalav would be Jalav's alone, to ride and do as she wished, to concern herself with neither gods nor warriors nor males. No delay to this end would I brook, no words of male-like caution would I allow to slow me, for males were well-known to dither and delay, as true warriors rode ahead boldly.

Rather than await further converse I put heels to my kan and moved ahead, finding that Ennat, Ilvin, Wedin, Dotil and Chaldrin accompanied me without hesitation. Ilvin had re-claimed her kan and rode beside Chaldrin, her hand going briefly to her sword to loosen it in its scabbard, her position to Chaldrin's left, where she might guard the male were we to abruptly find ourselves in the midst of battle. The male, of a size with Mehrayn and Aysayn, dark of hair and eye and powerfully built as warriors were not, smiled faintly at Ilvin's doing and made no attempt to deny it. Though he knew as well as I that his blade skill far outstripped that of Ilvin, he would not dismiss the Hitta's concern for him with a mere gesture of amusement. The protection offered by a Midanna warrior would be accepted in the spirit in which it was given, though no other males save Sigurri seemed able to do likewise. To all others Midanna warriors were wenches, a foolish male notion they would soon be abused of.

Before the brow of the rise was topped, our full set rode together. Aysayn and Mehrayn seemed concerned by the disturbance of S'Heernoh, yet not to so great an extent that they spoke of it. All eyes joined mine in looking ahead toward those whose ranks we approached, those males who had camped about the city in demand unknown to us. To our right were the males from the city of Galiose, the city Ranistard where the Hosta lay captive and unable to free themselves. Thigh-length coverings of cloth in many colors did these males wear, and among them moved those of Galiose's guard who were clad in metal and leather above their coverings. Most of them continued to sit and lie about the camp they had made, inert, no expectation that soon they would be called into battle. They lazed beneath the warmth of Mida's light, some attempting to follow what occurred nearer to the city, most more concerned with feeding.

To our left was the second force which had come to that place uninvited, a force different from the first. Clad in leathers were these males, silver belts glinting and flashing in the light, many bare-chested in the warmth they were surely unaccustomed to. Belsayah riders they were, and perhaps Neelarhi riders as well, those from the villages to the far north, those who followed Ceralt and Lialt. Those from Ranistard held my sister Hosta in captivity, and had held me as well; those from the villages had looked upon my capture among them as right and fitting, even honorable. Had my humor been sweet and light-hearted to begin with, surely would sight and memory of those males have turned it foul and black as Sigurr's soul. My left hand closed about the reins I held, forcing the thick leather into my palm and fingers, the distant knowledge of pain aiding me in keeping my right hand from my sword hilt. Were I to attack those males as I so achingly wished to do, the Midanna at my back and those in the city would surely join me, and at the moment I could not allow that. It remained necessary to consider the coming strangers, yet it would not be necessary to do so forever.

A space of surprising size separated the two forces, as though they who camped with a single purpose nevertheless did so as reluctant allies, and it was this space toward which we rode. A good deal of movement was to be found in both camps, some moving about on foot, some riding upon kand or lanthay, few looking about behind themselves, for where would come a force able to threaten them? Males are foolish, most especially in their smug assumption of superiority despite evidence to the contrary; my set was already within the space and riding toward those who led the two forces before most were even aware of our presence. That we rode briskly and with purpose yet not in attack set them to staring rather than preparing for defense, and their foolishness brought a curl to my lip even as Ennat snorted in scorn. Does one stand behind those one follows, purportedly guarding the back of one's leader, and allow strangers to approach without challenge? Does one assume that a small force is not the vanguard of a larger force without carefully looking about? The males we rode past were, like all males, thoughtless and foolish and completely lacking in all battle knowledge, fit only for standing aside while true warriors saw to the safety of all.

Nearly had we reached the front of the host before any thought to bar our way. Two hands of leather-and-metal-clad males ran from our right, an equal number of village riders appeared to our left, and no longer was there a clear path to those we sought. The males stood with swords drawn, grimly challenging our right to advance farther, mindlessly discounting the fact that we were mounted and they on foot. I considered showing them how badly they would fare against mounted, galloping attackers without the aid of spears, however I did not come to battle with them. If we had to engage them before we faced the strangers, they would learn soon enough.

"Halt!" shouted one of Ranistard, standing somewhat ahead of his set, obviously outraged as he looked at Aysayn and Mehrayn, who rode to my left. "Who are you, and what do you do here?"

"We seek Galiose and Ceralt," said I, drawing the male's eyes as we slowed and halted not far from him, the others making no attempt to respond. "Should you wish to inform them of our presence, you may do so; if not, step from our path so that we may announce ourselves."

"I know you, wench," said the male in a tone of impatient dismissal. "Even if I could not see you, your arrogance would shine forth clearly. The High Seat will deal with you in his own good time, and till then you will remain silent. You there, you men! Who are you, and for what reason do you come here?"

Aysayn and Mehrayn grinned with the amusement of children of the wild before the launching of feral attack. To my right, Ennat growled deep in her throat, keeping herself silent only through warrior strength. Chaldrin sat with his big hand about the arm of Ilvin, lending his calm to ease her fury. Had my Midanna not been warned of the insolent, insulting words which would likely be addressed to me, surely would battle have been joined upon the moment. Such a doing I had refused to them and to those others who rode with us, for there were matters of greater moment than insult before us.

"They come here in company with me," said I to the male, letting him know that I alone would speak for my set. "Will you inform Galiose of our presence, or must the High Seat discover us through his own efforts?"

"The High Seat will find great delight in discovering *you*, wench," returned the male in a growl, his gaze having once again returned to me. "There is much yet to be given you for the difficulty you caused him, and wise would you have been had you continued fleeing from us. The High Seat is not a man to be denied his due."

With such words did the male address Jalav, war leader of the Hosta and of all the Midanna, chosen of Mida and the dark god Sigurr, she who had raised the legions of Sigurr to ride to battle beside the warriors of Mida. When in capture in Ranistard it had been necessary to swallow such insult for I

had been unarmed; no longer was the war leader Jalav unarmed, no longer did she have the patience for swallowing
insult. Slowly yet with great deliberation did I allow my
yellow and brown kan to dance forward till I stood no more
than a pace from the male, and then looked down upon him.

"Jalav has ever been willing to give males their due," said
I with great softness, holding his gaze as a frown formed
upon his brow. "Have you skill with that weapon you hold in
your fist, male, or do you merely wave it about in an attempt
to frighten? When one speaks words of insult and challenge,
one had best be prepared to stand behind those words with
sword in hand."

"I see," said the male with an impatient nod, his fist
tightening about the hilt he held. "You now have men upon
whom to call, therefore do you feel free to increase your
insolence with other men. So you believe a captain of the
High Seat's guard would refuse challenge, do you? Learn,
then, how greatly you err. Which of you men mean to face
me?"

The male had turned his demand toward Mehrayn, Aysayn
and Chaldrin, glaring about at them as though it had been
they and not I who had spoken of challenge, leaving me to
look upon him with a lack of understanding. The male did not
seem prepared to refuse challenge, and yet he looked about at
others rather than toward she who had issued that challenge. I
had allowed my temper free rein so that I might more quickly
win our way through the obstruction in our path, in no
manner expecting confusion to ensnare me more strongly than
would the presence of eight hands of males rather than four.
Behind me Chaldrin's deep chuckle sounded softly, oddly
joined by the same from Aysayn and Mehrayn, and curiosity
gave voice to my confusion.

"For what reason do you look toward others of my set?" I
asked, seeing the male before me also appear confused,
seemingly at the amusement of the three Sigurri. "Should
you feel that those others would be bested more easily than I,
allow me to assure you that you are mistaken. Although they
are male, they are warriors as well, and easily able to best
any who stand before them. You gain naught by seeking to
face them rather than this warrior."

"You believe I would face a female?" demanded the male, outrage so thick upon him as he glared at me that those who had chuckled earlier now did so again. "Even were there sufficient females about so that all men might have their own, still would I refuse to face one over a sword! You and your wenches are arrogant and insolent and greatly in need of firm punishment, girl, yet to be sworded is not to be punished. And even were it so, I would not slay the one my woman has such great regard for; such a thing would sit ill between us."

Still did the male glare upon me with anger, now firmed to decision. Within me I felt the surge of anger which ever came at the belief of males that Jalav would fall before them, yet was the anger this time smothered beneath the ache of another thing.

"You—are one of those who hold a Hosta?" I asked, also finding myself startled. I had not thought any save hunters and some few warriors had taken the Hosta, none of those of the metal-and-leather ilk among them. The male gazed deeply into my eyes at the query, and faintly did a smile touch his lips.

"The wench became mine when the hunter who had brought her to our city gave up all claim to her," said he, the memory deepening his amusement. "He had attempted to teach her to obey him, had not succeeded, and had grown weary of hearing his lacks recited by the High Seat. As I had no woman of my own I requested and was granted her, and immediately began teaching her the manner in which a man and a wench might live together with peace between them."

"Aided, no doubt, by a lash," said I, my words turned bitter at memory of my own time in Ranistard, the pain and shame and thought of captivity without end—and Nolthis, he to whom I had been given after Ceralt had been put out of the city, he who had also been called captain of the High Seat's guard. My kan danced uneasily as my knees tightened about his barrel; I was so furious that the palm of my hand ached to hold a hilt. So great was my need to face that Nolthis again, that it was nearly as great as my need to free the Hosta. That the Hosta must await my victory over the coming strangers before freedom might once again be theirs was demanded by

Mida, and likely this facing of Nolthis would be delayed as well. Once the strangers were seen to, however. . . .

"The lashing you were given by command of the High Seat should not have been, wench," said the male, no longer amused. "This was spoken of by Galiose himself, his regret clear to those of us he addressed. He. . . ."

"His regret will not be truly clear till he and I have spoken of the matter," said I, unwilling to hear words of should-not-have-been. There had been full agony for me in my refusal to heed the commands of Galiose, and to speak of that agony as given in error did not remove its memory. I would have his life for the doing or he would have mine, and the knowledge of this was surely in my eyes for the male to see. The swordpoint he had allowed to fall was abruptly before him again, his visage paled somewhat as he backed a step. His lips parted, to speak words of denial of my intent, I think, yet another spoke before him.

"And of what will our converse consist?" asked the voice, strength and calm and ease of command to be heard in it. "Will it be said that the lashing need not have been, had a stubborn she-gando merely retreated a pace or two from that stubbornness? Will such a truth be mentioned, wench?"

Galiose pushed himself through the growing number of males who had gathered and stood before them, others of his metal-and-leather-clad males following behind. Large was the High Seat of Ranistard, dark-eyed and broad with much male strength, his long dark hair bound at the back of his neck in the manner of male warriors of the cities, the blue of his covering and leather marking him as leader to those of his city, the metal upon him and the well-worn hilt of his weapon marking him as one who was no stranger to battle. His hands rested upon his swordbelt as his eyes held mine, and well did I recall that gaze as he took in the black of my eyes and thigh-length hair, the bareness of my breasts, the breech I wore beneath my swordbelt, the dagger in my leg bands about which was wrapped the leather of my life sign, the lack of a leather city-male seat upon the kan I bestrode—though the male looked up he clearly looked down as well, seeing naught save the wench he had named me and truly believed me to be. As I thought of the time I would be free to face him, I felt my hand curl to a fist.

"You speak the truth," said I to Galiose, aware that those who accompanied me now moved their kand to where mine stood. "It is true that this Midanna refused your commands and was therefore lashed, yet is it also true that I could not have done otherwise. Did I not come to you of my own will, acknowledging you the war leader who held my oath of fealty? Did I not offer you the right of challenge, the sole manner in which a war leader might be made to obey another? As you refused the challenge, you also forfeited all right to command, therefore was there no more than deceit in the lashing. One must pay for deceit, Galiose, in the manner in which you shall pay."

"Have you never heard of the rights of capture, girl?" said the male, annoyance in his tone, no notice taken of the balance of my words. "You and yours lay in capture to me and mine, therefore obedience was required of you. In the absence of obedience, punishment—a punishment which might easily have been avoided had you not striven so diligently to show how slight was the respect you afforded me."

"One gives respect to those who do not fear to earn that respect with a sword," said I, seeing the flash of anger in the dark of his eyes. "To give obedience in captivity is to be a slave, and never shall Jalav be a slave. For what reason have you left the safety of your city's walls to visit this place? There are things which must soon be done, and the aid of you and yours is not required."

"The High Seat of Ranistard goes where he wills!" returned Galiose harshly aware of my attempt to provoke him. Mida might well have been angered if I paused to slay the male, yet were he to attack this Midanna, I must respond in kind. "I scarcely had need of further difficulties in these times of ill, yet did those from the farms hereabout call upon me to free their city from they knew not what. Now that I see you, wench, and other wenches upon the walls, surely do I begin to believe— Had you grown so fond of dwelling in a city, more easily might you have remained in mine."

"Should one be so foolish as to wish to dwell within walls," said I, seeing the depth of the look he gave me, "best is to find walls of one's own. There was little difficulty in taking this place, yet may you set your mind to rest. We mean to remain no more than a short while longer, and then will the city be returned to those who dwell within it. You may now take your males and depart."

"May I indeed," said Galiose with a growl, advancing another step toward me, his dark eyes bright with anger. "And should it be my wish to see this city returned to its own upon the moment? For how long will those within find it possible to remain, should we disallow hunting parties to emerge? In the two feyd we have already been here, none have come forth to hunt, neither have the farm herds been driven in to market. Should the need arise to do battle, how well will your wenches fare on empty bellies? And what number of them hold that city? As many as half the number of those who follow me? Look around you, girl."

Indeed did I allow my gaze to rove about among those who came with Galiose, confirming my previous estimate of the number of those who followed him. The High Seat had perhaps half again the number of those who awaited me within the city, less than the total force of Midanna I led. Many of those males I was able to see more closely were clearly slighter than those in leather and metal who, I had learned, were little enough themselves. The males about me seemed more prepared for camping than battle, and small difficulty would I have found in leading those who had once been enemy clans against them. My gaze brushed Ennat, who sat her kan to my right, and amusement shone in the dark of her eyes as she saw my own faint smile. Well she knew any battle would be ours, and eager would be the blades of the warriors of her clans.

"I suggest that you withdraw your wenches immediately, girl," said Galiose, a heavy satisfaction now to be heard from him. "When they emerge from the city they must surrender their weapons, and then we shall see what is to be done with all of you."

"Midanna do not surrender," I remarked, continuing to take note of the doings of the males who were encamped to my right. The small number of spears I was able to see amused me, so male-like was the lack. "Your numbers are scarcely as impressive as you believe, male, scarcely great enough to bring about consideration of dismissal concerning battle.''

"And yet his numbers are enhanced by mine," came another voice, disallowing me the opportunity of suggesting that Galiose himself consider surrender. "As my forces are even greater in number than his, you shall indeed dismiss all consideration of battle.''

There was little haste in the manner in which I turned back to regard the one who had spoken, the one whose appearance I had known would come. Ceralt had come up to stand not far from Galiose, his large, broad body clad in the leathers of those who followed him, his silvered belt gleaming in Mida's light, a swordbelt clasped about him below it. Firmly were his booted feet planted upon the ground; in his eyes, the look of command, a lock of dark hair, as ever, falling toward those eyes. Had I not known he would appear I would surely have shamed myself voicing a sound of pain at sight of him, a sight I had hungered for so often since we had parted in Mida's realm upon this world. While there, I had sent him word that we would not meet again save above the blades of our swords, and although I had since learned what pain he had accepted to keep similar pain from touching me, I had come to the decision that to speak of my knowledge before the battle with the coming strangers was joined and ended would be foolish. Ceralt would not stand in that battle, yet *my* sword would be well occupied. To speak sooner upon that which might well be ended by an enemy edge would be foolishness indeed.

"Your arrival is most timely, Ceralt," said Galiose, gazing with strong satisfaction not upon the male beside him, but upon me. "The foolish wench again contemplates disobedience, and requires a strong hand to teach her better.''

"My thanks are yours for having notified me of her arrival, Galiose," said Ceralt, his eyes, too, only upon me, his arms folded across his chest. "Many feyd gone, Lialt informed me that I would discover her here, yet the Snows are no longer accessible to him. As I now have what I came for, my riders and I will withdraw as quickly as you no longer require our support. When we have discovered the location of the battle

to come with those who threaten us, I will be certain that you
are informed."

"For that you will have my gratitude, Ceralt," said Galiose,
a flicker of trimness briefly darkening his eyes. "We must all
stand together in these times, else shall none of us survive.
You shall now call your wenches from out the city, girl, and
then you may depart with the man who has made you his. As
he means to speak sternly with you concerning the manner in
which you disobediently left his side, I shall not find it
necessary to do the same concerning the manner in which you
departed my city. You will be occupied quite enough with
what is given you by him."

The male seemed amused as he spoke, an amusement
shared by those who stood with Ceralt. Lialt, Ceralt's brother
by blood and Pathfinder for him, and Telion, male warrior
from Ranistard who had joined his fate with Ceralt's, stood
grinning with their eyes upon me, likely recalling the difficulty given me by them during the journey we had shared.
That Ceralt felt more anger than amusement gave them greater
amusement still, yet I, too, recalled our journey together and
felt no amusement whatsoever.

"Jalav is already well occupied," said I coldly to Galiose,
ignoring the others. "There are matters of import to be seen
to, and the presence of pretend warriors would be a hindrance, therefore shall you command your males to return
from whence they came. You shall do so immediately, for
there is little time to be spent upon foolishness of this sort."

"Pretend warriors?" demanded Galiose, furiously. "You
dare to speak so to *me*? I am the High Seat of Ranistard with
fifteen hundred men behind me, girl! Beside me is the Belsayah
High Rider with nearly two thousand! What number of men
do *you* command?"

"For what reason would I wish to command males?" I
asked, with private amusement. "Your greatness turns me
humble in your presence, Galiose, for I am no more than war
leader to every Midanna who rides. The command of males
should be left to other males."

At my earlier nod, Ennat had raised a fisted hand in
prearranged signal, bringing to sight those Midanna who
waited behind us. Clan after clan rode their gandod to the top

of the rise, pausing there in anticipation of the signal to attack, their clan colors bright, their eagerness impossible to dismiss. A mutter went up all about as those before me stared in frowning shock, and when their eyes returned to me another shock awaited them.

"The wench does indeed believe in leaving the command of men to other men," said Aysayn from his place to my left, also amused. "However, as she is the chosen messenger of Sigurr the great, we feel it only fitting that Sigurr's legions stand with her own."

The fist of Mehrayn was already in the air, bringing forth the Sigurri as the Midanna had been done. More than twice the number of Midanna were they, black body cloths wrapped about their loins, kand dancing beneath them, battle-readiness and delight clear in every line of them. Far longer did the Sigurri take the stares of those before us than had the Midanna, and then did Ceralt turn cold and frowning pools of blue upon Aysayn and Mehrayn.

"Who are you?" he demanded, the words nearly a growl, his anger strangely great. "From where do you come?"

"I am Aysayn," said Aysayn, taking no note of Ceralt's displeasure, "he who is Sigurr's Shadow upon this world. We come from our homelands at the behest of Sigurr himself."

"And I am Mehrayn, Sigurr's Sword and Prince of the Blood, he who is privileged to lead our warriors into battle," said Mehrayn, an odd expression holding him as he looked down upon Ceralt. "Your journey has been for naught, High Rider of the Belsayah, therefore would you be wise to depart as quickly as may be."

"Ceralt, they are warriors of Signurr, the aid we must have against the coming strangers!" said Lialt eagerly to his brother as he looked upon the Sigurri. "Our journey to Sigurr's Altar has borne the fruit we require."

"Such is to be seen," said Ceralt in a mutter, his stance straightened to his full height, his left palm caressing his sword hilt as he held the green gaze sent him by Mehrayn. "For what reason would they appear here, before the gates of a wench-taken city, rather than at the place of appearance of the strangers? How might they—"

His words, spoken half in annoyance, ended abruptly, and then he frowned at Aysayn.

"You come here at the behest of Sigurr himself, were the words you spoke," said he to Aysayn, palm no longer upon sword hilt. "Is this, then, the place where the strangers will appear? Have we all been sent here by the gods to welcome them in the sole manner they must be welcomed?"

"My sister has been informed by her lady Mida that this is the place they will appear," affirmed Aysayn. "As for the gods having brought you others to this spot, that is surely unlikely in the extreme. What need of others, when Sigurri and Midanna ride side by side?"

"You would have *wenches* do battle beside you?" demanded Galiose, glaring in outrage at Aysayn. "For battle a man requires other men like himself, not wenches with half the force of his own!"

"The city contains the balance of my Midanna," said I. I had not expected the words Aysayn had spoken, and they had warmed me for the insult they returned to those who had given it to me. "In the city is a matching force to that which you see before you, therefore need you be unconcerned with what number of Midanna shall ride. You may have what hind you require to take your followers from here, yet would it be best if you used no more than the hind of this fey. The new fey may well bring the strangers, and little joy shall you find should you discover yourself between them and the warriors come to slay them."

"You shall not dismiss us!" shouted Galiose in a rage, and, "I care not what number of Midanna ride!" shouted Ceralt upon the words of Galiose, and then was all further sense lost to their shoutings, although in truth there was little sense to begin with. Lialt and Telion shouted as well, as did certain of those with Galiose, and our kand danced in upset at the mindless uproar. Aysayn glanced briefly toward Mehrayn before shaking his head, and then did he lean the nearer to me.

"Agreement is hopeless in surroundings such as these," said he, his voice raised above the deafening din. "We must take them into the city with us, and there convince them to step back from doings which do not concern them."

"Sooner would I leave them here to shout to the skies,"
said I with a headshake, greatly displeased with so foolishly
male a suggestion. "We have not the time to tickle and coax
them."

"Would you prefer that they come at us in affronted
attack?" Sigurr's Shadow maintained, reasonably. "No, you
need not answer for I know you well enough, and also know
that we would have little difficulty in besting them. The point
I would have you see, sister, is the question of what number
of us will be required to best the strangers. Should we lose
even a dozen of those who follow us, in a battle which need
not be, will it be the lack of that dozen which gives victory to
our enemies rather than to ourselves? May we risk such an
outcome when it need not be?"

So earnestly open was Aysayn's gaze upon me, that I knew
at once he sought to snare me. I looked at him loweringly,
unable to deny the words he spoke—as he had known would
be the case—and yet hesitated to give him the agreement he
wished. I had been disturbed by the manner in which Ceralt
had looked upon me and the words he had uttered, and I had
no wish to allow him entrance to the city. It was Bellinard in
which he and Telion had traded for me as a slave, and
memory of the time angered me.

"Should you wish them within, *brother*, you may take
them there yourself," I replied after a moment, the previous
foulness of my humor returning two-fold. "I shall have naught
to do with them, for I have already had more of their presence than ever I wished. They are city males, not warriors,
and know naught of the proper manner in which to address a
war leader. I have no desire to treat with them and shall not."

"Do you wish them to believe you fear them?" asked
Aysayn in the softest of voices, his hand upon my shoulder
keeping me from turning my kan toward the city gates.
"They will see your refusal in no other light, wench, and I
would not have you appear so before them."

"Indeed do I fear them," said I to Aysayn, looking upon
him so sourly that he grinned. "I fear that what assurances of
safety are given them will be spat upon by my probable loss
of patience with their foolishness, and guest-blood will stain
the floors all about. Should it be your wish to see your word

broken in such a manner, so be it. The word will not be mine.''

"I shall rely upon my sister's honor to see that her brother's word is kept,'' said he with gentle laughter. "And should you be wise, wench, you will allow Mehrayn to return to your furs. When out of your sight, his humor is as foul as yours. The need of each of you to see to those who follow may now be put aside for a time.''

Rather than allowing me opportunity for finding insult in his words, the Mida-forsaken male turned from me and held a hand up, attempting to stem the flow of rantings which continued to pour from Galiose and Ceralt and their ilk. Those before us paid little heed to his attempt, however, therefore it was necessary for him to add to the uproar.

"Hear my words!'' said he in a voice which carried over the shouts and rumblings, drawing the eyes of those to whom he wished to speak. Though the shouts abated the rumblings continued, yet was Aysayn able to speak above them.

"The war leader of the Midanna and I have conferred, and now ask you to join us in the city her wenches hold,'' said he, his eyes going first to Galiose and then to Ceralt. "There we may take our ease the while we discuss the path the gods wish us to tread, with cups of falar to aid our agreement. Each of you may be accompanied by a hand of those who follow you, and you will, of course, have our word as to your safety. How say you?''

"I say I will require more,'' growled Galiose. "Once I accepted safe conduct from that wench, and discovered only after I had entered her coils that safe conduct failed to include the right to depart when I willed it. Is this instance to be the same?''

"You will not be detained beyond your decision to depart,'' said Aysayn, a twinkle of amusement in the glance he sent to me. "Do you accept our offer?''

"To confer?'' said Galiose, with a belligerent set of his jaw. "Certainly. Beyond that, I foresee little agreement. I will have my kan brought.''

"And you?'' asked Aysayn of Ceralt, drawing the dark-haired male's gaze from the war leader. "Is it your decision to join us as well?''

"Oh, indeed," said Ceralt with a judicious nod, folding his arms as he gave the Sigurri his full attention. "I shall certainly join you, if for no other reason than to—confer."

Aysayn nodded, well pleased with the agreement he had received, yet I was considerably less pleased. My head was filled full of the need to consider countless things before the appearance of the strangers, yet was there now a prior need to calm the insult of city males. Sooner would I have faced them in battle, yet Aysayn had spoken sooth and I would not put our victory in jeopardy when it might be avoided. I merely sat my kan in silence and awaited the fetching of mounts for the others, at last recalling the need to send word to the clans behind me of my intentions. Wedin and Dotil were returned to their sisters with the command that the clans were to remain alert yet do nothing more unless attacked, and then were Gidain and Rinain returned to the Sigurri by Mehrayn with similar directions. By then were our—guests—mounted; therefore did I lead them all toward the gates of Bellinard.

2.

Discussions— and a doing of fools

The gates of the city were opened when we had approached near enough, allowing us to enter by twos. Ennat rode beside me as I passed through first, she looking in open curiosity at what lay within the walls, pleased by the sight of the Midanna who awaited us. With the rose of the Hunda was the violet of the Homma, Palar and Gidon directing their clans as was fitting. The two war leaders greeted me with joyous shouts, and once our entire set was within the gates and they closed again and barred, the two came to stand before my kan.

"We have sent a runner to inform the others of your return, Jalav," said Gidon, her green eyes filled with pleasure as she tossed her heavy, golden hair. "All has gone well for us in your absence, and has clearly done the same for you. The males, we saw, have come to stand with us."

"Also have we seen another thing," said Palar, stroking the neck of my kan while her eyes rested upon Ennat. "The enemy clans ride as well? They showed themselves at your signal, it seemed; can it be they follow you as we do?"

"It was Mida's will that they do so," said I, pleased to once again be among my own. "This is Ennat, Keeper to those who are no longer enemy to us, and I have brought her here so that she and Rilas might speak."

"The Keeper will surely be awaiting your arrival at the overlarge dwelling, Jalav," Palar said with a nod as she and Gidon backed a pace from my kan. "We give Mida our thanks that you have returned, and will hear the tale of your journeying when our presence here is no longer required."

"And perhaps share a cup or two of daru," said I, more than warmed by their welcome. "There is much to speak of before the arrival of the strangers."

I turned my kan from them and once again led the way, through the narrow, choking, smooth-stoned paths that were city ways. Surprisingly there were many city folk about, keeping themselves from the gate and warrior doings, yet frankly staring. They gestured boldly and spoke curiously among themselves, male and female alike, little ones running here and there among their elders. They buzzed with questions as we rode among them, clearly sharing an excitement of sorts, eager as though they, too, anticipated glorious battle. These city folk had not seemed the same when last I had ridden among them, and I knew not what had brought such change to them.

The narrow city ways took us through the city, and then did they widen to pass larger, more isolated dwellings, grander by far than those which stood one upon the other. A distance ahead of us was visible the largest dwelling of them all, the dwelling which had once belonged to the High Seat of Bellinard, the dwelling which now housed my Midanna. Here and there among the city folk had I seen Midanna warriors, their hands raised in greeting as I passed, their faces grinning, their attention sought by many of those about them who clearly meant to question them. Again I had been uncomprehending, for the city folk had shown no fear of those warriors, and had I had no other thoughts to occupy me, I would surely have spent many reckid in wondering.

At last we came to the overlarge dwelling called the Palace of the High Seat, seeing the orange of the Hersa and the gold of the Hulna where those warriors stood guard at the city's second gate, not far from the dwelling. Before the dwelling itself was an expanse reached by many steps, white against the pink of the dwelling, now well peopled by Midanna warriors, in their van no other than Rilas. Our Keeper remained tall and straight, yet were there streaks of white in her golden hair, showing the number of kalod she had held the honor of her office. Her long covering contained all the colors of our clans, and her thin face smiled greeting as I drew rein and slid from the back of my kan.

"So, Jalav, once again you return to us with victory in your hand," said she, her voice warm and filled with great pleasure and pride. "Truly are you a daughter of Mida, blessed many times over by the mother of us all."

I gave my kan to the Helda warrior who happily stood awaiting the honor of tending the mount of one so well loved by Mida, and mounted the steps to where Rilas awaited me. Had I been less pleased to be among my own again, it would have been considerably more difficult to return Rilas's smile.

"Blessed is she who has those she may return to, those with whom she may share her victories," said I to Rilas, putting my hand to her shoulder as she put hand to mine. "I bring with me a new sister, Rilas, one of many new sisters whose presence I relish. I would have you know Ennat, once of the Sidda, now Keeper to all of her clans."

"I give you welcome, sister," said Rilas to Ennat, who had climbed the steps to stand beside me. Larger even than I was Ennat, and she returned the smile Rilas gave with even greater warmth.

"I am honored to stand before you, Keeper of those who were once enemy to us," said Ennat, speaking in a voice smaller than usual. "The heart and wisdom of Rilas have long been known of among all Midanna, even those who looked to another as Keeper. I would learn what I might from you, Keeper, so that I, too, may bring comfort and aid to the warriors about me."

"I have no doubt that you already bring such comfort and aid, Keeper," said Rilas, with a gentle amusement in her eyes. "You are welcome to stand beside me, Ennat, to see that we all abide by the will of Mida—as does Jalav, for whom the will of Mida seems to be a demand that she surround herself with larger and larger numbers of males. The four you departed with have now become considerably more, Jalav. Have your needs grown so large that you require such a number?"

"Some blessings have their dark side as well, Rilas," said I, aware of the greater amusement within her as she allowed her gaze to acknowledge those who rode in my wake. "It has been my lot to find myself among males without number, a doing I would have quickly ended had it not been demanded of me. There are others I would have you know, those who are indeed male, yet who have proven themselves something more."

I turned to where the Sigurri and S'Heernoh awaited upon
the stones below, their eyes busily taking in the warriors all
about, and gestured them to me. Ilvin had ascended the steps
in the near wake of Ennat and myself and continued to
receive the greetings of those Hitta who were present. When
the males were about us, I returned my gaze to Rilas.

"Keeper, I would have you know those who are followers
of Sigurr, and one who is not," said I, indicating the males
who had grown respectfully silent. "This one is Aysayn,
called Shadow of Sigurr, a Keeper to those who follow the
dark god. He of the blazing hair is Mehrayn, called Sword of
Sigurr, war leader to his males. The third is Chaldrin, a true
keren among males, more foolish than others in that he insists
upon following a war leader of Midanna and raising his
sword beside hers. Mida alone knows for what reason I call
him brother."

Chaldrin chuckled softly, possibly at the startlement to be
seen upon Rilas. She had looked upward at the males as I
named each of them, and had frowned somewhat at the
manner in which Mehrayn had gazed upon me.

"The last of the four is S'Heernoh, one who travels far
from the land of his people," I continued, bringing Rilas's
attention to the tall, gray-haired male. "Though warrior skills
are not among those he possesses, he has become a true
companion to us all, providing aid and information which no
other might have done. Should he learn to curb his amusement at those things which fail to bring amusement to others,
he may well remain living among us a time longer."

S'Heernoh showed his amusement then, as the other males
chuckled, yet Rilas remained untouched by it. Her frown now
rested upon S'Heernoh, composed in large part of puzzlement.

"In some manner do you seem familiar, male," she said to
him, her eyes seeking to plumb the depth of him. "And yet,
the thought of lack of warrior skills does not seem equally
familiar. Have we met in the time gone past?"

"Never before have I been given the honor of being presented to you, lady," said S'Heernoh, smoothly. "Should
such honor have been mine, I would surely have recalled it."

"Perhaps," said Rilas in a mutter, her thoughts clearly
upon the past, yet were there others about whom her curiosity

had not yet been satisfied. Those Aysayn had urged to join us now stood a short distance beyond the set we had formed, and her eyes went to them.

"Those males will not long remain among us," said I, losing nearly all of the welcome-pleasure I had felt at sight of how close Ceralt and Galiose had grown. The two stood shoulder to shoulder, Lialt and Telion with them, the other males they had brought ranged behind. Once Ceralt had demanded to know the size of the thing which stood between Galiose and himself, a demand brought about by knowledge of the lashing I had been given by command of the High Seat of Ranistard. Now it seemed the size of the thing was small indeed, so small that it was easily ignored so that naught would mar the closeness of the males. Memory of the shame and humiliation I had had at Ceralt's hands returned, unsoftened by an awareness of the pain he had attempted to keep from me.

"And yet, while they remain, the war leader will surely not deny me knowledge of them," said Rilas, her soft words striving to soothe my anger. "Speak to me of these others who follow you, Jalav, so that I may know them as you do."

"You would not care to know them as I do, Rilas," said I, sending my gaze to the four who had stepped nearer when the Keeper's attention had come to them. "The one in blue cloth and leather and metal is Galiose, called High Seat of Ranistard, he who holds the Hosta captive within the walls of a cursed city, he who had their war leader lashed for failing to obey him as would a city slave-woman. Beside him is Ceralt, High Rider to Belsayah village males, he who sought to ensnare a war leader of Midanna with stolen vows, he who sought to make a city slave-woman of her in truth. The one who seems so like Ceralt is his brother Lialt, Pathfinder for their village and also their healer. He of the red-gold mane is Telion, called warrior of Ranistard, chosen brother to both Galiose and Ceralt. Lialt and Telion found great amusement during the journey to Mida's realm upon this world, taking pleasure from one who had been declared no more than a wench commanded to obey them. When the strangers have been seen to, then shall there be challenge given aplenty."

A great silence had fallen at my words, words which

turned the looks of Galiose and Ceralt and Lialt and Telion odd indeed. They seemed taken aback by the truths I had voiced, truths they no longer seemed able to deny. Galiose avoided my eye and Ceralt stared with pain-filled intensity, Lialt flinched as though a lash had touched him, and Telion gave the appearance of a small child whose trust had been betrayed.

"Wench, do not speak so," said Telion in a rush, as though the words poured of themselves from his lips. "Such bitterness and pain! By the Serene Oneness, there are none here who would see you cut so deep from such memories. Are there no other, warmer memories with which to replace them? Was there not laughter and joy as well as hurt for you among us?"

"What laughter and joy might a wench find among the followers of the accursed Oneness?" asked Chaldrin in a growl, his left fist nearly white about the hilt of his sword. "I have heard her speak before concerning her time in your midst, and were you not in possession of the word of Sigurr's Shadow concerning your safety—"

"And what might her time have been like among the followers of Sigurr the foul?" demanded Telion, straightening to the fullness of his height to meet the blaze in Chaldrin's dark eyes. "For what reason do you all ring her about so closely, as though fearful of what words she would speak were none to halt her? Does she truly wish your presence, or does fear of you keep her from sending you all from her, so that those who truly care for her may stand beside her? I am unable to believe . . ."

"Those who truly care for her already stand beside her!" snarled Chaldrin, so completely bereft of his usual calm that he seemed nearly a stranger. "Were you familiar with the true nature of this wench, you would know that fear is no part of her! Neither in battle with words nor in battle with swords does fear touch her, and never shall it. . . ."

"To allow a wench to enter battle with weapons is to show naught of true care for her!" snapped Ceralt, adding his heated glare to that which Telion already sent Chaldrin. "Should a man's feelings be truly deep, he will keep her from danger of maiming or death! For her sake and his own will he do the thing, accepting her wailings and moanings concerning his cruelty with the strength of knowing he labors in the cause of right!''

"The cause of right!" echoed Mehrayn in full ridicule, standing himself beside Chaldrin to draw the gaze of Ceralt. "Should one consider one's own comfort as the cause of right, then to behave in such a manner would indeed be the thing he claims. To be truly a man is to know that one may not keep a wench from doing as she must, just as he does as he must. And in being truly a man one refrains from handing his wench about, else is she not his and he no man at all. A true man needs no aid from others to bring his wench to satiety.''

"What satiety might be gotten from a sword's edge?" demanded Ceralt, furiously. "Should what the wench must do include lying half dead in her own blood, covered by the wounds of uncounted spear thrusts, does one merely step to the side and smile fondly, allowing the thing? Truly would such an action prove the doings of a man—were he a man with no thought for the wench save her use! He would then find little difficulty in keeping the taste of her his alone. Few others would so relish the use of one about to be taken to the arms of the gods.''

"Such things occur at times with one who is by birth a warrior," said Mehrayn, his voice bleak as he looked at Ceralt. "Should a man be other than a warrior himself, he will find himself lacking in understanding of this truth—and would do well to take himself from warriors' concerns.''

"One need not be called warrior to be well-versed in weapons use," said Ceralt bleakly. "To turn from what another declares to be truth is to fail to face it and prove it a lie. Should the name warrior conceal a lack of stomach for keeping a willful wench from risking herself as she pleases, I find myself inordinately pleased to be called other than that.''

"One called warrior will stand beside the wench, raising his blade in support of her, seeing that she comes to no harm from her willfulness!" growled Mehrayn, he and Ceralt nearly nose to nose. "To feel it necessary to bind a willful wench is to declare oneself no warrior, no man, no thing of any sort worthy of notice! Should she overstep the bounds of good

sense, she need only be punished somewhat to restore her
sense of the proper. She need not be bound hand and foot!''

"Should binding her be the sole manner in which she
might be kept unharmed, no *man* would hesitate!'' returned
Ceralt, his growl as deep as Mehrayn's. "Nor would he
hesitate to give her a good taste of the leather, should that be
what she requires! Willful wenches must be tamed and taught
to live in a man's world, else shall the hands of all men be
raised against her!''

"No *man* would allow the hands of other men to be raised
against his woman, were she the most willful to have ever
lived!'' countered Mehrayn, fists upon hips as he glared upon
Ceralt. The male who was the Belsayah High Rider stood the
same, and no longer did I bother to hear the great foolishness
they both spouted. Males were filled with incredible foolishness, and one must truly be bereft to give heed to them.

All those who stood about were deeply engrossed in the
words exchanged by the two males, each according to his or
her place. Rilas listened avidly with a great attentiveness
upon her, Ennat gazed upon the two with bemusement and
lack of understanding, Aysayn seemed nearly prepared to
intrude upon the disagreement, Chaldrin stood at Mehrayn's
elbow, Telion and Lialt at Ceralt's, and Galiose appeared to
be both listening closely and lost in thought. S'Heernoh alone
found naught save amusement in the antics of the two, a soft,
secret chuckling to be heard from him, in no manner the same
as the low, ridiculing laughter of those warriors who stood
about. Warriors will often find amusement in the foolishness
of males, but this fey I did not. As it was necessary to have
those males about, it was equally as necessary that they be
taught a proper manner of behavior.

Without hesitation I moved to the nearest warrior who held
a spear, took the weapon from her, then made my way to the
disputants. Telion and Chaldrin stared with surprise when I
halted between them, yet could do no more than stare. Quickly
and with the strength of my annoyance did I use the haft
portion of the spear to rap sharply at the shin of first Ceralt
and then Mehrayn, ending their exchange and sending them
back from each other with yelps of pain. Save for the two
males and myself, all those standing about laughed heartily

as I looked with little approval upon the two who hopped about one-legged, holding or rubbing their injured limbs.

"Should the matter of safe conduct be ended, the war leader Jalav shall see first to the spilling of blood," said I, sending an icy gaze first to one and then to the other of them. "Even warriors-to-be, not yet large enough to lift a sword, would know and understand the need to see to the strangers before other considerations. Long have I known that males are less than the youngest of warriors-to-be, yet had I not expected proof of that at so poor a time. Should you all wish to squabble among yourselves, the Midanna are well able to see to the strangers with none save their own."

"No no, wench, we shall not allow this to occur again," said Aysayn, clearly attempting to swallow his laughter as he put a hand to Mehrayn's arm. Galiose, one hand arub upon his face, held Ceralt in a similar manner, the while the two who had faced one another now looked angrily upon she who had separated them. "Perhaps it would be best if we were to take a short while apart," said Sigurr's Shadow, "and only then attempt discussion upon the matter foremost in our minds."

"Before that, we must discuss the coming strangers," said S'Heernoh with such bland innocence that all of the males save Ceralt and Mehrayn again began chuckling. Clearly had the comment meaning for males, yet such are the minds of males that they are able to see meaning where those of fuller reason find none. I spent no useless thought upon the matter, turning instead toward Linol, war leader to the Hersa.

"Sister, we have those who require places to rest themselves," said I, moving forward to return the spear to the Helda warrior I had taken it from. "Conduct them to those places, and allow them their rest. Should any join again in heated exchange, however, show them the dungeons instead, and make no great effort to recall the cells in which they are left."

I turned about to gaze upon the males as Linol chuckled her agreement and gathered a number of her warriors to her with a gesture, seeing that the greater number of males chuckled as well. Again Ceralt and Mehrayn alone found no amusement in the happenings, a thing Ceralt made clear as he and his companions reached the place where I stood.

"I trust the—war leader will graciously find a pair of reckid later, so that she and I might speak," he murmured, looking down upon me with a look I well recalled. "It has clearly been too long a time since last we did so."

The look was then gone, as was the male, he and the others following after Linol and her Hersa. Lialt grinned well as he passed, clearly having heard Ceralt's words, the insolence of both doing well with increasing my annoyance. At such a time one has little need of additional sources of irritation, yet at such a time one need not look far for them.

"I find little amusement in your manner of doing, wench," said Mehrayn in a growl, his green eyes full displeased as he looked down upon me. "Once before we spoke of your raising weapons to me, yet clearly the matter requires further discussion. When once I am able to walk again, I shall seek you out for the discussion."

Then did the Sigurri and S'Heernoh follow after the previous set of males, blessedly leaving behind no others than Midanna. The clamor of them all had brought a throbbing to my head, as though many males stood within and hammered to be released. I put a hand to the throbbing and sought to rub it from me, yet Rilas appeared before me with the rubbing only just begun.

"Truly do some blessings have their dark sides," said she, looking up into my eyes with an attempt at understanding. "For what purpose have these males been brought here, Jalav?"

"Surely for the purpose of stealing my reason and leaving me gibbering," said I with an edge to my voice which nevertheless brought amusement to Ennat. "Should I continue to find victories which involve males such as those, likely will I fail to survive."

"I believe the war leader would do well to seek rest of her own, Rilas," said Ennat with a smile. "And surely are there words which you and she would wish to exchange, alone and uninterrupted. You and I may speak later, after I, too, have rested."

"Ennat, your wisdom has no need of enlarging," said Rilas, turning to her sister Keeper with a smile of gratitude. "Already does it encompass understanding beyond the efforts of those about you. Please accompany us till we reach the place you may rest yourself."

With a nod of agreement Ennat stepped back to allow me to pass her, a thing which I did with both eagerness and hesitancy. My eyes found little pleasure in the glaring brightness of Mida's light, yet was the thought of being enclosed within the walls of a dwelling dispiriting. So pleased was I to be rid of the males and in a place where they might not force their presence upon me, however, that the walls we stepped within were welcome. Cool was the air between the pink stone of walls, floor and ceiling, blue cloth hung about upon some of it, small and large platforms standing here and there along the halls, some with seats, some without. Also were there those who were city males and females, moving about the dwelling with as much confidence as those warriors who did the same. No collars nor chains were there upon those who moved about so, yet did they look upon me with a deference which was nearly slave-like.

"Those who see to this dwelling for us seem somewhat in awe of you, Jalav," said Rilas, noting where I looked as we walked the halls. "Surely do they recall you from our time of having first taken this place, and know you as she who commands those who command them. In accordance with your will, no longer are they slaves, a thing which filled them with joy when it was done, and now fills them equally with awe. Much do they prefer being servants to slaves."

"Only the city-bred would find a difference in the states," said I, increasingly annoyed. "Ever are those of the cities chained in one manner or another, and those of towns and villages as well. We, ourselves, will do well only when we have left them all far behind us. I live for the fey as I live for few others."

No response came from Rilas, Ennat remaining silent as well, therefore did we continue along the hall, turning every now and again, until we came to a number of steps leading upward. Ennat continued to look all about her with endless curiosity as we took ourselves to the floor above, and when we reached a door not far from that which had been mine when first my warriors had taken the dwelling, Rilas halted and threw it wide.

"Accept this chamber as your own, Ennat," said she, gesturing over a passing servant male. "This male will fetch daru and provender to you, and should you require aught else, you have only to speak of it to him."

"You have my thanks, Rilas," said Ennat, looking upon the male who had smiled at her before taking himself off to do the bidding of the Keeper. "There may perhaps be another thing he might see to."

"The warriors he has already served have found him able to give much pleasure," said Rilas, smiling with amusement at the manner in which Ennat followed the departing male with her eyes. "He feels neither humiliation nor resentment in being commanded to the service of warriors, therefore is the pleasure he gives unrestrained and untainted."

"Should he have half the vigor of the Sigurri, I will indeed be well pleased," said Ennat, turning to the chamber which had been given her. "May Mida guard you both till we stand together again."

"And you, sister," said Rilas, the warmth of her words unfeigned as she closed the door through which Ennat had passed. With that done her eyes came to me with a questioning frown, yet I avoided her gaze and strode off toward my own chamber, unwilling to answer the questions she would have attempted. The cloth beneath my feet was soft and warm, but little comfort did it provide for one in the midst of such turmoil as I.

No guard males in leather and metal stood before the doubled doors of my chamber as they had when the former High Seat had dwelled there, nor were there Midanna warriors in their place. I opened the doors and went in, fully expecting the windowless outer chamber to be dark and silent with disuse, instead finding many candles lit about the walls, illuminating the large chamber and the board piled high with provender and drink. My stride slowed as I looked about at the blue-silk-hung chamber, wondering at what use it had been put to in my absence, and the answer came without my having to voice the question.

"I ordered your chamber lit and provisioned as soon as word was brought me that you had been sighted without the city's walls, Jalav," said Rilas, the sound of the doors swinging shut accompanying her words. "Perhaps you would now care to sit and share daru, and speak to me of what occurs all about us."

"The will of the gods occurs all about us," said I, moving toward the board and the daru it held. "How has the time passed for you behind the walls of this city, Rilas?"

"The time has passed with surprising ease, war leader," said she, coming to stand behind me. "The males called Council of the High Seat at first tried to prescribe what must be done by our warriors and what must not, yet were they quickly taught that warriors do as they are bidden by their war leaders. The fey after your departure saw three males give challenge to three of your war leaders, they apparently believing that to claim war leadership of a clan was a mere matter of donning a blade and declaring one's intentions. When the three lay unmoving in their own blood, those of the city who had come to see their victory turned away silent and frightened, no longer of the belief that Midanna war leaders are to be bested by any with no more than a will to do so."

I turned from the board after removing and placing my swordbelt upon it, in my hands the two cups of daru I had poured. I then gave one to Rilas, kept the other, and gestured her to join me upon the floor cloth. The daru had cooled from the time it had first been heated, yet was most welcome as it slid down my throat.

"For a number of feyd thereafter, there was naught to be heard from those of the city, save the unending requests and suggestions from those termed the Council," said Rilas, sipping from her own cup as she looked upon me with lidded eyes. "I spent considerable time upon the question of which males the clans were to free and which they were to retain, having naught else which required consideration, and then came a male asking to speak with you, one of those who had been released from the place beneath this dwelling."

I nodded my understanding, recalling those unfortunates who had been enclosed in cells beneath the dwelling of the High Seat, that place called dungeons by males. None were able to discover what grievous acts had been committed by those so imprisoned, save that they had in one manner or another displeased the male called High Seat. I had decided to release the lot of them, and those males called Council had assisted me.

"When the male learned that he would be unable to speak with you," said Rilas, "he agreed to speak instead with she who was left to consider matters in your place. He seemed not yet past the ordeal he had been made to suffer, his body thin, his eyes filled still with the memory of pain and terror, although he spoke warmly of the kindness he had been shown by those warriors who had seen to his well-being when first he had been removed from his confinement. He had thereafter returned to his home in the city, yet had he found much amiss. With the absence of the males called guardsmen, those who had found defeat at our hands during the attack, none were about to halt those few who preyed upon the many. Indeed had the most of these who took from others banded together, and although one or two might have the courage to resist them individually, none were able to stand against the entire band. Urgent pleas had been put before those males called the Council, yet had this male who spoke and the others like him been told that naught might be done till the Midanna had departed and the Council ruled the city. What would be done at that time was not spoken of, yet would all be seen to once the invaders were gone from the city."

I leaned down to my left elbow upon the soft blue floor cloth, smiling faintly at the way those unskilled with weapons nevertheless attempted attack against those who had defeated them. The males of the city had little or no ability with the swords they often wore, yet were their numbers far greater than the numbers of the victorious Midanna. Had the males of the Council succeeded in arousing deep anger within the breasts of those greater numbers, they might well have seen the Midanna overwhelmed. The perpetually craven are well used to stabbing the back of one they had not the stomach to face, no matter the harm brought to others by such an action.

"My course of action then seemed clear," said Rilas, looking toward me as she spoke of her decision. "As it had been our doing that these males and their slave-women no longer had the protection of those in leather and metal, it was demanded by honor that we, ourselves, stand their protection. Tilim agreed at once to lead her Happa into the city to where the male would direct them, and once they had departed I saw Katil and her Harra gone silently after them. I knew not whether the male had spoken the truth, you see, and could not allow a single clan to enter an area where they might be taken by greater numbers lying in hiding.''

I nodded in understanding and allowed my smile to warm in approval, showing Rilas that she had done as I would have. Had I been there I, myself, would have accompanied the Happa, yet were Rilas's warrior days a far distance behind her. Her own presence would have been more hindrance than help, and she had been wise indeed to acknowledge that fact.

"The Happa found that the male had spoken the truth," said Rilas, strengthened, now, by my approval. "Those who had formerly taken no more than unliving possessions were in the process of taking a small number of slave-females for their own use when Katil and her clan arrived, a doing which was quickly ended by Happa swords. One of those who had come to steal was no more than knocked senseless, and when the others were seen to he was revived. The daggers of two of the Happa convinced the male to reveal where his brothers waited, and then did the Happa go there and see to the balance of them. No single thief-male escaped their swords, and those who had been prey to the set sent up a joyous yelling and shouting that nearly tore down the dwellings all about. A feast was then declared, and the Happa were stuffed nearly to bursting by those who cavorted and sang.''

Rilas drank deep of the daru she held, looking down upon it, then sighed wearily.

"It was then necessary to seek further for what mischief those Council males might well have been brewing," said she, rubbing at her eyes with her free hand. "With the aid of Drilinar, the male who had come seeking our assistance, I was able to learn of the doings of those of this city. I shall not weary you with each point brought forth for me, Jalav, yet must I ask you to believe me without doing as I did, demanding to see with my own eyes that which I found incredible.

"City males are divided into many small groups, each group performing a chore which needs seeing to, each taking that which is termed payment from his brothers for doing what they have neither the time nor the skill to see to themselves. The division seems necessary to the city males, and also do they look upon it as desirable, for none of them would wish a—seat, let us say, made with less than utmost skill, even should they lack that skill themselves. The difficulty which then obtained was that all seat-makers—and hunters, and warriors, and those who engaged in trade, and those who repaired dwellings, and those who offered any skill of any sort—allowed no more than a set number to join their group, and all others were forbidden to engage in the practice without their let. These groups are termed 'guilds,' and none cared that others might face starvation and death through their denial; too many members would lessen payment for each. Should one wish a seat one could not build for oneself, one must trade with the seat-maker's guild, accepting what was offered, for no others were permitted to offer as good or better. All were caught up in this mindlessness, and none seemed able to end it, not to speak of seeing the need for ending it. Far better to watch the suffering of others, give them crumbs from the feast you yourself indulged in, then smile with the pleasure such generosity brought. To aid them to stand alone was too great a risk, for once standing those who were looked down upon might well prove as tall and strong as those who had previously laughed and sneered.''

Rilas rose to her feet to refill her cup of daru, and I was able to see the anger which now accompanied her weariness. I had no true understanding of those city-male doings of which she had spoken, yet did I deem it unwise to interrupt her speaking. Our Keeper had not had so effortless a stay in that city as she would have had me believe, but Midanna rarely acknowledged pain and difficulty. Far better to deny it in silence, and thereby find victory over the memory of it the sooner.

"Suffice it to say that the guilds are no more," said Rilas, turning back to me with her cup refilled. "It took the presence of more than one of the clans to see it so, yet are all now free to do as they will, be it seat-making or trading or hunting or what have you. Those who wish to do a thing simply do it; should they possess the skill to do it well, many come seeking their services. For those who do the thing badly, there are none about to protect them from their lacks. They either seek out another thing to do, else do they, themselves, face starvation. A number of those without skill chose instead to take what they might no longer demand, therefore was it necessary to have warriors ever about, to keep the helpless from again becoming prey. A large number did we eject from the city, those who although without skill of their own, were masters to others who labored at various chores. These masters attempted to incite their followers against us and the folk we protected, but I refused to allow that to continue. Also did I deem it wise to have other warriors begin the training in weapons of those who showed the most promise. When once we depart from here, those who look to us for protection will no longer be able to do so, therefore must we leave those in our place to do the thing for us."

"Males," said I with a good deal of distaste, swallowing my daru to chase away the flavor of the thought. "City males who will wait no longer than the moment the gates close behind us to do the same to their brothers as was previously done. Who will the helpless then weep to?"

"Jalav, we cannot turn city folk into Midanna, even were we to make the attempt," said Rilas, once more seating herself opposite me. "We are able to do no more than allow them the opportunity to see to themselves. Perhaps by then they will have learned not to place themselves in bondage to others. Would you now care to speak of the disturbance you feel, the disturbance which sits so heavily upon your shoulders?"

"Certainly," said I with a shrug, watching her as she looked concerned even as I sipped again at my daru. "Which disturbance would you hear of first, Rilas? As there are so large a number of them, the choice of which to begin upon may as well be yours."

"War leader, I do not seek to intrude," said she softly. "Well aware am I of the error I made when I last insisted that you speak upon something you clearly had no wish to discuss. Had the males drawn weapons the fault would have been mine, yet I still do not understand the basis for their disagreement. It *was* you they discussed, was it not?"

"Indeed," said I, grimacing with disgust. "Indeed was I

the object of their discussion, for each of the males believes I am his alone, his to possess no matter the will of others. Such is the male manner of doing, a thing I have long since lost patience for.''

"They look upon a war leader of the Midanna as though she were a city slave-woman?'' demanded Rilas, indignation straightening her where she sat. "They would dare so mindless a thing in the presence of her warriors? With her weapons and the love of Mida wrapped firmly about her? Have they no further desire to continue with their lives?''

"Their desire has little to do with continuing their lives,'' said I, annoyed. "My time of capture to Ceralt you already know of, the manner in which he attempted to keep me from warrior doings during the occasion of our journey to Mida's Realm upon this world. My time with Mehrayn was not the same, for the male truly wishes to see me with the prerogatives of a warrior—yet not with the prerogatives of a war leader. The use I have from him is strong and bold, ever-eager and ever-pleasing, yet does he refuse to accept that another might momentarily interest me, if only for the comparison. Nearly a hand of feyd past, the while we brought Midanna and Sigurri toward this city, I came upon a Sigurri warrior I had not previously seen. The male was not so large as others, yet was he more well-endowed than any other I had ever seen, and curiosity overcame me. The male swam in a stream a distance from his brothers, his golden body completely unclothed, and when he saw me gazing upon him from the bank, he swam to where I stood and pulled himself from the water.''

I sighed deeply, recalling the time most clearly, and Rilas smiled knowingly, for she, too, had been a warrior.

"He stood before me, the water falling from his pale hair, a smile of willingness upon the broadness of his face, and then he reached out a hand to put a finger to my swordbelt,'' said I, sipping from the daru to cool the warmth of the memory. "His smile turned quickly to a grin of challenge, for he dared me to put away the trappings of a warrior and join him in a battle of another sort; I discovered willingness within me, therefore did I remove my swordbelt, and then moved forward to press my body to his. The strength in his arms took no note of my weight as he put me to the grass with him, and then was my breech opened and pulled away, to allow his hands to move about me more easily. Soon were we joined in the battle of pleasure, and although I found the time enjoyable, I discovered as well that he had not the ability which Mehrayn possesses. We each found release, lay a moment beside one another, then went our separate ways as is done after a pause such as that.''

I rose to my feet as Rilas nodded, refilled my cup with daru, then turned again to look down upon her.

''I know not how Mehrayn learned of the time, yet did he certainly learn of it,'' I continued, remembering the annoyance that I had felt then. ''He pulled me to the back of his kan, rode a good distance from the presence of both Midanna and Sigurri, then attempted to berate me for having taken another in *his* place. I cared little for such male foolishness and spoke my own words in anger at his gall, yet did he refuse to heed the voice of reason. He gave ear to none of it and instead took himself off, leaving me to return to our camping place on foot. My fury had grown so high by the time of my return, that I set Renin and her Sonna all about the place I had chosen to take my rest. When, after we had fed and all about sought their sleeping leather, and the male appeared to join me as always, the Sonna, obedient to my word, refused him passage through their ranks. Surely did the male howl in anguish for hind, yet was refused that darkness and each darkness thereafter. Males!''

''Indeed are they best avoided when not giving use,'' said Rilas, thoughtfully. ''Only now do I find meaning in the heated words exchanged a short while ago. He of the dark hair wishes to see you kept from all battle, the while he of the flame hair wishes to see you kept from all other males. They are both of them mad, to believe Mida would allow her chosen to be subject to such denial.''

Rilas then looked toward me with the scorn she felt, believing I would show the same, yet had she touched upon a point of much graver concern than the doings of males. I put the daru to my lips and drank deep of it, and when I lowered the cup I saw that she stared with something closely akin to fear.

"Surely did I misread your expression when I made mention of the goddess," said she, her voice as soft as her eyes were widened. "Jalav, you are Mida's chosen, sworn to her till the end of your feyd, more beloved than any before you! You have gathered and led the host which will vanquish her enemies! I could not have seen the look of blood-feud upon you at mention of her name!"

"Indeed shall I vanquish Mida's enemies," said I, turning from the wounded gaze which held to me so tightly. "I shall find victory over the strangers as I have vowed to do, at last completing this task which has become well-nigh endless, and should I survive the doing, I will then see the Hosta freed. Once that, my final duty, has been seen to, I shall then return to Sigurr's Peak, where Mida's Realm upon this world may be found. Once there—once there, she and I will speak of denial, and of the giving of pain, and of the spilling of blood. Jalav will be free to ride and do as she wills, else will she be one with the endless dark."

"Jalav, no," whispered Rilas from behind me, having stood from the floor cloth to place a hand upon my shoulder. "No mortal may do battle with a god!"

"So had I thought," I responded grimly, gazing upon the blue silk which clothed the wall opposite to where I stood, no more than silver wall sconces breaking the span of it. "No mortal may do battle with a god, yet have we mortals been set by Mida to meet and best the strangers. In her wisdom, Ennat spoke a truth which I had not previously seen: are not the enemies of gods themselves gods? Should it be beyond possibility for mortals to find victory over gods, for what reason have we been commanded to battle with the strangers? No, Rilas, battle is more than possible, and I shall have it even should it be the end of me."

"I find it impossible to comprehend for what reason you have been brought to such sacrilegious determination," said Rilas, her hand gone from my shoulder, the greater part of upset gone from her voice. "That Mida allows and demands such beliefs from you is clear, yet do I fail to see the purpose of it. Well may such purpose even include the males."

"It cannot be that Mida desires battle thought in me," said

I, turning to look upon a now thoughtfully vexed Rilas. "For what reason would she wish to face me?"

"For what reason would she not?" demanded Rilas in turn, annoyed at having been drawn from the depths of her thoughts. "Is a goddess to fear the skill of a mortal warrior? Is Mida to back in uncertainty from one whose every breath is taken in accordance with the will of that goddess? I now see the basis for your disturbance, Jalav, for you have forgotten, in your upset, that all which occurs is by Mida's will. You, and I, and all those about us, act only in accordance with that will."

Having spoken the words which were to her merely explanation, Rilas then turned from me and sought again her place upon the floor cloth. Her thoughts had already resubmerged her in private considerations, therefore did she see naught of the annoyance which surely flared within me. For what reason it had not occurred to me that my thirst for vengeance might well be inspired by the goddess herself, I knew not, yet did I certainly know that I had no wish for it to be so. To encourage a war leader of Midanna to stand before one in challenge as though that war leader were no more than a warrior-to-be was deep insult; more than enough insult had been given me during the task which now neared completion. Little desire had I to find more.

In continuing annoyance and growing frustration I turned to the board of provender, chose a wing and leg of roast lellin, and began to eat. For what reason would it be Mida's wish that I challenge her? Should it be the goddess's desire to see me fall, the doing might more easily be accomplished in the battle which was to come. It might well have been that Mida wished me in her Realm so that I might be punished for insolence and sacrilege, yet would she be well aware of the fact that I would accept the final dark sooner than submit to such a thing. That I could not be forced to bow to her was clear from the fact that I had clearly seen to the task given me according to my own preferences, and that would not have been permitted had I merely moved to the desires of she for whom I rode. To believe I was determined to give challenge only through the will of another was infuriating and I refused to entertain the possibility. The wisdom of Rilas was well known to all, yet did I refuse to believe that she was right this time.

I had put aside my pot of daru so that I might clean the meat from the lellin bones, yet was my interest in feeding gone after no more than a few bites. I returned the section of lellin to the board with an impatient toss, took a cloth upon which I wiped the grease from my hands, then retrieved my daru to accompany me as I prowled about the chamber.

What purpose other than my own would be served by my challenging Mida? The thought nagged at me as I paced from the board of provender toward the raised area of the chamber, a platform upon which the former High Seat of Bellinard was wont to display himself. I recalled how he had appeared when my warriors and I had first entered the chamber, carelessly unconcerned in his arrogance, sprawled at his ease in the large, intricately carved, silk-covered seat, surrounded by slave females who instantly saw to his every wish. Much alike are males everywhere, seeking always to be served, taking for their own the females they desire—

I stopped abruptly, the cup of daru poised nearly at my lips. Suddenly it occurred to me what purpose other than my own would be served, should I challenge Mida. I would then be *there*, in Mida's Realm upon this world, a domain which stood beside that of—Sigurr. Once again I would be there, yet where Mida's protection had been mine when first I had visited there, a second appearance would not find it the same. Only Mida's will had kept me from claiming by Sigurr a fate the shadow of which had nearly ended me. To recall the time was to taste of terror, to shudder in revulsion and horror, to swallow down in vain the illness which rose with bitter bile.

Quickly I crouched where I had halted, head swirling dizzily, heart pounding as though I ran headlong, the air in the chamber suddenly insufficient for my lungs. Could such a thing truly be Mida's purpose, to lure me with foolish thoughts of challenge to a place where I might be taken by Sigurr? Much unexpected pleasure had Sigurr had from me, so Mida had said. The dark god of males had been—taken with me, I had been told, his interest high in she who had given him deeper release than any other mortal female. I swallowed down my daru quickly, emptying the cup and then dropping

it, then wrapped my arms about myself in an effort to free my
body of the ice deep within. Sigurr would seek me again, so
Mida had said, and perhaps do a thing never before done.
What that might be I had no wish to know; what I had already
learned of Sigurr was more than any mortal *should* know,
more than any would care to know.

Again my thoughts returned to my time in Mida's Realm
upon this world, a realm which lay beside that of the dark
god. At first I had thought that the two domains were kept
from one another save when captives were taken, yet I had
learned there were other times when they were brought together. Few indeed were the outsiders who found their way
through the cold and snow of the north to reach the caverns
below Sigurr's Peak, however those who were called Midanna
and Sigurri had need of new lives to maintain and increase
their numbers. I had stood watching from the shadows when
goddess and god summoned all who followed them, bringing
male and female together in a great cavern and commanding
them to their duty. I had thought to see pleasure indulged in,
for in such a manner are new warrior lives brought forth, yet
had there been no trace of pleasure, neither for Midanna nor
Sigurri. In truth it had chilled me to see that no single pair
failed to find discomfort, disgust, and even pain at the cou-
pling, all suffering grim and hated requirement rather than a
sharing of eagerness. It had come to me then with a flash of
understanding that the gods themselves kept pleasure from
their followers, allowing them such feelings only when they
forced use from captives and slaves, as the two gods demon-
strated when the grimness was completed. The male chosen by
Mida had attempted to contain his fear, but the female claimed
by Sigurr had screamed and screamed and screamed. . . .

And yet, I thought, throwing off the distraction of memory, Sigurr might be avoided simply by failing to stand before
Mida in challenge. The goddess's feelings of insult were
clearly deep, yet should I refuse to place myself within
Sigurr's easy reach, I would then be a source of frustration
rather than satisfaction—yet would my *own* frustration remain! I had no wish to forgo the giving of challenge, however I failed to see how it might be done save by standing too
near the one I wished to shun.

I sat up upon the floor cloth, my knees drawn up, my arms about them, my annoyance burning higher and higher. Never would I or any Midanna warrior seek safety by standing behind the presence of another, yet was I able to see Mida's actions in no other light. To taunt the one who was war leader to every Midanna who raised sword, to cause that war leader shame and pain, to inflict agonies and humiliation, to deny her the males she would have chosen, and then to refuse challenge! No Midanna would ever have acted so, and to think that Mida herself would engage in so foul a doing was nearly inconceivable! I had wondered at the temerity of inspiring such anger in a Midanna war leader without thought of consequence, yet had the consequences been well thought upon—and likely laughed at. What need to fear the anger of a war leader, when that war leader would be too well occupied with the doings of another to consider anger?

And for what reason had Ceralt been led to that place, just at that time? Mehrayn accompanied me out of necessity, yet the presence of Ceralt was not the same. For what reason had both of the males I found interest in been brought together, the males Mida had wished to deny me? I no longer believed in the innocence of such happenings, that no purpose was to be served through their occurrence. There was purpose aplenty—which must be discovered before it might be understood and countered. For this foolishness to be sent to bedevil me now, when the strangers were nearly upon us, was a distraction I had no need of, yet could not avoid. I would not allow the goddess, in her anger with me, to bring harm to others who were, in essence, blameless. That would be dishonorable.

I had stretched out upon the floor cloth on my back, left leg raised and right extended, unseeing eyes upon the chamber's ceiling, thinking of the strangers, when yet another distraction came. Into my sight stepped a male, his face expressionless about eyes filled with hunger, his gaze coming down to me where I lay, his tongue moistening his lips. Although the previous serving males I had seen had been clothed with blue tied about their waists, this male who looked down upon me wore naught in the way of covering, nor was he free. The slave collar clasped his neck, and he seemed somehow familiar. I frowned at his abrupt appearance; however he, himself, showed only the trace of a smile.

"Mistress, I have been sent by the master called Aysayn to ask a thing of you," said he, his voice rough despite the softness of his tone and words. "The master would know what place is to be used for the meeting soon to be held, and would know as well if you agree that all participants should appear unarmed. I am told that you will be aware of the reason why that might be best."

"I am indeed aware of such a reason," said I, frowning, raising myself to sitting as the male crouched beside me. "In what manner were you given permission to enter this chamber?"

"Mistress, I am a slave," said he, seeming amused. "Slaves have no need of asking permission, for their presence is not merely required, it is demanded. Also did I rap first upon your door, in an effort to keep from intrusion, yet no answer was vouchsafed me. As I was charged with bringing you a message, I considered it my duty to enter without specific response. I offer my apologies for having taken you from what were surely considerations of great import."

Despite the smoothness of the slave's speech, I forebore giving him answer as I twisted about where I sat, seeking the place where Rilas had been. No longer was the Keeper there, nor was she then within the chamber; clearly had I been so deep in thought, that I had heard no more of her departure than I had heard of the arrival of the male. For what reason she had departed without speaking further words to me I knew not, yet was that a question the answer to which must be sought out another time.

"You may take my reply to the male Aysayn," said I, straightening again to search the floor cloth for the emptied cup I had earlier dropped. "Tell him that the meeting may be held here, where there is provender and drink aplenty, and also that I concur with his thoughts regarding weapons. Should he have difficulty extracting agreement from our guests, have him recall to them the number of warriors in this place. Should it be necessary to state the request more than once, the second instance will no longer see it as a request."

I began, then, to raise myself from the floor, my intent

being to refill the cup I had retrieved, yet the left hand of the slave came to my shoulder, his right to the cup I held.

"Allow me to see to that, Mistress," said he, taking the cup with a strange smile. "I will, of course, deliver the message—once I have seen to the needs of my mistress."

He straightened from his crouch and stepped past me toward the board with provender and daru, taking no note of the way my eyes followed him. I had a great dislike of slaves, male and female both, yet the actions of the male seemed somewhat strange, even for one in bondage. Silently I rose to my feet, walked behind the male to the board, then stood awaiting the end of his task. When he turned again with the cup refilled he started, nearly spilling the daru, greatly surprised that I stood so near behind him.

"What is it you seek here, male?" I asked, taking the cup from him before he regained his composure. The male stood perhaps three fingers above me, broad enough of shoulder yet more slender than muscled, dark hair with dark eyes as well.

"I seek only to serve you, Mistress," said he, with difficulty. "I would serve the mistress completely, in every way demanded of me, in every way I might." And then he had gone to his knees, bent, and pressed his lips to my foot. "I beg you to command me, mistress," he whispered, his eyes no longer upon me. "A slave begs for the favor of his mistress."

The male remained upon all fours, his head bowed, his body held in the tension of misery. I stepped back, surprised, and looked down upon him with curiosity.

"In a dwelling filled with Midanna warriors, what need would there be for a male to beg use?" I asked, sipping at the daru I held. "Have my warriors been too immersed in other matters to take note of you?"

"So you do, indeed, fail to recall me," said the slave, raising his head slowly to bring his gaze to my face. "I had thought you merely toyed with me, sought to have me beg for that which I—" His words ended as his head shook briefly, a negation of the useless, and then he sighed deeply. "I was a slave here in the palace when you and your wenches took it," said he, a good deal of bitterness to be heard in the soft pain of his voice. "I attempted to secure my freedom through service to one of your wenches, but you discovered my attempt and ended it before it might achieve its goal. As you see, I continue to find failure in achieving it."

"Now do I recall you," said I, gazing down upon the male who knelt with head hanging and defeat all through him, a large measure of satisfaction accompanying the memory. "It was you, was it not, who attempted to force a vow from my warrior through the use of your body? That I aided her should give you no surprise, for I am the war leader of her war leader. In what manner should this have brought you to your present state?"

"Are you unable to recall your commands?" demanded the male, his skin darkening as he continued to avoid my eye. His state was clear enough to any who looked upon him, the smell of need strong beside the look, unable to control what he felt despite his humiliation. "It was your command that I not be used save with that drug in me, and with the number of men taken as captives, your wenches found no need for the drug!" he cried. "At first I was well pleased to find no need for tickling wenches who arrogantly strode about, and then the feyd passed and more feyd beyond those. I—am a man, with the needs of a man, unable to be among nearly naked wenches, seeing them give release to other men, and feel naught myself! It was occasionally possible, then, to catch a slave wench and use her to see to my need, and then the slave wenches and a good number of the men slaves were freed to become servants! It was then no longer possible to touch the ones I had previously used, for they would have run weeping to your warriors. I have not had a woman in more feyd than I am able to count, more feyd than I am able to bear! No man should be done in this way!"

The male wept in truth then, his fists clenched tight as his head lowered to his knees, his shoulders rounded and shaking, his body racked by sobs. I had not envisioned such an end when I had given my commands concerning him, and I stood a moment studying him, sipping my daru, before giving voice to my thoughts.

"I see your punishment has been truly fitting, male," I said at last, finding little sympathy within me which might have softened the words. "To use pleasure to achieve one's

ends is dishonorable and merits failure and punishment. Had
you sought to give no more than pleasure, you would have
received the same, and likely your freedom as well; as you
sought only baseness in use, so have you received only
baseness. Rarely is an open hand shown to a stranger by
Midanna; should that open hand be spurned and spat upon, it
will not be offered a second time."

"And yet, wenches may use their bodies to secure what
they desire!" rasped the male, his voice rough yet with the
moisture which covered his cheeks, his head raising though
he continued to avert his eyes. "They prance before a man
and lure him, graciously allow him their use, then wheedle
and demand all he is able to provide and more! Why should
not men do the same? You warrior wenches take what you
will as men would; for what reason may I not use my body to
obtain what *I* desire?"

"What privileges a warrior has she has earned," I replied,
seeing in the slave the same lack of reason typical of all
males. "You now reap what wrongful use of your body has
earned you, just as wrongful use of a sword would earn for a
warrior her enemy's point in her belly. For what reason do
you bemoan your lot, a lot which was earned, when a warrior
does not?"

"A wench with a sword asks for a point in her belly,"
muttered the male, wiping at his face with a forearm as he
rose slowly to his feet to face me. "I did not ask to be done
as I have been, I only sought a path to freedom. To be free is
the right of a man."

"To seek an honorable end through dishonorable means
sullies the purpose as well as the seeker," I returned, gesturing my loss of patience with the fool of a male. "Many seek
to avoid the path they find themselves upon through their own
actions, yet to no avail. You must walk your path till you
have learned what place you walk through your own efforts,
male, and then, perhaps, you will find a branching. You may
return now to Aysayn with my reply."

Annoyed, I began to turn from him then, but he reached
for my arm, halting me before I had taken more than half a
step.

"Perhaps I have already found a branching," said he, and

his gaze no longer avoided mine. "First I shall have what has so long been denied me, and then will I be accompanied by a well-used, black-haired wench beyond the gates of this accursed city. None will think to stop or question me as I command all others, and once I have attained my freedom, I will allow you the opportunity to earn your own. For now, however, I will allow only one thing."

The male then began to pull me toward him, his intentions unmistakable, his courage clearly bolstered by the fact we were alone and my sword was out of reach. He was scarcely larger than I, yet were his shoulders broader by far, his strength the strength of a male with a female, his determination and need adding the push of desperation. Clearly the male anticipated victory in his efforts, and if I had not already been taught the usefulness of unarmed combat by the Sigurri, surely would he have had his victory; however, Chaldrin had not spent his breath in vain.

Though my left hand held a cup of daru and the male's fingers held that arm, I was able to drop the cup, thrust my arm forward out of his grip, and then bring the elbow back with strength into his middle. Shocked, surprise was barely born upon his features before lack of air bent him double, and then I turned and brought my knee up sharply under his chin, straightening him once more and overstraightening him. Flat to the floor cloth was the male thrown, upon his back, much in the same position he had thought to have me. Pain brought his knees up somewhat as he rolled to his side, and dazedly he touched a finger to the blood on his lip.

"The war leader who commands all others is not so easily bested, male," I said, distastefully. "Raise yourself to your feet now, and take to Aysayn the reply you were given."

"But—I do not understand!" the male blurted, shock widening his eyes. "You will not call your warriors and have me thrown in chains and lashed? You will not take up your sword and spill my blood? Why do you fail to do so?"

"Because I shall not allow you to escape your punishment," I replied, watching as he struggled to regain his feet. "Should you learn from that punishment and eventually regain your freedom, we will speak then of swords and of

spilling blood, but never of chains and the lash. Now, take
yourself from here.''

"I do not understand," muttered the male, putting his hand
through his hair and attempting to straighten himself as he
made unsteadily for the door. "I do not understand now, nor
do I expect to understand."

With a final look of strangely composed expressions the
male at last left to do my bidding, allowing me to retrieve the
cup which had fallen to the floor cloth. Not far from the cup
were the remains of the spilled daru, turning the blue of the
floor cloth black, clearly showing the bounds of the spill. Less
clearly defined were my reasons for having allowed the male
to live, for the ways of the Midanna give the life of an
attacker to she who is attacked, hers to take if she is able.
Had I wished it, my dagger might have slid beneath the chin
of the male as easily as my knee, perhaps even more easily,
and yet I had not done him so. The true reasons for my
having withheld death were not within my grasp, and I
frowned as I went to pour more daru. Clearly I had spent too
long a time among males, for much of their thoughtless
foolishness had come to color my own doings.

The time was not long before the males began arriving.
First to be heard was the sound of voices raised in disagreement, and then the doors to my chamber were thrown wide to
allow the entrance of Galiose, Ceralt, Lialt, and Telion, with
Aysayn, Mehrayn, Chaldrin, and S'Heernoh behind them.
Galiose seemed greatly vexed, his walk an indignant stride,
his grimace a declaration of his displeasure with the world
about him. His dark eyes quickly found me where I sat at
ease upon the floor cloth, beneath the bottom step of the
platform which held the seat once used by the High Seat, my
back against the tread of the bottommost step, my left leg
drawn up so that my arm might rest upon it. His anger
quickly brought him forward, and he halted perhaps two
paces from where I sat.

"The foot of a man's throne is the proper place for you,
wench, yet not in such an insolent pose," said he in a growl,
putting fists to hips as he glared down at me. "Is this the
manner in which your word upon our safety is kept? By

denying us the possession of our swords? By denying us the presence of those brought with us?''

"You are guests within this dwelling, and guests have no need of weapons for their safety,'' said I with a shrug, answering that part of his speech which held meaning for me. "To say that weapons are indeed required is to say your host is without honor, her word untrustworthy. As for the balance of your males, I have no knowledge of them.''

"The suggestion that they remain behind was mine,'' said Aysayn, stepping forward while Galiose continued to glare at me, this time wordlessly. "There is little need for so many others to be about while we discuss what requires discussion. Should you later discover a need for their presence, you may send for them.''

"Send for them,'' echoed Galiose in a grumble, sending toward Aysayn a look considerably darker than that which he had sent toward me. "And of what use will they be, as disarmed as the balance of us? For a wench to know naught of proper male dealings is to be expected, yet for a man to do the same as a wench—'' Though outraged, Galiose's sense of propriety kept him from being even more insulting, then his attention turned to me again. "Where is the High Seat of Bellinard?'' he demanded. "Have you slain him?''

"The High Seat of Bellinard is indeed no more,'' said I with a further shrug, rising to my feet so that I might more easily see he who was High Seat of another place. "Earnestly was I assured that the male held his place through the blessing of his god, an approval which kept all others from challenging him for it. To test that I, myself, challenged that blessing, and met the High Seat's chosen champion with swords. When his champion fell, the High Seat did the same, and was thereafter sent to the fate he had so often given to others. Whether he remains alive I know not; should it be your wish to take yourself beneath this dwelling to see, you have my permission to do so.''

The face of Galiose worked in silent agitation. Some paces behind him were his three companions, Telion in some manner amused, Lialt faintly annoyed, and Ceralt—expressionless despite the trace of anger in his light eyes. To the left of them, at a distance of no less than three paces, stood the three

who accompanied Aysayn, their eyes as directly upon the
first males as the gazes of those three fixed on me.

"As the matter of challenge has been mentioned," I said,
looking up into the disturbance of Galiose's eyes, "perhaps
you would be kind enough to say where the male called
Nolthis is. It was my intention to seek him out when once the
strangers had been seen to, yet there may be time enough
before their arrival for a bit of—dallying."

"Dallying," echoed Galiose, looking down at me quizzi-
cally, no longer angry, yet more disturbed. "Since the fey I
learned of what he had done to you, I well knew what sort of
dallying you would seek with him were you ever to encounter
him again. For that you have more than my apologies, wench,
for I had never meant such a thing to be."

"And his current whereabouts?" I pressed, uninterested in
apologies. Words do naught to calm the battle lust in one, the
need for vengeance, the memory of agony. No less than a
meeting of swords will accomplish such an end, and I wet my
lips in anticipation of such a meeting.

"He undoubtedly burns in the dark god's realm," said
Galiose with a shrug of indifference. "I, myself, faced him
when I learned of his doing, the fool eager in his belief that
he might best me. So I informed Ceralt when he came
seeking him, and now do I so inform you."

I then looked at Ceralt, seeing the way his head came up, the
way he looked upon me. Galiose had stolen the satisfaction
which rightfully was mine, and the look Ceralt sent said he
would have done the same, proudly, happily, despite the lack of
honor in such a doing. That's how males regard vengeance, as
though it were free for the taking. Midanna knew that vengeance belonged first to she who had been wronged, yet were
these males far from the true honor of Midanna.

"Perhaps it would be best if we all now partook of what
food and drink there is," said Aysayn as I did no more than
bring the insulted annoyance of my gaze back to a Galiose
who saw naught of it. The male was well pleased with what
he had done, unsuspecting of the additional debt now between us, yet Aysayn saw what Galiose did not. One must
enter battle beside another in order to truly know them, and
Aysayn and I had stood so together twice.

"At last we find a subject upon which we might agree," said Galiose to Aysayn, a hint of humor now to be seen upon him. "Let us indeed fortify ourselves for the coming discussions—and against a possible extension of hospitality. It has come to me that those who are called High Seat are not looked upon with favor in this place."

Aysayn chuckled with amusement at Galiose's sally, and then did the two males take themselves off toward that place where the provender lay, drawing others with them. As I continued to hold a cup of daru I felt no inclination toward joining them, therefore I seated myself upon a step of the platform to sip from the cup, attempting to calm the frustration which filled me at thought of being deprived of Nolthis's life. It would soon be necessary to speak with those males about the strangers, to ease their outrage and see them quickly upon their way, and for such a thing one cannot join their feelings of outrage. Soon enough the strangers would arrive, and there would be time enough for outrage.

"I saw you found the need to put my teachings to use, wench," said Chaldrin in his calm, familiar rumble, sitting on the step to my left. "Did the slave attempt to do you harm?"

"The slave sought a different path from the one he strode," I said, seeing the amusement in the dark of Chaldrin's eyes. "Merely did I give him a glimpse of what other path he might find himself upon. For what reason do you fail to take sustenance, Chaldrin?"

"Perhaps for the same reason you fail to do so," replied the male, still amused. "Ilvin sought me out in the place I had been given to take my rest, and with her were a number of those wenches who were closest sisters to her among her Hitta. The wench had spoken so highly of my prowess in the furs that the others were of a mind to try me themselves, and all had come to ask if I were willing. I have not yet given them my decision, for I had hoped to have Ilvin alone this darkness, yet has the proposal centered my attention upon hunger for other than that which your table provides."

"Should you agree, I feel sure you will not damage Ilvin's estimate of you, brother," said I, sharing his amusement. "Should you feel uncertain as to your capacity, however, you have only to ask and I will have you provided with a small supply of that which is used to sustain what sthuvad are taken to serve the clans. Once in the grip of the drug, service to the entire clan of Hitta will not be beyond you.''

"My sister's generosity is greatly appreciated, yet have I heard of this sthuvad drug from Ilvin and Wedin and Dotil,'' he said, dryly. "As it is scarcely my wish to *need* to serve so large a number of wenches, I shall make do without. I wonder, however, if your thoughts have also been drawn to considerations of things other than sustenance, and yet also other than pleasure. You knew from S'Heernoh that these men would be here; is their presence the reason for the foulness of your humor these past feyd?''

"For what reason should it not be?'' I demanded looking down at the cup I held. "Much shame and humiliation was mine through the efforts of each of them, and deep insult as well. Would you have me greet them as brothers, only just returned home after too-lengthy an absence?''

"And yet, they look upon you as something other than an enemy,'' said he, his voice now soft. "Even he of the blue cloth and leather, despite his displeasure, has no true wish to see you harmed. Can it be your agitation stems from a source other than anger?''

"You believe I feel no anger at those about me?'' I asked with a snort of ridicule. "Should that truly be your belief, brother, best would be that you decrease rather than increase your time in the furs. Clearly have you already performed too often, to the detriment of your intellect.''

"I believe you feel *too* great an anger at those about you,'' he said calmly, ignoring my words. "So great an anger often conceals feelings of another sort. It also seems clear that your anger at Mehrayn these past feyd is meant to keep him at a distance from you. Are you unable to decide between the Sword and that dark-haired High Rider of the Belsayah?''

"All males are fools,'' I muttered, staring malevolently at the one who called me sister. "What decisions Jalav must make over males are concerned only with their battle disposition, naught to do with individuals. She who leads all of the Midanna has little time for thoughts of dallying.''

"Should you mean to ignore the matter in the hopes that it

will soon disappear and cease to be, you delude yourself, girl,'' said he, a faint annoyance beginning in voice and eyes alike. "Neither Mehrayn nor that other will allow you to avoid decision, and best would be that you reach such a decision quickly. Should they come to the point of facing one another, the decision will have been taken from you.''

"Sound advice,'' said another voice before I might reply to such an absurdity. I turned my head quickly to see Telion where he stood near enough to hear Chaldrin's words. The male held a cup of daru and a half-eaten leg of lellin, and he sat himself beside me with a nod for Chaldrin.

"You must indeed come quickly to a decision,'' said Telion, looking upon me with the light eyes I recalled so well. "Had Ceralt not had concern over the strangers to distract him, he would surely have gone mad the while his wounds healed. Ever were his thoughts upon you, ever were his fears tormenting him. Often, in the beginning, he would awake crying your name, the pain of his wounds fashioning danger and disaster for you in his sleep. He would shout and attempt defiance of Lialt, and then would Lialt and I find the need to force sleeping potions down his throat. Lialt had thought *you* were difficult to tend; Ceralt proved much the worse for him, and there was but one thing which kept him in his furs till his health returned: the promise that Lialt would search the Snows for your whereabouts when Ceralt was again able to ride. He has missed you sorely, wench, and will not depart without you unless he is made to believe another holds your heart—and then he will go only to await his ending.''

"Mehrayn, too, has had difficulty bearing your separation,'' said Chaldrin, his words coming as I gazed silently upon an uncharacteristically sober Telion. "His sleep, too, has been disturbed, I am told, with the belief that for some unknown reason your feelings for him are no more, and you mean to turn your back on him. Much has he agonized over that, sitting unspeaking for hind and staring into nothingness, yet he refuses to burden you with his fears. In your presence he is as he ever was, and fades to a ghost of himself only when you are elsewhere.''

"Therefore must you come to a decision,'' said Telion, his

gaze now more felt than seen. "Ceralt and that red-haired Sigurri know well enough of their rivalry, therefore is it only a matter of time before they do as your large friend suggests and settle the matter between them. Do you truly wish to see one of them lying slain at your feet?"

Chaldrin attempted to add even more words to those already spoken, but I stood abruptly and walked away, unwilling to hear more. Had I wondered at Ceralt's presence earlier, I now no longer wondered; he and Mehrayn were meant to face one another, and both were likely fated to fall. Had it been possible to walk the Snows all of us would have had warning—and yet, what likelihood was there that they would have heeded such warning? As males, they determined that none would presume to take that which they considered theirs? I raised the cup of daru to my lips and drained it, but that did not cool my quickly mounting rage. Mida would see the males destroy one another in contest over me, the males themselves would obey her wishes with pleasure and glee, and I—I was to favor one above the other, giving pain in the choice no matter how it was done, foolishly believing my decision would be respected. Clearly the goddess knew Jalav less well than she believed, less well than Jalav had grown to know males. Were I to reject one of the males, thinking to give brief pain and then see an end to the difficulty, I would quickly learn that was not the end of it. Males were stubborn, Mehrayn and Ceralt more so than most, and neither would walk away quietly. No matter the beliefs of Chaldrin and Telion, weapons would indeed be raised, and this I would not allow. The wishes of the goddess would *not* prevail, and the thought came that if I brought her sufficient frustration and anger, perhaps it would be unnecessary to seek her out afterward to give challenge. Best would be were she goaded into seeking *me* out, leaving Sigurr far behind in his own foul domain.

I looked up to find that all eyes rested upon me expectantly, as though all were warriors eager for battle, awaiting the word of their war leader. I looked from one to another with a snort of derision, avoiding only Mehrayn and Ceralt, then walked among them all to the board and the daru it held. Many pitchers of daru had been provided for those who would drink with the war leader, but the males had taken little of it. Perhaps they disliked the strength of the drink, and wanted something a bit less potent.

"Am I mistaken in believing I heard words concerning your decision?" asked Aysayn at last, his eyes on me as I turned from the board with cup refilled. "We will, of course, allow you the time to see to any matter which needs attending, before we begin discussion upon the point which brought us together. Most especially should the matter be a serious one."

A stirring came at the end of his words, as though all those who stood about wished to speak and yet dared not; only Chaldrin and Telion moved, as they brought themselves nearer to the board. I grew annoyed at such foolishness, for they waited, so they thought, to hear which male I would choose to follow, which male I would give my oath to obey. Were I to choose one over the other in accordance with their demands, such would be the decision I rendered, for no other sort of decision was acceptable to males. Clearly they failed to recall that Jalav was a warrior and war leader.

"The decision is of small consequence, and has already been made," said I to Aysayn, sipping from my daru and giving no indication that I noted his increased attention. Indeed, the attention of all of the males was now even more completely upon me, as though I discussed the fate of our world.

"As the decision has already been made, perhaps you would care to share it with us," said Aysayn, attempting a smile of comradeship through obvious symptoms of strain. "Has it to do with any of us who now stand within this room?"

"Oh, indeed," said I with a judicious nod, returning Aysayn's smile. "It was necessary for me to decide upon one who would share my sleeping leather this darkness, and the decision was easily made. Shall we now talk about the strangers?"

"Perhaps it would be best if we were first to hear which of us has been—honored," said Galiose with odd heartiness as he stepped nearer to me, his dark eyes eager. "The one who has been chosen will surely wish to prepare himself, and we others would wish to offer him our congratulations. Will you speak his name?"

"Certainly," said I, smiling at Ceralt and Mehrayn. The

two males stood together, somewhat apart from the others, dark-haired Ceralt bare-chested above his leather breech and leggings and silver belt, red-haired Mehrayn equally bare-chested above the black of his Sigurri loin covering. Truly tempting were the two, large, well-muscled, broadly inviting and able to give great pleasure, yet did they both wish to see me denied in one manner or another. As that was so, I considered it only meet that they taste of the thing themselves for once, and smiled instead at the one who stood beyond them.

"My choice for this darkness is S'Heernoh," said I, inspecting the male as a Midanna was wont to do. "My warriors speak highly of his ability, and I have decided to see the thing for myself."

Ceralt and Mehrayn seemed to cease breathing till my words of decision had been uttered, and then they turned with incredulous looks toward the one I had named. So quickly did the change from silence to uproar occur that I blinked, at once besieged from all directions. The protests from the males all about were clamorous and unintelligible, none permitting another to speak ahead of him, all deeply outraged. In the midst of it all I was able to see the manner in which S'Heernoh flinched, and then his eyes were covered by one hand, as though to shield him from pain. Although the looks given him by Mehrayn and Ceralt were not tender and brotherly, I failed to see what manner of pain there might be for him.

"Absolutely not!" thundered Galiose from beside me, his anger at last rising above the din of the others. "Have you no sense of propriety, girl? You may not look to another when there are two who have already spoken of their desire for you, two who will not be ignored! To allow a wench her say is ever an error, Aysayn, for she will ever make of it the sort of mockery now before us."

"You fail to understand, Galiose, that this wench is not merely a wench," said Aysayn, his dark eyes flashing with annoyance. "Are you unable to recall that the forces she commands are larger and more experienced than yours? That she rides in the name of the gods? That you now stand within a city held by those who follow her without question? How can you believe a decision may be forced on her?"

"She is a wench, and a wench must ever obey the men about her," returned Galiose in a growl, his stubbornness refusing to allow any to take the binding from his eyes. "That you permit her to do as she wills is no kindness, Aysayn, for she will never learn her proper place amid such doings. Join me, instead, in commanding her to a proper choice, one which will allow us to move on to matters of greater import."

"Blessed Signurr, deliver me," muttered Aysayn, his head ashake as he turned from Galiose to reach for some daru. Though he clearly wished to hear no more from Galiose, the other male stepped past me to join him at the board, his voice lowered and changed to coaxing. Briefly I considered summoning warriors to show Galiose the true meaning of obedience, yet was it necessary to recall that Ranistard's High Seat had Aysayn's bond as to his safety. Perhaps, after he had been permitted to quit the city as had been promised him. . . .

"Your sense of humor has scarcely improved since last you exercised it," said Telion, he and Chaldrin and Lialt stepping forward to take the places abandoned by Aysayn and Galiose. "You cannot mean to continue in such a vein."

"Ceralt will not allow it," said Lialt, his annoyance clear as he looked down upon me. "Don't you recall what his displeasure has meant to you in the past?"

"What number of times were you used by Mida's pets, Lialt?" I asked, looking up into the lightness of eyes so like Ceralt's, and yet so very different. "Were you pleased with that use? Mida's pets, I was told, were greatly pleased with your efforts, but remember they are scarcely warriors in truth. Would you care to experience use by those who are truly warriors?"

"We were given safe conduct, wench," said Telion when Lialt failed to reply, the Belsayah Pathfinder merely darkening at the reminder of his own embarrassment. "Though we appreciate the generosity of your offer, we must unfortunately decline. What do you plan for Ceralt?"

"And Mehrayn," came Chaldrin's rumble. "And for what reason have you ensnarled S'Heernoh in this madness?"

The large, dark male looked upon me with a vexation close to Aysayn's, the eyes of Telion and Lialt lending their import. I didn't have to discuss my decision with any of them, yet it suited my humor.

"It came to me that amongst all of you, S'Heernoh alone had not been tasted by me," said I, drinking from my daru and looking from one to another of those who stood about me. "I am a war leader of Midanna, and therefore must consider my actions carefully, giving no unintentional insult. Do you then believe S'Heernoh so much less than the rest of you, that he should not be done as you?"

"The worth of S'Heernoh is scarcely in contention," said Chaldrin while Telion shook his head in annoyance. "The matter before us at this moment concerns the Sword and the High Rider, both of whom are prepared to contest for you. Do you truly wish to see which one will survive the meeting?"

"What matters which survives, when there is naught to survive for?" I asked, knowing the simplicity of the statement would surely appeal to these males. "The two have presented themselves to the war leader Jalav, and that war leader has rejected them both. My choice will stand as stated, and none may deny me."

"Alas, my lady Jalav, that is unfortunately not so," came the voice of S'Heernoh. He stepped between Lialt and Telion, halting directly before me, and as strange as ever was the amusement in his dark eyes. "I would find it a great honor to attend you this darkness," said he, "and yet must I regretfully decline. There was a lovely warrior in the corridor through which we passed to reach our rooms, clad in red, of the Happa clan, I believe she said, and her request was most courteous—and interesting—and—" Much did the male attempt to appear shame-faced, yet he was too amused. "Already have I given my word to attend another. Would you see me forsworn?"

Silently had Mehrayn and Ceralt come up to stand themselves behind S'Heernoh, their eyes showing naught of the amusement of the elder male, the gaze of each of them resting no place other than upon me. Light was the gaze of each of them, Ceralt's blue and Mehrayn's green, and well did I recall the look of laughter in each pair of eyes. How deep was the touch of the look of laughter, and how rarely it occurred in the sight of a warrior.

"My lady Jalav, have you heard my words?" asked S'Heernoh, returning me to the fact of his presence. Again the male seemed amused, yet I knew not why.

"Indeed have I heard your words, S'Heernoh," I said, taking care not to look again upon the two who stood just behind him. "You need not fear being forsworn, for the Happa warrior who approached you will doubtless release you from your vow when she learns of my interest. You may, if you wish it, promise yourself for the following darkness."

"And who, if not S'Heernoh, will occupy your sleeping leather the following darkness?" asked Chaldrin at once, the accursed male unable to hold his tongue still. "Am I to be honored, or Telion or Lialt, or perhaps Aysayn or Galiose?"

"Surely not you, brother," said I quickly, wishing him to see my displeasure. "You, I am sure, will be far too weary from having served so many so well. The following darkness I will perhaps take a slave to my sleeping leather, for never have I had the taste of a slave. Perhaps it will prove a taste to build an appetite upon."

"Surely do you sound the city wench incensed over not having been courted," said Telion with a snort of derision. "What deference will you have from us, girl, and how soon will it bring you to sufficient maturity that lucid and adult actions will come from you rather than childish tantrums?"

"You dare to liken the doings of a Midanna war leader to those of a city slave-woman?" I demanded, my rage taking me a step nearer to Telion, my right hand already beginning to reach for my sword hilt. I understood naught of what the male had said, and yet I was certain from his tone that insult was intended. So often had insult been given me by those males during my time of capture, that they now believed themselves safe from my wrath. Indeed I meant to show the male how greatly he erred, yet had I forgotten that my sword had been put aside with theirs. My fingers closed on air, enraging me yet further, and the Mida-forsaken male folded his arms across his broad, leather-clad chest, and smiled arrogantly.

"Should a Midanna war leader indulge in tantrums, it is scarcely I who likens her actions to a city wench," said he, caring naught for the continuing insult he gave. "Do you also mean to spit upon the promise of safety given us, as if you had no idea of honor? Your posturings demand no respect, wench, solely do they call for a strip of leather to be applied to your insolence, with strength and with frequent repetitions. Surely do you. . . ."

"Enough, brother," came another voice, and I stood before Telion with fists clenched, my fury attempting to burst out of control, looking up into the mockery in his eyes, so greatly enraged that at first I knew not who had spoken.

"What reason is there for me to cease, Ceralt?" asked Telion. "As I raise no weapon they none of them may halt me, therefore may I address her as I please."

"You forget that *I* gave no such vow, Telion," said Ceralt very softly, so softly that the male before me lost the power of his anger. "Though we have truly become brothers through the trials we faced together, I cannot allow you to speak to her so. You give her uncalled-for pain, brother, and I will not allow her to be given pain."

"I had not seen it in such a light, Ceralt," returned Telion in a murmur, a quiet smile now upon him as he moved away from me. Ceralt then stood in his place, directly before me, no ridicule or condemnation in the light eyes which looked down upon me. "As you demand it of me," said Telion, "I shall certainly cease at once."

"Satya," said Ceralt, his hand raised to my cheek, his gaze held to mine, his voice striking me motionless with all the emotion to be heard therein. "It has been a lifetime and more since last I touched you. Are you well?"

So few words he spoke, this male who had done and been so much to me, the tips of his fingers to my face like burning brands, draining my strength and again beginning to make me his. My body cried out silently, demanding the feel of his arms about me, the touch of his lips upon mine, the ecstasy of his desire and the glory of his strength. A truly great need did I feel for the male, and yet was it far from the crippling desire in which I had been held the while I remained his captive. No longer was Jalav made slave by the goddess she rode for, and at last did she see the true reason behind the doings of Telion. He had deliberately insulted me, knowing Ceralt would intervene, thinking I would pay greater heed to one who stood himself in my defense when I could not, in honor, give proper reply myself.

"Jalav is quite well," said I to Ceralt, refusing further nearness and the indescribable pleasure that putting my hands to the firm, broad strength of his body would bring. "Perhaps it would be best to show exactly how well."

The softened look Ceralt had worn changed to a puzzled frown. With no hesitation I moved to where Telion stood happily sipping his daru, and quickly kicked out, catching Telion in the middle with the thrust of my heel. The daru sprayed from the mouth of the male as he flung his cup away and bent double from the strength of the kick, a strength which was no more than half of that which I had learned to deliver. It was not my desire to give true harm to Telion, no more than it had been his desire to give true insult, yet had each thing been given and also received. One who gives must ever be prepared to receive as well.

"A Midanna is pleased to take note of those who do not raise weapon to her," said I, looking down upon a Telion who knelt with one hand to the floor cloth, the other at his middle, a greenish pallor having settled upon his features. "Should you again wish to approach me without weapons, feel free to do so."

The daru remaining in my own cup had not been spilled, therefore did I turn from Lialt and Ceralt's attempts to aid their brother and swallowed it down, taking no note of Chaldrin swallowing down a chuckle. That S'Heernoh had also found amusement in the foolishness failed to surprise me, nor did the glint in Aysayn's eyes, nor the annoyance in those of Galiose. These males each had their own interest in foolishness, and I found I had forgotten the last of them till a hand touched my shoulder.

"Your ability has grown since last I saw it put to use," said Mehrayn, his wide hand gentle where it rested upon me. "I see it will be necessary to guard myself more closely in future."

I turned my head to his calm, faintly amused regard, recalling the time he spoke of, the time I had not been able to best his strength and keep him from me. So deeply had I desired his arms about me then, as deeply as I desired them that moment, yet no more might I acknowledge this of Mehrayn than I had acknowledged it of Ceralt.

"The male Mehrayn need not concern himself," said I, meeting the nearly fierce green gaze. "This warrior deems it highly unlikely that the need shall arise."

With little difficulty did I walk from his hand then, toward the board and further daru. Never before had I had so great a need of daru, yet was it also true that never before had I been plagued by so large a number of males close about me. Was this the manner in which Mida meant to end me, surely was the likelihood of her doing so quite excellent.

"The wench herself proves my words true, Aysayn," said Galiose as I reached to the daru pitcher. He and Sigurr's Shadow stood there together, and little amusement touched the High Seat of Ranistard. "None of us will find it possible to give full minds to matters of import till she has declared her true intentions. How is a man to do as he must, when thoughts of a woman constantly distract him? She must declare herself, I say, not behave as though she has never before laid eyes upon them."

"Perhaps it would be best if matters were permitted to continue in just such a manner," came another voice, the voice of S'Heernoh. I turned to see the grateful relief with which Aysayn looked upon the gray-haired male, for Sigurr's Shadow had clearly grown as weary as I at Galiose's constant carping. Galiose, however, was less pleased.

"I find no understanding of so unenlightened a view, man," said he, attempting to take the Walker's measure with his eyes. "Your disagreement with me indicates a lack of feeling toward those who now suffer needlessly. Should the wench be made to declare herself, the matter will be settled."

"Surely would it be far beyond my place to voice disagreement with the High Seat of Ranistard," said S'Heernoh, the smoothness of his voice and the small bow he performed causing Aysayn to drink from the cup he held, to try to hide his amusement. "Merely do I point out that we have scarcely come together here to discuss the doings of a wench and those men who desire her. Should the coming strangers not be adequately seen to, the declaration you now seek so earnestly will surely be of little interest even to those quite intimately concerned with it.''

"Your view no longer seems quite so unenlightened," said Galiose wryly, looking upon S'Heernoh apologetically. "Should those whose arrival we anticipate *not* be seen to, likely shall we none of us be free of suffering. Perhaps, Aysayn, you would begin by speaking of how you and yours come to be here.''

"I would be pleased to do so," Aysayn replied, equally surprised to see that there appeared to be more to Galiose than it had seemed at first. And as Sigurr's Shadow spoke the tale which had been requested of him, I was able to swallow my daru in peace.

"I had not thought that inquiring after your health would be so hazardous an undertaking," came a sudden voice from behind me striving not to sound stern. "I believe, in future, I shall avoid such controversial issues.''

"There are many things one would do best to avoid," I returned, making no effort to look upon Ceralt where he stood so close to me. And then, as I found I could not silence myself, added, "Your wounds are properly healed, I trust?''

"My wounds have been healed for some time," he replied, unfortunately coming about to where I might see him. So large and strong he was, his dark hair falling to his eyes, his gaze coming down to me as his hands toyed with the goblet he held. "I have missed you sorely, Jalav, and though I will surely bring pain to us both, I must tell you the reason for my having done to you what I did upon the journey to Sigurr's Peak.''

He was solemn, filled with the pain of difficult memory, doubtless reflecting my own memories.

"I am already aware of what reasons you had," I said, beginning to turn with the thought of joining Aysayn and Galiose, yet did a large hand come quickly to my arm to halt me.

"You could not be aware of my reasons," said he, a faint smile coming to him as though he anticipated speaking a truth too long held silent. "No others save Lialt and Telion were told of my doings, and they would not have betrayed a secret entrusted to them. You see, wench, Lialt had walked the Snows, and had discovered that. . . .''

"That you were to die," I interrupted, making him look serious. "It was you I learned the thing from, overhearing the words you spoke to Telion. And yet Lialt misread the Snows, for the thing which was so certain was, in the end, avoided.''

"Narrowly," he stressed, moving a hand to the thick lock of hair which draped my shoulder. "I had feared that I would not survive to touch you ever again, to put my lips to yours, to—I sought to breed hatred within you against my ending, so that you would not be given the pain of mourning me. Were my attempts too successful, Jalav? Is that the reason you have allowed another to take my place?"

Soberly did the male look down upon me, pain in his light eyes. I, too, felt pain, yet not for similar reasons.

"What place there is beside a war leader of Midanna is not meant to be filled by males," I said, taking my eyes from his and attempting to free my arm. "It was this that you were unable to accept, was it not? That I am a warrior and war leader, not a village female all aquiver to do your bidding? The place you took was not freely given, nor is it meant to be given to any."

"There is a place beside any wench for a man willing to take it," said he, refusing, though gently, to release my arm. "Indeed do I insist upon seeing you as other than a warrior, for you are, in truth, more woman than war leader, more mine than any other's. Have I not drawn you from the circle and declared you mine before all those who follow me? When the discussions here are done, you will again be mine."

"Just so easily?" I asked, looking at him again to see the blaze in his light eyes which declared he would be obeyed no matter the will of others. "And what of the goddess, and the task I see to for her? Have I been named Mida's chosen and the messenger of Sigurr merely so that I might be claimed by a male? Are the Midanna to face the coming strangers with no war leader to direct them? Have you so quickly forgotten the manner in which Mida deals with one who attempts to deny her will?"

"There are sufficient men about to see to those who come to do us ill," said he, stubbornness ablaze in the eyes which looked down upon me. "There is no need whatsoever for wenches to enter battle, therefore no need of one to lead them. It is more than past time that you be permanently claimed, woman, and I am the man who will see to it."

"Forgive the interruption, yet I could not fail to overhear the fact that some task requires doing," came another voice, an innocently helpful voice, causing Ceralt to release my arm. "Might I volunteer my services in seeing to the thing?"

Needless to say, Mehrayn wanted to join us, pleasantly smiling at those he addressed. Ceralt seemed immediately prepared to take insult at the jocular offer, yet quickly mastered his emotions.

"I give you thanks for your generous thoughtfulness, yet is assistance unnecessary," he returned in a manner similar to Mehrayn's, looking directly upon Sigurr's Sword. "The task is not so difficult, therefore shall I find it more than possible to accomplish it alone."

"Strangely enough, I, too, have a task to accomplish which I prefer seeing to alone," said Mehrayn, showing continuing pleasure in the face of Ceralt's smooth mannerliness. "Certain undertakings are more satisfying when seen to in such a way, are they not? Tell me, Jalav: which of those dishes upon the board do you find most palatable? As you and yours have done so excellently well in taking and holding this place, I will accept your recommendation without hesitation."

Now was Mehrayn looking upon me rather than Ceralt, with an interested attentiveness, his words having put a silent, jaw-clenching fury upon the other male. I did not know why Ceralt would be so upset, nor was I able to fathom the reason behind Mehrayn's asking such a thing. Surely the male was able to know of his own self which of the provender appeared tempting.

"I, too, would be pleased to have such a recommendation," Ceralt said nearly at once, quickly changing his scowl to a smile as he looked upon me. "So truly excellent were your efforts in preparing provender upon the journey we shared, that a man would be a fool to doubt your ability to know the finest. Let us move nearer to the board."

No longer was Mehrayn quite as pleased as he had been, most especially as he was nearly left behind when Ceralt put his arm about me to guide me toward the board. In one stride, however, Mehrayn was again to my right, and then there were three who halted before the provender.

"What of this?" Mehrayn asked at once, reaching toward the roast lellin. "It appears much as the lellin we shared in the forests between Signurr's city and the lands of the Midanna, when you rode to claim the leadership of those who were then enemy to you. I believe I shall never forget how fine it was, seeing you astride your kan, your swordbelt firmly upon you. . . ."

His green eyes looked upon me rather than the provender, his words recalling the closeness we had then shared for a time, his body calling out to mine as ever it did. Had he pulled me to him then I could not have refused him, yet was there another who stood with us.

"Perhaps you would recommend this nilno," Ceralt said before Mehrayn's words might continue, his arm about me turning me from the contemplation of Sigurr's Sword into which I had fallen. "I had not considered uncooked nilno, yet does sight of it recall to mind the time when first we met— and also the journey we shared in traveling between Bellinard and Ranistard. Never had I thought it possible for a wench to eat uncooked fare, and yet you did so without hesitation when the need arose. Never shall I forget how magnificent I then considered you—and how much more magnificent I found you to be after that. Our time together was unparalleled pleasure for me, far beyond anything I envisioned as possible. It was no less than. . . ."

It was light eyes beneath dark hair which held me then, bringing to mind the time I had so wished I might be Ceralt's. The concern of the male was ofttimes smothering, yet was it a concern which came from within him, one which truly put this warrior before his own beliefs and wishes. Perhaps it was that which caused him to release me from the vow he had stolen, the desire to see me kept from harm. Sooner would he have me free of the bond which held me beside him, than given hurt and humiliation through being forbidden to touch hand to weapon. His arm about me spoke of how truly long it had been since he had held me to him, and surely did I then wish it might be two arms about me rather than just one—had there not been others about.

"Have I ever spoken to you, of the time I fought for the place of Sigurr's Sword?" Mehrayn asked, he in turn treading upon the words of Ceralt, his arm about my waist turning me toward him again. "The one who held the place then was skillful indeed, yet I met him before all of the city, intent upon striving to the utmost to make the honor mine. No more than a breech of red cloth was I permitted to wear about my loins, to show, should I fail in my attempt, that it was a lowly slave who had foolishly sought to advance himself rather than one who had been a warrior of Sigurr. The fey was hot and bright when we stepped out to face one another, all those looking on silent with the tension of the moment. . . ."

"I believe you know, wench, that my father was Belsayah High Rider before me," Ceralt quickly put in, turning me again from the red-haired Sigurri. "Although the place was mine by right of birth, still was it necessary that I travel from village to village, answering any who might wish to challenge me for the honor. Were I to have fallen in such a challenge, the one who bested me would then be High Rider in my place. I had already faced two challenges and had stood victorious, when I came to the fifth village and a third who put himself before me as was his right. The first two had been naught, no more than fools believing themselves able to swing a blade, yet the third was considerably more. A man who had traveled widely and had been a captain in some High Seat's guard. . . ."

"And there we stood, gazing upon one another across our weapons," said Mehrayn, adding to my dizziness and dismay by turning me again in his direction. "The skies were dark and threatening, speaking of Sigurr's presence and his displeasure with one of the two who stood in challenge beneath his eye . . ."

"I had thought you spoke of the fey as hot and bright," remarked Ceralt, an odd tone to his voice. "As I, myself, felt very little fear and uncertainty, the times of my challenges are quite clear in my memory."

"A true warrior knows no fear and uncertainty," returned Mehrayn somewhat stiffly. "There is, however, the matter of wariness, which any with intelligence will feel. Most especially before one such as the previous Sword, who was . . ."

"My third challenge, once answered, brought unexpected results," said Ceralt, and once again I looked upon him rather than Mehrayn. "Immediately were there more wenches about me than ever before, battling one another for my attention, seeking to serve me, begging my favor. I laughed indulgently at the display, of course, for I knew as well as a man might that it was another sort of wench I sought, one who stood so far above the others that . . ."

"Although there was ever a shortage of wenches in Sigurr's city, I was sought out by them even before I became the Sword," said Mehrayn, once again adding to the whirling in my head. "Once the honor was mine, however, they were constantly about me, begging me to use *them* in my devotions rather than slaves. Even the slaves wept when I chose them, yet did I know full well that my heart would not be given till I found one so far above them all . . ."

"One would have little difficulty in picturing the weeping of slaves who were chosen to serve a follower of Sigurr," said Ceralt, immediately drawing the green of Mehrayn's gaze. "The Belsayah hold no slaves, nor have they interest in doing so. The wenches they draw from the circle of choice more than suffice."

"As those wenches are held even more closely than slaves, why should they not suffice?" asked Mehrayn, his tone as even as Ceralt's had been. "Men require slaves to share when there are too few wenches for each to have his own, yet are some possessed of sufficient honor to keep from using those who are free. To hand a free wench about is to shame and demean her."

"And to allow her to risk her all with a weapon in hand is to show her honor and concern?" demanded Ceralt, his blue eyes cold and unmoving from Mehrayn. "All men should be possessed of the sense to see the wrong in this; for those without sufficient wenches of their own, to do such a thing is inexcusable. Sharing will scarcely end a wench, yet battle . . ."

Already were their arms gone from about me, therefore was there naught of obstacles to keep them from standing toe to toe once again. Each spoke while giving no heed to the other, their tempers flying, and at last I was able to turn about of my own volition and walk a number of paces from them before swallowing half the daru in my cup. The foolishness of their previous exchanges had made my head pound, and memories of the times I had spent with each of them disturbed me greatly. So much anger and hurt had Ceralt given me, and yet, when I had thought myself forsworn and shamed beyond bearing by doings of my own, he had reassured me.

"How might there be shame for you in a thing which gave me such joy?" he had asked, holding me tightly to him in his furs, his gentle touch attempting to soothe away my misery. "Do you not know, woman of my heart, how long I waited to hear you call upon me in need, rather than bear the load yourself, alone and in silence? My heart leaped with greater joy than it had ever known—and you found naught save shame therein? Can there be shame in giving another such joy?"

To that fey was I unable to truly answer the question he had put, yet did I recall the strength he had given me when mine had not been sufficient, the arms which had held me to him without condemnation. And Mehrayn. How deep had been the confusion and hurt I had felt when I thought him chosen willingly by the goddess, and how clearly he had known of my pain.

"Jalav, my beloved, are you unable to see that such a thing is not so?" he had cried, holding me to him with all the strength in his great arms. "Never would I choose another before you, sooner would I see my soul irretrievably lost! Though you have come to expect much pain from men, I would give you the brief pain of death before I would give you the agony of turning from you when you would face the gods for me! And *never* would I find it possible to give you death."

I had been able to do little more than hold him then, just as I had done with Ceralt, and now they demanded that I choose between them, sending one of them from me forever. How great was my hatred of the goddess for bringing them together: beyond the bounds of simple blood debt, larger than the demand for vengeance. The cup of daru I looked upon moved as the hand which held it trembled with the rage which gripped me, turning red-tinged as the kill-lust sparked briefly, then wavered and lost reality as I pictured the journey trail which would bring me to the place I might realize my life's last, most stringent desire. No other thought save killing filled me then, and when Aysayn put a hand to my arm, the

look I gave him took some bit of the color from the tanned
face which regarded me.

"Jalav, what ails you?" he asked in the softest of tones,
his touch quickly withdrawn from my arm. "It had seemed
that you roved elsewhere in your thoughts, yet now do you
appear— Is there aid I might offer?"

"None may aid me now, brother," I replied, feeling the
overwhelming desires drain from me as quickly as they had
come. My head ached unbearably. I was to be forced to face
the goddess, in the place of her own choosing, in the place
where Sigurr waited. Once before had I faced him and withstood him to gain what I wished; this time was the need as
pressing, and I would surely be drawn again into his Realm.
Survival was unlikely, yet was I unconcerned with survival,
so long as that Other also failed to survive. I drew an
unsteady breath into my lungs as I looked again, differently,
upon Sigurr's Shadow, and shook my head at his concern.
"Perhaps I have partaken too freely of this daru," said I,
gesturing with my cup before draining it. "How went the tale
upon the reasons for your presence?"

"More successfully than the time spent by you, I would
venture," he said, turning to look upon the two males who
were then being separated by those about them. Lialt, Telion
and Galiose fought to take Ceralt to the left of the board, the
while Chaldrin and S'Heernoh did the same in an effort to
draw Mehrayn to the right. "Should peace ever be restored,
Galiose wishes to be allowed to tour this house."

"Knowing Galiose as I do, the wish was more likely a
demand," said I, at once seeing my conjecture confirmed in
the dark of Aysayn's eyes. "Have you thought upon a means
as yet of removing him and his ilk from our path other than
through battle?"

"There may perhaps be a way," said Aysayn with a nod.
"As the others are so deeply engaged in considerations of
another sort, let us take the opportunity to discuss the matter."

We both took more daru then sat upon the floor cloth and
began our discussion. Aysayn's thoughts had gone much in
the manner of my own, therefore I found no disagreement
with his words. Numbers are often critical in battle, yet are
numbers for the sake of numbers worse than useless. To take

into battle those who are not truly warriors, those who are as likely to cut and run as stand and fight, is most often to give victory to one's enemy. For that reason were all Midanna blooded warriors, and for such a reason were none save Sigurri warriors permitted to raise a blade. For the sake of victory was it necessary that Ranistard and Belsayah males return from whence they had come, and Aysayn's thoughts as to how this might be accomplished showed full understanding of the nature of those males. I listened closely, upon occasion nodding in agreement, and therefore was unaware of the approach of Galiose till that male interrupted Aysayn's words with a noise made in his throat.

"Tranquillity and peace have once more been restored—for this moment, at least," said he when Aysayn and I looked. "Perhaps I should begin my inspection of this place. I will surely find sufficient things amiss to distract nearly all those who accompany me, which is certain to be a far safer distraction than what now concerns them."

"Have you not yet had your fill of foolishness, Galiose?" I asked, looking up toward him. "It suited you to bring your males to this place; will it suit you equally well when you see them fall from lack of sustenance?"

"Of what do you speak, wench?" asked the male with a snort of ridicule, clearly lacking the ability to think as a true leader of warriors. "Has the great pleasure of being ardently sought after brought you fantasies? My men will hunt for their needs, just as they have till now."

"Along with the hunters of the Sigurri and my Midanna?" I countered, at last seeing his amusement falter. "Think you the forests hereabout are able to support so many? Think you your males will find targets for their arrows when they must hunt in competition with those who live within the forests? Do you mean to concern yourself with foolishness till their bellies rumble with hunger, and they turn avid eyes upon the kand which brought them?"

"There is place here only for warriors," said Aysayn, his tone firm though gentle. "We need not stand and shout the virtues of our respective warriors till all about are deafened to find a solution; there is a way we may prove the thing to the satisfaction of all, before we starve in the way spoken of by

Jalav. I had not seen the need in such a light, yet is she undoubtedly correct. We must settle matters as soon as possible."

"And how do you intend seeing them settled?" Galiose growled, his eyes hard upon Aysayn's. "Are we to be sent packing with the threat of having provender kept from us?"

"There is little need for childish threats," said I, rising from the floor cloth as Aysayn did the same. "Sigurr's Shadow has had a thought with which I completely concur. As it is the question of warriors which concerns us, we will see whose force possesses the largest number of them. Each of us will choose fighters from the other's ranks, of a set number previously agreed upon, and then will those fighters face one another with blunted weapons. Those who stand victorious will remain, those who have been defeated depart; the thing will in that way be proven beyond doubt."

"You are to choose the fighters from my force, while I choose those from yours?" demanded Galiose, looking from Aysayn to me and then back again. "Why would we not choose among our own followers? How are you to know which are the best among mine, when you will do no more than look upon them?"

"We do not mean to choose the best of yours," said Aysayn with a sigh, clearly having expected so—*male* an objection. "Nor are you to choose from among the best of ours. War leaders of the Midanna wear the second silver ring as Jalav does, Princes of the Blood among the Sigurri bear the mark of Sigurr in the flesh of their left shoulders as Mehrayn does. The remainder of those who follow us are warriors, and it is from their ranks that you must choose. For our part we will choose among those who are not well armored, those whose swords are not as well worn as those of their companions. Just as you may choose from any of ours, so will we choose from any of yours."

"You will deliberately choose new men and volunteers?" demanded Galiose, again near to the point of outrage. "You will seek to steal my place from me through the choice of those who are less than their brothers?"

"Are you unable to see that the very presence of those you describe weakens your force?" I demanded in turn, well out of patience with the fool. "Search about among Midanna and Sigurri, seeking the same, for you will have the same opportunity as we. Seek the *least* of our forces—and learn that they far outshine the best of yours. No chain is stronger than its weakest link, no force stronger than its weakest fighter. Your forces cannot hope to compare to ours."

"You believe your least will outshine my best?" said Galiose with barely controlled anger, yet with the sense of having found victory. "You demand a meeting to determine who will stay and who will go? Very well, I will agree to such a meeting—on the provision that the matter is seen to in exactly that way: your least against my best. Only then will I admit defeat as telling, only then will I return my forces to Ranistard. Now what say you?"

The belligerent male before us sought to force us to a protest of his proposal, clearly without understanding that Aysayn and I had expected his demand. Had we, ourselves, proposed it, Galiose would surely have grown deeply insulted and likely stalked out immediately to give the challenge. As it was he who voiced the doing, however, there was naught for Aysayn and myself to do save accept.

"Our least against your best," Sigurr's Shadow agreed, making no effort to glance at Mida's chosen. "Should we not emerge victorious even in such a meeting, we do not merit the honor of standing before the strangers."

"There must be one further provision," said Galiose of a sudden, his pleasure at our acceptance well hidden beneath the shadow of abrupt, uneasy suspicion. More indeed was there to Galiose beyond constantly grating verbiage, for it had quickly come to him that there had been no protest over so patently dishonorable an arrangement. "The meeting must be between my force and yours, Aysayn, none of the wenches to be involved. Too often will a man hold his stroke against a female, putting him at a great disadvantage. Ceralt, I feel sure, will ask the same."

"Indeed," said Ceralt with a nod from where he stood, between Lialt and Telion. "I will send my best against your least as Galiose does, in a meeting with blunted weapons, but the wenches must be excluded. To prove a man will not swing upon a woman proves naught concerning his fighting skill."

"A male who will not protect his life no matter who seeks to take it is a fool deserving to be ended," said I, looking upon Galiose in increased annoyance. "The Sigurri, at least, know better than to indulge in such mindless foolishness. What will occur should you somehow best Aysayn's warriors—and the strangers who come show themselves to be female like the Midanna? Will you merely step back from them and allow them to do as they please?"

"We will, in that event, allow your wenches to step to the fore," said Galiose, an odd look about him as he threw off his previous doubt. "For what other reason might the Serene Oneness have allowed you all to gather here? I, myself, would not merely stand by and allow a wench to attack me, nor would most of my men; in mock battle, however, where a man's life might not be lost, to attack in return with full strength would be dishonorable, and I will not handicap my men in such a way. Do you both agree?"

This time Aysayn did indeed look upon me questioningly, the calm in his dark eyes showing he would stand with me were I to voice a refusal. Though I felt the urge to do so, also did I feel the effort would be useless, for I recalled the doing of Galiose's male, he who had halted our approach when we had first shown ourselves. These males were, like all city males, completely lacking in reason, however there was little call for Midanna to be the same. To agree to the demand was to take a point of contention from Galiose against the time his males were bested, therefore did I nod sourly to indicate my reluctant agreement.

"Very well," said Galiose briskly in acknowledgment. "When is this meeting to be held, and where?"

"Surely not before the new light," said Aysayn, again looking to me with raised brows. "We must each of us choose those who will meet after agreeing upon their number, and then must we find or make sufficient blunted weapons for their use. The place may be chosen when these other matters are seen to."

"My warriors have given training to certain of the city males," said I, thoughtfully swirling the daru remaining in the cup I held. "They, perhaps, found it necessary to employ shielded weapons, for city males have not proven themselves able to stand against Midanna in any other way. I will inquire among my war leaders, and perhaps in such a manner will the number to face one another be decided on.''

"By the number of weapons available," said Galiose with a nod. Briefly did he look upon me with annoyance, and then he turned to Aysayn. "As there is a good deal of time remaining before the meeting," said he, "we may as well begin the inspection. You have told her that she is to accompany and guide us?''

"I have the desire neither to accompany nor guide you," I informed the fool of a male, in no manner willing to remain in the presence of Mehrayn and Ceralt. "Should it be your intention to see this dwelling, you may wander about as you will; perhaps fortune may then smile upon us, and you will become irretrievably lost. Now may you all take your leave, for I have war leaders to meet with and a battle to prepare for. Perhaps, Aysayn, you would care to bring a portion of your legions within the walls of this city, so that those of my warriors here may grow to know them as brother warriors. In battle, one should know those who stand at her back.''

"An excellent thought," said Aysayn at once, likely to cover the black look sent to me by Galiose. "Mehrayn will choose those he wishes within the city, and once chosen we may speak of a time for their entry. You will see to their billeting?''

"We will house them here, in this dwelling," said I, turning to replace my cup upon the board. "There is surely ample space for all, yet should there be. . . .''

"You cannot refuse," said Galiose from behind me, caring naught for the words of mine he trod upon, his voice somewhat lowered. "So long as those two are able to attempt to take your attention, they will not attempt other things with each other. *You* are the sole distraction currently able to hold them, no matter my previous words upon the point.''

The male attempted to force my agreement with the sternness of his gaze, yet was I of a different mind than he. To allow the two males their attempts was to encourage their belief that I would choose between them, a thing I most certainly would not do. To say again I would not held little meaning; far better to take myself from their company, and allow actions to stand in place of words.

"There are matters of battle preparation I must be about," I said, looking at Galiose with resolve. "Find one to distract you males who has interest in them."

The male clearly meant to speak further, yet did I turn and walk from him before he might do so. My feelings toward the goddess and her aims continued to twist me about, therefore was I nearly to the door of my sleeping chamber before a hand upon my arm told me of one who had followed and now sought to halt me.

"A moment, wench," said Chaldrin very softly, looking down upon me with an odd-seeming gaze. "S'Heernoh has told me of what the one called Galiose intended, yet does it appear that you have refused him. Is this so?"

"Indeed I have refused him," I agreed with a nod, wondering that he would question me upon the matter. "We all of us stand about engaged in foolishness, and should Galiose be allowed his will, the arrival of the strangers will find us still engaged so. There must be one among us who sees the thing done otherwise."

"But the strangers have not yet appeared," said Chaldrin, "nor may they do so for kalod yet. Are we to spend kalod doing naught save anticipating their appearance?"

"Such is foolishness," I retorted with a sound of scorn, sending him a glance of impatience. "For what reason are we gathered here, if not to meet and face the strangers? Did Mida not speak of this as the place they would appear? The time will not be kalod, Chaldrin, of this am I certain."

"Perhaps there is more hope than certainty in your convictions, girl," said he softly, a hint of sadness in his voice. "I, too, had hoped— You are truly unable to decide between them, is this not so?"

His great hand came to smooth my hair then, seeking, through the gentleness of the gesture, to lend strength where it was lacking. There was little doubt I had need of strength just then, but I found it within myself.

"I have no need to decide between them," said I to the broad, bare-chested man before my eyes. "A war leader need not take notice of those males who petition for her attention, for she is Midanna, not city slave-woman. When the matter of the strangers has been seen to, then will there be ample time to consider other things.''

"Should we all of us survive," said Chaldrin. "Should they appear before we are all too infirm with age to cause harm to any save ourselves. Are you aware of the fact that during this inspection Galiose proposes, you will have both Mehrayn and Ceralt before you as you have not previously had? And that they also will not face one another? You need to see them both together, Jalav, to weigh the words and actions of one against the other, before you know which one you wish. Should the wait for the strangers truly become kalod, would they not pass more easily with a man by your side?''

I moved an additional step backward to lean upon the silk-covered wall with my shoulders, looking down upon the blue floor cloth we stood on. I attempted to keep my temper in hand, for Chaldrin was truly a brother to me, one who believed he moved in the manner which was best for his sister. Much like my experiences in leading war leaders was this dealing with Chaldrin, for I had learned that to command war leaders was to be at times commanded by them. Though Chaldrin followed me, he, too, at times sought to command me to the path he considered best, an annoyance I found difficult to bear just then.

"It has unfortunately become the will of the gods that I have many males by my side," said I at last, raising my head to regard the one who gazed upon me so earnestly. Those others in the chamber paid our soft exchange no mind, they being then engaged themselves in converse of their own. "I have learned much in the time of my journeying for Mida, yet has one learning stood itself far above the others: the use of males is pleasant, their constant company a hindrance and annoyance. The two you spoke of will not face one another, for naught would be gained by the doing, a fact simple enough to be comprehended even by males. I have determined to grant neither of them my notice, and shall not.''

"No matter the amount of time you have spent among men, you continue to remain the innocent," said Chaldrin with a growl. "Ceralt, Telion says, has thought of little else these many hands of feyd other than recovering the woman he wishes for his own. Mehrayn, a man of great determination, will not allow another to claim the wench who has become his chosen. Have you not spoken to me of the manner in which Ceralt held you captive? Was I not able to see with my own eyes the manner in which Mehrayn took you to serve him? Think you your lack of notice of them shall keep them from considering the same again?''

"They may do no more than consider it!" I snapped, beginning to feel true anger at such foolish persistence. "Ceralt took me when I was wound-weakened and unarmed, Mehrayn when I believed I obeyed the commands of Mida. Now I stand in the midst of my warriors, and shall not allow the same again!"

"You will not allow it?" asked Chaldrin, his softened tone continuing even and remorseless. "In what manner do you believe you might halt it? Will you stand many of your wenches all about you when you sleep? Will you keep the same number about you when you walk the halls of this palace or the ways of this city? How many will you take should it be your desire to ride the forests hereabout? Think you such constant guarding will not be noted by those who follow you? Will you not lose face before them when they learn you fear the doings of 'males'?''

"I fear the doings of no males!" I spat, my hands clenched into fists, the anger likely blazing from my eyes. "Nor do I need to be guarded! Jalav is able to see to herself!"

"Asleep as well as awake?" pursued the wretched male, undaunted by my anger, folding his massive arms deliberately across his chest. "In an untenanted corner of this place, where any might appear silently behind you? In the thick of the forests, where each bush you pass many conceal one waiting to leap upon your kan? Which of them attempts the thing first depends only upon which has the smaller amount of patience, which takes the idea first into his head. Is this what you wish?''

The words he spoke rendered me well-nigh speechless with anger. None other save males would consider the doings Chaldrin spoke of, yet was there a thing he had failed to recall.

"They shall not do as you suggest, for they may not," I

snarled, feeling the desire to rend and tear with teeth and claws. "I am war leader to all these Midanna hereabout, and must lead them in battle against the strangers. Neither Ceralt nor Mehrayn would see the battle lost merely to satisfy their own desires."

"Indeed they would not," returned Chaldrin immediately, the manner in which he refused to take his eyes from me bringing me increasing upset. "However, it must be recalled that one named Jalav was necessary to bring them together, yet now might any lead them. The presence or absence of one additional sword will not turn the battle, wench, and this they understand more clearly than you. Well might that one called Galiose be set in your place."

"Galiose!" I echoed, so outraged that I nearly choked upon all I wished to say. Jalav unneeded, and Galiose to be set in her place? Chaldrin sought to give me outrage, as deliberately as Telion had sought to insult me, thinking I would likely speak agreement with his demands to keep so mindless a thing from occurring. He watched me carefully as I fought to separate one word from the next, faint amusement and hidden satisfaction in his gaze, while I strengthened my determination that never would I do as he wished.

"I shall not choose between them," I said from teeth tightly clenched. "I shall not allow this—'inspection'—Galiose demands, and I shall not take notice of males I wish no part of. Jalav has spoken, and so shall it be!"

"Jalav is stubborn, and ever shall it be," said the male, his rumble filled with great annoyance as he straightened even further where he stood. "I sought to guide you from the pit you stroll toward blindly, wench, yet do you refuse to open your eyes and see. As I have vowed to keep what harm from you I might, I must now see to the matter in another way. You will take yourself to the others and agree to the time among them, else shall I claim the right given me by you just after the battle with the followers of the foul Oneness."

So strongly determined was the gaze now upon me that I blinked, taken aback by his unrelenting manner. Quite often had Chaldrin and I disagreed, yet he had not appeared as he did now since the time I had been captive to him in the Caverns of the Doomed.

"Have you learned me so poorly, brother?" I asked, faintly hurt that he would consider me as so many other, unknowing males did. "Do you believe the thought of pain to be given will turn me from the path I have chosen? Should this be your thought, do what you must; Jalav, too, does as she must."

"Brother me no brother, wench," said he, again with a growl. So large was the male, the massiveness of his muscles doing naught to slow him in battle, his agility remarkable both with sword and barehanded. Foolishly had I given him my let to take what vengeance he would from me, and now would he see the thing done with none to deny him. Foolish indeed was the war leader Jalav, who required the giving of pain and humiliation to keep firmly before her eyes the true nature of males.

"I have no need to hear of a bond between us, girl," said he, lacking all sign of hesitation. "You think to bear what punishment I give you in silence, as you have done in the past, and then have it over and behind you. Perhaps you have forgotten what that punishment will be."

His eyes sought memory of the vow he had given, that time in the forests in the dark before dawn, not far from the visiting place of those who had been enemy Midanna. He had learned then of Mehrayn's doing, how the other male had taken me over his knee and brought a great ache to my bottom, and had nodded in approval and said he would do the same, yet not with so "light" a touch. Sooner would I have had the touch of a whip to my back, yet was there too little humiliation in a doing such as that for one who was male. I took my gaze from he who had once been leader of those in the Caverns of the Doomed and stared down instead upon the floor covering, speaking no word which might again be seized and used against me.

"I see you do indeed recall what punishment you must face," came the grimly satisfied tones of Chaldrin as he stood before me, a faint stirring to be heard as he shifted in place. "I have no doubt as to the silence it will be received with, and yet will silence avail you naught—should the thing be done before the eyes of your wenches. How firm does your resolve stand now, sister?"

So great was the terrible shock I felt, that nearly did my

breathing cease in the horrified stiffening of my body. Many
and many a time had I been given such shame and humiliation
by males that I thought myself unable to bear it, yet were
those things as naught when compared to that which Chaldrin
proposed. Of what use would I afterward be, if those who
followed me were to see me done as a slave female of the
cities, and then unable to even contemplate vengeance in the
light of the vow I had taken? How might I ever again meet
the eyes of any other, speak words as equals, seek out the
companionship of those like myself? There would be none
like myself, so terribly shamed that their souls had flamed to
dark ashes and were no more, and also would there be none
to lead the clans in battle. Each war leader would direct her
clan sisters as she saw fit against the strangers, and so many
would fall that even were victory to come, the Midanna
would be no more. I put a trembling hand to the deep,
burning illness in my middle, unable, through the wild, wailing
scream in my mind, to conceive of any other movement or
thought, and again words were directed toward me.

"You see, then, that you must obey me," said the one
who once had held my trust, the one who once had been
looked upon by me as a brother. "The walking about will not
be nearly so devastating an experience, and surely will you
soon see of your own self the need for it. Once you have seen
enough to speak a final word in choice, it will matter not if
weapons are resorted to; you will have learned that Mehrayn's
is the truer love, that he alone merits your presence beside
him. That other, that follower of the Oneness, will then be
seen for what he is; should he be foolish enough to challenge
the Sword he will fall, never again to bring you grief and
harm, never again to cast confusion over your mind. You will
then not seek to turn from Mehrayn for what he has done, but
will see it as the only fitting reply to one who has caused you
such pain. Would that I might do the thing myself."

How soft the words had been, how gentle the hand which
came to stroke my hair. I felt the smooth, warm floor cloth
beneath my feet, the unyielding wall which was again at my
back, and also the chill of my flesh which overrode an
awareness of other, lesser things. At last had my thoughts
ceased whirling in all directions, for no longer were there

thoughts left within me. No more than the pain of great hurt was there within me, a pain I had no true understanding of. I looked down upon hands which remained unmoving at my middle, feeling no desire to seek my lost thoughts, and again the same hand came to stroke my hair.

"You are upset now, I know, therefore shall I spare you the need to speak of your agreement," said he. "I will speak of it for you, and once you are in the midst of it you will no longer be upset. Have no fear, sister; all will surely turn out for the best."

He turned about and took himself toward the others. I stood by the wall alone. Deep within I now felt a hollowness where earlier had been pain, a hollowness which would never again be filled. There was the place where one called brother had dwelled, one who had betrayed me with the word I, myself, had given him so that the bond between us might not be shattered. How great a fool is the warrior who believes there might ever be such a bond between warrior and male, herself and a reasonless, honorless male. No other than Midanna would from then on call me sister, and I—never again would I speak the despicable word *brother*.

3.

Inspection—
and a cause for challenge

I had little stomach for walking about with those males, yet had it come to me that I had bought back my word with the agreement which had been forced from me. I stood beside the wall for no more than a moment or two, hardening myself to the necessity, only to discover that the males were not yet prepared to depart. Ceralt and Mehrayn had apparently failed to feed earlier, and now saw to the omission in company with Lialt, Telion and Chaldrin. At the doors to the hall stood only Galiose, Aysayn and S'Heernoh, and the first of them looked upon me with a mixture of satisfaction and annoyance as I came up to them.

"I congratulate you upon having learned at last to bow to reason and necessity," Galiose said to me, his tone somewhat dryer than I cared for. "Had the thing occurred sooner, surely would there have been far less difficulty between us. Now there is but one further matter I must remark upon, and that is the dagger you continue to wear in your leg bands. As we, your guests, must walk about unarmed, I consider it no more than fitting that you do the same."

"The dagger shall remain as it is," said I, stiffening somewhat at the reminder of the weapon—and the life sign wrapped about it. From Mida and Sigurr had my altered life sign come, and truly had it proven itself a device of the gods.

"For what reason do you refuse to remove the dagger?" asked Galiose, eyeing me in a curious manner. "Do you perhaps contemplate ridding yourself of a certain number of unwanted guests?"

"The life sign wrapped about it must be touched by none save myself," I replied. "It was given me by the gods as a

93

sign that I ride in their names and is capable of performing
wonders, yet is it also capable of performing horrors. No
other must be allowed to touch it.''

"Such is foolishness, girl," replied the male with an amused
snort. "There are none about with signs from the gods,
therefore do you merely seek to excuse the reason for retaining your dagger. If this were not so, you would need do no
more than replace the life sign about your neck, where it was
worn when you resided in my city. Give over the dagger
now, and no further foolishness from you.''

"It is scarcely foolishness," said Aysayn where he stood,
a sobriety upon him which Galiose clearly had not expected.

"The lady war leader may not give up possession of the
sign, nor may it be demanded that she wear it," said S'Heernoh
to a now-frowning Galiose, his manner as sober as Aysayn's.
"The sign of the gods is a jealous possession, allowing no
other to touch it, keeping the war leader in its thrall when she
wears it. It would be best to allow it to remain as it is and
speak no more about it.''

"S'Heernoh's words are true, Galiose," said Aysayn. "We
who have seen this truth wish we had not, therefore must you
consider yourself fortunate that you continue in skepticism.
Allow the dagger to remain as it is.''

"Very well," said Galiose with a sigh, scarcely pleased
with the need yet unwilling to press the matter. "I understand
naught of this, yet shall I say no further about it. We shall
depart as quickly as the others have seen to their hunger.''

I turned as he did to look upon Ceralt and Mehrayn, yet
was I filled with considerably less satisfaction than he. I had
no wish to continue in their presence, but I had to rid myself
of a more restrictive circumstance. When once the walk was
done my oath to Chaldrin would be done as well, and I need
not give heed the while to the maunderings of the two males.
Should they continue as they had earlier done, I knew the
thing would not be difficult; to that moment, I had not the
least idea of what they had attempted, nor the reason for it.
Indeed are males strange, and truly is that strangeness best
kept well away from warriors.

I had expected Mehrayn and Ceralt to indulge in a leisurely
feeding, yet did they heal their hunger quickly, and seem-

ingly with careful scrutiny of one another. Neither of them looked upon the other directly, yet they were done at nearly the same instant, quickly swallowing the daru they had poured. It was clear all were at last prepared to depart, therefore did I move to the doors and begin that departure without further delay.

There was little to be seen upon the floor which held my chamber, therefore did I lead the males to a stairway which led below, yet not to the nearest stairway. It had come to me that much time might be spent upon no more than moving from place to place, allowing Galiose to look his fill at empty halls, and then would I have fulfilled my commitment to accompany the set. I had little wish to take those males among warriors, most especially as my sword remained behind me in my chamber. In honor I could not refuse them guest-protection, and that despite the fact that should need of it occur, it would likely be brought about by their own actions.

"What has become of the slaves who are meant to see to guests upon this floor?" asked Galiose, his gesture indicating the abandoned platform once surrounded by slave females which stood in the corridor near to the stairway. "Also were they absent upon our arrival."

"What slaves remain likely have duties elsewhere," said I with a shrug, then did I recall something. "Earlier was a slave sent to me by Aysayn, none came to offer you their services?"

"The servant who came was male, as was the slave who passed my door in search of Aysayn," said Galiose, his gesture this time discounting those he spoke of, his eyes upon me rather than upon the steps we descended. "I would know what became of the collared wenches once to be found here, the slave females who served men. Your own wenches would have little need of them, I know, therefore do I find myself curious as to their—disposition."

The male looked upon me with little expression, yet were his dark eyes anticipating my response with something akin to upset. Galiose clearly considered it possible that the slave females had been done away with in some manner, perhaps put with the former High Seat in that place called dungeons.

Truly were city males without the least concept of honor, for what true warrior would do such a thing to so low and helpless a creature as a slave female?

"The slave females have been freed," I informed Galiose stiffly, attempting to deny the insult I felt at thoughts which had been, in truth, unvoiced. "You must recall, male, that Midanna are warriors possessing honor, not males who steal forever the freedom of others. Sooner would we give the kindness of death."

"Those who look upon death as a kindness have not yet learned how precious life may be made to be," said Galiose, his hooded look of relief mixed well with an appealing oddness. "Also does it seem that freedom concerns your warriors only when it is that of wenches; had that not been so, there would be no slaves of any sort about. To keep men imbonded is clearly acceptable to you, for men bring you pleasure which wenches do not. A pity you have never learned that men are far more than the bearers of that which brings pleasure to females."

Those who moved about the lower floor looked with curiosity upon those who had just descended, yet they all continued about their business rather than intrude. Perhaps what warriors were there and those called servants had pressing tasks elsewhere—or perhaps they were able to see how the words of Galiose had affected me. I would not speak of the reasons for retaining some few of the males as slaves, for Galiose was not one to whom a Midanna must account, yet had I another matter upon which I would not refrain from speaking.

"Jalav has been given many opportunities to learn of those things males are capable of aside from pleasure," said I, sending to him a look filled with memory. "Would Galiose care to see the leavings of some few of those doings?"

"Enough, wench," said the male at once, his eyes quickly leaving me, his voice heavy with something very like defeat. "I have spent too many reckid hearing first from Ceralt and then from Aysayn of those things which have been done to you by men. I, myself, stand as guilty as those others, and knowledge of this fact sickens me. There is no apology which might be offered for such a thing, save possibly to give aid where I might, such as with Ceralt and that other. Perhaps, should the Serene Oneness smile upon us all, you will become deeply enough enmeshed with them that you will find yourself with no spare moments to give men challenge. Certainly such an end is worthy in itself.''

Again his eyes were upon me. Well did Galiose know that I deeply wished to give him challenge; the male thought to distract me with foolishness in the hopes of thereby extending his life, yet were his thoughts as badly formed as those of all males. When once the matter of the strangers was done he would be the same, but it was idle to repeat the thing again at that time; the male would not believe till my sword point stood at his throat, and then would all save ending be behind him. This I spoke of with a look of my own, then did I turn to continue us on our way.

Galiose walked quietly beside me for some small distance, his silence seemingly filled with inner agitation, and then did he appear to take himself in hand once more. He looked about at the pink stone of the dwelling, as though seeking a sign of familiarity in the midst of strangeness, and then gestured toward the cross-corridor we approached.

''We shall take the left-hand turning there, rather than continue straight ahead,'' said he, much as though he walked the halls of his own dwelling. ''There is likely to be little of interest in the direction we now move in, and also little to inspect.''

The male spoke with a conviction born of knowledge, and it came to me then that he likely knew the dwelling well, for he had surely been within its walls upon other occasions. I had no wish to abide by his desires, yet was it now clear that to refuse would be to speak of the delaying tactics I had attempted. Galiose would take the direction he desired, and I would find it possible to do no more than regret again the sword left behind me.

The turn to the left was far too easily accomplished, those others with us following after without comment. I strove to recall what might lie in the direction we now took, then found it best to silently admit that I no longer knew, even had the knowledge been mine to begin with. To take a dwelling of such size had proven far easier than to learn its twistings and

turnings, most especially for one who had spent so little time
within it. Likely even Galiose knew the place better than I,
which turned my former intentions to no more than foolishness. It would be best to merely accompany him as had been
agreed, all the while looking not once upon . . .

"Do not seek Aysayn for a short while, wench, for he will
not be with us," came a voice nearby, a voice which seemed
pleased to have a reason to speak. "He has asked me to
inform you that he goes to inquire about the availability of
blunted weapons, and will return as soon as he can. Should
practice weapons not be available we will need to fashion
them, therefore does he feel it best that he begin now while
you are otherwise engaged."

"Otherwise engaged," I echoed in a mutter, finding
Aysayn's message near as annoying as Mehrayn's satisfaction. Others moved about at necessary tasks, while I did no
more than accompany males through corridors I had no knowledge of, so that one of their number might look critically
upon those who had accomplished what his own force would
surely find beyond them. Great fools were males, and Jalav
scarcely different for endlessly permitting herself to be thrust
into their presence.

"What is it that you seek, Galiose?" came another voice at
my side, the speaker stepping smoothly between myself and
the High Seat of Ranistard. "This place seems well-kept and
efficiently run, much like your own palace. The servants are
numerous and pleased to do what they might, and even the
warrior wenches seem alert."

"To seem alert is not to be alert, Ceralt," replied Galiose,
his eyes narrowed as he looked ahead. "Neatness and servant
efficiency do little to protect a palace, and this place may
well be under attack very shortly. I would see what precautions have been taken, and how well they have been maintained after so many feyd of quiet and peace. That doorway
just ahead to the right is the armory, yet does it stand open
and unguarded. Apparently any who wish weapons need only
enter and take them."

"Surely there are none about these halls who have proven
themselves untrustworthy in such a way," said Mehrayn, his
intention to lodge a protest somewhat dampened by the obvi-

ous truth spoken by Galiose. "What need to guard weapons in the midst of one's own?"

"What better way to find victory over a sleepy-eyed force, than to appear unexpectedly in their midst?" countered Galiose, his eyes unmoving from the open doorway we had approached and stopped before. "And, adding insult to injury, using their own weapons to best them? Only wenches would gift their enemies quite so well and so thoughtlessly, yet what else might one expect? To teach them better, I may well enter and arm myself from that which fails to be properly guarded."

Galiose had found an inarguable point of contention, and fully intended using it to replace that which had been taken from him.

"You have not my permission to appropriate what you will from that place," said I to the look he bestowed upon me, showing no more than the mild refusal I spoke with. "Not till you have been given that permission may you arm yourself."

"And I say a man who finds the soft underbelly of a guard beast, may pierce that underbelly at will," countered the male, his full-grown determination now bringing him pleasure. "The sword I strap about me will speak more fully of your lacks than a thousand words, and not soon will you forget such a lesson. When I have chosen the sword I wish, you may then send for wenches to guard this place."

With such words did the High Seat of Ranistard turn from me and begin to stride into the chamber, a chamber invitingly open and unguarded. Ceralt looked toward me with a faint air of hesitation, likely considering how he might join Galiose without bringing anger to she who stood beside him, and also did Mehrayn seem of two minds. As Galiose sought a weapon, they also wished the same—and their hesitation alone kept them from sharing the lesson their brother male had earlier spoken of.

Galiose was no more than three steps within the chamber, his gaze already moving about the rows and stacks of weapons, when the net fell upon him. Large and heavy was that net, meant to be used upon more than just one, and its weight and the surprise of its abrupt drop sent Galiose down to the stone of the floor with an outraged shout. Even as the net settled about the male and bore him down, brown-clad

Harra and gold-clad Hulna appeared to surround their captive, some armed with spears, some with unsheathed blades, all grinning widely. Galiose attempted to struggle beneath the net, furiously seeking to free himself, yet was he no more successful than I had been in a similar circumstance. When it was clear he could not escape, I walked slowly forward to stand over him.

"When one is surrounded by those who may be blood enemies, one takes certain precautions," said I, the patient explanation drawing a dark-eyed glare from beneath the net. "What is barred may be unbarred, and clearly seen guards standing a post become no more than targets for those who attack. Far better to keep those guards well out of sight, and use what may be coveted to draw enemies out from behind dissembling obedience and friendliness. Before riding to Sigurr's city, I offered prowess standing to any warriors who were able to take a guarded point from those who guarded it. Any warrior caught unawares by her sisters loses a great deal of standing, therefore would I venture to believe that they remain alert. Have you concluded your inspection of this chamber?"

"Yes, I have concluded my inspection of this chamber," replied Galiose with jaw clenched tight, fingers curled to claws in the netting, skin darkened in response to the sounds of muffled chuckling to be heard from those who had remained outside the chamber. "Perhaps you would be so kind as to order me released."

"Sooner would I indulge in the kindness of city males, and keep what was captured as it is," I said, nevertheless gesturing to my warriors to remove the netting. "A pity males have not the capacity for honor possessed by warriors."

I turned away then to leave the male to be freed by those who had netted him, and returned to the others who awaited an end to foolishness. Mehrayn and S'Heernoh grinned openly, Ceralt, Lialt and Telion attempted to swallow down their amusement, and no others stood about with them. Two were gone from our set, then, and earnestly did I wish that those two had been accompanied by the rest.

"Your security arrangements seem well thought out, wench," said Mehrayn as I came to a halt before them, reluctantly awaiting the release of the last of them. "I find them no less than what might be expected from one such as you."

"Indeed are your safeguards impressive," said Ceralt with a glance for Mehrayn, yet otherwise taking note of none save this warrior. "It gives a man a good deal of pleasure, to see a woman with so great an amount of talent as well as beauty."

"And skill," said Mehrayn, refraining from a glance toward the other, expending much effort in maintaining an air of pleasantness. "Talent, beauty and an unmatched skill, things one finds but rarely in a wench."

"And grace," said Ceralt, his smile strained yet attempting great warmth, his gaze remaining upon me. "The grace of a woman who stands far above all others, and who is . . ."

"Who is the image of a superb child of the wild," said Mehrayn warmly. "All grace and suppleness, and filled with . . ."

"There was little need for so humiliating an incident, girl," said Galiose in a growl as he came up to my left, apparently seeing naught of the manner in which I had closed my eyes. Soon would Ceralt and Mehrayn be at one another again, and I had no wish to watch. My patience was also wearing thin, and even as I rubbed at the weariness in my eyes, the voice of S'Heernoh came between the two at the brink of challenge.

"Forgive me, Prince, Lord High Rider, yet must I speak," said the gray-haired Walker, the smoothness of his tone offering no more than apology. "Should it be the intention of either of you to find approval in the eyes of the lady war leader, such constant bickering will not accomplish the aim. Surely the wench look upon a man who is the master of his emotions with more favor, will she not? Few find interest in uncontrolled boys—would you wish a woman who desired such a one?"

My eyes had opened to see the manner in which the two had looked with little friendliness upon the Walker who stood between them, then they glared at each other. It seemed that they wished to argue more, yet had S'Heernoh's words given them pause.

"Is there not truth in what I say, Blessed One?" S'Heernoh continued to Galiose, disallowing the second male the pursuit

of his previous anger. "Is the wench not more likely to look
with favor upon those who court her interest, than upon those
who are constantly at each other's throats? And also would
she not find more interest in men when not in the midst of
being berated?"

Galiose, who had seemed rather intent upon voicing his
grievances, also paused, looking first upon S'Heernoh, then
upon Ceralt and Mehrayn, and lastly upon me. Clearly the
male was not pleased, yet did it appear that he was again
trapped in the coils of a net.

"Most certainly would a wench prefer the courting of gen-
tlemen to the roistering of brigands," said he after making a
sound in his throat, his glance to S'Heernoh much like that
bestowed upon the Walker by Mehrayn and Ceralt. "A man
incapable of properly paying court is a man who deserves to
forfeit what he seeks. Let us now continue with the inspection, and those who wish to leave us may do so."

With a hand to my arm Galiose then led me through the
others, who gave ground with rather peculiar expressions
upon them. Perhaps Ceralt and Mehrayn had garnered as little
from what had been said as I, yet their faces showed more
determined frustration than bewilderment. S'Heernoh, as ever,
seemed more amused, and Telion and Lialt strove to appear
uncaring despite the deep interest shining in their eyes. The
Harra and Hulna warriors we left continued chuckling with
amusement, a thing which failed to lighten my humor; I had
hoped Galiose would grow angry enough to stop his charade,
yet were we now to "continue."

Galiose held silent for a short distance, as though he
considered some matter in his thoughts, and then was there
the sound of a noise in his throat once again.

"So your wenches are encouraged to constantly test the
alertness of each other," he said, his glance to me in some
manner disturbed. "Slackness after victory then becomes
impossible, as does the loss of battle-keenness. Those who
know an attack will surely come cannot be surprised."

"Surprise remains possible even then but requires quicker
response," I replied, at last understanding that the male
strove to appear unimpressed. "Surely the same is done
among your males."

"Ah, most certainly, most certainly," agreed the male, once again finding great interest in the corridors about us, attempting to conceal the fact that he spoke a falsehood. Likely victory brought a slovenliness to city males who found it, as though none would then attempt to take that victory from them, and these were the ones Galiose would see in the place of my Midanna.

"I understand that the gardens of this place are quite lovely," said another voice, and then was Ceralt again between Galiose and myself to the left, his light eyes looking down upon me. "Perhaps you will be kind enough to show them to me when this inspection is done."

"I, too, would find great interest in such a stroll," said Mehrayn from my right, a smile accompanying his gaze. "Second, of course, to the one whose original suggestion it was."

"And I, of course, would have no more objection to a second stroll than another objects to the first," said Ceralt, also smiling. "The wishes and desires of the woman of my heart are foremost in my thoughts."

"As is the pleasure of that woman foremost in mine," said Mehrayn, the utterance which was so filled with warmth an apparent agreement with that of Ceralt. "Harmony is what she wishes, therefore is harmony what she will receive."

Both males, greatly pleased with themselves, then joined Galiose in looking about, apparently unaware that each took one of my hands in his own, nearly simultaneously. So large were the hands which took mine, in proportion to the males themselves, seeming as vast as the confusion which had returned to descend upon me. I knew not what those males were about, yet was it unlikely to bode well for the warrior who walked between them.

The time I had hoped to see greatly curtailed lengthened itself instead, growing and growing as we walked from one corridor to the next, Galiose peering into each corner it was possible to approach. The chamber which held a great number of sleeping males puzzled him, yet only till he was informed by a Homma guard that the males rested and gathered their strength against the time they would be summoned by warriors. Then was the male greatly indignant, most espe-

cially when the Homma suggested he might wish to join
them. None were captives, she assured him, she and her
sisters present only to be sure the males were not disturbed
before they were well-rested. Her grin was wide when Galiose
stalked from the chamber, and the manner in which she
closed one eye to me behind his departing back brought a
good deal of amusement I had not earlier felt. Galiose huffed
and muttered for a number of reckid thereafter, apparently
berating himself for having looked upon the Homma warrior
with interest before she had spoken. The interest of a male in
a warrior was acceptable; the reverse evidently was not.

That the incident was amusing was undeniable, as undeniable as the fact that the balance of the time was not. Mehrayn
and Ceralt continued with the newest of their strangenesses,
uttering not a single word in anger to one another. Indeed did
they strive to be most pleasant, praising this or that doing or
appearance, this or that guardpost or gathering. That I gave
almost naught of words in return disturbed them not at all,
they were able to parade their intentions and observations
before me, with none to halt the flow.

Had the two restricted themselves to words, perhaps the
barrage would have proven more bearable; they began, however, to do more than just talk.

It was Mehrayn who started it, an opportunity presenting
itself which he chose not to overlook. Galiose had paused to
enter a large chamber where warriors of many clans loosened
their swordarms in practice duels, and had called Ceralt to his
side to share his observations. The others had entered the
chamber as well, eyes narrowed as they sought points for
criticism, therefore were none save Mehrayn and myself left
in the corridor. Without warning was I suddenly in Mehrayn's
arms, my body pressed to his, his lips warmly upon mine.
The kiss was not given but taken, surprise holding me still,
and then were his lips beside my ear.

"Best not to mention this wench," he said in the softest of
whispers, gently kissing my ear. "That I found myself no
longer able to keep my hands from you would likely be
insufficient reason to keep further difficulty from occurring. I
would welcome such difficulty, however for your sake I shall
attempt to avoid it."

I was then directed into the chamber by the hand of the male, no indication upon him of what had occurred, no more than the thumping within me as a sign that there had, indeed, been a thing to consider. My anger was great that the male would dare do me so, then bind my actions against all protest; had I attempted to remonstrate with him, Ceralt would likely have made himself a party to the dispute, and I did not want that. Also I was annoyed that the male had stirred my blood at a time I might not see it cooled again, unless I pulled him into a quiet corner as he had done with me. The glint in his glance said he would not be averse to such a happening, yet his attitude did nothing to alter the situation. I might not choose between the males, and that despite the urgings of heat.

Shortly thereafter was it Mehrayn who stepped within a chamber which would likely house a number of his Sigurri warriors, accompanied by S'Heernoh and a now-returned Aysayn, followed by Galiose, Lialt and Telion. Before I might also follow, I was quickly pulled into wide-muscled arms with my back to the stone of the wall, and then were warm, hungry lips upon mine. How long it had been since last I had tasted Ceralt's kiss I knew not, and I could scarcely pull away with my back to the wall. My paltry attempt was completely unsuccessful, and deep was the kiss the male took before his lips left mine.

"Forgive me, Jalav, yet I could no longer keep from taking a small taste of you," I was told in a soft, pleasure-filled voice which caressed my ear. "Likely it would be best that we keep this between ourselves, however, for the sake of the peace you desire. Should your desire at any time change, speak to me of it and I will do the same again, with eager heart, before the others."

And again was I assisted after those who had gone ahead, unable to speak a word of complaint, even more aware of the demands of my body. Never before had I denied myself so, and I found the experience one I could easily have done without.

Nearly another hin passed then, and it quickly appeared that Mehrayn and Ceralt now sought all opportunities to put hands to me. A query upon something observed brought an arm about my shoulders or to my waist, a compliment drew a hand to my hair, and the departure from one post to another most often required a pat on my bottom. As the time passed my anger grew even greater than the stirring of my blood, for had I not been forced into their company by another, the two would have had little opportunity to do me as a city slave-female, theirs for the stroking. Though they gave no outward sign of it the others about us were well aware of the doings of the two, their glances constantly revealing amusement, and at last I was able to bear no more of it. Galiose had led us outside the dwelling through a small side door, checking what would be faced by those attempting entry past the Happa who stood their post there, providing me with the opportunity to merely turn and walk away. Turn I did with no effort whatsoever, yet no more than three steps brought me to Aysayn, who stood unmoving in my path.

"Where do you go, sister?" he asked, seeming all innocence. "I feel sure Galiose does not mean to take this direction next."

"I care naught for what direction Galiose means to take," I replied, disdainfully. "I go now to see to other, more pressing matters."

"You go now to avoid further time with Mehrayn and Ceralt," he corrected, the pose of innocence dissolved as he folded arms across his chest. "You err in seeking to avoid them, girl, for now is the time best suited to choosing one above the other. They have made you desire them, and in deep desire does one learn one's true feelings."

"My true feelings are indeed known to me," said I with a nod of stiffness, folding my arms as he had. "I wish neither of those males, therefore shall I not choose between them."

"You have so little wish for them that you nearly moaned with each of their caresses," said Aysayn with a snort of ridicule. "That you are a wench made for the use of men and one who finds too great a pleasure with them is known to me, yet does this go far beyond the heat needs of a wench. Remain with the two a short while longer, and then you will know which of them you must have to ease you."

"I go now to see to pressing matters," I said again, the

fury rising so high within me that I well-nigh choked upon it. "Step from my path, male, before I hurl you from it."

The Happa warriors, who had not heard the balance of the exchange between us, nevertheless heard the last of my words and stepped forward to stand at my back. Aysayn looked first upon them and then upon me, at last understanding that the fury I felt would send the eager Happa against him without hesitation, no matter the closeness which had previously been ours. With great reluctance he stepped away from me, far too wise to put himself, weaponless, against armed and skilled warriors, and with a gesture which returned the Happa to their posts, I at last managed to slip away, filled by fury. I should have set my warriors upon him no matter his capitulation, for daring to speak so to me, a lack I regretted as I made for stairs which would return me to my chamber. A wench made for use by males indeed!

So great was my anger that I had stalked well within the chamber before it came to me that others awaited me there, others who were not male. Rogon, war leader of the Hirga, and Palar, war leader of the Hunda, stood by the board with cups of daru in their hands, their brows raised at the manner of my entrance. Rather than speak I stalked to the board, poured daru of my own, then swallowed it down without pause. The drink did naught to cool the flames which raged within me, and this the others were able to see.

"War leader, may we assist you in any manner?" asked Rogon, her head to one side in unspoken curiosity. Not so large as other Midanna was this Rogon, yet was her sword swift and deadly, she having bested all who had ever stood to face her. She accompanied me when first we had taken that city and had proven her courage and strength without question. Now I attempted to keep the heat of my anger from her, as I attempted to relate in some manner what had occurred.

"Never, Rogon, never allow those who are male to speak with you upon any subject," I growled, reaching to a pitcher to refill my cup. "Should you fail to heed my words, you will surely regret it."

"Jalav, never have we found more than a single use for males," said Palar, amusement to be heard in her voice. Both taller and broader than Rogon was Palar, hair of a brown touched less with red, eyes as dark, sword as quick. "Should those who returned with you be too great a bother, my warriors would be pleased to see to them for you."

"Indeed," said Rogon with a grin, exchanging glances with Palar. "We are warriors of Mida, are we not, and it was at the behest of Mida that these males were brought here, was it not? What, then, would be more fitting?"

"To see them strung above a slow fire would be more fitting," I replied, speaking the words with such distinct vehemence that the two war leaders laughed. "Should the strangers take much longer in arriving, surely will I greet them as sisters, rather than lead attack against them. Their appearance will cause the males to ride out immediately, and how might one attack those who take so great a stone from about one's neck?"

"The males seem much involved in courting you, Jalav," Rogon observed, her amusement continuing as she sipped at her daru.

"Males have little reason," said I, taking my cup of daru as I seated myself cross-legged upon the floor cloth. "They seek to have me do what I would not. One would believe they had no knowledge of the coming battle."

"They are males, Jalav," said Rogon, "and ever do males seek to avoid thoughts of battle." She seated herself before me as she spoke, Palar also doing the same, and only then did I see that she waited to speak with me regarding some matter. Custom dictated that a warrior not attempt to speak before her war leader was prepared to listen, and although Rogon herself stood as war leader, also was she a warrior of Mida under my command. I had done little for those who followed me since my return; now I must lay aside my own concerns for a time.

"How may I assist you, Rogon?" I asked, looking upon the small Hirga war leader. "Has something gone amiss here in the city?"

"Our doings here in the city proceed with little difficulty, Jalav," said she, naught of concern to be seen in her smile and headshake. "Palar and I were asked by Rilas to give sword training to those males here who wished it, and gladly did we assist the Keeper. At first were the males rowdy and

ill-prepared to benefit from instruction, yet Palar and I soon
saw them settled down.''

"Rogon bested the loudest of them with the swords of
wood we had made," said Palar, with a grin of amused
remembrance, ''and then I drew my edged blade and asked if
any there dared to face me. The males looked from Rogon, to
the male who sat upon the ground cradling head and arms, to
the gleam of Mida's light upon my blade, and then were we
no longer disturbed by rowdiness.''

"Those who are prepared to give difficulty rather than
accept it seldom have the bother," said I, nodding in approval. "As city matters cause no difficulty, for what reason
have you come to me?''

"I have come, war leader, so that proper form may be
observed," said Rogon with sobriety. "These males who
accompany you are free, I know, still do they indeed accompany you, and I would not have you believe that I sought to
take what was yours without first speaking of it with you.''

''You would have one of the males?'' I said, surprised. To
seek out one of those males when one had no need to do so,
struck me then as a doing fit for one who was bereft.

"Not for converse, Jalav, merely for use," replied Rogon,
a twinkle in her eyes. "The male came to speak of those
training weapons which we had made for the city males we
taught, and when he had gone I thought upon what pleasure
he might be able to give. Large was he and exceedingly well
made, broad of shoulder and chest, well-muscled—a male fit
for a war leader, I think. Do you object?''

"Not at all. I'm relieved," I returned, then did I look upon
Palar as well. "Should you also wish to be a true sister to
me, war leader, you may also take one of the males. Or,
perhaps, two or three. It had not occurred to me to rid myself
of them in such a way.''

"I regret, Jalav, that I may not be of such aid to you,"
laughed Palar, Rogon chuckling beside her. "I have long
since chosen three of those whose use I most prefer, and have
not the time for another. One may not spend all the hind of
each fey in one's sleeping leather.''

"Certainly not with battle in the offing," I agreed, joining
their amusement. How good it was, to be returned to the

midst of one's own! "Which of the males will you have,
Rogon?"

"I would have the light-haired one, Jalav, he who is also
dark-eyed," she replied, sipping the daru she held. "The
covering he wears is black, and I believe he is called Arsan."

"Aysayn," I corrected, a sudden, unexpected delight filling me, my own daru sliding down my throat nearly unnoticed. So the male would see matters done according to his
own will, would he? So he would speak to Jalav of what she
might be and do? The Sigurri felt secure with his warriors so
near at hand, however they had not yet been allowed entrance
into the city. He who had spoken so well of my power in that
place would learn the truth of the words he had uttered.

"Rogon, how do you mean to use him?" I asked. "Do
you mean to have him, or is he to use you?"

"Much do I prefer the taking of males, Jalav," said she,
surprised. "Why do you ask?"

"I ask for the reason that I am acquainted with Aysayn,"
said I, unfolding my legs and leaning down to one elbow so
that I might consider the matter more comfortably. "Should
you approach the male as one who is free and request his use,
he will either refuse you or see the thing done to his own
tastes, he taking use from you. Far better that you visit him
with a number of your Hirga, approach him closely, then ring
him with daggers. Take care that he not be allowed to move,
however; the male is possessed of great speed, and is skilled
in a form of battle which requires no weapons."

"You would have us make a use-captive of one who has
been given assurance of his safety?" asked Rogon; she and
Palar both looked bewildered. "War leader, I do not
understand."

"War leader, the male was given no such assurance," I
replied, looking upon Rogon and recalling the use once taken
from me by Aysayn. "What assurances there were, were
given by him to the other males who accompany us. Naught
was said concerning his own safety."

"Much does it seem that Jalav would have more of the
Hirga take use from the male than merely their war leader,"
said Palar, amused again. "Is there, perhaps, a thing owed
this male, Jalav?"

"Indeed, Palar," said I, again raising my cup to my lips, feeling gratified. "Indeed is there a thing owed the male."

"Then it will be my pleasure to see to the matter for you, Jalav," said Rogon, raising herself to her feet so that she might return her cup to the board, Palar following suit. "Should it be your wish to see any other without assurances done so, you have only to speak of it."

"And so I shall, Rogon," I said, then allowed them to take their leave. So pleased was I with that particular turn of events that I rose and went to the board, finding that a good appetite had returned to me. I fed upon what tempted me, primarily nilno, wrettan eggs and a slice of baked grain, then finished what daru I had left before putting the cup aside. Too much of the daru had I swallowed that fey, and done too little thinking upon the strangers.

Thought of the strangers took me from my chamber once more, to seek out my war leaders and speak to them of those things which had occurred to me, yet was my choice of direction surely Mida-sent. The males I had left should have been elsewhere than the corridors I took, yet did I round one turn and find myself before them.

"Ah! So there you are, wench," said Galiose, halting before me with a look of satisfaction. "We felt it likely that your task had already been seen to, therefore have we come to seek you out so that we may continue. The others have gone in another direction in pursuit of you, and we shall come upon them by going that way."

He touched my arm, the look in his dark eyes silencing my protests. My word had been given, his look had said, and to be forsworn was the sole manner in which I might refuse. I had required a time alone and had been granted that time, now was it necessary that I resume the place brought me by a vow. I sent Galiose my own look, one which spoke of a vow of another sort, then moved off in the direction he had indicated.

"It seems, Jalav, that I now have you to myself for a time," said Ceralt, appearing near me and matching my pace with no difficulty, referring to the presence only of Galiose, Lialt, and Telion. "Had the gods favored that other over me, surely would it have been he who found you first. With the aid of the gods, then, I best him now as my men and those of Galiose shall best him and his upon the morrow.''

"You believe your village and city males will best Sigurri warriors?" I said with great incredulity, at once annoyed and amused that he considered such foolishness. "No more shall you best them than you would best my Midanna, for the Sigurri are every bit as well-trained warriors as we. You will have naught to do with the battle, male, and for this you may thank your invisible god.''

"The Sigurri," growled Ceralt, suddenly angry. "I grow exceedingly weary of hearing the virtues of these Sigurri extolled. Warriors are the Sigurri, and welcome at the side of Midanna are they, and ones to sit with and speak to as equals! Even does one stand so high in your favor that you agreed to this looking about as a boon to *him*! Come the new light, the Belsayah will show them for what they truly are: boasters and braggarts who prefer wenches beside them for wenches may be used as men may not! No true man would allow a wench to stand beside him in battle, nor will you be allowed to do so when once my men and I have won.''

"To count a meeting won even before it has been begun is the sign of one who either rides for the gods or has no true knowledge of battle," I said. "As the new light will show the truth to all, we need no longer discuss it.''

Surely would I have preferred leaving the male entirely, yet I could not, for I had given my word. Also I felt an undeniable attraction to this male that caused me only annoyance and bewilderment. The large hand that took mine returned to me memory of the manner in which he held me to his body, his lips fiercely taking mine, his caressing hands bringing to life the roaring flames of desire. I thought upon what would occur if I were to emerge victorious from all I attempted, free, then, to accept what males I would. In what manner might a Midanna accept one such as Ceralt, and continue to be what she was? How might she deny the strength of him without giving challenge? Such a thing did not seem possible. What need of burning thirst for victory, then, when victory will not bring what one desires most?

"Tell me of your time among these Sigurri," said Ceralt of a sudden, as though leaving off thoughts of his own which had grown unpalatable. "You seem quite close to the one named Aysayn, he who informed us of the task you left to see to. For what reason does he consult with you so closely? Has he an unvoiced desire to taste you?"

"Aysayn and I have stood in battle together, and I am the messenger of his god," I replied, glancing over to see that those light eyes rested upon me once again. "When his enemies sought to bring him down with the coward's stroke, I agreed to stand with him in defense of his place, and all of our lives were nearly lost. To share such a thing is to share more than a common beginning, more than may be described to one who has not experienced it. He would not be possessed of an unvoiced desire to taste me, for he has already done so, thoroughly and at length. Should he ever wish the same again, he need only speak of it."

"I had nearly forgotten that Midanna are wenches able to see to the needs of any men who desire them," said he, chuckling lightly as his hand closed briefly tighter on mine. "This—sharing you speak of, the sharing which must be experienced. Have we not a similar sharing between us, one which we found during the journey to Sigurr's Altar? Did we not all face battle at the end of it, a battle which was only barely survived?"

No longer did Ceralt's voice sound amused. Upon the corridor wall was an excellent rendering of the beauty to be found in the forests, yet was it unable to cause me to believe I stood any place save within a dwelling. There were those, I knew, who took the rendering as the forest itself, however the truth was that to appear as a certain thing was not to be that thing in reality.

"The battle beneath Sigurr's Peak was not a sharing, Ceralt," I replied after a moment. "Those who share stand beside one another, facing together what comes, each willing to accept the fate of the other. When one stands himself before another, the presence of that other unwelcome beside him, what might there be of sharing between them?"

"Perhaps it is joy alone he wishes to share with that other," said he, his words soft. "Perhaps he stands himself before that other so that danger and difficulty might be kept from her, to spare her what need not be?"

"How might there be true sharing between two, when one experiences nothing other than ease and joy?" I asked, somewhat surprised that so self-evident a truth need be mentioned. "To share danger brings a greater joy to shared pleasure, for have the two not then shared the worst and the best? In such a way is a deep bond forged, in pain and pleasure both, else is the bond too weak to withstand the rigors of time."

"And is this what you share with that other, the one called Sigurr's Sword?" Ceralt asked, his hand coming to my face to turn it toward him, allowing me to see the painful fear which now filled his eyes. "Is there a bond between you forged in pleasure and pain? Has he, too, stood beside you in battle?"

I looked upon him as he awaited my answer, and much did it seem that he would have been far happier were I to speak no words at all. I knew not why he would put a question he would prefer remained unanswered, yet were all males touched with a similar lack of reason.

"Mehrayn has no difficulty in seeing the warrior who is Jalav," said I, attempting to put from my notice the warmth of Ceralt's hand upon my face. "More than once has he stood himself before me, yet not when my own blade was free to leap from its scabbard. To aid one who is unable to aid herself, takes naught from that one; to give aid when it is unsought and unwanted is to take the pride from she who is aided, as though she had not the skill to do the thing herself. Aid which becomes insult is no aid at all."

"I—cannot understand what insult a wench might find in protection," said he, confusion now holding him as tightly as it most often did with me. "Ever have I been taught that a man must put himself between his woman and that which would bring her harm, no matter what that thing might be. How am I now to see the doing as insult?"

The final question he spoke was not addressed to me, and strongly did it hold him as we continued up the corridor. The others had made no attempt to quicken their pace and join us, therefore were we the first to come upon Mehrayn, Aysayn, and S'Heernoh as we turned into yet another corridor. Sigurr's Sword frowned at the abrupt picture presented him, yet was Ceralt far too withdrawn to take notice. He released my hand as I halted and continued on alone, his eyes seeing naught of what occurred about him.

"Now that we are reunited, the inspection may continue," Galiose greeted the Sigurri and S'Heernoh with expansive good humor, striving to keep his eyes from a deeply withdrawn Ceralt. "We have so far seen naught of the east wing, therefore shall that be our next objective. Follow me."

The male then took himself off, drawing Ceralt with him by an arm about the shoulders, causing the others to follow. But I was not alone. Mehrayn had allowed the others to go before him, and when he fell in beside me to my right, he lost no time in taking my hand.

"I find myself greatly surprised that you accompany us once again without the use of chains," he murmured. "Had I known how demurely agreeable walking about would make you, I would have seen it done much the sooner."

"I find little amusement in this state of affairs, male," I informed him coldly, immediately seeking to take my hand from his. "This walking about does no more than try my patience, a thing which would be seen by any but the greatest of fools."

"Your description of me clearly indicates keen insight," said he with a nod of agreement, gripping my hand so I could not free it. "Also is it undeniably accurate. I am indeed a fool, yet not so great a fool as to release what portion of you I now hold. Later I shall seek a much greater portion."

"Later I shall be happily engaged with another," I said, finding it more pleasant to look upon the corridor walls than the male I walked beside. "Both you and Ceralt would be wise to seek out warriors for this darkness, else shall you find no more than sleep in your furs."

"Another," growled Mehrayn, no longer calm and amused. "For what reason must you embroil S'Heernoh in this? Such behavior would be fitting in a child, and ill becomes one who stands as leader to warriors. Leave the man be, and we shall speak no more of it."

"Indeed shall we speak no more of it," I said, meeting his annoyance. "In point of fact there is naught to be spoken of, for this leader of warriors has already heard enough from one who leads males. Greatly more than is sufficient."

"For what reason do you continue to seek other men, while I seek only you?" he asked, a softened reply to my anger. "Do you feel so little for me, then, that you would do such a thing?"

"Why would I do otherwise?" I demanded with great exasperation. "I am a war leader of Midanna who has ever taken what males pleased her, and shall ever continue to do so. For what reason should I not?"

"For the reason that there is one about who would have *all* of your attention," said he, exasperated as well. "You have never known such a thing, I know—men having so often handed you about, yet am I not the same as they. I would keep you to myself alone."

"There have been those, in the past, who wished the same," I replied with a shrug. "But no male may keep a warrior from seeking out those who interest her."

"And her interest may extend even to one who follows a god of abominations?" he asked very softly, finally releasing my hand, green eyes showing no hint of amusement. "Have you not had sufficient ill from those who bow to the One-ness? The matter will, at the last, stand between this other and myself, yet would I have you know what I mean to do. Even were he a follower of the true god, I would not allow him to touch what is mine."

"Jalav belongs to no male," I growled, fully out of patience with these males and their beliefs and graspings. "Jalav rides for the gods and will do battle with their enemies, and in no other manner might she be claimed. To believe otherwise is to believe foolishness."

"To believe men will allow the matter to lie so is even greater foolishness," said he, again calm. "The battle to come will not last for all time, and when it is done those who survive will return to the lives they led before it. I choose to believe we both will survive, and afterward I will stand before you and demand my due. Should any attempt to halt me, they must face my blade."

The eyes of the male were now fully calm, his straightened shoulders a challenge in themselves, and again I thought upon victory and the fruits it brought. All saw victory as a means to ends of their own, yet was Jalav not to have an end but *be*

one. Ever would males pursue her to suit themselves, unaware of the fact that Jalav was a Midanna who would see to
her own suiting.

"With the battle done, I will then be free to accept challenge," I said, the shrug I made full clear as we continued up
the corridor. "I will not again be taken by a male to be done
as he sees fit, to be allowed no say of my own. Sooner will I
see my blood upon the ground—or the blood of another."

"It was not you I envisioned when I spoke of facing
opposition with my blade," said he sternly. "You I will deal
with in another manner, one which may be avoided should
you come to see the sense in joining with one who is a
warrior like yourself. As you have said, no warrior may be
denied."

The male then strode ahead of me, rapidly closing the gap
between himself and the others, ending the discussion which
had nearly sent me away instead. Now had both of them
spoken of their intentions, their determination refusing all
attempts at denial, their blind stubbornness set to the path
which was meant to destroy them both. Surely would I have
been far wiser to allow them that path and thereby rid myself
of two who were no more than breathing mounds of vexation
to a warrior, yet was I unable to do so. Jalav, ever a fool,
ever one to wish for that which she might not have, would
face a goddess and likely fall, yet would the males thereby
find survival. It was vastly important that they survive, no
matter that neither would ever be mine. Should victory come,
that was what it would see accomplished, the survival of two
I could not bear to have ended; my life had become no more
than a burden, yet theirs were precious to me beyond words.

Sunk in the morass of wishing for what might never be, I
followed silently and sightlessly after those who followed a
confident Galiose. Indeed did the male know the dwelling as
though it were his own, yet the accomplishment did naught to
raise the spirits of one who would have far preferred losing
herself in unending corridors for all time. I knew naught of
their discovery that I was not more fully in their midst till I
returned to myself to find Ceralt and Mehrayn in their now-
customary places to either side of me, the one no longer
distracted, the other no longer filled with annoyance. Both

blue eyes and green looked down upon me with something
very like guilt, their concern reflected clearly upon the faces
of the others.

"I ask you to forgive my outburst, Jalav," Mehrayn said at
once when my eyes were upon him, his big hand coming to
smooth my hair. "It was not my intention to cause you pain,
which clearly shows how great a fool I am. A wise man sees
more carefully to his intentions."

"Should he be a fool, then I am surely the same," said
Ceralt, drawing my gaze in turn to his sobriety. "I, too,
should not have spoken as I did, yet was I too deeply
wrapped in my own thoughts to consider the one those thoughts
concerned. There are two now who must be forgiven."

"There is naught to forgive when males behave as males,"
said I, looking away from both, truly in no humor to hear
further from them. "Where is it that we go now, Galiose?"

"Our destination lies just ahead," replied the male, his
words gentle as though he spoke to one sorely wounded.
"Perhaps fortune will favor us and I will be netted again,
which surely will return the smile to your face."

The others chuckled their appreciation of the comment,
even Aysayn, who had undoubtedly been told of the thing,
with an amusement I could not share.

"Sooner would I have an end to this inspection of yours,"
I informed the male, my impatience sounding clearly in the
words. "There are many other things which await my attention, things of far greater import than . . ."

"No, no, wench, this too is of great import," the male
hastened to assure me, unwilling to hear words in contradic-
tion. "Your reluctance to continue in our company is understandable, for rather than amusement and diversion, you have
found sadness with us. For shame, you men! Is there naught
you may do to brighten the mood of this wench you both seek
to pay court to?"

His final words were to Ceralt and Mehrayn, who looked
upon one another with expressions of consternation, which
more properly should have been ones of blankness. I had not
the least understanding of what Galiose was about, save that
it was not his intention to allow that foolishness to end. With
a sound of further impatience I began to move more swiftly in

the direction of the male's objective, seeking to hasten the arrival of my own, and thereby found that such an end was not soon to be.

"Would you hear an amusing tale, wench?" Ceralt asked as he regained my side, an odd eagerness upon him. "Once there was a warrior who roved all about, and one fey he happened upon a farm in the wild. Tending this farm was a man and his wife, aided in their efforts by their three lovely daughters. The first of these three had hair of gold, and so large were her . . ."

"No!" hissed Mehrayn from where he walked to my right, looking upon Ceralt as though he were bereft. "What amusement is there likely to be in that tale for one who is female? Would you next have her stalk off in search of a sword?"

"Clearly did I fail to think the thing through," Ceralt agreed in a mutter filled with heavy self-annoyance, glancing first at me then Mehrayn. "What, then, *are* we to tell her?"

"What of the daughter with the hair of gold?" I asked Ceralt after seeing a look of vexed puzzlement take Mehrayn, a sudden curiosity upon me. "What was it that she possessed that the male found so great in size?"

"Ah—her hands!" replied Mehrayn when Ceralt merely looked upon me without words, his gaze suggesting that I had put a sword to his throat the while he remained weaponless. "The wench had hands so large that surely did the warrior believe she, too, was a warrior."

"Indeed," said Ceralt with an immediate nod, his look of relief beside the one of gratitude. "The wench had hands so large, that well might she have been a warrior."

"In what manner might the size of hands indicate a warrior?" I then asked, finding naught of reason in the tale the males attempted to tell. "There are those with hands far larger than mine, yet am I alone war leader to all Midanna who ride. What has hand size to do with skill?"

"The tale is no more than foolishness meant to amuse, girl," Ceralt said with something much like desperation, Mehrayn filled with equal upset. "Likely I should not even have begun such a tale, and will therefore take it no further. Perhaps there is an amusement *you* would care to relate, man."

"I?" asked Mehrayn in even greater upset, for it was he whom Ceralt had addressed. "What tales I am acquainted with are of the sort *you* began, far too foolish to be related."

"But what of the female with overlarge hands?" I asked again, this time addressing them both. "In what manner might such hands be amusing? Were they far too large for the size of her, therefore making her an object of ridicule for the male?"

"No, wench, no," said Ceralt, desperation having entered his tone, yet was he kept from further words by the intrusion of Galiose. The High Seat of Ranistard seemed barely able to keep sobriety upon him, and then did it come to me that the others fared far worse. Lialt and Telion hung upon one another with tearful eyes, struggling to keep their laughter soundless, the while Aysayn stood with back turned and shoulders ashake. Even S'Heernoh, so often amused yet never beyond control, had halted with head down and one hand to his middle, the other hand pounding upon his thigh as he laughed with the silence of Lialt and Telion. For what reason all seemed so amused I knew not, yet was I of the opinion that Ceralt and Mehrayn were the objects of it rather than myself. Apparently the two males drew the same conclusion; once they had glared about, they looked upon Galiose with little which might be construed as brotherhood.

"Forgive my interruption, yet have we now reached our destination," said Galiose hurriedly, indicating a doorway just ahead, bringing to the attention of all the four Hitta warriors who eyed the males with expressions of incomprehension. "Perhaps the tale of amusement would best be left for another time."

"A pity the suggestion of it was not done the same," growled Ceralt as he looked upon Galiose in some manner increasing the second male's amusement. Mehrayn, however, was more taken with recognition of the doorway we had nearly reached. He, as I, now knew the place, a chamber filled with memories.

"For what reason did you wish to come here?" he asked Galiose as we all resumed movement toward the doorway. "Had I known that this was our destination, likely would I have found other tasks to occupy me."

"The place is where slaves were formerly kept," Galiose replied, again proving his knowledge of the dwelling. "Merely did I feel curiosity as to what purpose it now served."

"The purpose it serves now is the same," said I, aware of the sudden silence of the males as we crossed the threshold past the four Hitta. Within were a large number of males in collars and without covering, their doings watched over and directed by many warriors. Some of these males were seated or lying flat, some restlessly upon their feet, all appearing weary as though they only now rested after having seen to many tasks. In a far corner a small number of them labored over the cleaning of a large pot of metal, likely a pot which had recently allowed them all to feed. The torches upon the stone of the walls were many and bright, clearly illuminating the empty enclosures of metal which filled more than half of the place.

"I had thought you had no love for slavery," remarked the High Seat of Ranistard in an uninflected voice, looking about at those who also looked upon us. "Apparently the belief indeed holds true for females alone, for I see none of them about."

"The forces of the High Seat of this place contained few females," I replied, nodding acknowledgment to the greetings of the warriors who guarded that chamber. "Many of these are of the metal and leather ilk, others they who guarded the slaves held here, all familiar with the use of weapons. To return their freedom was not possible, therefore were they given the choice between slavery and individual combat. Some few accepted the offer of battle, and were thereafter allowed to face my war leaders. I was no longer present when the meetings took place."

"And what was the outcome of those meetings?" Galiose asked, somewhat subdued.

"The outcome, I must assume, was the one which was expected," I replied with a shrug. "All of my war leaders remain in the places they held before my departure. When we have left this place, those who dwell within the city will decide the fate of the balance of these. Should it be their decision to free them, it is they who will need to live beside them."

Galiose nodded in silence as he again looked about, and then was his attention taken by some occurrence to my right. I, also, turned about to look, and saw that Mehrayn had left my side to wander some small distance away, to stand below a suspended bar of metal which had once had chains hanging from it. The male looked up in contemplation of the bar, as though considering it through newly uncovered eyes, and then was a decision of sorts made. Mehrayn crouched a small amount and then leapt, catching at the bar with the backs of his hands to those of us who watched. The muscles in his arms stood out as he slowly raised himself till his chin appeared above the bar, then did he just as slowly allow himself to sink down again. When once he hung flat he dropped lightly to the flags once more, then brought his eyes to us with a grin.

"Once was I suspended from that bar to be whipped," said he, rubbing his palms one with the other. "To shout out the pain would have been humiliating, therefore did I set my thoughts to what effort it would take to chin upon the metal I hung from. It pleases me to learn that chinning requires less effort than the acceptance of leather across one's back."

Mehrayn's grin had not faltered, most especially in view of the manner in which I had not been able to keep myself from looking upon him, and then was he suddenly not alone. Ceralt abruptly appeared beside him, looked up to the bar, then looked upon Sigurr's Sword with the faintest of smiles.

"Indeed does the thing appear tempting," said he, and then had he, too, leapt up to grasp the bar. Again muscles surged in arms as a large body was raised and lowered, and then was Ceralt again upon his feet beside Mehrayn. "Also is the execution of it pleasing," he added.

Mehrayn had glanced to me as I had watched Ceralt, and no longer was he possessed of a grin. Annoyance had once again taken the Sigurri, and with that annoyance he looked about himself, at once seeing a large, heavy rack of wood, one which had formerly held whips. No word did he speak as he moved to that rack, bent to settle his broad shoulders beneath the inner top of the thing as he held to it with his hands, and then he straightened again. With a creak of effort from the wood and the straining of arms, legs and shoulders,

Mehrayn raised the weighty rack from the flags, held it till he was fully straightened, then slowly lowered it once more. This time had it been Ceralt who had glanced to me as I watched, and when Mehrayn stepped away from the rack with a renewed grin, Ceralt stalked over to take his place.

As the Belsayah raised the rack as Mehrayn had, I looked upon him with the puzzlement I felt, understanding naught of what his and Mehrayn's intentions might be. A number of the warriors who stood guard about the chamber watched the two males with broad grins and deep chuckling, evidently enjoying the exhibition, yet was I unable to comprehend what it was that they exhibited. I moved somewhat nearer the two as Ceralt replaced the rack and straightened to send a look of grim pleasure toward the Sigurri, then did he turn and take himself toward a long, heavy chain which was secured to the ceiling a few paces off. The thing hung nearly to the floor, and once Ceralt had pulled upon it with strength to be certain that it was well fastened in place, he immediately began to scale it. Up the chain he went as though he scaled knotted leather, and even as I watched I saw that Mehrayn moved slowly in that direction as I did.

Needless to say, once Ceralt had descended it was then necessary that Mehrayn ascend, and once he, too, had descended the two stood upon the flags and regarded one another with straightened shoulders and heads held high. I continued to have no understanding of what they attempted, yet was I just as well pleased to have watched them without understanding. How stirring to the sight of a warrior are the doings of healthy, vital males, how pleasant to stand and observe them in their strength and arrogance. I might have stood so for considerably longer, save that the males had approached one another a good deal more closely and then began an exhibition of another sort.

Till then each had matched the efforts of the other, and apparently such a state was unacceptable to both. Now as they stood toe-to-toe they raised their arms so that they might lace fingers, left hand to right for each of them, the grips upward and firmly intertwined. Again I had no notion as to what they were about, and then were they abruptly in the midst of it, arms and shoulders straining, legs braced and

locked, their efforts swiftly making clear of their intention.
Hand-to-hand did they test their strength, each attempting to
overcome the other, the object of the match clearly being to
drive one's opponent to his knees, his hands bent backward at
the wrists and helplessly trapped. No more than soft grunts of
effort came from the two as they strained, yet had those very
efforts turned the chamber more bleak than even my memories shadowed it. They had found a way to face one another
without weapons, a manner in which they might give each
other hurt, and no longer had I the least desire to look upon
them. My presence was surely the cause, and that was easily
remedied.

I turned about and immediately left the chamber, paying no
mind to Galiose's attempts to halt me. I had pulled my arm
from his grip with practiced ease, and was not even long
delayed by the slave male who attempted to take advantage of
the distraction of nearly all in the place. The slave's arm
came swiftly about my throat as I passed him, his intention of
taking me hostage clear, yet was I not of a mind to allow him
the opportunity. An elbow in the side loosened his grip, I
slipped swiftly out from beneath his arm the while bringing it
back and to the side with me, and then did I put my knee with
the strength of anger into the back of his own elbow. He
screamed wildly as the arm broke, a not-quite-innocent victim
of the churning within me, and then was it all left behind as I
strode up the corridor and away. Males must ever be males,
good and evil alike, and no more than great agitation did they
bring to warriors.

I had returned to the upper floor and the doors to my
chamber were just ahead, when I noticed the appearance of
another, one I had not thought would dare appear before me
again. Beside the wall not far from the doors did he wait,
immersed in thought. At sound of my approach his dark eyes
came to me, and a gentle smile softened the features of he
who was called Chaldrin.

"I have come to see when you would have your next
lesson, sister," said he, straightening from the wall as I
halted not far from him. "Should the walking about occupy
you too fully, however, the practice may be left for another
time."

So easily did the male address me, as though naught had occurred to change what had stood between us. That he had told the others my agreement to the inspecting was done as a favor granted to a brother meant naught; it was truth which rose above all else, and well did I know the truth of the thing. No matching smile did I send him, no warmth of any sort to be thrown away upon one who had betrayed me.

"The walking about is done, the learning is done, and these are the last words which shall ever pass between us," I said, seeing the smile depart from him at my cold, distant manner. "The debt which stood between us is now met, all vows complete and all words returned. No others save Midanna may address me as sister; I shall not have the calling from one without honor. Never again are you to approach me, male, save with sword loose in scabbard; should it fail to be so, your life will surely be forfeit."

Having said all there was to say I began to turn from him, yet did his hand come to my left shoulder to halt me.

"I sought no more than your happiness, yours and Mehrayn's," said he, his voice truly soft, nearly a whisper. "There is naught I would cavil at to keep pain from touching you, naught I would not face to save you from hurt. I have given my vow to stand beside you always; you cannot send me from you."

For answer I merely walked from his hand, telling him his words were no longer heard, the sight of him no longer accepted. Honorable had I once thought him to be, and honorable had he been—till honor became too cumbersome a burden. Sister he had called me, and I, like a fool, had believed; never again would I believe such a thing, most especially not from a male.

I pushed through the doors of my chamber quickly, once again seeing little of what stood about me, and therefore was I nearly to the board before I became aware of those who this time inhabited the place. Rilas and Ennat sat upon the floor cloth, clearly awaiting me, cups of daru in their hands, the intent to see deep within me in their eyes. The penetrating gaze of a Keeper had ever been a marvel to me, an ability never made the most of, yet was I just then more in need of solitude and daru than marvels.

"You seem disturbed, Jalav," said Rilas, truly concerned. "What has occurred to cause you disturbance?"

"How might I not be disturbed," I asked, "with so many free males about?" I took a cup and poured the daru I desired, then turned again to the Keepers. "You have come to speak with me?"

"Indeed," said Rilas, her calm only then pointing up the agitation in Ennat. "The Keeper Ennat and I have exchanged information, and there is a question we would put to the war leader to all Midanna: why was Ennat not told that Mida has demanded the slaying of the Sigurri once the strangers are seen to? You told me of this charge when first you returned from her domain; surely the command remains?"

I looked upon Rilas with consternation, well aware of Ennat's dismay. I did not recall that command of the goddess—a command which I had acknowledged and agreed to—but clearly Ennat did.

"Jalav of the Midanna, may such a thing truly be?" asked Ennat, unable to remain silent any longer. "The Sigurri— Our freedom and lives remain ours through their efforts; to repay them with death would be the height of dishonor! Are we truly bidden by Mida to slay them?"

"Such a command was indeed given me by Mida," I admitted with reluctance, finding Ennat's beseeching words well-nigh painful. "She, however, clearly judged them by those who attend the dark god in his domain, males of low doings and no hint of honor. The command was given in the belief that the Sigurri would attempt to see the Midanna done in such a fashion, a doing *I* truly believe would be beyond them. There is little honor in raising sword against those who mean you no harm."

"What honor is there in denying the will of the goddess?" asked Rilas, frowning, as Ennat showed relieved agreement. "Are we not sworn to follow her every command and decision, sworn in blood to see her will completely done? Scarcely is it our place to speak of what was meant rather than what was commanded, Jalav. Was the slaying of the males commanded of us, or was it not?"

Again did I regard Rilas in silence. Ennat had returned to the grip of deep disturbance, for she, too, was a Keeper. No

Midanna was meant to defy the will of Mida, Keepers least of all, none, perhaps, save she who thought to challenge a goddess. As I had begun, so would I continue, and give nodding thanks to she who had forced me so often among those who twisted truth to suit their own ends.

"Would you have me say the goddess has commanded dishonor, Rilas?" I asked in turn, swallowing down the distaste of the doing as I had swallowed down the drink. "Is a Midanna warrior to say such a thing concerning the mother of us all? More likely does the error lie with me, for having misunderstood the words spoken to me. Mayhap it was the males of the cavern we were commanded to slay, those who stand ready to heed the dark god's commands. Surely would Mida find herself able to best him, were we to account for those who would come to his aid."

"In place of those called Midanna who are no more than pets," said Rilas, startled. "Then would she and the god of males no longer stand in contest, for Mida would be supreme. Now do I see the reason for your wish to give challenge, Jalav. You erred in understanding the command of the goddess, and in such a way did Mida seek to return you to her. You are indeed meant to stand in challenge, yet not before Mida and not alone. All the clans of the Midanna will stand behind you, and the one to be challenged will be the god of the males!"

Truly pleased did Rilas appear, the glow of her gladness taking kalod from her shoulders, Ennat also eager and filled with pleasure. The two Keepers rose from the floor cloth to finish their daru and put hands to my shoulder in farewell, then did they take themselves from the chamber, deeply immersed in a discussion concerning the necessity for searching long and well before finding the true will of Mida. I waited till the doors had stilled their swinging, staring the while into the depths of the cup I held, then did I throw the daru, cup and all, into the wall behind the board with all my might.

Mida! The fury I felt was so great that surely would I have faced even the dark god without hesitation at that moment. To hear again that my thirst for challenge was no more than the will of the goddess, and to have the thing proven with the

words I had spoken as lies! I began to stride about the
chamber, seeking to cool the rage which flamed so high
within me, feeling no other thing than a screaming ache to
rend and tear. Again was I to be denied, this time of the need
to ride from those who wished to follow, the need to seek
alone a reckoning with she who cared naught for the anger of
a war leader of Midanna. Also was there fear beside the rage,
fear that Rilas was indeed right, that all I felt and thought and
said was solely at the behest of she who had chosen me to
ride in her name. Such a complete captivity would truly be
unendurable, for after the strangers and the cavern followers
of Sigurr there would be others, tasks without end and demands undeniable. Never would Jalav be free of the will of
Mida, never would she be shut of the demands of duty— The
thought was one which could not be borne, no simple denial
sufficient to keep the lash of its likelihood from rending my
flesh. No other thing than the absolute refusal of she who was
war leader to all the Midanna might best it, and such a thing
did I then raise as shield before me. With head held high did I
throw such refusal to believe in the face of the fear which
sought to back-stab me, and then did I return to the board and
what daru it continued to hold.

4.

Sleep—
and the foolishness of
overindulgence

A faint sound brought me somewhat awake, though I felt the
drag of far too much daru. I lay upon the sleeping furs in the
second chamber, not far from the fire, somehow knowing that
darkness had fallen without and had not yet ended. So soft
were the furs beneath my face and belly and breasts, so
strongly did they call to me to return to the comfort of sleep
that nearly did I do so, and yet there was something I must
recall. I thought upon the thing with mind unmoving and eyes
closed, and then did I become aware of the hands at my
breech. So taken with daru had I been that I had not removed
it before falling to the furs, yet were quiet, gentle hands
doing it for me. The vague question as to who it might be
reminded me that S'Heernoh was to have come to me at
darkness, and then was the breech pulled away and a hand
boldly astroke upon my now bare bottom. I moved in displeasure, having no true wish to be touched in such an insolent
manner, annoyed that the heat would begin to build so quickly
within me from so small a thing. Made for the use of males,
had Aysayn said to me, made to feel too great a pleasure at
their touch, yet was S'Heernoh there at my command and
easily sent away again in the same manner.

"I no longer wish the use of a male," I said with some
difficulty, the words soft even in the silence of the chamber.
"Take yourself from me, and wait for another time."

My eyes had not opened and my face had not abandoned
the softness of the fur, and indeed did I begin to merge once
more with the darkness all about—till the hand of the male I
had sent from me slid down to my thighs. Greatly pleased
with the feel of me did the touch seem, a faint sound of

129

delight coming from the throat of he who sat or lay beside me, the fingers of the hand quickly seeking what might be found between the thighs he had caressed. Again I moved in protest, this time dragging my head up, what little strength the daru had left immediately taken by the touch upon my desire. In desperation I attempted to turn from the sensations and face the one who dared to refuse my commands, however a hand came to rest itself upon the fur to my free side, the arm keeping me from turning as I wished. With very little effort was I held in place for what continued to be done to me, and anger rose beneath the growing waves of need.

"Release me, accursed male," I said with a slur of effort, without the snap I had wished the words to have. "You have been given my command, S'Heernoh, and I demand that you obey."

"Most certainly would S'Heernoh obey—if he were here," said a voice softly, a male voice, one I knew. "Such a man is not for you, wench, for you require a man who will instead see that *you* obey. Have you no desire for me after so long a time?"

Indeed did my body flare with uncontrollable desire even in the midst of the vast confusion I felt, for it was Ceralt who had come to me, Ceralt who now touched me as he had so often done in the past. My face returned to the fur as I strove to crawl from the touch which so easily brought forth the moisture from my body, yet did the arm about me tighten and again was I held.

"Were you given my permission to move about so?" the Mida-forsaken male asked with a chuckle, the strength in his arm seeing easily to my struggles. "You may not deny me, you know. As I am your guest, such a denial would be quite dishonorable."

"You are—the guest of—Aysayn," I gasped out, searching frantically amid the fog in my mind for that which would free me. "Seek—him out instead—for I wish—naught to do with—a male."

"For one who has no desire for a man, you respond with astounding speed," said he, refusing to halt that which brought me such weakness. "And what man would seek out a follower of the dark god, when he might have a follower of the golden goddess instead? And I *shall* have you, wench, for I have come for no other thing."

I knew a moment of relief when his hand finally left me, yet was the moment very brief indeed. The next saw me turned quickly to my back, and then was I held in the arms of the male, my body pressed to his, naught left of the leathers and furs and belt he had worn. So warm and strong was the body against mine, so broad and hard and impossible to ignore. The flames of the fire illuminated half of the face so close above mine, yet was the brightness shown in the light of his eyes arisen from another source entirely.

"Have you any conception of how sorely I have missed you?" he asked in a voice like smoke, soft and light yet impossible to avoid. "In my dreams you often remained beside me, and when I woke, held by the pain and strength-lessness of wounds, I wept to find you gone. No longer am I hampered by wounds, yet I continue to weep at thought of losing you. Sooner would I have wounds impossible to recover from."

His lips came to me then, softly demanding, refusing to be denied, allowing me no words of my own. Indeed was it difficult to know what words I would speak, for I might not accept this male who held me so tightly. Were I to do so his life would surely be lost, his and Mehrayn's as well—and yet the feel of him against me, the taste of his lips, the touch of his hands to me! In the name of all those who had gone before me, I could not refuse the demands he put, could not keep from allowing my own hands the hard-muscled feel of him. His lips left mine to go to my breasts, and my fingers tangled in his dark, unruly hair, a moan forced from me by the lightning he so easily evoked. Had he left me then I would surely have died, charred to nothingness by the heat which lapped so high about me. Feyd had it been since last I had had the use of a male, and no Midanna was made to go so long without. I moved upon the softness of the lenga fur, held in his arms, consumed by the need he had put upon me, and moaned again when his hand stroked my middle.

"So long has it been since last I had this belly and these breasts to lie upon," he murmured, the heat clearly a part of him as well. "I shall now take you, woman, and show th you have always been mine and ever shall be."

With great deliberation did he then put himself ab‑ve me, spread my knees with his hands, and bring his manhood to my desire. Sudden memory of the vow he had stolen caused me briefly to attempt to deny him despite ny need, however the strength of his hands upon my thighs refused denial, as did the quick thrust within me. I gasped as he made me completely his, and then was I again held in his arms, his lips to mine as his hips began their movement I longed for. The male took me completely, made me his despite my wish to protest, turning all struggle to mist and memory. Well used was I for uncounted time, and then was I permitted to find sleep again.

Much did it seem that a very long time had passed, yet did the time also seem very little. I awoke a second time unable to consider the confusion of time, for the need I had thought so well seen to had in some manner returned to me. And then I knew it had been returned, for hands and lips touched me all about where I lay on my back in the furs, hands and lips which took what they wished. At last had S'Heernoh appeared, then, bringing desire to me before bringing wakefulness. Again I felt annoyance at such presumption, for one summoned by a war leader did not presume to take. It was he who would be taken, and this would I make certain he knew as soon as I was able to open my eyes and speak. Again the hands upon me forced me to move as they willed, and this at last brought words to my tongue.

"Enough, S'Heernoh," I said, speaking with the same difficulty I had earlier had. "You may now lie back, and this Midanna will use you."

I attempted to raise myself to sitting without opening eyes which lacked all will to open, knowing I had no need of sight to find and use a male, yet was I unable to do so. Much did it seem that I was held close to the fur by the hair, as though the male leaned upon it, and also had he failed to obey my command to cease his touching. Truly was I unable to bear being done so and I struggled to free myself, and then came a chuckling which increased my distress.

"I am not S'Heernoh, I shall not lie back, and no Midanna will use me," said he who had chuckled, one whose voice I had reason to know well. "S'Heernoh is to be left in peace, for the man who claims you will allow no other in his place."

It was, of course, Mehrayn who spoke, a thing my body had known even before I awoke. Ever was the male able to bring need upon me, fully as easily as Ceralt; for what reason they two were best able to do so I knew not, yet did I know well the anger the realization brought.

"Release me," I demanded with what strength I was able, groping back to the wide hand which rested upon my hair, seeking to free myself. "I will have naught to do with males, therefore must you release me."

The breathless scratchiness of my voice caused the male again to chuckle, yet no other thing was accomplished. The wide hand remained immovably firm upon my hair, I remained flat to the furs, and in no manner did I find easing from the touch which moved me to madness.

"I am pleased to hear you will have naught further to do with other men," said Mehrayn, his voice low and murmuring as his lips came to my throat. "Your squirmings indicate you will not deny *me*, however, which is as it should be. You may not deny me, for you are mine and ever shall be."

"Mehrayn," I gasped, and then was I well beyond the ability to speak. Though I moved in desperation I could not escape the arousal of his touch, nor was I able to make him cease. I fought in vain with the hand which held my hair, and then were there lips upon mine, demanding a response to their commands, demanding all I had no desire to give. What I would not have given was taken from me, and then was there no longer a hand between my thighs but the male himself, preparing to take even more. As slowly as always did he approach and begin to enter me, forcing a moan from me which was a plea for greater hurry, a plea the male refused to hear. The use was his and his alone, a matter well proven before he was fully within; truly was I unable to deny him, just as I had been unable to deny the other, and then came the storm I had whimpered and begged for. Completely swept up by the storm was I, and then, after uncounted time, I was not.

5.

*The meeting of males—
and an inconsolable loss*

At last did I awaken to the urging of none save myself, an awakening which returned memory to me of what had occurred during the darkness. I lay upon the lenga pelt upon my left side, staring at the fire which had clearly been fed during that same darkness, fully disgusted with the sense of satisfaction my body luxuriated in. By two males had Jalav been used, and the body of Jalav delighted in having been used so, no matter her own will to the contrary. I rolled to my right to let the dimness of the chamber take my sight instead, reaching for a fistful of lenga fur to aid me in calming the rampaging of my thoughts.

Jalav had come to Bellinard to battle the strangers who were enemies to the gods, yet were there others Jalav must do battle with as well. Males there were who refused to heed the words of reason, who proposed all manner of foolishness and demanded that Jalav join them in it. Keepers there were who concerned themselves with naught save the will of Mida, ignorant of their lack of knowledge where the goddess was concerned and serenely sure in that ignorance. Warriors there were, and war leaders as well, who would all demand to follow Jalav when they learned she was to return to the place which was Mida's Realm upon this world. The goddess Mida herself there was, and the male god Sigurr as well, both of whom wished Jalav ill, in one manner or another. And two males were there, both of whom wished the possession of Jalav, both of whom would fight for that possession, no matter her denial of them both. And indeed had Jalav denied them during the darkness; indeed had she shown how little interest they held for her. Surely had that been a doing of the goddess, a doing which could not now be undone.

A sigh took me as I rolled to my back, a sigh of weariness and frustration and annoyance. How large a number was a warrior to face, before she might find a time of rest? How often must she stand alone in opposition to all others, before the need to do so was no more? The strength and patience which had once seemed unending no longer seemed the same, and well convinced had I grown to be that I would not be permitted to fall during the battle with the strangers. Battle's end would bring no more than the beginning of many other tasks, tasks either sent by the goddess or performed because of her very existence—yet this I could not allow. In what manner I would see it otherwise I knew not, yet must it be seen so.

I raised myself to sitting upon the lenga pelt, finding no more than the shadow of heaviness remaining from the daru I had swallowed, shaking back the hair which draped me about as the blue silks draped the walls. My breech lay to the left of the fur where Ceralt had thrown it, the dagger wrapped about with my life sign upon the floor cloth not far from it. No other thing than my leg bands had those males left me, that and the smell of their satisfaction with one who had not been able to deny them. Annoyance flared even higher at these thoughts, at myself as well as the males. She who drank so great an amount of daru with free males roaming about surely earned what was done to her, and not again would I indulge in such foolishness. Should those two come to me again, my greeting would be different.

With breech and dagger replaced and swordbelt closed firmly about me, I took myself to the outer chamber to find that those city-folk called servants then fetched fresh provender for the board beneath the eyes of watchful warriors, and when once those warriors had given me greeting for the new fey, I sent them to gather my war leaders to me. There were a number of matters which required seeing to, and that before foolishness attempted to distract me.

I had already partaken of the fresh provender when the last of my war leaders appeared, she who had been in the midst of assigning guardposts to the back of the dwelling. Cenir of the

Helda had, of course, first seen her task accomplished before
bringing the yellow of her clan colors to join those of the
other war leaders already in attendance. It was then that I
informed them of a good part of what had occurred while I
had been gone, of the way those who had once been enemies
had nearly been taken by cowardly trickery, of the way the
Sigurri had aided them and myself, of the way I had won the
war leadership of those who might no longer be called enemies. Also did I inform them that half of the Sigurri would
enter the city that fey, so that their warriors might become
acquainted with those who would stand beside them in battle.
Grins of approval and anticipation showed from faces of the
nine who sat with me upon the floor cloth, however Tilim of
the Happa raised a point to be answered.

"Jalav, what of the meeting between these Sigurri and
those other males who have come of their own?" she asked,
the red of her clan covering sharp against the blue of the floor
cloth. "Should the Sigurri be bested, will it not be they who
must depart?"

"The Sigurri will not be bested," I assured her, sipping
from the small amount of daru I had allowed myself. "The
Sigurri are warriors as those other city males are not, therefore is there likelihood that they will find victory. When once
their legions have been given place here in this dwelling, all
of you must meet with those who are war leaders to them,
and guardposts must be assigned for watching the skies."

They were silent briefly, staring out in lack of understanding, and then did many begin to speak at once. Words were
not easily distinguishable in such an outburst, therefore did I
unfold my legs and lean down to my right elbow till their
exclamations had sorted themselves out.

"The skies, Jalav?" demanded Gidon at last, her voice
rising above those about her. "You believe the strangers will
come from the skies?"

"They are the enemies of gods and therefore gods themselves, Gidon," I replied with a shrug, having considered the
point at some length. "In no manner am I able to visualize
such a thing, and yet must it be considered. Our new sister
clans and the balance of the Sigurri will be set all about this
city from without, to stand before any who attempt to take it

from the forests. Had that been the sole concern, it would not have been necessary for us to take this place, and yet were we bidden to do so. As the outward approach to the city is already guarded, from what other direction might an attack come? Are we to be taken unawares simply because we are unable to accept such a possibility?''

"In what manner might they come from the skies, Jalav?'' asked Rogon, and truly did the Hirga war leader appear incensed and outraged. "How might such cowardly attack be accomplished?''

"Perhaps their gandod or kand will have the ability to fly as though they were lellin,'' said I, looking about to see that most felt as Rogon did. "Perhaps they, themselves, are possessed of wings, or have not the need for wings. Mida and Sigurr appear among those they wish to visit surrounded by a mist of gold or black, a mist from which they seem to form. This, too, must be watched for, and also must it be recalled that first may the mist be seen, which will give warning of impending arrival. When once a form has grown to solidity within it, then might that form be faced with weapons.''

"Mida's will make it so,'' muttered Katil the Harra, quickly draining the cup of daru she held. Quite shaken did the brown-clad war leader appear, and she was not alone in feeling so. To battle the gods is no easy thing, for Midanna no less than for others.

"That they may be bested with weapons may not be denied,'' said I, raising myself again to sitting, speaking the words with all the assurance I, myself, felt. "Had our swords been useless, would we have been set here against those who come? Surely the glory of death in battle is the right of all Midanna, yet what glory would there be to stand against those who might not be bested? What glory in merely falling, and what sense? No, sisters, greater glory is to be ours, the glory of standing victorious over those who would dare to face us. Do you doubt this?''

"No!'' they chorused, heartened by the words I had spoken, grinning about at each other with great gladness. Battle was to be ours, and victory as well, and none doubted that it would be so.

"For what reason do we guard this place, Jalav?'' asked

Linol, she of the Hersa. "For what reason would the strangers wish to take it?"

"How may we know, Linol?" I asked in turn, unconcerned over so minor a point. "It was here that Mida said the strangers would appear. The reason for that appearance was not told me, nor need we know their purpose in order to halt it. Perhaps they have heard that the use of these city males is sweet, and wish to taste of them themselves."

"Then we save them from a great disappointment, Jalav," said Palar amidst the laughter of the others. "At first does one find the use of city males sweet, but that wears off. To find true enjoyment one must keep more than one of them, for one has not the ability to meet the demands of a warrior. The three I have hold my interest now, yet will I likely soon tire of them."

"You will not find the Sigurri the same," said I with amusement of my own, noting the quick interest in the eyes of those who looked upon me. "Be certain, however, that the tasting of them is left to a time when alertness is not required of those who indulge in such tasting. The Sigurri have great capacity, and will hold a warrior's attention often and well. An interruption at such a time will not be welcome, most especially if those who interrupt are the strangers."

"Indeed do the Sigurri have great capacity, should that light-haired male be a true sampling," said Rogon, a look of amusement upon her as she sipped at her daru. "I had not thought he would be able to serve as many of my warriors as he did, and that after I myself had used him. He disliked giving service with a dagger at his throat, yet was he most easily aroused and not easily drained. It was some time before we had all he was able to give."

"He pleased you, then," said I with a smile of satisfaction, amused that Aysayn had been made to serve so well. Too often had it been he who took service, and most fitting was it that for once he had been made to give.

"Indeed," said Rogon with a grin for the look upon me, as well pleased with my satisfaction at the task given her, as at her satisfaction with the male. "Surely will my warriors seek out those who enter the city, to learn if all have the ability of . . ."

"Well, well, I see I should have arrived a good deal earlier," came the interruption of a voice, one which had no place among us. Few would have had the temerity to interrupt a meeting of war leaders, for few would have been so addled or bereft. Galiose, however, was undeniably oblivious to the manner in which he intruded.

"Truly should I have arrived much the earlier," said he, his eyes moving from one to the other of my war leaders. "To lose even a moment from being in the company of so large a number of lovely wenches is truly inconsolable loss, and had I known you all gathered here I would not have denied myself."

"In such a manner do certain of those of this city also speak," said Palar to me, a dismissal in the tone she used as she took all attention from the male. "Most often do they prove pitiful in the sleeping leather, for words are the sole thing they have learned to use in a proper manner. Are there other matters you would discuss with us, Jalav?"

"For now I shall merely caution you and your warriors to be as alert as possible," said I, seeing that Palar's comment and the chuckling agreement of her sisters had taken the grin from Galiose. "The time of the meeting of the males will surely be a time to expect those who may seek to catch us unawares, and for that reason shall your warriors not attend the doing. Set your guardposts, sisters, and we may speak again when this fey has ended and those who are meant to depart have done so."

I rose to my feet amid the nods and words of agreement to be heard from those who followed me, they taking themselves from the floor cloth as well, and once the daru they held had been swallowed and their cups replaced upon the board, they took their leave. As the last of them made for the doors Galiose approached me, and once the chamber had been emptied he turned to me with a grimace.

"Undoubtedly their foul dispositions may be attributed to swallowing down that distillation of fire so early in the fey," said he, eyeing the cup I continued to hold. "For what reason you wenches do so is beyond me, save that you know no better. You may now give over your own cup, for I mean to continue with my inspection of this place as quickly as the others arrive. It will, of course, be halted for the contests, and then be resumed once the disagreement is settled.''

"The thing called inspection will not be resumed, now or later,'' I informed him, allowing the smooth strength of freshly brewed daru to slide down my throat. "Males, perhaps, have naught better to do with their time, yet the same is not true of Midanna. I shall spend no more upon such foolishness than the time already given, and wish to hear no more about it.''

"Do you mean to spit upon the word you gave?'' he demanded as I turned from him, seeking to return my cup to the board. "You were to continue with me in the company of the others, till a certain decision was made by you. I know of no decision having been reached.''

"And yet I have indeed made a decision,'' said I, turning again to look upon him as I folded my arms below where my life sign had once hung. "My decision is as it was to begin with, that I wish neither of those males. Also, should one believe that an oath has been broken by another, one speaks of challenge rather than decisions. Do you mean to speak to me in such a way, male?''

Indeed did the thought of challenge from Galiose please me, as he must surely have been able to see in my eyes. A frown took him as he looked down upon me, rising annoyance and anger beginning to touch him, yet did another speak before he was able to voice the words I most wished to hear.

"No father would speak of challenge to his daughter, lady Jalav,'' came the voice of S'Heernoh, causing Galiose and myself to look to the doors where the gray-haired male stood with Aysayn, Lialt and Telion, they four having clearly just arrived. "The High Seat of Ranistard is filled with no more than fatherly concern, therefore does he speak to you as he does. He would see you touched by happiness rather than misery.''

"Should that be so, he would surely give me challenge,'' said I, my tone souring to see that Galiose was no more than annoyed. The anger he had felt was gone, and all knew that no male would give challenge save that his usual reluctance was overcome by the heat in his blood. Had the interruption come but a pair of moments later I would have had what I sought, yet was the time now lost to my purpose.

"Sooner would I give the wench the hiding she merits," growled Galiose, folding his arms as he looked down upon me with great displeasure. "Did you hear that she refuses to allow us to continue with our inspection?"

"We heard," agreed S'Heernoh with a sigh, he and the others coming forward separately from the door. Lialt and Telion shook their heads as they made for the board, Aysayn took himself to a seat to one side of the chamber, S'Heernoh alone walking forward to stand beside Galiose. "Perhaps it would be best if she were allowed a longer time for consideration," said the Walker to the High Seat. "She is surely unused to such things as close association with men, and must be accustomed to them slowly, and with patience. Perhaps another fey will find her agreeable once more."

"Never will there be such a fey," said I distinctly to both males, increasing the annoyance in Galiose and causing S'Heernoh to close his eyes with a further sigh. "Those who wish to indulge in foolishness may do so alone, for this Midanna will have no more of it. Also have I decided that the forthcoming meeting will be held outside the city. Those who are defeated must see the defeat with their own eyes, and I shall not have all manner of city males parading about within the gates. Those of the city who wish to attend may take themselves outside."

"And then, when we have found victory, we will accompany them back in," said Galiose, a stiff nod of compliance joining his words. "My men have not had wenches in too long a time, and yours will do them nicely. Then will we at last be able to see properly to the matter of the coming strangers."

With such foolishness did Galiose then take himself to join Telion and Lialt at the board, caring naught for the insult he left behind him. Surely, then, did I know regret for the victory the Sigurri would have, a victory which would take from my warriors and myself the pleasure of seeing to such boasting fools with swords. Swords which were in no manner shielded.

"For what reason must you speak with such absolute cer-

tainty, lady war leader?" said S'Heernoh from where he
stood, now beside my right shoulder. "A perhaps here and a
likely there would see to the determination of the High Seat,
with insult neither given nor taken. Would you sooner risk
yourself by facing him in challenge, and that before the arrival
of the strangers?"

"There is *likely* to be little risk in facing that one in
challenge," said I, turning to raise my eyes to the ones which
regarded me so closely. "*Perhaps* S'Heernoh would now
care to discuss his whereabouts of the last darkness. Surely
was I of the belief that he had been summoned to the sleeping
leather of a war leader."

"And surely would I have attended that war leader, had I
not been taken ill," said the male, the sincerity in his dark
eyes somehow difficult to accept. "The servants who aided
me will gladly speak of how suddenly the illness came upon
me, and how strongly it held me in its grasp. Was this not
explained to you by the servant I sent with word of my
indisposition?"

"No servant came, nor was I given explanation," said I,
sensing the odd amusement of the male that lurked behind his
eyes and words. For what reason he would feel amusement
was one with the doings of all males, yet did I believe I saw
the true reason for his "illness." "Do you fear Ceralt and
Mehrayn so greatly, then, that you would obey them sooner
than this war leader? Are you not aware of the fact that there
is naught they may do to you that I may not also see done?"

"My lady Jalav, how might I explain?" said he, frustrated
now. "The Prince and the High Rider— Neither of them
merely indulges in a pleasant pastime, caring little for the
outcome of the thing. Each of them seeks to possess the
woman he may not continue on without, and this is what you
would place me in the midst of? For no reason other than that
you feel annoyance toward *them*? To feel the wrath of a man
and warrior about to descend upon one is not the same as to
feel the like from a wench and warrior, no matter the ability
and skill possessed by that wench. To feel the thing from two
men and warriors—! Sooner would I have my ending from
your hands, lady, for then I would no longer need to peer
about cautiously before daring to depart from my room—or

attempting to enter yours. Indeed did I seek to obey your command last darkness, fully twice did I seek to do so. The first time I nearly trod upon the High Rider, who had stood himself before your doors; my second attempt found the Prince in his place, equally as large and equally as imposing. Should I have continued on, neither you nor any other wench would again have had pleasure from me—even had I lived.''

The fiercely hissed indignation of the male was nearly laughable, that and his attempt to confine his words to my hearing. Indeed did he fear Ceralt and Mehrayn, as many males seemed to fear them, yet was Jalav in no manner a male.

''Once this fey is done, the Prince and High Rider will no longer concern us, S'Heernoh,'' I reassured the male, putting a hand to his shoulder. In some manner the quiver of his fear had not reached his flesh, for the shoulder beneath my hand seemed solid and sure, and more firmly muscled than his leanness would lead one to expect. ''With his males defeated Ceralt will need to return them to their villages, and Mehrayn will find that those of his legions and my Midanna who remain without the city will require a leader to be ever with them. I, myself, shall direct those warriors within the city, therefore shall the place beyond the walls be his. At that time I will send for you again—with none to stand before the doors of my chamber.''

''Quite interesting intentions, lady,'' muttered the male, taking his eyes from me not soon enough to keep away sight of his vexation. Tall and lean and gray-haired was S'Heernoh, dark-eyed and ever filled with odd amusement, yet not at that moment. Surely did it seem the male had no wish to serve a war leader, and yet such was foolishness. He had served two Summa warriors on our journey to the visiting place of those who had once been enemies; for what reason would he hesitate to do the same with a war leader?

To find reason in the doings of males had ever been beyond me, and surely was S'Heernoh male; therefore did I make no attempt to divine the reasons for his distress, doing no more than taking pleasure from the feel of his shoulder and arm beneath my hand. To put hands upon a well-made male will bring a hum to the throat of any warrior, yet was

the time of my diversion most short in duration. The male
seemed unaware of my doing till the doors to my chamber
opened once again, and then did a glance show him the
arrival of Mehrayn and Ceralt. I cared naught for the appearance of those two, yet S'Heernoh felt the weight of their
immediate stares and abruptly attempted to brush my hand
from him, much as though he were covered with insects. As
his eyes were upon the two males rather than upon me I was
able to avoid the brushing a short while, and then was my
hand at last caught the while rarely-seen-before annoyance
flashed from his gaze to mine.

"*Perhaps*, lady, the High Seat has the right of it, and you
do indeed deserve a good hiding," he growled, his eyes
unmoving from my face. "You may not treat such men so,
nor may you so unthinkingly place another between you and
them. Should you have a reason for refusing them speak to
them of it, and perhaps an acceptable path may be discovered
which skirts the morass of your refusal."

"A warrior is to speak with males?" I asked scornfully.
"No male will give ear to the wishes of a warrior, those two
least of all, and surely would I prove to be as great a fool as
they were I to attempt such a thing. And should S'Heernoh
wish to range himself with one such as Galiose, surely would
he be wise to first don a weapon."

Then did I take my hand from his grip with a jerk and turn
from him, allowing him to speak no further, as he had so
clearly intended doing. The seething anger this brought him
was no less than his due, in payment for that which he had
brought to me. Speak to those who were bound to see their
own will done, indeed!

In great annoyance and mounting anger did I look about
the chamber, then, to see that Ceralt had gone to those three
who stood before the board, and Mehrayn had joined Aysayn
where the latter had taken seat. It came to me then that I was
soon to be shut of all those males, soon to be free of their
constant, abrasive presence, soon to be done with the need
for having them about and under foot. Ceralt would be gone
and Mehrayn unable to enter the city, the strangers would
come in their turn to be seen to, and then might Jalav do as
she must, to free herself or end in the attempt. The matter of

Sigurr continued to intrude upon my thoughts when they concerned themselves with the challenging of Mida, for it had not yet come to me in what manner I might avoid him. After consideration, surely had it seemed that the beliefs of Rilas had been sent to her, to insure that Jalav would indeed be brought where the male god might reach her, a thing which was. . . .

"There are words I would have with you, girl," came a growl of a voice, causing me to raise my eyes to the face of Mehrayn. So intent upon my own thoughts had I been that I had not seen him approach; now he stood directly before me, wide arms folded across broad, bare chest, strong displeasure in the green gaze which came down to me.

"What is it you wish, male?" I asked, annoyed that my thoughts had been interrupted. In no manner was it to be believed that males were capable of such thoughts of their own; had they been, they would have spent more time in the doing and less bedeviling warriors.

"I *wish* to know for what reason Aysayn was set upon by those wenches of yours," said Mehrayn, clearly angry. "Did it amuse you to have him put to use as a temple slave, a dagger at his throat, all refusal denied him?"

"Indeed did Jalav find amusement in the thing," I allowed, meeting his gaze as a warrior and war leader. "For what reason should she not? Did Aysayn not use her in a similar fashion?"

"Did he?" asked Mehrayn, his anger unabated. "With no weapon free to your hand with which you might defend yourself? With a blade at your throat? Till you were nearly unable to walk? Had that been so, I doubt you would have stood with him upon the sands against his enemies. Should the strangers appear this fey, he, too, will stand; and fight; and mayhap find a glory come too soon. All through believing a young girl child was possessed of a true sense of honor."

The words, bitterly spoken, a matching bitterness beside the anger in his gaze, ended as he turned abruptly from me, his broad stride returning him to the side of Aysayn. In no manner had he given me opportunity to reply, and yet had he done so, I knew not what I would have said. Much did I feel

as I had when first I began to travel through the land of
males—confused, all certainties become unsure and unsupported. In deep, enmiring confusion I turned then, only to
find another no more than a pace from me.

"Wench, you must cease this at once," said Ceralt, halting
just before me to put his fingers to his swordbelt. "There has
already been far too much of it, and I will have no more."

"Of what do you speak?" I asked, in my disturbance
paying little mind to what was said. "There are other things I
must see to, things of importance. . . ."

"Naught is of greater importance than the halting of the
slaying of a man bit by bloody bit!" he snapped, one hand
coming to my face so that I must look up at the anger in his
light eyes. "No man lives without ever having erred, no
leader leads without commanding that which makes the man
in him weep! Galiose erred in having you lashed, and you
must indeed hear his words of regret!"

"Regret!" I echoed, understanding naught of the anger he
showed. "His words of regret will remove the pain of the
lash, the agony of its touch? No longer will memory of the
thing come to me because he has spoken of remorse?"

"There is greater pain in memory than that which comes
from physical hurt," said he, a bitterness much like Mehrayn's
in his voice. "Should a man cause agony in a soft, helpless
thing through anger and deep indignation, he will soon thereafter find himself without the shield of such emotions, and
then must consider what he has done. He must live with his
guilt for the rest of his feyd, and to live with a blade in one's
flesh is less painful, for even should the small, soft thing
forgive him, no man is ever able to forgive himself. And
should she show him bitterness and hurt for the doing instead,
surely does a part of him die with each word spoken, each
accusation unspoken. To bring hurt to another may at times
cause greater agony in oneself; should you be unable to see
this and appreciate it, do not speak to Galiose again."

He withdrew his hand and took himself from me, returning
to those he had left as Mehrayn had returned to Aysayn.
None in that chamber looked upon me, not even S'Heernoh
who stood with back turned and head down, leaning with his
fists upon the board above a cup of daru he had poured.

Males were they, all of them, wishing to give no more than confusion and pain to a warrior, wishing to see her lie broken at their feet. Soon would that warrior be rid of them, however, all of them, and never again would she enmesh herself in their doings. Hurriedly did I then take myself to the doors to the corridor and through them, speaking no word, knowing I would not be pursued. I was no longer of interest to those males, and how pleased was I at that!

Little difficulty was there in finding a far, quiet chamber in that dwelling, one where none would intrude, one where I might sit undisturbed. Not even thoughts of the strangers came to me there, and I sat for far more than three hind upon the thick blue floor cloth, beside a hand of tall, wide windows made like doors which were covered with maglessa weave, seeing little or naught of the chamber. Neither platforms nor seats were to be found in that place, no more than silks and candle sconces upon the walls, the tall, wide windows, a large section removed from the center of the floor cloth. Oval was that section, as a shield is oval, the smooth stone of the floor ashine amidst the thick, soft floor cloth. For what reason the chamber had been done so I knew not, nor did I care; that none other was there more than sufficed, allowing me the time of nonthought.

At last did memory return of those things requiring attention, stirring me in the place I lay upon the floor cloth on my back, bringing again awareness of my surroundings. One knee had I raised and then left so, hands unmoving upon my middle, leather-bound hair a smoothened lump beneath me. I had no wish to return to that place and time and the requirements of duty, no desire to do other than ride from each of the demands upon me and make them no more; had I been other than a war leader of Midanna I would surely have done so, yet was I solely a war leader. It angered me that this must be so, for the weight of the chains of duty had grown, bringing a heaviness to my soul rather than my body. It angered me also that the strangers had not yet appeared, those on whose behalf I had had so much difficulty so that I might be prepared to meet them. Were they to be much longer in arriving my fury would be difficult to contain.

I sat abruptly upon the cloth and then rose to my feet,

resettling my swordbelt before taking myself toward the doors
to the chamber. Those matters which awaited would not see
to themselves, and best would be to have them done and over
with. I descended to the floor below and sought without the
dwelling for that place where the kand were kept, passing
warriors of many clans who moved about upon tasks of their
own. One Hulna warrior assured me she knew the whereabouts of my kan, therefore did I stand and watch the doings
all about the while she went to fetch him. It was, perhaps, the
latest doing which brought the Hulna such eagerness to take
herself to that place where the kand were kept, yet was she
scarcely alone in feeling so.

Many grins and murmurs of approval greeted those Sigurri
warriors who had been sent within the city, hand upon hand
of warriors standing looking upon or advancing with their
slowly moving column of twos. From the second, nearer gate
did the Sigurri come, negating the need for their traversal of
the city, allowing them to look upon those who watched their
arrival with matching grins. Had it been possible I would
surely have had them sent elsewhere than within the city, and
yet in what other manner might I have divided their force to
negate what was, without the city, a vastly greater numerical
superiority? Truly had I little doubt as to their intentions,
being certain they would not turn upon those Midanna they
had aided, and yet of what certainty were certainties? Had it
been their wish they might easily have taken those warriors
who had come to the city with them, and then turned their
numbers toward those who held the city. In allowing half
their number to enter the city, their numerical superiority was
no more; should it be their will to face Midanna with blades,
those Midanna would no longer be at so great a disadvantage.
The safety of many Midanna lives rested in the hands of one;
was that one to turn them to naught through a blind belief in
the honor of others?

Not many reckid passed before the Hulna returned with my
yellow and brown kan, and then was she off again, to assist
with making place for the kand ridden by the Sigurri. A good
portion of the grounds of the dwelling nearest the palace had
been marked off for that purpose, leather strung between
spears driven into the ground serving as an enclosure for the

mounts. Quite large had that enclosure been made, to fit the number of kand brought within, and would certainly do for the time that was. Should the feyd begin to stretch unending, other provisions would need to be made.

I mounted my kan in a single leap, settled myself upon his back as he danced beneath me, then turned his head toward the second gate, that which lay beyond the ways of the city. Little desire had I to depart through the lines of the entering Sigurri, and also did I wish to see what occurred before the far gate. I rode beneath bright skies, anticipating with distaste the ever-present throngs who lined and clogged the ways of the city, finding surprise when no more than a double handful of males and city females were to be seen at once upon those ways. Before the gate itself was a strong contingent of Harra and Hersa, alert for any who would enter the city without leave, yet were the gates opened wide to allow departure, and city folk yet trickled through as they gestured without, eager to see what occurred so near. Most departed on foot, hurrying to add themselves to the circle about the area within which moved fewer than four hands of males, each armed with a sword of wood. Large wheeled and covered conveyances had also been taken without, to be placed beyond those who stood, males upon them who had drawn back the coverings and then shouted below to those who stood before them. A number of males had climbed to the beds of the conveyances from where they might see above the heads of those before them, and yet each new male to do so was required to give over what was not easily seen to the one whose conveyance it was, before he was permitted to ascend. I knew not what those city folk might be about, yet it was scarcely likely to be of great importance.

I had halted at the gate to look about before riding through, finding the noise and shoutings of those who watched unexpected, and a Hersa warrior detached herself from her sisters and approached me.

"War leader, the doings have been greatly amusing," said she, putting a hand to the neck of my kan as she looked up with a grin. "Those in leather and metal, and those in leather with furs upon their legs, have been able to do naught against those in black body cloths. Much do they seem as warriors-

to-be standing against war leaders, and should true weapons
have been used, the sweet ground would have long since run
red with their lifeblood. Those in black are true warriors; the
others are not.''

I nodded in silence to hear that which I had known would
be, seeing as I did so the victory of yet another Sigurri. Small
was that black-clad warrior, considerably smaller than the
city male he faced, undoubtedly chosen for that very reason.
How foolish city males were, to be ignorant of the fact that a
warrior smaller than her sisters must be a good deal more able
than they, else would she be unable to hold her own against
their greater size and strength. The ability of a warrior lay not
in her size but in her skill, a thing clearly known to any
warrior. To speak of oneself as a warrior was not to be that
thing, a lesson now learned by those who were no more than
city and village folk.

I gave thanks to the Hersa who had spoken to me, and then
did I make my way through and behind those who watched,
taking myself toward those Midanna who also watched the
goings-on, yet from the shoulder of the rise. In no manner
had they attempted to draw nearer, unsurprising in that they
were warriors alert against attack, yet were there a large
number of Sigurri in their company, the two groups warriors
all, finding amusement in the futile efforts of those who
would have the calling without first developing the skill. I
rode from clan to clan and gestured my war leaders to me
before dismounting, spoke a short while concerning the manner in which their warriors and the Sigurri were to circle the
city once the defeated village and city males had departed,
then answered what few questions there were. Provender
would not be a difficulty for a time, I was also told, yet was
the daru long gone and lamented. I smiled at the sighs of
longing to be heard, knowing well the needs of warriors, then
allowed that I might speak with those war leaders within the
city. Surely would they share what daru they had with sisters
who were bereft, and should the amount to be had prove
insufficient, I would see the renth of the city added to it.
Wide smiles and grins quickly replaced sighs, and then was I
able to remount in order to return to the city.

Much did it seem that the numbers of those who watched

the contests had increased, spreading themselves all about, keeping one from riding among them save with much difficulty. Also moving about were those with wide boards of provender, small cups of that which smelled of meat, somewhat larger cups of that filled full with sweetness. Behind those with provender came those with skins of drink, to the left renth, to the right what seemed much in appearance like that called thrai, a drink I had thought was only of the Sigurri. No presence at all had thrai, its composition no more than heated and colored water, a sweetness added to sicken any who had grown warrior size. Far more of the males about chose to trade for the renth, yet were there those who sought no more than the thrai to trade for their metal, a foolishness to be expected when one considered its source. A shout went up from those nearer the contests, showing yet another victory had been achieved, and then was my kan halted entirely. Deliberately had a hand grabbed my kan's reins, no uncertainty in the dark eyes which regarded me.

"You ride unconcernedly without me, wench," said Chaldrin, his calm rumble perhaps a shade less calm than usual. "And yet, for what reason should you not? There are none about here capable of harming you."

I had no wish to speak to the male—nor any male, for that matter—therefore did I attempt to pull my kan from his grip. What words there had been had already passed between us, yet the male would not allow the thing to lie undisturbed.

"None about capable of bringing you harm, indeed!" said he with a sudden mockery, closing tighter the fist which held to my reins. "These are men about here, and you no more than a wench, and surely were they to take you you would squirm well beneath them. No wench may ride about without a man to protect her."

A chuckling came from those males who had turned about to see us. All looked upon Chaldrin, large, broad, thick in the waist, a swordbelt closed about the white of his loin wrap, leather bracers tight about his wrists, and then all looked upon me and chuckled. Indeed was Jalav of a lesser size than the male; yet however he bore a scar attesting to the keenness of her blade. Though angered, I simply tried once more to free my mount.

"For what reason do you seek so eagerly to ride from me, wench?" pursued the male, a grin accompanying his rumble, his hand immovable from before my kan. "Do you fear I will take you as I have in the past, forcing obedience and response from you, with none about to give you assistance? Do you seek to flee because you fear me?"

"Jalav fears no male!" I returned in a snarl, truly feeling rage at the strengthened laughter. "No others need be about to give her assistance, for she requires none—as she required none when last she faced you."

"For the reason that I allowed her her victory?" asked the male in derision, his own laughter even more infuriating. "Think you he shall do the same again, and permit her to fatten the falsity of her pride? In no manner might you best me, wench, save that I allow it."

Calmly sure and comfortable was the male, greatly amused and strengthened by the raucous calls supporting him, sending his gaze to move over me with the intrusiveness of one who looked upon a slave. So that was the way of it with males, then, the manner in which they boasted and bragged at the expense of one who had once been fool enough to believe them something more than simply male. All males gave pain, as often as they might, and shame and humiliation as well; easily might such things be given to one who was slave, yet was Jalav war leader to all the Midanna.

"As you allowed me my victory, you will feel no hesitation, then, in facing me again," I returned at once, sliding quickly from my kan to stand and face my challenger. "Your weapon hangs at your side as does mine; withdraw your words or draw your blade."

"To withdraw the words would not remove the truth of them," said he, giving my kan's reins to one of those who stood about. Then did he turn to face me once more, moving till he regained the place he had stood, at last putting hand to hilt. "I shall not this time spare you, wench, therefore had you best look closely to your defense."

As his sword slid free of its scabbard mine was also in my fist, the two weapons drawn so quickly that those about us backed with a many-voiced gasp, seeking distance between themselves and any soon-to-be-executed backswings. Neither

Chaldrin nor I looked upon those who ringed us; one does not look upon any save the one who faces her in challenge, else is she scarcely likely to survive the meeting. The male stepped forward filled full with confidence, his dark eyes marking each movement I made, and then did he swing toward me, casually yet with strength, and made a sound of scorn when I ended the swing with my blade.

"Barely adequate for one of supposed skill, girl," said he, his tone relentless. "Is this the manner in which you mean to best me? With the movements of an awkward, unschooled child? Perhaps I should have first demanded that you earn the right to face me."

Again the males about us laughed, some voicing loud agreement, yet did I know that already had I earned what right was needed. No rage came from his taunting but pain, the pain of knowing how great a fool I had been, the pain of memories I had believed to be truth, now turned achingly all to lies. Never had the male felt what I had felt, never had he truly been one with a Midanna. For what reason he had done as he had I was unable to fathom, yet was I more than able to put an end to more of it.

Words were unnecessary to add to the speed of my swing, the strength of my attack. With speed and strength I had at him, then, seeking to cleave his head or slice off an arm or sever the dark-haired visage of him. So furious was my attack that I drove him back, his sword striving in a blur to keep my edge from him, amusement no longer to be seen in his eyes. Shocked were the utterances which now came from all about, yet was I aware of no more than the grass beneath my feet, the hilt in my fist, the male before my blade. Swiftly did his weapon seek to reply, attempting an entry through my guard, but I kept him from it. Almost without thought did I repulse his attempts, sneering at their inadequacy, and then I was suddenly, shockingly aware that he no longer guarded himself. My point flashed toward his middle far too late to understand his purpose, far too late to halt the stroke. Into the middle of him did my sword jar with strength, with naught to deny it, naught to bar its way. Though uncounted enemies had stood so before me, never before had it felt as though I, too, were transfixed. In wild, unreasoning confusion I pulled

my blade from him, in some manner certain that doing so
would negate the entrance of the blade, yet the great gout of
blood released belied that. Pale had Chaldrin gone at the first
touch of sharpened metal, a grunt torn from him at its removal, and yet did he look upon me with the warmth of old,
and smile the faint smile I had so often seen upon him.

"More than adequate, sister," he whispered, as the lifeblood poured from him. "Truly the doing of one of great
skill, a warrior and war leader without equal."

"Chaldrin," I whispered in answer, watching helplessly as
he slid to his knees, the sword already fallen from his fist. I
could barely bring myself to speak his name, yet he, himself,
was not done with speaking.

"My life was not mine but yours, sister," he breathed, no
more than the breath of a breeze upon the grass. "To be no
longer fit to ride and stand beside you—is to no longer be
deserving of the life you returned. The shame I gave you is
now no more—for you have wiped it away with my blood.
Also—do I hope—that I may—have your—forgiveness as
well—"

"Chaldrin, no!" I cried as he fell forward; I dropped to
catch him up in my arms. So heavy was he, and so covered
with the blood I had spilled! "Mida, no! Leave him and take
me instead!" I screamed, struggling to keep him from the
ground, knowing that were I to release him to fall all the
way, surely would he be gone from me forever. I fought to
keep him erect, by my soul do I swear I fought, yet the
weight of him took me down and down, and then was there
another who grasped my arms with fingers of rock and threw
me from the one who was truly my brother.

"What have you done?" demanded S'Heernoh with a cry,
appearing from I know not where, bending quickly over the
one I had not been strong enough to keep from the ground.
His hands went uselessly to one already gone to the endless
dark. Without thought did I regain my feet, find and resheathe
my bloody sword, and run to my kan so that I might vault to
his back. A pull turned me about and a kick sent me agallop
through those hastily making way, and then was I racing
toward the forests not far from the city, flying with every bit
of speed my kan possessed. Tears flew as well, tears of

agony I could not halt, and the forests, when I reached them, were no more than a blur. Without slowing I rode into the blur, caring naught for what might happen, hearing only the cry which wailed and echoed inside me: Chaldrin! My brother Chaldrin! Forever gone, forever no more!

How long I rode and where, I know not; from out of the blur came a low-hanging branch, and then happily I, too, was no more.

6.

An awakening— and a fruitless search

I awoke with a heavy throbbing in my head. I lay still without thought and without an awareness of what was about me, seeking to retain my tenuous hold upon wakefulness, seeking to escape the throbbing. When at last the ache did indeed ease its grip I slept awhile, knowing I did so only when I awoke for the second time. Distant and receding had the throbbing grown, so much so that I was able to begin to move where I lay; only upon beginning the attempt did I discover I was unable to do so.

Confusion swirled me thickly about as I at last looked to where I lay. Belly down was I upon a thin, much used fur, my cheek to the thing, my wrists and ankles held tight by leather. From all about came the sound of creaking, and I raised my head with some effort to see the wood of the closed conveyance I lay in. The sway and creak spoke of the fact that the conveyance was in motion, and indeed was I then able to see the presence of leaves and branches as we passed them, through the gap in the cloth at the end of the conveyance. The rising and movement of my head showed another thing, that the war leather was gone from my hair, and this, too, I was unable to understand. Many things stood all about me, sacks and square constructions of wood, high piled sleeping furs and bulging drinking skins, mounds of cloth coverings and further sacks. The smell of provender and the heavier smell of salt came from many of these mounds, and in no manner was I able to envision how I had come to be among them. I attempted to part the leather which held my wrists behind me, struggled to loosen it even some small amount, admitting the uselessness of the efforts only after the passing reckid proved the thing beyond doubt. The manner in which I had gotten there was just then unimportant; that I was unable to free myself to depart again was considerably more to the point.

I had again been attempting to free myself, when the conveyance slowed and came unsteadily to a halt. The memory had come to me of the time I had been taken by Ceralt to his village in a conveyance such as that, yet had I then been wounded rather than bound. It seemed unlikely that Ceralt had again done the same, nor was I to be proven wrong; sounds came of one approaching from the front of the conveyance through its cargo, and then was a male crouching beside me who seemed somewhat familiar.

"Ah, you have returned to yourself, wench," said he, a great deal of satisfaction upon him, his hand reaching out to stroke my hair. "I had hoped you would do so before we had reached our destination."

"Release me at once!" I snapped, looking upon the dark-haired, dark-eyed, wide-shouldered form of him, attempting to recall why he seemed familiar. Clad in a dark red covering of city males was he, strapped leather coverings upon his feet, a swordbelt closed about his waist. It seemed the swordbelt had seen little use, a thing most fitting for one of a city.

"Release you?" echoed the male with clear amusement, his hand moving to stroke my bound right arm. "When I have waited so long for the Serene Oneness to grant you to me? You were told, were you not, that this fey or the next, this kalod or the next, you would at some time be mine? The time has now come, wench, and never again shall I release you. I will bring you such pleasure that you will not wish to be released, and gladly will you bear what sons and daughters I give you."

"Relidose!" said I, abruptly recalling the male. He had it been who had first approached the palace of the High Seat after my Midanna had taken it, he who had offered to stand for me against the chosen champion of the High Seat, he who had afterward asked to follow me. Not long had the male followed, not long had he been able to efface himself sufficiently to please a war leader, and from that moment to this I had not again thought of him.

"Aye, Relidose," said he, undisturbed that I had not at first known him. "Little reason was given you to recall me, wench, yet shall that omission now be repaired. You will not again be allowed forgetfulness, for you will know yourself mine alone."

With soft laughter did the male then reach to his swordbelt, opening it so that he might put it aside. Again I angrily fought the leather which held me, yet no more did I accomplish than increasing the laughter of the male. I had rolled to my side when first he had crouched beside me, in order to more easily look upon him; this the male now undid by pushing me flat to my belly again, so that he might move from his crouch to kneel across me, one knee to either side of my body. Between his thighs I struggled to free myself, furious at his continuing laughter, attempting to keep my face from the aged sleeping fur beneath me, and then his hands came to my sides. Slowly were the ties of my breech opened and as slowly was it pulled away, and then was my hair parted and thrown to either side of me.

"How round and lovely a bottom you have, wench," said Relidose with a chuckle, the insolent, intrusive touch of his hands coming with the words. "Sight of it inspires me to seek you elsewhere, an elsewhere equally as lovely and far more enticing. Your softness calls me, girl, and never shall I refuse to answer."

The hands of the male then went to my thighs and raised them up, forcing my face to the fur as he did so. I turned my head to the side and fought to keep from being raised so, yet the leather would not allow me to struggle. One arm of the male went about me, holding me so that I might be touched in another manner, and nearly did a gasp escape from me.

"Ah, what lovely softness," crooned the male, disallowing the twist of my hips as I sought to avoid so distressing a touch. "How long I have dreamt of possessing this softness, of caressing it and bringing it to heat. Do you desire me as yet, wench? Are you yet prepared to receive me? I shall not bring you pain, you know, no more than pleasure shall I give. Are you as quick to heat as those others of your wenches?"

My wrists pulled at the leather which held me, my fury growing beyond all bounds that I might not refuse what the male did, yet all effort continued to go for naught. Well stroked and caressed was I by the male who had taken me, and then was I held so that he might use me as well. Little difficulty did he find in entering me despite the leather on my ankles, yet was the time more discomfort than pleasure; the male, however, found pleasure aplenty, and once he had found release as well, he withdrew and allowed me to lie flat again.

"Fully as delightful as I had anticipated," said he, a pat to my bottom added to the words as he reached for his sword. "Had I the time at present I would have you again, yet shall there be many later opportunities. I truly give the deepest thanks that the Serene Oneness put you in my path, knocked senseless from your kan by a tree branch. My prayers have now been answered in full, and never again shall I ask another thing."

Chuckling, the male then left me, to return from whence he had come. A moment later was the conveyance again in motion, leaving me to move angrily upon the aged sleeping fur. To believe that my presence was a gift to him from his god! To claim to have found me lying senseless after having fallen from my kan! What Midanna warrior would fall from so trouble-free a mount as a kan? In what manner would I have allowed a tree branch to knock me from my—

The raging in my mind ceased as memory abruptly returned. Indeed had I been knocked from my kan, for I had not seen the branch which struck me; I had not seen the branch because of the presence of blurriness, caused by tears, which in turn had been caused by—

I could not complete the thought.

A shivering took me as my cheek returned to the fur, a shivering from the terrible chill I felt. Much did I wish I might sit and put my arms upon my head and wail out my soul hurt as I had once seen a village female do, rocking back and forth at the unbearable pain in an effort to ease it. In Mida's name did I wish I might do so, and yet I had in no manner earned such easing. It had been I and I alone who had caused the agony, I and I alone who might be held culpable. Many times in the past had I seen the occurrences about me as due to the will of Mida, yet in no manner might this doing

be lain at her feet. It was Jalav's anger which had caused the
challenge, Jalav's hand which had held the sword hilt; had I
not fallen to anger I would have seen Chaldrin drop his
guard, welcoming the thrust which never should have been.
An ache was in my chest and throat, one so great I was nearly
unable to breathe, yet did I do no more than lie upon the
sleeping fur, belly down, cheek to the fur, eyes closed, no
longer struggling against the leather upon me. I no longer had
the desire to struggle, no longer the will to do other than lie
there; perhaps, were I to lie there long enough, my brother
and I would soon again be one.

I know not the number of reckid which passed the while I
lay unthinking, yet were there far too few before the conveyance again slowed and came to a halt. Without was I able to
hear the murmur of many voices, and then one rose above the
rest.

"Wagons!" exclaimed the voice of a male, surprise most
evident in that voice. "How were you able to get wagons past
those savages, Relidose?"

"The gates have been opened this fey to allow exit to one
and all," returned the voice of Relidose, followed by a sound
which seemed to indicate his jumping to the ground. "The
letter I dropped over the wall with your supplies two feyd
agone told you of those who had appeared before our gates,
did it not? Truly did many of us believe there would be battle
between them and the wenches who held the city, yet did the
light of the last new fey bring unexpected surprise: the black-
haired leader of the wenches returned from whatever place
she had journeyed to, and with her were equally as many
wenches as already occupied our city, and a matching force
of men. With so great a number behind them, those who led
the men before our walls were able to enter the city in
company with the wench and the men who rode with her,
supposedly to speak of what might be done to avoid battle
between them."

"But they are warriors and men!" came the outraged voice
of a female. "For what reason did they not merely engage
and best those savage sluts? Were they, too, unable to see
beyond their own filthy needs?"

"You forget the presence of the men who accompanied the

wenches, sister mine," said Relidose, a dryness to the words.
"These men, it was said, are followers of the dark god
Sigurr, warriors who sacrifice virgins to him to assure their
prowess in battle. In some manner were they made to agree to
a contest between certain of their warriors and a chosen
number of those who are civilized, practice weapons to be
used in place of true. Before the last darkness were the
combatants chosen, the contests beginning not long after the
arrival of the new light of this fey. As the contests were held
beyond the walls of the city, the gates were thrown wide to
allow those who wished it to attend the doing."

"And those who would have supported the savages were
defeated!" said the male who had spoken earlier, a great,
grim delight taking him. "Our city is soon to be ours again,
and you have brought the wagons to allow us to return there
in comfort!"

"No, Kadimone," said Relidose with a sigh, a sadness of
sorts to be heard. "Right from the first the followers of the
dark god stood victorious, and the doing took the heart from
every good man who saw it. I knew at once that those who
had come to free our city would soon depart in order to retain
their lives, and that my sister, and you, her husband, and all
these others who had been put so cruelly out of their own city
would not be allowed to return to it. I had secured these
wagons in anticipation of victory, to fetch you home as you
suggested, and nearly wept when I saw the thing become
impossible. It was then that your sole course of action came
to me, therefore did I use the lack of vigilance brought about
by the contests and take what you would require from the
stores put aside for the palace, and quickly brought them
here. You all must take these wagons and journey to the
settlement."

"The settlement!" came the shocked echo in many voices,
upset and indignation and disgust to be heard. A muddle of
words came from a muddle of voices, and then the voice of
the one called Kadimone again rose above them.

"You would have us go to the settlement?" demanded the
male, outraged. "Where they are far too primitive to appreciate the merits of a guild? Where they each make whatever
they would have, without first seeking guild permission?

Where they would demand that we do more than practice the art of our several crafts?''

"They dwell in crude, nearly empty cabins, Relidose!" said the female who had been called sister by the male, her indignation well mixed with disgust. "They would be no better than these caves we have been forced to take shelter in, with none to see to the cleaning and cooking save myself! And what of all the lovely possessions we were made to abandon? I have been sustained through this horrible ordeal only by thought of the fey when I might return and reclaim my possessions; you would now have me abandon them forever?''

"Orlinia, your possessions may not be returned for," said Relidose, "not so long as those wenches hold the city. And none of us knows how long that will be. And you, Kadimone, may teach those of the settlement the benefits brought by a guild, just as you taught the members of your own guild. You may not remain here in these caves, for who knows when it will no longer be possible to supply you with food? My savings were modest to begin with; to spend my last copper on provisions for you would benefit neither of us, and you will not hear of my selling what was left behind.''

"Certainly not!" snapped the female Orlinia. "Were you to sell our lovely things, there would be naught to return to when we did return! Kadimone has assured you that your paltry coppers will be replaced immediately upon our return, has he not? Would you have him tell you where our silver is hidden, so that the unscrupulous might cozen its location. For what reason must you be so foolish, Relidose?''

"Who is that who drives the second wagon?" demanded the male Kadimone in abrupt interruption. "That cannot be a slave collar upon him.''

"Indeed is it a slave collar he wears," said Relidose, his voice tight, restrained. "To drive two wagons alone would not have been possible, therefore did I cast about for one who would aid me. Would you have had me choose a free man, one who might well have had his lot improved through the meddling of those wenches? I would have learned of his true feelings only when they came with spears to take me up. Instead I looked upon those who had been set to the task of selecting what portion of the stores would need to be sent to the palace, and realized that those slaves struggling beneath the selected burdens would have no love for the wenches they served. Had their loyalty not been in question, they would have been given their freedom and made servants instead. I was able to approach this slave when those who directed him took themselves off to watch the contesting, offered him his freedom were he to assist me, and was accepted. We found a tunic too large for him which hid his collar, and were able to drive through the gates with none the wiser."

"You need not apologize, Relidose," said Kadimone, his tone now thoughtful. "There are many tasks here a slave may be set to, and should he see to them properly he will be allowed a regular portion of scraps from our provender. You, yourself, mean to return to the city, of course."

"That was my original intention, yes," replied Relidose, the vexation clear in his voice. "An unexpected occurrence during my journey here has caused me to rethink my position, . however. Kadimone, the man was given my word that his freedom would be restored! You cannot. . . ."

"Not return to the city?" barked the female Orlinia, again with disapproval. "If you were to remain, who, then, would secure the supplies we require? Are our children to be abandoned to starve? The children of the blood of your own sister?"

"Orlinia, my silver is nearly gone!" replied Relidose in exasperation. "Had it been necessary to purchase what these wagons contain, I would not have been able to do so! All of you here must go on to the settlement, and I shall go with . . ."

"What occurrence during your journey?" demanded Kadimone, greatly annoyed. "I am unable to conceive of what might possibly have occurred to cause you to turn your back on the plight of your own."

"I have been given the gift I have long prayed for!" said Relidose. "Am I to spit upon the blessing of the Serene Oneness, and return alone to a city where I might no longer do as I have done since your banishment? Rather than that I shall join you, and make a place for myself in the new settlement, where I may live in peace with my woman. After all I have done for you, would you deny me a place in your midst?''

"What you have done for us is abandon us!" shrilled the female Orlinia, nearly beside herself. "You selfishly think only of yourself, and then ask to be accepted among us?"

"To have been allowed to aid us is not to be one of us, Relidose," said Kadimone with stern disapproval. "A wise man seeks not to overstep himself. What foolish little peasant wench have you found, that you are too greatly shamed to show to the city of your birth? And what leads you to believe that we would permit her presence among decent folk even should *you* be allowed to remain?"

"Adjust your tone or face my wrath, Kadimone," said Relidose, drawing gasps with the coldness of his vow. "The girl is soon to be my wife, and I will permit none to speak ill of her. And as the matter disturbs you so, allow me to assure you that shame has naught to do with my inability to return to the city with her. If I were to do so, she would surely be taken from my side no matter her own wishes to the contrary, for those wenches are jealously possessive. They would not allow her to remain with the man of her choice, and I will not see her lost to me again."

"What nonsense do you speak, Relidose?" asked Kadimone with more bluster than bravery. "What female might you have found, that you need fear her being taken from you?"

"Come and see for yourself," said Relidose, and now did he seem pleased. I heard the sounds of many feet, as though all moved about to the back of the conveyance, and then was there further sound, as of the cloth there being opened and drawn away. All these things I was fully aware of, yet was none of it able to touch me; I cared naught for the doings of mortal nor god. I lay belly down and bound with leather, one cheek to the fur, my eyes continuing closed. No wish had I to attempt escape, for how might I escape from what I had done?

"Do you see her?" asked Relidose, triumphantly. "Do you understand now why I am unable to return to the city?"

"Why—that great mass of black hair!" exclaimed Kadimone, shocked. "See the size of her! She cannot be—the one who leads those savages?"

"Indeed is she Jalav, the one who once led them," said Relidose with soft laughter. "Now is she Jalav who will soon be my wife. We will build a life together, and never will she leave me."

"Relidose, are you mad?" demanded Kadimone in a voice so high it nearly squeaked. "Most certainly she will not leave you, for she is bound hand and foot! Do you believe an elder will wed you to a woman who is bound? And what if she should become unbound? She is a savage and will surely take all our lives!"

"When she is unbound she will do naught, for she will then be too deeply in love with me," said Relidose with a chuckle, indulgent toward one who clearly feared naught save mist. "I have given her pleasure no more than once, therefore is it too soon to expect such a thing as yet, however the following hind and feyd will see that changed. I will give her such pleasure that she will ache to serve me, beg to do nothing but obey me completely. She will plead to be stroked, and I, of course, will. . . ."

"Relidose, you sicken me!" shrilled Orlinia, aghast at what she had heard. "What disgusting things you have done with that savage, we none of us wish to hear! I have no doubt that it pleased her; after all, what else is one to expect from a slut? You will not, however, perform any further perversions, for we will not allow such a thing in our presence! The very idea, a man with a sister of such high station, to do such. . . ."

"Indeed should she be stroked," said Kadimore, suddenly venomous. "Is she not the one who led those savages to our city, those savages who dared to see *us* sent into exile? I would have her stroked with the heaviest whip I might, to repay her in some small measure for the injustice she caused to be perpetrated!"

"I asked that you not speak of her so," said Relidose with anger, above the growl of agreement to be heard from the others he stood among. "She is the woman fated to be my wife, and I shall not allow. . . ."

"She is a savage fated only to pay for her crimes!" screamed Kadimone, truly enraged. "Stand back and do not attempt to halt us, else shall you share in her punishment!"

"No!" shouted Relidose with ragged desperation, the sounds

of struggle accompanying his cry, yet did those sounds of struggle increase, with no further words to be heard. A number of moments passed so, with savage grunts and exclamations of fury, and then was silence returned, no more than harsh breathing to be heard. A scuff came, as of a single movement, and then a horrified female gasp.

"Do not distress yourself, Orlinia," said Kadimone, his reassurance stiff and still filled with anger. "The man had ever been an embarrassment to you, and also to me as your husband. As madness took him there at the end, we are fortunate indeed not to have suffered even more. The Serene Oneness now shelters his soul, and we are no longer required to bear it."

"Your patience with him was ever a comfort to me, Kadimone," said Orlinia, sobbing. "Even as a child he would cause me embarrassment, and father refused to punish him properly. He was my brother, yet surely will this prove for the best."

"And now for the wench," said Kadimone with relish. "If not for her, he would have returned to the city, if not for her, we could remain here. Bring her out where we all may see her, and after having seen her, punish her."

The conveyance moved then, as though there were those who boarded it, and then were there hands upon me, clearly the hands of males. Once the leather had been removed from my ankles the hands lifted me to my feet, thrusting me forward and pulling me along, both at one time. I had no true interest in opening my eyes, yet did they open of themselves to show me those who were about.

Three there were who had come into the conveyance, clad in the coverings of city males, yet were these coverings somewhat longer than those others I had seen. Taken with anger were the males, their hands upon my bound arms far from gentle, yet were their grips lacking in the strength I had come to expect from males. Less than a hand of the steps forced upon me brought me to the end of the conveyance, and then was I pulled quickly to the ground below—and those who waited.

The kand which pulled a second conveyance were perhaps two gandod-strides back from the conveyance I had been in, the space between filled with city folk. Mid-fey-light shone down upon more than two hands of males, a like number of females, a lesser number of those who were children to them, all of whom gasped or exclaimed in some manner when I was brought before them. Too well overfed did these city folk seem, no more than two or perhaps three of the males lacking the roundness of the others, their females the same beneath long, city slave-woman coverings. Even the young appeared less than they should be, without vitality and without true life. Never before had I seen such folk, their presence at the caves I once had known seeming very much out of place.

"Disgusting!" exclaimed a female to the fore, one who seemed older than she appeared. Dark of hair and eye was she, no prettiness to her round, puffy face, great disapproval thickening her gaze. The shrillness had apparently left the female Orlinia, as had her deep sobs of personal loss.

"Kadimone, her nakedness is an affront to those of us who are decent women!" snapped the female, her hands flat to the heavy, rose-colored cloth of her covering. "You must do something, and that at once!"

The male she addressed stood to her right, a male no longer in his prime, had such a one ever had a prime. Soft were the hands beneath delicate gold wristlets, the fleshy neck hung about with glittering stones, a blue covering worn rather long upon the flat chest and swollen belly of him. Not so dark of hair and eye as the female was he, yet was there more intensity in the gaze which moved all about me, a wetting of thick lips accompanying the inspection. I looked down upon the male and his slave-woman as I stood before them, then allowing my gaze to follow the others, finding that none there stood to a greater height than me, few so much as possessing a matching size. Small were these city folk, soft and unprepossessing and scarcely worth the notice of a warrior; had I had any true interest in what befell me, surely would I soon have been free of them.

"See the bruise upon her brow," said the male Kadimone in a murmur, taking no immediate note of the protests voiced by his female. "Now do I believe I understand the manner in which your brother was able to take her. Surely was she senseless when he came upon her, else would she have taken him instead.''

"See how arrogantly she dares to look upon us, Kadimone!" shrilled the female, again taken with great indignation, her small, overfleshed form fairly quivering with outrage. "I will not be looked upon in such a manner by a naked, savage slut! You must see to her at once!"

"And so I shall, my dear," said the male who had not taken his eyes from me, a faint smile moving the fleshy creases of his face. "You, however, and our other ladies, shall not remain, for true men do not parade indecency about before their women. Take the children and return to the caves, and begin at once the gathering of those things to be taken with us to the settlement. We men will see to the punishment of this slut, and then shall we rejoin you and inspect your efforts.''

Feeble protestations came from the females at being commanded to depart; however, all the males stood firm by the portly Kadimone. When once they and their young began withdrawing toward the upward trending path which led to the caves they had taken shelter in, I was able to see the remains of he who had been Relidose. Battered and bloody was the body of the male, as though struck many times by each of those who had stood about him, as silent and unmoving as another had so recently become. So great a fool had the male Relidose been, to believe he might claim undisturbed one who had gained the enmity of his people. Far better that life was no longer left to him, that he be spared the pain when the same was done to she whose possession he had coveted.

"My dear wife would have me see to you, savage," Kadimone murmured, drawing my gaze back to him. "Would it please you to have me do so?"

With the query came the puffed up fingers of the male to touch my breast, the moisture of his palm dampening my flesh. Low, coarse laughter came from the others of the males, laughter heavy with the sound of need, striving to bring anger to the one in their capture. Little of anger was left to their captive, however, therefore did she do no more than step back from the touch, immediately dismissing it and the male as well.

"The insolence of the slut!" gasped another of the males, taller and thinner than his brothers, with stooped, rounded shoulders and large, light eyes in a long face. "She dismisses you as though you were a slave, Kadimone! Has she no concept of how great an honor you do her?"

"Clearly not," said Kadimone in a near growl bespeaking cold humiliation. "The low, savage look of her for the moment caused me forgetfulness as to what she was, yet shall I from now on keep it firmly in mind. It is more than time that her punishment began. Bring her."

Two of those who had brought me from the conveyance again took my arms, forcing me to follow after the male Kadimone. To the side of the conveyance did the male go, seeking all about himself, and then did his gaze touch the large rear wheel, one of four the conveyance needed. At the male's command those who held to my arms attempted to put me to my knees before the wheel, yet were they possessed of considerably less strength than was usual with males. It had ever been my desire to meet the final dark with head held high, proudly erect before that which none might defeat, therefore did I strive to keep myself from being put to my knees. Three other males were called forth by Kadimone, however, their annoyance as great as his, and quickly was I put to my knees, than thrown to my belly in the sparse grass which grew in that place so near the stone of the caves. I had not thought my wrists would be released, yet was the leather indeed taken from them briefly, so that my arms might be brought forward and above my head. The leather was then quickly replaced, my head kept low the while by my hair having been pulled forward and held to the ground before the wheel. When once my wrists were again held by the leather, they were tied to the wheel by the end of that very same leather, the mass of my hair beneath my upstretched arms having been released by those who had held it. Attempting to raise my head proved fruitless, however, for my arms rested upon the hair, and the mass of it allowed me sight of naught else.

"Have you found the strips of leather we will require in addition to the one already upon her?" asked Kadimone of those about him, a cheerful pleasantness to his voice. "Ah, excellent, excellent. You may now attach each to one of her ankles."

Hands took my ankles and brought the feel of leather, yet were my ankles not tied one to the other. Upon each was knotted a length of leather, each length taut as though held by the hands which had tied it, keeping me truly flat to the hard, stony ground. I knew not what these males were about, yet was it clear that there was to be pain before my ending.

"And now for the punishment," said the male who was Kadimone, eagerly panting anticipation upon him. "Soon will we hear the screams of her anguish, and know ourselves to be truly revenged."

Amid many murmurs of equal eagerness was the sound of the whip nearly lost, the sound which presaged its approach to my flesh. The sound and feel of its striking, however, was another matter entirely; the flare of pain brought my head up and caused me to pull at the thong which held my wrists to the wheel, mindlessly seeking to twist from the searing touch which spread like flames in dry grass. Directly across my back had I been struck, and although it was not like the feel of the lash, the pain it brought would not be denied.

"There and there!" grunted the male Kadimone, gloating freely as the whip struck me two times more. "See what lovely stripes redden her flesh, my friends, see how she attempts to turn from the blows. Hold the leather tight now, men; we would not wish her to escape her just desserts. Soon she will be howling and begging an ending to it all."

The onlookers laughed in agreement, and then fell silent, save for the grunting and panting of Kadimone and the striking of the whip to my flesh. The first stroke had truly been painful and the second nearly the same; although I could not keep from twisting about upon the sparse grass and hard stone-strewn ground, seeking to avoid the efforts of the male, no longer was the pain as great as it had been to begin with. I had no understanding of why this should be so, and then, after perhaps two hands of blows, the male abruptly ceased.

"She makes no sound, Kadimone," came the voice of he who was tall and thin, and surely did the male sound reproving. "Strike her again, and with greater strength."

"I have seen myself that she makes no sound," grumbled Kadimone, gasping as though taken with exhaustion after great exertion. "I have already struck her with what strength I possess, and shall now give the pleasure to another. Take the whip and beat her."

"I?" said the tall, thin male, with a squeak. "Never have I used a whip such as that even upon kand. I would not know how to wield it."

"Surely there must be one among you eager to bring screams and pleadings to this savage," said Kadimone, still panting. A number of voices spoke at once, all in demurral, and I raised my head as far as possible to ease the ache in my back. Truly difficult did I find it comprehending what sort of males these were, but I was glad my face was not visible to them. Had they seen the expression of disgust I wore, surely would a greater number of them have been willing to wield the whip.

After a number of reckid of heated discussion, one of those standing about was persuaded to take the whip. I had spent the intervening time seeking to understand how such as those had bested and slain a male such as Relidose, one who was scarcely a warrior yet far superior to the ones who had ended him. My thoughts were brought to a halt by the return of pain, yet this male, much like Kadimone, had not the vigor to long continue as he had begun. I pulled at the wrist leather which bound me to the wheel as the blows fell one after the other, then at longer and longer intervals, until, at last, they ceased.

"Still she fails to cry out," observed the male who was tall and thin, now deeply disturbed. "What are we to do, Kadimone? Bind her and take her to the forests for the beasts to consume?"

"No," came the voice of Kadimone, petulantly angered. "She is to cause us such travail, and then be allowed so easily to escape? I shall not permit such a thing, the Serene Oneness take me if I do! Bring closer that slave."

The sound of footsteps came as I again raised my head and sought to free myself of the hair which blinded me, dismissing the pain of my back so it need not be considered. Surely had I expected an eventual ending from these males; how long was it to be before they roused themselves to so simple a doing?

"You may kneel before me, slave," came the haughty voice of Kadimone. "I am the leader of these good people, and therefore your master."

"I was promised my freedom," said another, a male who somehow sounded familiar. "A free man has no need to kneel before another."

"Your insolence is objectionable, slave!" snapped Kadimone with severity. "Should it be your wish that you now be granted freedom, it will certainly be yours! I will see you free of our company and our provender, our shelter and our weapons, that tunic which was given you by one of ours and also the wagons. The sole thing I will not see you free of is that collar, and also, perhaps, the fate which awaits you alone in the forests. Is this the freedom you demand so eagerly?"

A silence of hesitation ensued and then was there a sound of vexation.

"It was not my intention to exchange one slavery for another," said the second male with frustrated anger. "Sooner would I find an ending in the forests, than continue forever in servitude."

"No, no, fellow, your time of servitude will not be forever," returned Kadimone, a great heartiness now his. "We soon depart for the settlement begun by our city a kalod ago, a journey of perhaps three feyd, and once we have arrived there safely, we will no longer have need of the services of a slave. We will remove your collar and give you what provisions you require, and also what weapons. Is three feyd too long a time to await freedom with pleasure?"

"Three reckid is too long a time, for one who has so long been enslaved," growled the other, though a good deal of firmness had left his voice. "For what reason might I not be given my freedom now, and simply accompany you in such a way?"

"We are to believe that once having your freedom you will not desert us?" asked Kadimone with a sound of scorn. "Do we appear to be the innocent children? And for what reason should we not demand payment for the things we will give?

Are they so valueless that they need not be paid for? Are they so valueless to *you* that you will refuse our offer?"

Again a silence came, one in which the male undoubtedly considered what he had been told, clearly having learned naught in his service to warriors. To pledge oneself as slave, even for a short time, is to pledge oneself to that slavery forever. Should one allow reasons to be found for the shorter servitude, surely might further reasons be found for extending it and then again and again, till one's entire life is gone beneath chains, commands, and the lash. That lesson would not need to be told to a warrior; it had never been told the male.

"Very well," said the male at last, little pleasure to the sound of him. "I will pay for what I will be given with three feyd of servitude. In what direction does this settlement of yours lie?"

"It lies to the west," replied Kadimone, with mocking satisfaction the words nearly a chuckle. "Think you you might find reason to kneel to me *now*, slave? Your payment must be as full as that which you expect to receive for it."

"And you may address each of us as master," said the male who was tall and thin, his smirk clear enough to be heard above the sound of brief scuffing. "Also must you request permission before putting a question to your masters."

"Yes, master," responded the male who had again allowed the chains of slavery to bind him, an odd lack of emotion to the words. "May this one ask the reason for his having been summoned?"

"I was about to discuss that very point," said Kadimone, his thick satisfaction undiminished. "You see, do you not, this savage slut we have captured?"

"Yes, master," replied the male, briefly clearing his throat before speaking the words.

I, myself, knew not what Kadimone was about; surely the slave had been present when Relidose discovered me senseless in the forests. For what reason, then, would the male speak such lies?

"Her punishment and disposition will be a major part of the tasks assigned you," continued Kadimone, his words so self-important that nearly were they a boast. "When you are given permission to rise, you will take up that whip and beat her. Also—you were not—altered in any manner during your service to those savages? You were not—made other than a man?"

"No, master, I was not—altered," said the slave, and now indeed did he sound amused.

"Excellent," said Kadimone with a sigh of relief. "One may never be sure what savages will do. As the wench has refused the favor of a free man, she will be made to regret the insult through being forced to the frequent use of a slave. You may take first use from her when you are done with her beating."

"Yes, master," said the slave in near to a whisper, his acknowledgment to being commanded suddenly heavy with great anticipation. I, myself, pulled at the leather which bound me, attempting to free myself—yet such a thing was not possible.

"The command to rise was clearly given by gesture. First did I hear the sound of footsteps beside me, and then came the crack of the whip as its movement was tested. This one, I knew, would not strike as lightly as had the others, and quickly was I proven right. The next crack of the whip brought flashing pain, spreading pain, growing pain; I raised my head and attempted to roll from it, yet did my ankles continue held by leather. Again was I struck, and then again and again and again, a full hand of strokes before it ceased.

"Master, I had best not continue with this now," said the slave the while I gasped and attempted to deny what he had given me. "That the wench refuses to cry out the terrible pain given her by you and that other master, is not to say that she fails to feel it. You wish her conscious during the humiliation of her use, do you not?"

"Most certainly, most certainly," replied Kadimone at once, his great pleasure evident. "How clever of you, slave, to consider such a thing. Very well, put the whip aside now, and get on with the rest."

Of a sudden was the leather upon my ankles reversed, twisting my legs about, forcing me to my back, my hair thrown even more fully upon my face. The short, stiff grass against the welts of the whip was like dagger points in my flesh, yet was I unable to pull up or aside from the feel of it. Again I struggled, silently cursing the male who had put those welts upon me, and then strange hands suddenly threw the mass of hair from my face.

"Do not struggle so, fool of a wench," said the slave male very low, seemingly reaching to my hair to arrange it to suit himself. "Do you seek to open the welts and cause them to bleed? This time you may not deny me, therefore need you do no more than simply lie still. I will see to the rest."

"You!" I breathed, recalling the male at once, now that I was able to look upon him. Though he now wore a covering of brown, long and loose and ill-fitting, clearly was he the slave who had first begged my use in my chamber, and then had attempted to take it. The male had found his way from the city as he had wished, however he had not yet found an escape from slavery.

"I am now prepared to take her, master," said the slave, glancing over his shoulder at a smirking Kadimone. "Hopefully my performance will not be too brief by cause of the presence of all those who stand about and watch. Surely a lengthy use will bring her the greatest punishment."

"To be used so by a slave will bring her all of the humiliation we wish," said Kadimone with a chuckle and a heavy-fingered gesture of dismissal. "Short use or long, the use itself is the thing. You may now proceed, for we wish to see it done."

"Yes, master," acknowledged the slave with faint resignation, as though he had attempted a thing which he had not accomplished. I knew not what the thing might be, yet did I know well enough that I had no desire for his use.

"I believe she seeks to refuse you, slave," Kadimone observed with further chuckling. "Lean back for a moment, and those with the leather will open her for you."

"My thanks, master, however I have no need of such assistance," returned the male in a murmur, looking down upon me from where he knelt across me. He stroked my sides, gently and softly, and then as gently came to my breasts. Again I attempted struggle despite the pain I had been given, yet was not able to deny his touch—nor the manner in which his knee parted my thighs. Quickly, then, were both knees between mine, and then his head lowered to put his lips to my middle.

"You *will* respond to me, wench," said he in the whisper he had earlier used, his lips trailing up my body to the place his hands continued to hold. "Should you wish to retain your life, you must allow the humiliation; deny them that, and they will surely end you."

I, too, believed the same, that to deny those males again would bring what I ached for, therefore had I determined that it was necessary to thwart the slave. To that end I renewed my struggles against the leather which held me, using the pain I felt to negate the doings of the male who now kissed all about what was held by his hands, and briefly, stingingly, victory was mine. My flesh failed to respond to his ministrations, and then, abruptly, he became aware of my intentions.

"I should have known," said he, the anger in his eyes clear as he raised his head to look down upon me. "One such as you would surely prefer death to brief humiliation, yet I shall not allow it. For long has this body been in my thoughts; now shall I be long in this body."

His hands left my breasts to go to my thighs, and then were they forced wide for the presentation of his manhood. Indeed was the male prepared for my use, a thing quickly made clear to me, and then he had thrust deeply within, to take what pleasure he willed. Again I attempted to deny him with the movement of pain, yet his hands came to my upstretched arms and grasped them tightly.

"No other movement than this shall you make," he said, beginning the in and out thrust of his hips, bringing me feelings I could not refuse. "Ah, wench, how sweet is the taste of you, how succulent the feast which breaks my fast. You will respond, of this I have no doubt, for already the moisture begins to flow from you."

I tossed my head in anger, determined to deny the male whatever response I might, yet was he far more male than those others who stood about, and I the possessor of warrior blood. Greatly did the male relish the use he took, striving steadfastly to give pleasure as well, and slowly, slowly, my determination was no more.

"Hah, see how her eyes have closed!" crowed the voice of

the male Kadimone, nearer than it had been. "No longer is she cold and distant, for her femaleness will not allow it. The wench has been mastered by a slave!"

The lips of the slave came to mine as the laughter grew all about, silencing of whatever words I might have spoken. Truly would I have wished to rage at the ridicule, calling down all manner of curses upon the males, and yet was I unable to do so much as deny the slave the tasting of my tongue. His manhood took the strength from me as it fired my blood, the demand he put to me a command I must obey, and although I wept inwardly to be humiliated so, all save moaning was outwardly beyond me.

"Ah, yes, sweet wench, now do you truly welcome me," murmured the slave, his thrusting so deep that nearly was I unable to meet it. "You squirm and sigh and beg to be filled, and I, of course, shall not deny you. The masters who stand here must see you thoroughly taken, else shall they not allow you to live. I, however, will not allow your death, therefore must you dance and well. Ah, yes, rise to meet me, wench, for there is much yet for you to try. For now you are mine, and I shall not release you before I must."

Thus did the words of the male flow, now intelligible, now beyond understanding, and through it all was the laughter of those who watched beyond eluding. For quite some time did the slave continue on, far beyond the capacity one denied should have had, yet had his purpose been accomplished long before he was no longer able to keep from release. Well shamed was Jalav before those parodies of males, and no longer was the final dark to be inarguably hers.

7.

*Punishment—
an an unlooked-for visit*

The late-fey light had grown low and cool, most especially
beneath the trees of the forest. The clearing the city folk had
this fey found was one of a series, one beyond the next like
rooms of a dwelling. Greatly delighted had the males and
their females been, thinking only of their comfort, naught of
the difficulty in guarding so spread-out a camp. I was unsure
as to whether or not guardposts were set each darkness, yet
I could not consider such a thing. Neither leadership nor a need
for concern was mine, and had I had the ability to consider
the matter clearly, surely would I have gloried in the lack.

I attempted to move my wrists in the leather which held
them, finding only the beginnings of familiar numbness to
greet my efforts. For what reason I made the attempt I knew
not; no desire had I to find escape, nor even the strength had
desire been present. I hung from my wrists by the leather
which bound them, suspended from the limb of a tree, just as
I had at the ending of each of the preceding two feyd. My
feet, just short of the ground, were ankle-bound as well,
disallowing me stance as well as movement. No city-folk had
come as yet to halt beside me, likely for the reason that they
had not yet prepared their camps, therefore did I do no more
than hang in place and make vague attempts to move my
wrists.

"How do you fare, wench?" came the low-voiced query, a
voice I had long since grown to know. "Have they had at you
as yet? Are you in great pain?"

I made no effort to raise my head and look upon the slave
male, nor did I make answer to the questions he put. At the
end of each of the two previous feyd, when once I had been

suspended from a branch, the females and young of the city males had come to give laughter and ridicule to their captive. Also had a good number of them struck me with branches and leather and such, showing, in fine, better arms than their males had shown. My hair had been parted and brought forward to cover my breasts, and a scrap of cloth had been bound about my waist, these things done so that none of the females would be outraged by the sight of a "clothingless savage." That I gave them no more sound than I had given their males incensed them, yet were they city slave-women, with naught of true strength to them. Their arms grew weary before their anger faded, therefore had their males allowed them to watch the use their slave put me to. Truly was it a pity my pain had been too great to permit them to see me fully shamed.

"You must not allow yourself to fall to hopelessness, girl," came the voice of the male, intense despite its softness. "Upon the new fey will the settlement be reached, therefore is this the final darkness to be spent in the forests. I have listened to them discussing the matter, and they mean to sell you for the highest price they might to those who inhabit the settlement. It had been their intention to sell your use alone, yet are their womenfolk insistent upon having you out of their sight for all time. I shall not allow them to do such a thing, therefore. . . ."

"What do you do here, slave?" demanded the voice of Kadimone, arrogant and haughty as always. "Why do you not attend to the tasks you have been given?"

"I have already seen to them, master," returned the slave, complete deference to the sound of him. "I was merely crossing the clearing to return to the wagon, when my eyes fell upon the savage. Truly is it a blessing from the Serene Oneness that your vengeance has been taken from her in full, for she will clearly not survive much the longer."

"Not survive?" echoed Kadimone immediately, a sudden fear in his voice. "For what reason do you speak so, slave? For what reason will she fail to survive?"

"One need only look upon her to see the thing, master," answered the slave with deference. "She has been made to walk behind the wagons these three feyd past, she has been

soundly beaten by you and your ladies upon several occasions, and also has she refused to take any sustenance whatsoever. No more than water have I been able to force between
her lips, and little enough of that. To be hung so by the wrists
is both painful and draining, and soon shall your ladies make
visit again. Clearly, master, the wench will likely not survive
the darkness.''

"Remove her from there at once!" commanded Kadimone,
a bluster in his tone to cover the fear. "You, slave, are to
tend her carefully this darkness, and with the new light is she
to be placed in a wagon for the end of the journey. She is
valuable merchandise, and one does not treat valuable merchandise in so offhand a manner."

"You would even have me place her upon a sleeping fur
for the darkness?" asked the slave. "And feed her proper
provender rather than the scraps heretofore thrown her?"

"I most certainly mean no other thing," affirmed Kadimone,
his arrogance returned. "See to the commands you have been
given, slave, else shall you be beaten in her stead."

"At once, master," murmured the slave, the words following the sound of Kadimone and those with him moving off
through the clearing. Then were there no further words, no
more than the sound of two hurried steps before the leather
upon my wrists jerked. With the jerk came a lowering, and
then was the slave's arm about my waist, his other hand
moving to free my wrists. With that done he bent to sling me
over his shoulder, and then moved purposefully across the
clearing.

Once at the conveyance the slave lowered me to the grass,
disappeared briefly within, then returned with a thick sleeping
fur which he began spreading beneath the conveyance. Each
darkness had I spent that conveyance, bound so that I might
not escape, beside the slave who was to have used me as he
willed. Indeed had he used me freely at first, taking what he
wished, yet had he then halted that use, doing no more than
that required of him by Kadimone and the others. I lay upon
my side, feeling the life slowly returning to my hands, watching the slave spread the fur beneath the conveyance, wondering for what reason he continually spoke to me. No more than
a single word had I addressed to him since the thing began,

yet did he speak to me as though countless hands of words had been exchanged between us.

"There," said he with satisfaction, emerging from beneath the conveyance to bend to me once again. "You have need of the small comfort of this fur, and now may have it. When their tents have all been erected and the darkness meal prepared, I shall fetch you some decent provender. How great is the pain you feel? Nearly did you fall from your feet before we reached this place; will you be able to stand and walk?"

Closely did the male look upon me as he placed me upon the fur, a frown of concern darkening his features as his hand came to smooth back my dampened hair. My arms and body ached, my legs and feet were leaden with weariness, my insides hollow and no longer twisting with hunger. All these things touched me but lightly; no concern had I over what would befall me.

"You must rouse yourself to some sort of effort," insisted the male, vexation and disturbance clear in him as I took my gaze from his. "Do you wish to be sold to some lout of a settler, one who dwells in a crude city-to-be, there to be used and beaten by him till the wench you were no longer is? One after the other will he fill your belly with his get, brats to be raised up in a city with no name of its own. Not till a thousand men inhabit the place will it be called other than Bellinard settlement, for the city which began it. Is this what you wish? To dwell in a hovel as a slave to the one who buys you, never again to be free and proud as you were?"

The urgent challenge of his words caused me to close my eyes, too weary to listen further. He knew not that no war leader of Midanna might bear daughters to her clan, for she chewed the leaves of the dabla bush to prevent that from happening; nor did he seem to know that Jalav would indeed find the final dark before any city male might claim her. Pride and freedom had he spoken of as well, as though those things were truly meaningful. Again I turned to my side upon the fur, drawing up my bound legs so that I might lie with the least amount of pain. True freedom was the illusion of fools, for none were so chained as they who sought their freedom above all others; pride, too, was as futile a striving, for no more than a single, thoughtless act was able to shatter it as a heavy spear shatters a thin target board. What need for pride, when one no longer has that which one is proud of?

"Very well, perhaps you do indeed require rest more greatly than lecturing," said the male with a sigh, smoothing my hair. "Sleep and gather what strength you may, wench, for once those fools are all asleep, you and I will leave this place. Were I ignorant enough to believe I would be given freedom rather than permanent slavery when once the settlement was reached, I would deserve no other thing. Sleep now, until I return with your provender."

Briefly did I open my eyes to see the male crawl from beneath the conveyance, taking himself off I knew not where. So he knew, after all, that Kadimone and his ilk coveted his service and would not release him as had been promised, no matter the sweetness of the words which had been used. As he knew the truth I wondered that he had remained, yet was such a consideration unimportant; that darkness would he regain his freedom—without Jalav's company.

Sleep found me rather easily then, yet did it seem far from restful. Pain pursued me in my dreams, as did one who was dark and filled with fury, each striking me with whips and seeking to make me run in fear. That I felt no fear and would not run enraged them more, for none had ever been so uncaring in their presence. Once I would have laughed to see them so, helplessly raging, yet laughter no longer filled any part of me. Weariness and disinterest I felt now, and soon would come the endless comfort of the final dark.

"For what reason do you merely lie there, wench?" demanded a disapproving voice. "Are you as helpless as a small girl-child, that you fail to bestir yourself?"

I frowned with the effort to recall that voice, for it seemed familiar. The voice of a male it was, far from the near whisper of the slave, a voice strong and alive, confident and demanding. I moved upon the sleeping fur, unsure as to why I felt such upset, then struggled to force open my eyes. Darkness had fallen complete by then, the only thing readily distinguishable the looming bulk of the conveyance above me, and then another thing grew clear. He stood with feet spread and fists on hips, the white of his body covering a smudged lightness in the dark, his sword hung sheathed at his side, his wrists held tight by their leather wrappings. The dark of his eyes showed the disapproval he felt, and achingly, chokingly, I whispered, "Chaldrin!"

"Have you taken too greatly to heart the doings of city folk, wench?" he demanded, his gaze unmoving from mine. "Will you lie in your furs like a slug-a-bed, weeping softly till your life has been stolen from you? Will you greet the endless dark on your back, no more than a slave wench set to use, accepting all which comes with no more than a whimper?"

"Chaldrin, I cannot," I whispered, raising a hand toward him in supplication. I knew what he wished of me, yet was the doing now beyond me. "Wait for me, brother, for soon I shall join you, and together we may continue on to the dark."

"No, wench, such a thing may not be," he replied, sadness now to be seen in the eyes which held to me. "Well do I know what pain you have, and also do I know of your weariness; the time has not yet come for your rest, however. There continue to be tasks which are left undone, therefore must you seek within for the strength you require. You have my word you will not regret the effort."

"Already do I regret the effort," I whispered, permitting my hand to fall. "And if my strength should prove insufficient?"

"It will not," said he, coming nearer to crouch beside me, reaching out to stroke my hair. "Your strength will prove itself more than adequate, and soon will you find the rest you crave. Just a little while longer, sister, and all you desire will be yours."

"Will you give me your word, brother?" I asked, closing my eyes to keep the tears of disappointment within. "Will you wait till I have seen to the last of these things? I shall miss you sorely, brother; will you wait?"

No reply came to the query, none, at least, I was able to hear; instead I heard the shift of his weight beside me, and again his hand touched my hair.

"Will you not reply, brother?" I asked, opening my eyes again to seek sight of his form. He crouched beside me as before, yet had he darkened to appear as no more than a shadow.

"I shall be pleased to reply to any question you put, wench," came an answering whisper, yet not in the voice I had expected. "First, however, I must see this provender within you, and then we may hold converse. Are you able to sit?"

With the aid of the slave I sat upon the fur, understanding naught of what had occurred. Where had Chaldrin gone, and how had the slave been put in his place? My mind, so long prepared only for death, found thought an unexpected effort. I was dizzy and confused as well, but I knew I might no longer passively accept what came.

The provender brought by the slave was a stew, thick enough but too salty. I fed upon what part of it I was able, then was given a waterskin to drink from, the while the slave swallowed down the balance of the stew. No more than shadows were we to one another, yet when I had drunk my fill of the water I looked upon him.

"For what reason do you remain among these useless folk, male?" I asked, hearing the soft sounds of his feeding. "For what reason did you agree to act the slave among them?"

"For the reason that I know their sort well," said he, the words indistinct as he continued to feed. "I truly had no wish to go naked and collared and weaponless into the forests, not when I might obtain all I required by remaining. That leech of a former guild head lied when he spoke of what service would earn me, yet do I mean to see him held to his word. For the service I have already given I shall myself collect my earnings, and this darkness will see me begun upon the journey home. Also, of course, did I remain to give you assistance."

So easily had the male added the last of his words, that I could not make sense of them. With a last scrape of the spoon he put the bowl aside, then groped for and took the waterskin from my hands. I watched his shadow raise the skin more easily than had I, and then he lowered it again and replaced the plug.

"Your silence tells me you doubt my honorable intentions," said he, faintly chuckling. "Should the eagerness with which I took your use be the reason for your doubt, kindly recall the state in which I had been in, and try to understand. Also do I give you my word that I would have remained and aided you even had I been forbidden your use.''

Again the last of his words were measurably different, this time sobriety having entered his tone. For some unexplained reason I did indeed believe, yet did I continue to fail to understand.

''I see naught to explain so selfless a doing,'' said I after a moment, attempting to pierce the darkness with my gaze. ''One who was done as you should not give thanks to his captor by aiding her.''

''My life was left mine through the doings of that captor,'' said he, his tone continuing sober and even. ''Had I attempted a similar attack upon the High Seat, surely would I have been ended with torture, not merely struck and kicked and then sent about my business. Still I have no clear understanding of the reason you behaved so, yet am I aware of having my life returned when it was forfeit. I could not allow one such as you to remain in the hands of ones such as they.''

The determination of the male was less clear to me than to him; however, aside from curiosity, it mattered not. What was of more concern was the reason why none would let me rest, yet that, too, was beyond my ability to discern. No more than a little while longer would bring me what I desired, I had been told, therefore would I continue on as far as I was able. The stew had returned to me some small measure of strength; I tossed my head to shake back the hair from my arms, and raised my knees so that I might more easily reach the leather upon my ankles.

''What do you do?'' asked the slave male, obviously having discerned my movement even in the darkness. ''I have already loosened that leather so that feeling will not be taken from your limbs. When the time has come for us to depart, it may then be easily removed.''

''No more easily than now,'' I returned, feeling about for the knot which held the leather closed. ''I dislike being bound, therefore shall I remove the leather immediately.''

''Therefore shall you not,'' countered the male, taking my ankles in his hands and pulling them flat again. ''It would be foolish in the extreme to give warning of our intentions, a thing which the removal of that leather would surely do. They will come a last time before retiring to see how you fare, therefore must you appear docile and obedient, in no manner a threat to their peace of mind. Sight of the leather upon you will accomplish these things.''

"They would believe a war leader of Midanna docile because of leather upon her ankles?'' I asked with a soft sound of ridicule, finding that the hands of the male would not allow me to raise my knees again. "No being who lives is so credulous.''

"Save for these city folk,'' said he, and then his hands left my ankles to come to my arms. Little strength was needed to push me flat to the fur again, and then he smoothed my hair. "Also must you lie here rather than sit, for they believed you to be close to the end. In reality shall you be gathering strength, for what must be done after all have found sleep.''

"For what *shall* be done,'' said I, making no mention of my painful annoyance. I disliked being bound, and disliked the manner in which the male had returned me to lying upon the fur, yet had I insufficient strength to refuse the doings. When once I had left that place, however, no longer would I need to consider such things.

"There remains a good deal of time before us before we might begin our final preparations,'' said the male after a moment, his darkened face looking down upon me where I lay. "It pleases me to see you so much more animated and vital than you were these past three feyd. Has your pain receded to the point where you might perhaps be able to feel pleasure again?''

Quite evident was the interest in the voice of the male, his hand again at my hair, his query having naught to do with willingness, only with what response he might expect. Clearly did he believe that my use continued to be his without question, a foolishness to be expected from one who was male and from a city.

"The sole thing I am able to feel is impatience,'' said I, shaking his hand from my hair with a short movement of my head. "How long till these city folk take to their furs? And what of those who stand guard?''

"There are none who stand guard,'' he murmured, taking a thick lock of my hair into his hands. "Of what use would a guard be, when they all would be as helpless awake as asleep against any who came? Also were there none of them willing to stand guard alone, without a tent and therefore the most likely victim of any beast which happened upon the camp. They will all take to their furs after they have had a final look at their captive and their slave, two who would surely be mad to venture into the forests during the darkness, and who may therefore be left entirely unguarded while they sleep. Were they to find us in the midst of pleasuring ourselves, they would retire more quickly, knowing us well and fully occupied for a good portion of the darkness.''

''Were they to find us pleasuring ourselves, they would watch,'' I returned immediately, exasperated. ''Never have I known males to take greater pleasure in watching than in doing, yet am I able to recall the avidity with which they observed your obedience to their commands. Their females, too, take great pleasure in watching, and not again shall I provide amusement for them all.''

''Were you wed to one such as they, would you, too, not find greater pleasure in watching than in doing?'' he asked, amused. ''The men are soft and find greater interest in salable merchandise than wenches, and the women are grown fat and lazy and uninterested in all things save the silver they use to buy what will make them fatter and lazier. Their complaints these past feyd over all things including having to cook over open fires have been unending, more than enough to slay the interest in any man foolish enough to approach them. You, however, speak only of impatience, therefore is my interest far from ended.''

''Perhaps I should speak as well of the sword soon to be returned to me,'' I said in the light of the soft laughter in his words. ''Also, possibly, of the dagger which was taken, the dagger I carry always in the leg bands which are still upon me. You have not my permission to use me, male, and best would be that *that* be your sole interest and consideration.''

''Best for one is not at all times best for another,'' said he with no lessening of amusement, and then did he suddenly release my hair. ''I see the light of a lantern approaching, wench, therefore do they likely come now to see how you

fare. Show them naught save weakness, and do not speak. I
shall speak for us both.''

I quickly turned my head to the right, and saw the small
flame-within-a-box which the male had seen, now hearing the
grass-softened footsteps which any save city folk would have
known better than to allow. One walks the forests with as
little sound as possible, calling as little attention to oneself as
possible, else does one go hungry therein or possibly end as
prey to that which is larger, swifter and stronger. Had these
city folk not been given provender to carry with them, surely
would they by then be screaming with hunger.

Another moment saw the light directly beside the conveyance, and then were there five who bent to look upon me.
Kadimone was beside the tall, thin male, the latter having
been given the task of carrying their light, and also were there
two others of the males, neither retaining youth and fitness.
The fifth of the set was the female Orlinia, looking petulant,
her roundness undiminished by the terrible ordeal of that
journey, a thing she had often screamed and wept over during
the feyd just past.

"How does she fare now, slave?" demanded Kadimone as
quickly as he had bent, a grunt for the effort. "Surely has rest
and nourishment restored her to some extent?"

"She is improved some small amount, master," responded
the slave, deferentially. "She continues to be greatly weakened, but she seems further from ending."

"Certainly she seems further from ending!" snapped the
female Orlinia, sending to me the venom of her glare. "Has
she not been privileged to eat what *I* prepared with my own
hands? She may now see *herself* as the lady, and *I* as the
captive! There, Kadimone, see the look in her eyes! See how
she dares mock me to my face!"

"You may not beat her again, Orlinia," replied the male
Kadimone with something of a frown. "We must have the
silver from her sale if we are to survive in Bellinard settlement till the guilds are established. And yet do her eyes
indeed seem insolent and mocking. . . ."

"That is only desire you see, master," said the slave in a
rush of words, filling the gap left by the thoughtful trailing
off of Kadimone's speech. "She has not this fey had her

usual use, and though she struggles to deny her need, in shame over having been mastered by a slave, she is unable to do so. Out of concern for your property I have not put hand to her, and yet, should it be your command, I shall keep her too well occupied this darkness to consider insolence. The masters and the lady may confidently return to the comfort of their tents, and leave her disposition to me."

"She does not appear to *me* to be in need," said the tall, thin male, leaning forward with the light he held to peer at me more closely. "Surely does she seem more taken with anger."

"Certainly, master, at the need which rises within her," said the slave again in haste, his fingers coming to my arm beneath my hair to pinch hard. "It angers her that she must give service to a slave, a humiliation which you, yourselves, have put upon her. How great must be your satisfaction, to be so fully avenged."

"I feel little satisfaction to be looked upon so by a savage," said the female Orlinia, her petulance continuing unabated, uncaring that it was now the slave I looked upon. For what reason he had pinched me I knew not, yet did I greatly dislike such a doing. "Do you mean to permit her such insolence, Kadimone?"

"She seems possessed of little strength for insolence," said the male to his female, his tone remaining thoughtful. "Also, however, does she seem to show little in the way of need. Do you, slave, seek to use her despite the damage she might sustain? Do you seek to have us fetch the whip, and give to you what was given to her?"

"No, master, no!" denied the slave, and much did a good portion of his desperation seem real as he looked pleadingly upon Kadimone. "Merely do I seek to serve you as faithfully as always, so that I might earn what shall be given me at the settlement. Should it be your desire that I not touch the wench, I shall certainly not touch her."

"And yet you insisted that she was in need," pursued Kadimone, greatly pleased with the manner in which he caused the slave to grovel. "Did you dare lie to us, slave, thinking that you would *not* be whipped? Do you think us such fools that we may be told what is patently untrue?"

"Yes, let us give *him* her whipping," said Orlinia, vengeful pleasure now touching her. "*He* was the one who came to take the food of free folk for the wench! His insolence is nearly as great as hers."

"Please, master, I beg you to hear me!" said the slave with deep vexation to Kadimone, his hand quickly turning my face from Orlinia. Such annoyance had I felt at the words of the female, that I had been ready to face her properly, to speak as a war leader should to one of her sort. The slave had again forced me flat with the arm of the hand upon my face, and once I was made to look upon him, his other hand came to my face as well.

"See how she looks upon me, master," said the slave hastily, his dark eyes now meeting mine. "Having tasted of her so deeply, well aware am I of the need she strives so diligently to hide. She sends to me the glare of hatred, yet am I able to see beyond the glare, to the shine of submission desired. Had you wished to lower yourselves and taken her in my stead, you, too, would see the same. The need she feels is present, and I have not lied."

"Solely are we able to see the hatred, slave," said Kadimone with a sniff, dismissing what he had been told. "Should she be in such great need as you say, it will not long take to set her writhing. Two hands of reckid shall I allow you, and then shall you either be permitted her use, or tied to a wheel to be whipped for lying. You may now begin."

Strongly did the vexation flare in the eyes of the slave as he looked down upon me, yet did he make no further attempt to speak against Kadimone's command. Instead did he seem to be searching my face, seeking for what I was unable to fathom. Was it my desire to stand with sword in hand before those city folk he sought, surely was the desire found without difficulty, however no satisfaction but a sigh escaped him, and then did he release my face.

"A pity dissembling is beyond you," he murmured so softly that surely none heard the words save myself. "Best you resign yourself to this, wench, for I shall not be beaten to keep you from embarrassment. One of us must have full strength for our undertaking."

I knew not the meaning of the words he spoke, yet was I

quickly apprised of his intent when his hand went to the cloth
tied about my middle and then beneath it. Surely did he mean
to shame me again before these city folk, and that I would not
allow. Again I began to raise myself from the fur, to reach
his hand and thrust it from me, yet did his other hand tangle
painfully in my hair, and in such a manner hold me flat.

"You see, master, with her ankles bound she may not kick
nor twist from my reach," said the slave the while he began
caressing me in a most distressing manner. "To do a woman
so is greatly arousing for a man, for he knows she cannot
escape him and he may do with her as he pleases. Also is
such a thing arousing for the female, for in knowing she may
not escape him, also is she forced to understand that she must
serve him whether she wills it or no. In such a circumstance
the female's body will prepare her of its own self, and when
the man at last deigns to take her, he will be amazed at the
warmth of her greeting. No man who has not taken his
woman in such a way has ever tasted the full sweetness of
her."

"See the manner in which she seeks to refuse him," said
Orlinia with a great smirk of satisfaction, unaware of the
manner in which Kadimone had turned his head to silently
regard her. "Her body now begins to move despite the grip
he holds her in, a complete and absolute denial of his will.
She fails to obey him now, and surely will she also fail to
obey him in two hands of reckid. Best you have the whip
fetched, Kadimone, to be at hand when we require it."

"The whip will not be required, Orlinia," replied the male
Kadimone, his eyes still upon the female. "Her squirming
began the moment he touched her, the squirming you prefer
to see as absolute refusal and denial. He spoke the truth
regarding her need—and upon another point as well, I believe."

"Kadimone, what has come over you?" demanded Orlinia,
her head now turned to see the manner in which she was
being regarded, her voice growing shrill. "What other point
do you speak of, and why must you look upon me so
strangely?"

"I look upon a woman I have not known sufficiently
well," said the male, smiling faintly at the disturbance of the
female. "I shall not have it said that a slave may know

greater pleasure than a free man. I believe the time has come
for us to return to our tent.''

"Kadimone, you cannot mean to— No, please!'' babbled
the female as her arm was taken to straighten her from
bending. "The slave spoke lies, Kadimone, only lies to
ensnare you! You must recall that I am a lady!''

"See how the lies of the slave have hardened the savage's
breasts," said Kadimone with a chuckle, turning a horrified
Orlinia away from the conveyance. "We shall see if they have
the power to do the same with the breasts of a lady. Niminore,
the lantern if you please.''

"Certainly, Kadimone," replied the tall, thin male with a
start, straightening and turning to hurry after the first male.
Also did the final two males depart, and the slave and I were
returned once more to the darkness.

"I give thanks to the Serene Oneness that I was given
sufficient opportunity to learn how quick you warrior wenches
are to heat,'' said the slave male, with a gloating chuckle.
"That Orlinia had best learn to be the same, else shall he
likely try the whip next. Were I convinced that he would,
surely would I be tempted to remain to see it.''

"Release me, accursed male!'' I hissed, reaching to the
hand which remained buried in my hair. I could not now see
the male, yet was his presence in no doubt whatsoever. He
had not released me, nor had he ceased in his caressing.

"Best would be that we wait till they have reached their
tents," said he, his voice now a murmur, his touch unceas-
ing. "Also must you recall that I have been permitted your
use by the one who calls himself my master. Do you urge a
slave to disobey his master?''

Nearly did a moan escape me then, so deeply did the male
touch me, and also was my strength nearly spent in struggle
against him. My hands at his fist made one last, futile attempt
to free me from his grip, and then did they fall away. Indeed
were Midanna warriors quick to heat, and that at times even
in the presence of pain.

"I hear no reply from you, wench," said the male, his
words soft as his lips came to my hair. "Would you have a
slave disobey his master?''

"You will do as you please no matter my words or lack

thereof," I answered with what strength I could, finding a lessening of need with the increase of pain. "You are no more of a slave than I, far less of a slave than those who call you theirs. You may do as you will, for there are none about to halt you."

"What has become of the sword soon to be returned to you?" he asked, amused and also pleased by the truth I had spoken. "Has the warrior wench given over thought of using her weapons?"

No further strength had I for speech, and certainly none for what weapons would be returned to me, therefore did I remain silent in answer to his amusement. What strength I required would be found within me, Chaldrin had said, yet had he failed to give me his word upon the matter. Perhaps he had not wished to be forsworn, a strong possibility suggested by the dizziness I felt.

"Wench, you do not respond as you did," said the male suddenly, no longer amused and taking his fist from my hair. "Neither your body nor your words acknowledge my presence, and this is not as it was. Have you been forced to too great an effort?"

Again I failed to reply, feeling that I could not even had I wished to, and the male was quick to see even in the darkness about us.

"Curse my stupidity and curse the demands of those with twisted souls," he muttered in deep vexation, both of his hands now coming to smooth my hair. "You need no longer be disturbed, wench, for I shall not touch you again this darkness. Seek sleep instead, and I shall awaken you when all is prepared for our departure. Sleep now, to regain what strength you might."

His words were as unexpected and strange as the balance of recent happenings, yet was I at that time unable to consider any of them. Sleep was indeed the sole thing to be considered, the sole thing which I could consider. As my eyes had not opened, it was not necessary to close them.

Some time later was I again awake, more easily than in the first instance, less confusion surrounding me. The fur I lay upon in the continuing darkness was soft and comfortable, yet did I find considerably more interest in the movements of the slave male. It had been his approach which had awakened me, his movements performed with a greater stealth than those of the cities seemed capable of, yet not so great that he was able to go unnoticed by a Midanna. Two large, dark shapes did he carry to a place before the conveyance to set them down, shapes which seemed not overly heavy, and then did he bend to crawl beneath the conveyance. He started when I raised myself to sitting, and then he sat beside me to touch his hand to my hair.

"You have awakened precisely on time, wench," said he, his soft voice filled with surprised pleasure. "Are you stronger than you were? Has the pain eased its grip upon you?"

"Again am I able to consider what weapons might come to my hand," I agreed, refraining from any attempt to move over-quickly. "How long a time have I spent in sleep?"

"Perhaps four hind," said he, moving his hands to the leather upon my ankles. "Our hosts and hostesses sleep soundly now, unaware of the imminent departure of their guests. I have gathered all we will require for our journey, which is, of course, considerably less than they would require. I have taken no more than a small amount of provender, to allow us to put sufficient distance between us and them before we pause to hunt. All of your belongings are in a single sack; mine in another. My service has earned me a sword and dagger and a bow and shafts, this tunic I continue to wear, and the kan I shall ride. The kan we take for you has also been paid for, with the pain and humiliation you were given. Will you find difficulty in sitting a kan?"

"There will be difficulty in naught which takes me from this place," I replied, finding great relief when the leather fell away from my ankles. I was then able to sit cross-legged as is ever my preference, the cloth tied about my waist notwithstanding. My own hands went to that cloth and in a moment was it gone from me, no more to mark me as a captive. Pink had that cloth been, an offensive, city-female pink, a color worn by none of the clans who followed me.

"We will also take this fur for you," said the male, clearly referring to the pelt we sat upon. "There should be ample room upon it for both of us, and you will require the comfort it provides for some feyd yet."

"There is a thing I still don't understand," I said, looking upon the dark shadow which was his face. "Your home lies east of here, in the direction of Bellinard? In some manner was I of the opinion that it lay elsewhere, other than near Bellinard."

"You are correct," said he, a nod moving the shadow. "My home lies to the west, beyond even the second Bellinard, else would I have taken you and left these folk the very first darkness. As they moved in the proper direction, and as I failed to realize how great an amount of pain would be given you, I made no attempt to separate myself from them at once. Last darkness we might also have gone, although last darkness you were held too tightly by the pain of the beatings. Taking you then upon a kan would only have increased that pain."

"As your home lies to the west," said I, taking no note of the balance of his words, "how is it that you continue to speak of the hunting we shall do, and the fur to be shared by the two of us? Are you not aware that I must return to Bellinard, to see to the tasks I have not yet completed? As we take separate trails, the sharing you speak of will not be possible."

"We do not take separate trails, wench," said he, his voice gently patient. "Never again shall I return to Bellinard the accursed, and you would not be able to reach it alone, without assistance. Instead shall you ride with me, to my home, and once you have grown strong again you may either remain or depart. In the interim I shall make every effort to keep you from the latter, for I find I enjoy the presence of a warrior wench in my furs. Remain here, and I will fetch the kand."

His hand found my face and his lips touched mine, and then was he crawling from beneath the conveyance, to stand once beyond it and take himself off. The kand were tied to a line not far from the conveyances they pulled, one set in this clearing, one set in the next. It would be no more than a short while before he returned, therefore was it necessary to make what haste I could. To ride with him to his home was not possible, a fact far better shown than discussed.

I felt slightly dizzy as I crawled from beneath the conveyance; however, I was able to thrust it from me as I crouched before the dark shapes which were the sacks the male had made mention of. The first I touched and opened contained a sword and bow, shafts and a dagger, a small bit of provender and a small drinking skin. The other sack, then, was mine, and I did no more than place a hand to hilt to assure myself of that before slinging the entire sack over my shoulder by the leather which drew it closed. Later would there be time to don breech and weapons in a proper manner, later when the forest darkness had swallowed me up against all pursuit.

Straightening from the crouch and shaking my hair back from my arms returned a small measure of dizziness, but I was still able to quickly and quietly take myself to the forest's edge, to the east, in the direction from which we had come. Direction in darkness is not easily discernible, yet had the conveyance been halted without turning when we had reached the clearings, and in such a manner was I able to know the proper route. When once the new light came, I would search out the track left by the passage of the conveyance and follow it as far as necessary, till I was once again able to look about myself without pain and dizziness.

Forest shadows accompanied me as I slipped through the darkness, all the sounds and life awake in it surrounding me immediately and making me a part of them. Leaves and branches caressed me as I slid by, unaware of the added pain their touches gave, grass moved soundlessly beneath my feet, the cool fingers of the air slowly released my flesh from their chill touch. I had thought to remain about the camp to be sure the male took himself safely upon his way, yet no more than a hand of steps showed me that without the remorseless pull of a conveyance, I would not long be able to continue on. Should there be difficulty my presence would avail the male naught, yet would my escape assure his if he were retaken. Once I reached Bellinard I would take warriors and return, and had the male been unable to escape his slavery, my warriors and I would then do it for him.

Rather short was the time before I began stumbling, the sack on my shoulder nearing the weight of a kan, the noise I produced sufficient to deafen any save city folk. The male I had left had attempted to follow me through the darkness, the kan he rode and his low, hissing call sending me quickly behind a tree until he had passed, watching as he rode on a short distance and then turned about. I waited till he had looked about himself for a final time with a low-voiced curse before riding away in the direction from which he had come, the pace of his kan saying he would not again turn aside, and then resumed my own journey. That had been perhaps two hind earlier, a far shorter time than I had hoped it would be. Surely if I had true interest in what I did the end of my strength would not have come so soon, however I felt no such interest. No more than resentment did I feel that I might not rest when *I* wished to do so, no more than annoyance with the now increased pain of my body.

I dropped the leaden sack to the ground beside a tree and then lowered myself after it, recalling only then that I had failed to replace my breech, leaning down to one elbow to spare my back, heaving a sigh of dismissal. I cared not that I had failed to cover my womanhood, for who was there about in that forest to take note of it? No others than city folk and males would find themselves disturbed, and happily none of either were about. A hunting cry sounded in the far distance, so faint I might have doubted its reality had I not been Midanna, the hunger in it doing naught to awaken a matching hunger in me. It would be necessary to look within my sack to see if it contained the provender the first sack had held, yet first would I take a short time of rest. Were the sack to be empty of provender I would need to hunt after fashioning a spear, therefore was it necessary that I first rest to restore my strength. First rest and then hunt. First fashion a spear and then hunt. First find no provender, and then hunt. Were I not first hunted myself. I found that my eyes had closed, and then I found that I slept.

8.

Discovery— and a less palatable capture

I awoke to discover that I had not slept but lain senseless, for it seemed that I no longer rested near the tree nor even lay beside it. In two arms did it seem I was now being held, carried about with little effort, the smell of a male strong from the leather-clad shoulder my head leaned upon. In truth was the smell of males all about rather than merely from the shoulder, and I moved in protest that I had again been taken captive.

"Put her here," said the concerned voice of a male, a voice I had not expected. "I shall have the lives of the ones who did her so, Sigurr take me if I do not!"

"I believe she wakens," said the one who held me, another I had not expected. "I give thanks to the Serene Oneness that we have found her and she lives."

Then was I lowered to the softness of a covered lenga pelt, the arms were withdrawn, and a hand smoothed my hair. Had I thought that what occurred about me was reality I would surely have leaped off the lenga pelt and run into the forests, yet had it come to me that such a belief would have been foolishness. No more than imaginings brought about by hunger and pain was I in the midst of, the voices no more than wind in the trees, the comfort of the pelt no more than grass grown thick in feylight. At times had I heard tell of such a thing, the imaginings brought about by weakness and need, and nearly did I smile with the relief I felt.

"For what reason has she not yet opened her eyes?" asked a third voice-of-the-mind, as concerned as the others. "Had Chaldrin not been so sorely wounded, he would have accompanied us and seen to her, and had your brother Lialt not been needed to tend him, he, too, would have been here.''

"Chaldrin no longer lives,'' said I to the wind voice, annoyed that it knew so little. In a moment I would open my eyes, and search through my sack for what provender there might be. "Chaldrin no longer lives, and I am the one who has slain him. Perhaps he will wait till my tasks are done.''

"Wench, Chaldrin has not been slain,'' said the voice, a great surprise now to be heard. "Open your eyes and look upon me, and then you will know that I speak the truth.''

So easily did the wind speak lies to me, thinking to bring me pain with its words, yet was I not to be gulled, like some warrior-to-be, to believe what was clearly not so. I sat upon the pelt which was no more than grass, raised my head in defiance, and opened my eyes to see—the face of a crouching Aysayn.

"Chaldrin lives,'' said he again, smiling at the way I stared at him. "Think you his slaying might be so easily accomplished? He lies sorely wounded and in great need of careful tending, yet does he live with Lialt's assurance that he shall continue to do so. Had he known we rode in search of you, surely would he have made the attempt to accompany us.''

So great was the relief and joy I felt that my eyes closed once again, to allow Aysayn's words to penetrate. Chaldrin was not lost to me forever, I had not slain in mindless anger the one who had vowed always to stand beside me. Chaldrin lived and my spirit soared, for he was far more deserving of life than I.

And then did my eyes open once again, for an unsettling thought had come. Clearly was that Aysayn who crouched at my feet beyond the lenga pelt, light-haired and dark-eyed and clad in black body cloth and swordbelt; as that was so, then the others who had earlier spoken were—

Without thought and quickly as I was able, I turned upon the pelt and attempted to scramble from it, to leave as far behind as possible those two who crouched at either side. Their surprise held them rooted the while I attempted my feet, yet was Aysayn not deceived as they; a large hand shot forth to close about my ankle, and no more than the lenga pelt with my face did I find.

"What foolishness holds you now, girl?" demanded Aysayn as he pulled me back to where I had been. "Where did you think to go as you are, bare as a nilno and all covered with welts? You, too, are in need of tending, and that as quickly as possible."

"I have no need of tending," said I, raising up on my elbows while keeping my eyes upon the lenga pelt. "Release me now, for I wish to don breech and swordbelt."

"You shall don no more than salves of healing," said Mehrayn from his place to my left, his voice heavy with scorn. "What ails you, wench, to believe yourself able to dress and bear weapons?"

"Clearly lack of sustenance ails her," said Ceralt from one side, clearly displeased. "See how thin she has grown in the past feyd, as though naught has passed her lips."

"I will fetch the salve, you the provender," said Mehrayn, to Ceralt. "Perhaps, between the two of us, we may quickly restore her to health."

"And retain our own health in the doing of it," agreed Ceralt dryly, as he rose. "Perhaps I shall one fey speak of what was necessary to restore her once before."

"And I of an incident in which I was involved," said Mehrayn as they walked from the fur to the kand which stood not far distant. No sooner were their eyes no longer upon me than I again attempted to rise from the pelt, yet had I forgotten the hand of Aysayn, which had not retreated far from my ankle.

"You shall not," said he in a softer voice, his grip as unbreakable as it had earlier been. "For what reason do you seek to run from them?"

"I do not seek to run from them," I returned just as low, attempting to free my ankle from the hand which held it. "Merely do I prefer being elsewhere, away from those who so disapprove of my doings."

"You would have them give approval to finding you beaten and starved and lying insensible and defenseless in a forest?" he asked, with a hint of amusement. "You ask no more of them than that?"

"I ask naught of them in any manner," I muttered, finding his hand impossible to escape. "Release me, male, for I shall journey with neither you nor them."

"Wise are you indeed to seek to avoid *me*," said Aysayn, his voice somewhat puzzled. "What I fail to understand, however, is the reason you would avoid *them*."

I, too, felt puzzlement, therefore did I turn my head to regard him over my shoulder. Lying so caused my body to ache, an excellent reason for asking the question I had as quickly as possible.

"For what reason would I wish to avoid *you*?" I asked, seeing that he had gone to one knee to hold my ankle more easily. "More so than any other male, that is?"

"For the reason that there is a matter which you and I shall speak of as quickly as you are once again as you were," said he, looking upon me with an odd steadiness. "Ever have I considered the use of wenches a great pleasure, yet not with a blade at my throat and not in such large numbers at once. When you are returned to yourself, we shall discuss the matter at length."

Well did I then recall the words Mehrayn had spoken, concerning the difficulty Aysayn had had by cause of his use by warriors. I turned to my left side upon the fur to ease the ache in my body, and looked upon the male with sobriety.

"The possibility of the strangers coming at that time in attack had not occurred to me," said I, shaking the hair back over my shoulder. "Had you fallen in battle due to the pain you were given, the fault would have been mine. Should you wish to face me in challenge when the strangers have been seen to, I will not deny you."

"Challenge," said he with a sound of scorn, shaking his head as he took seat upon the pelt beside my feet. "Should we all of us survive the coming of the strangers, you will likely spend the following two kalod seeing to challenges both given and allowed. Mine, however, need not be included among them, for I have no intention of seeking challenge. No call was there for having me done as you did, with the possibility of battle or without, therefore shall you face me not in challenge but in punishment, a fitting punishment for

so childish a doing. Also, perhaps, shall you receive what
was given the leader of that horde.''

Great indignation came to me at Aysayn's words, that he
would dare speak to me so, yet did I frown at a far
more important matter, and sit up to face the male more
directly.

"What have you done to Rogon?" I demanded, nearly
agrowl with the anger I felt. "Naught was she guilty of save
obeying my commands! Were you displeased with the actions
of a Midanna, your place was to speak to me of it!''

"Rogon, eh?'' said he, leaning down to one elbow as his
hand rubbed his chin. "I had not known what name was hers.
A small bundle, yet exceedingly well packaged. And that
wealth of dark red hair.'' His gaze, which had been turned
inward, now sought me with his grin. "Had she come to me
alone, it would likely have been she who found difficulty in
walking. And how was I to speak to you of my displeasure?
You had disappeared, none knowing where.''

"Now I am no longer disappeared,'' I replied, refusing to
be put off. "What have you done to my warrior?''

"No more than teach her to be cautious of what commands
she obeys,'' said he with a shrug of dismissal. "That first
darkness of your disappearance, I found myself restored sufficiently to seek the wench out where she walked about among
Sigurri warriors and her own wenches. Little difficulty did I
find in taking her from the fringes of them with none the
wiser, and thence to a place we would be undisturbed. She
struggled with the strength of one twice her size, yet was I
able to remove her swordbelt and take her in my arms. After
a short while she attempted again to use me, clearly unaware
of the reason I had brought her to that place, learning of it
only when she, herself, was put to use. Her struggles then
were of greater amusement and interest, yet failed to be of
much duration. When I at last left her, she had not as yet
returned to herself. I shall be sure to seek her out again when
once we have returned to the city.''

Again his gaze went inward, a faint smile on his face,
bringing me a greater disturbance than I had thought to have.
Clearly had Aysayn found a good deal of pleasure with
Rogon, so much so that he meant to seek her out a second

time. I knew not how Rogon viewed the matter; however, she had ever been one to take use from males, not herself give that use. Now I had, inadvertently, involved Rogon with Aysayn. The male was able to give great pleasure, I knew, and in such a manner was a warrior entrapped, through the pleasure brought to her. How could I assist Rogon to freedom?

"And just such forced service might I also take from you," said Aysayn, returning himself to my attention, his dark eyes again upon me. "To be given such additional punishment would be fitting, a thing likely to be agreed to by your two—suitors. And now tell me why you seek to avoid them."

His eyes looked up toward me from where he lay upon his right side, far greater demand in them than had been in his words. Truly concerned was the male, and that despite the fact that the concern was none of his.

"I dislike being importuned by those I have already refused," I said, making no effort to avoid his gaze. "For what reason has Ceralt not departed with his village males? They were defeated, were they not? And why does Mehrayn not direct those warriors who remain without the city? The place was meant to be his."

"Ceralt's villagers were indeed defeated," said Aysayn with a nod, his gaze unmoving. "Ceralt himself, however, and Galiose as well, being two of those who were chosen as best to stand against our least, were themselves victorious. Telion returns Ceralt's men to their villages, and one of Galiose's does the same with the men of Ranistard. Ceralt and Galiose, as victors, demanded the right to remain; therefore have they done so. Mehrayn has appointed one of the Princes of the Blood to direct our legions in his absence, a man with far greater skill than I, making my presence, too, unnecessary. For those reasons were we three all able to come seeking you, which we have done. Now, while Ceralt prepares provender for you and Mehrayn warms the salve, both over the fire they have built, I will hear for what reason you have refused them."

"A war leader of Midanna need not speak of reasons," I returned, stiffly. "No more need is there that she do than voice her preferences, which has already been done. Also is it

my preference to return to the city alone, which shall be done
as well."

"No, it shall not," said he, his calm denial nearly as
infuriating as his hand upon my ankle had been. "Do you
refuse to choose one to keep hurt from the other? Do you
forget that they, themselves, shall see to the choice, should
you fail to speak your own desire? I will do what I may to
help keep their swords sheathed; however, I may not stand
between them forever. Tell me of the difficulty you face, and
perhaps I shall find it possible to aid you."

The smell of the meat which then roasted upon the fire
brought an ache to my insides, one nearly as great as the
vexation which filled me. It continued to be beyond me why
males must ever make demands upon warriors, yet was understanding unnecessary to be the victim of the thing. Nearly
each male I came upon sought, for one reason or another, to
possess me as his own, a state so infuriating that rational
thought was well nigh impossible. For what reason would
they not leave me be? How was I to see an end to the thing,
save through sword-use? Even had I found it necessary to
skulk about in hiding, to rid myself of one who had accompanied me no more than a matter of feyd, one who had been a
slave in Bellinard. Great fools were all of these males, concerned with naught save their own desires, that and the
foolishness of what other might wish to possess what he,
himself, coveted—

Of a sudden did a thought come, about these males. I was
ordered to choose which male would be mine; the other,
presumably, having been spurned, would take himself off to
bedevil another. In reality would he who had been spurned
stand himself in challenge to the one chosen, a thing to be
expected from males. In what manner, however, would one
stand himself in challenge against another who was not present? In order to have battle one must have an available
enemy, else does battle occur only in one's thoughts. It
would be necessary that I again speak untruth, but that became easier each time it was indulged in. These males had
refused to hear the truth; what, then, was left save lies?

"None need give me aid," said I to Aysayn, looking again
to the dark eyes which regarded me. "I am Midanna, and a

war leader of Midanna, and have already done as I wished. The male I will have for my own has already been chosen.''

"Indeed," said Aysayn with an odd pleasantness to his manner, looking up at me in comfort from the place where he reclined. "And what man have you this time chosen? Is it to be S'Heernoh again? Or perhaps you have this time settled upon Galiose. Should your choice be Galiose, you will likely not be concerned with giving him challenge. There will be two others to do the thing for you.''

"Why would I be so foolish as to choose one I wish to challenge?" I asked, annoyed at so witless a suggestion. "The one I have chosen is the one who freed me from those in whose capture I lay.''

Again the aroma of roasting meat came, bringing dizziness and a faint trembling with it, therefore did I unfold my legs and lie upon the pelt upon my left side. I would take the provender these males offered for I had a great need of it, and then would I begin the return journey to Bellinard—a solitary return journey.

"What one who freed you from capture?" demanded Aysayn with startling abruptness, his face suddenly appearing directly above mine. "What capture were you in, and who was it who freed you from it?''

"I ended in the capture of those city folk who had been sent in shame from Bellinard by my Midanna," I informed him. "Great was the pleasure they took in beating their captive, and also was it their intention to sell me in Bellinard settlement once it was reached. The slave felt he owed his life to me, therefore did he aid me in my escape when he executed his own.''

"Slave?" demanded Aysayn. "What slave? For what reason did he fail to remain with you? In what manner did you return his life to him? How was he able to leave one so clearly unable to see to herself?''

"What occurs here, brother?" asked Mehrayn in a puzzled voice the while I attempted to construct suitable replies in my mind to the questions Aysayn had put. Mehrayn and Ceralt had come forward from the fire they had built, and now stood beyond the pelt near Aysayn, directly before me. No more than their legs was I able to see from where I lay, yet was that certainly more than sufficient.

"The wench claims to have made a choice in a man," said Aysayn in annoyance, pulling back from me to sit upon the pelt rather than kneel upon it, glancing briefly up at those who stood so near to him. "Would you have me repeat what I was told?"

"Indeed," said Ceralt after a hesitation. "The question has for far too long gone unanswered."

"Very well," said Aysayn, his eyes upon me rather than upon those he addressed. "The man she has chosen is—a slave."

A moment of silence greeted Aysayn's announcement, as though the words called for deep thought, and then Ceralt and Mehrayn spoke with nearly the same breath.

"What?" demanded Ceralt as though he had not heard correctly, and, "A what?" demanded Mehrayn, outraged. Then did they both speak at great length and together, so that the sound of each swallowed the sense of the words of the other. At once Aysayn held up a hand, and looked upon the two who stood beside him.

"The wench has chosen a slave," said he, his tone calm as theirs had failed to be. "The slave who aided her escape from those who held her captive. The slave whose life she returned. Perhaps it would be best if you were to give her that meat now, Ceralt, and then we may question her at greater length."

"I had nearly forgotten I held it," said Ceralt in a mutter of annoyance. "Sit now and take the meat, Jalav, and then we shall speak of what needs to be spoken of."

He crouched then and held out what was impaled upon his dagger, a large slice of freshly heated nilno. Clearly had the meat been cooked at another time and merely warmed in the fire, yet did it capture my attention for all of that. My insides truly twisted as I sat again upon the lenga fur, and no more than the briefest glimpse did I give the male.

"There is naught which needs to be spoken of," said I, taking the meat from the blade held out to me, finding it just cool enough to hold. "A decision was demanded of me, and I have made that decision."

"That was not the decision demanded of you, wench," said Mehrayn, mild reproof in his voice as he sat himself cross-legged upon the pelt, easing his sword to a position of comfort. "Your choice was between Ceralt and myself, and naught has occurred to change that."

"A Midanna war leader may choose any male she wishes," I said about a large bite of nilno, juices dripping down my fingers. "It has been said many times that I must have a male of my own, therefore have I chosen one. Now do I demand to be left in peace."

"Left in peace with your slave?" asked Aysayn, moving aside, to make room for Ceralt. "We are to believe that you have somehow been freed from capture by a slave who in some manner owed his life to you, and who then rode off and left you? After he became your chosen? Do you take us for fools?"

"I take you for males, which is often the same," I allowed, savoring the annoyance he showed. "You, Aysayn, know the slave yourself, for it was you who sent him to me in the palace of the High Seat. It was then that I allowed him to retain his life, which he chose to see as having had it returned after having forfeited it. For what reason he saw it so, I know not. Happily, I am not male."

"There are those of us who have already taken note of that fact," said Mehrayn, his eyes moving about me in the same manner that Ceralt's did. "For what reason have you taken no more than two bites of that nilno?"

"For the reason that I am able to hold no more," said I, reluctant to release the meat I held, yet unable to continue feeding upon it. The grease had added to my queasiness rather than easing it, and my throat would surely refuse another taste.

"I see now I should have prepared falum rather than nilno," said Ceralt, frowning. "That and broth must be her fare till she is able again to accept solid food. Also her hair should be braided, if that salve is to be applied to the cuts and weals."

"And she also should sleep awhile, to regain her strength," said Mehrayn, reaching to a small parsto-hide sack he had put in his swordbelt. Parsto-hide, unlike leather, may be heated near a fire without fear that it will dry out and crack. Brewed daru may be carried in it, or sword oil. "We may continue speaking of her slave after she has had tending and a nap."

"I have no wish for falum, salve, sleep nor tending," I informed them all, raising my head as I threw the nilno between Mehrayn and Ceralt. "I shall now take my belongings and depart, for there are those in Bellinard who await my return."

"Had we deemed you well enough to travel, you would have traveled with us," said Ceralt, rising together with Mehrayn as I shifted about in preparation for regaining my feet. The pain I had refused to acknowledge ruled nearly every part of my body, yet had it done the same the darkness previous, and I had still been able to continue on a while. That fey I would do the same again, and rest when adequate distance separated me from the males who were now too near.

"For now you will rest with us till you are able to travel," said Mehrayn, moving about to the opposite side of the pelt, Ceralt remaining where he had been. I had given more attention to my rising than to the males, a foolishness I would not have indulged in in a more clear-headed moment. Mehrayn went to one knee and reached across to my right arm, and before I knew aught was about he and Ceralt had put their arms about and beneath me, to return me to the lenga pelt on my back. With a sound of surprised indignation I attempted to raise myself once again, yet Aysayn had once more taken my ankles, and the others each kept a hand to one of my shoulders.

"Their whips were busy indeed," said Mehrayn, much of a growl in his voice as he looked down upon me. "The front of her is not as badly wealed as her back, therefore you and I will see to it first, Ceralt. When she sleeps, it will be best if she does so belly down."

"You continue to believe the sign of Sigurr will not aid her?" Aysayn asked Mehrayn, as I feebly attempted to kick from his grasp. "For what reason would it not?"

"For the reason that no other thing than major wounds and life threats have been seen to by it in the past," said Mehrayn, taking his hand from my shoulder to open the parsto-hide sack. "The wench herself has seen it the same, and the salve should heal her quickly enough, along with rest and proper nourishment. Would you have me place her in the power of the sign for naught?"

"I continue to find it difficult to believe that the wench carries a sign of the gods," said Ceralt at Aysayn's headshake, putting his free hand to my shoulder. "Ever had she insisted she rode for her goddess, yet had I taken the insistence for a female notion meant to be ignored."

"The will of the gods may not be ignored," said I with what strength I was able, to Ceralt and the others as well. "Best you release me and step from my path, to keep from being thrown from it."

"Were we meant to keep from your path at this time, we would not have found you," returned Mehrayn at once, seeing naught of Ceralt's frown nor Aysayn's faint air of disturbance. "The salve is warm and will not increase your pain, wench, but might hurt from the applying of it. Ceralt and I will work as quickly as possible, and then will you be able to rest."

My protests were as naught against the determination of the males, and once strands of my hair had been brushed gently aside, Mehrayn and Ceralt shared the applying of the salve. The males touched the marks upon me with great care, though I found it necessary to close my eyes and clamp tight my teeth and fists, to be sure no sound escaped my throat. Two of the city females had taken great pleasure in striking me upon breasts and thighs, and that despite the presence of my hair and the cloth tied about my waist. Had greater strength been theirs, surely would the weals and cuts have been considerably worse.

With the front of me seen to, all three males aided in turning me to my belly, and then Ceralt began plaiting my hair, just as had been done when I was his captive. Again I attempted to free myself from their attentions, yet to no avail. My ankles were held, the plaiting was done, and then the salve was applied. With fists closed tight about clumps of lenga fur, I was given more than enough opportunity to regret the two swallows of nilno I had taken; with each passing moment they threatened to return from whence they had gone. I strained to keep such evidence of weakness from shaming me, and in the straining at last found the ease of darkness.

Consciousness returned to me with the sounds of feathered children of the wild. I remained as I had been put, belly down in the furs, and another fur had been put atop me despite the warmth of the mid-fey light. I stirred a bit where I lay then raised up on my elbows to see what strength I had recovered, finding then that the salve had also been put upon my wrists where the leather had so often held me. A good portion of the pain I had had remained to plague me, yet was there some small easing beside the annoyance I felt. Had I not been weakened by capture, those males would not have been able to force upon me the treatment of a city slave-woman, an insult they cared naught for giving. Insolent were males, and forever giving insult, and a warrior did well to avoid them whenever she might.

The lenga pelt I lay upon had been placed in the shade of a tree, and it came to me then that I heard no voices from the fire which now was beyond my feet. Had the males gone hunting, I, too, would soon be gone, and that was as eagerly desired as the end of my tasks. It came to me then to wonder how it was that Chaldrin's spirit had appeared to urge me toward an ending to my tasks, when the male had not taken the final journey to the endless dark. It was not unheard of for the spirit of a departed warrior to return and visit those the warrior had been closest to, yet never had I heard of one returning who had not truly gone. Males, it seemed, were as strange in death as they were in life, and once I had returned to Bellinard I would be sure to speak to Chaldrin of the matter.

The fur beneath me urged me to remain upon its comfort, yet were there doings awaiting my attention. I began to turn to my left side, so that I might more easily kick off the covering pelt—and discovered only then that my ankles were loosely yet firmly bound in leather. The audacity of those males to do such a thing so angered me I tried to fling the covering pelt as far as possible, yet the sound of a voice stopped me.

"Leave the cover as it is, girl," said Aysayn, clearly quite near to me. ''The salve must be warm to be most effective, even after it has been applied.''

I twisted about, and saw that Sigurr's Shadow had seated himself not far from the end of the pelt. His dark eyes were calmly assessing, his back leaned against the bole of the tree we sat beneath, and absently did he chew the blade of grass he held.

''By what right have I been bound?'' I demanded, filled with even greater annoyance at the sight of his calm. ''Am I now to consider myself captive to you?''

''If you wish,'' he replied, quietly amused. ''It was the desire of none here to take a captive, however should you require such a state, we shall certainly not refuse you.'' He paused then to whistle the song of the nesting lellin, then added, ''The leather was put upon you to keep you from dislodging the covering fur, should you begin moving about in your sleep. Has some measure of the pain and weariness now been taken from you?''

''A Midanna war leader feels neither pain nor weariness,'' I replied, not at all mollified by the smoothness of his words. ''I shall now take my belongings and depart.''

''Before you have given thanks to those who aided you?'' he asked with feigned surprise. ''Before we have spoken further upon the matter of the slave you have chosen in place of Ceralt and Mehrayn? Surely you will join us for the mid-fey meal, which has already been prepared against your awakening?''

He made scant attempt to conceal the amusement he felt even as he rose to his feet, an amusement which showed in the mock courtesy he thought to cozen me with.

''There is naught I wish to join save the return trail to Bellinard,'' I said with all the annoyance I felt, making no effort to look up to the male where he stood. ''I find your attempts filled with little amusement, Aysayn, for I am not one such as Galiose, to be led about by the ears with the appearance of concession. I shall have my weapons and breech, and then I shall be gone upon my way.''

I began, then, to sit upon the pelt, in order to throw aside the cover and remove the leather which bound me, yet was I

again stopped, as Aysayn grabbed my hair to keep me unmoving till he had seated himself in the grass before me.

"Indeed are you not one such as Galiose," said he, no
more than amused by the fury with which I looked upon him.
"Galiose will accept the words of diplomacy for the sake of
peace, a state you have little or no interest in. As you seem to
require an exact description of the state of affairs you currently find yourself in, I shall no longer make the attempt to
spare your sense of pride. You shall remain in our company
and care till full health has been restored to you, and only
then shall you return to Bellinard—again in our company.
You may not refuse our aid nor may you depart, for Mehrayn
and Ceralt will not allow it, nor shall I. Have I spoken clearly
enough?"

So gentle and mannerly was his inquiry that one would have
thought he discussed the direction in which one must ride in
order to find the stream one has been seeking. So great was
my anger that I reached to his fist and attempted to loosen it
from about my hair, yet was it no different from the fist of
any other male, large and square and possessed of the accursed strength which warriors had been denied. He watched
in silence a moment as I pushed and struggled to part his
fingers, and then did he dare to reach over and sharply strike
my hands away with his free one.

"You need not waste what little strength you have in
activities such as that," said he, looking down upon me with
a critical eye. "For what reason do you attempt to refuse aid
when you are so clearly in need of it?"

"For what reason need I accept?" I countered, glowering
at him. "Have I given my vow to do so? Have I been
commanded by the gods to do so? I am a Midanna warrior;
should it not be my wish to accept what is offered, I need not
do so."

"So you continue to seek to avoid Mehrayn and Ceralt,"
said he with a sudden grin, amusement returned and enhanced. "Even are you willing to indulge in the actions of a
child to do so, for your steadfast refusals may be viewed in
no other manner. What will you do should they take the
notion to treat you as the child you seem?"

"Aysayn, release me!" I hissed, furious with his amusement, yet also greatly upset. "I have chosen to refuse both of those males, and have no desire to remain longer in their company!"

"By cause of the slave you have accepted in their stead," said he with a solemn nod. "As the two who have been rejected now approach, we shall first see you fed, and then shall delve more deeply into the matter of your chosen. Should you refuse what is given you, I feel certain your disappointed suitors will assist you in swallowing it."

So pleased was the accursed male to impart this knowledge, that he was unable to keep hidden the grin he had covered, surely anticipating the time when those others might again put their hands upon me. In helpless fury I turned my head as far as I might, and was able to see the approach he had already noted. Ceralt and Mehrayn had come from deeper within the forest, their strides wide and eager, their upper bodies and hair glistening wetly. Neither leather chest and leg coverings nor fur boots had been retained by Ceralt, both most obviously unnecessary in the warmth of the fey, his sword and Mehrayn's aswing at their sides through the vigor of their movements. Both had clearly bathed but recently, and I returned my gaze to Aysayn with resentment and rage.

"I am no longer able to bear the weight of these furs," I informed him, my gaze a promise of reckoning to come. "Release me so that I may remove them, and do so immediately."

"You must bear their weight for you may not remove them, child," said the male, his voice and amusement softened, his words spoken more slowly, as though he did indeed address one too young to easily follow his meaning. "The salve must be kept warm to do its proper healing, therefore must you remain in the furs. Your discomfort is not unknown to Aysayn, therefore shall Aysayn bring you a large sweet when the fey has ended, to reward you for your bravery and obedience. The sweet will please you, will it not?"

Had I then stood with sword to hand and strength unimpaired as I had a few feyd earlier, surely would I have striven to the utmost to see that Sigurr no longer cast a Shadow upon our world. Even so, with body aching and limbs weakened, with mind yet befogged and belly hollow, with ankles bound and

hair entrapped, still was I a war leader of Midanna. Although
it would have pleased me to use the learning I had had from
Chaldrin, I knew Aysayn's knowledge of the learning was far
more extensive than mine; therefore I must use that which
came from the living symbol of my life sign, the hadat. The
greatest portion of my strength was spent in bringing my
knees to the place my elbows had been, and that before
Aysayn knew what I was about. With the aid of my palms to
the lenga fur I was able to bend to the hand upon my hair and
sink my teeth into it, with all the fury I felt. The male howled
with surprise and pain, immediately attempting to withdraw
the hand, yet was I not of a mind to release him that quickly.
Aysayn, Sigurr's Shadow upon this world, had had great
amusement; now would Jalav, chosen of the gods, have the
same.

A great deal of shoutings and confusion then ensued, with
Aysayn thrashing about and Ceralt and Mehrayn suddenly
beside and between us, and then was my hair taken in a fist
just at my head, and fingers pressed hard between my jaws. It
was then necessary that I release Aysayn though I had no
wish to, and once done I, too, was released. Ceralt removed
his hand from my hair and drew me back upon the lenga
pelts while Mehrayn assisted Aysayn in examining his hand.
In no more than two places had my teeth broken the skin, and
the flow of blood was feeble indeed; had I had my full
strength upon me, well might I have attempted his throat
instead. I sat upon the lenga pelts with some difficulty, bound
ankles to the left, chest pounding with the small exertion I
had attempted, Ceralt's arm about my shoulders in support
and restraint, and Mehrayn glanced up from the hand he bent
over.

"Though it scarcely seems necessary that you give reverent
thanks that that is not your sword hand, brother," said he to
Aysayn, "still might you find it best to see the hand washed
and salved. What occurred between you that such strong
disagreement would arise?"

"Disagreement!" echoed Aysayn with a dark look for me,
rubbing his hand. "Your amusement is poorly considered,
brother. The wench attempted to command me to her will,
and when I refused to allow her to cause herself further harm,

she attacked me. Perhaps my choice of words were a trifle—lighthearted, yet even so— Are you quite certain that there is no hope of seeing her restored more quickly than will be accomplished through use of the salve? Her humor grows more foul with each passing fey.''

''Her humor will need to accommodate itself,'' said Mehrayn with a dour look. ''Perhaps, in future, it would also be best were you to speak with her in a less—lighthearted manner, to avoid inciting so vigorous a return.''

''A vigor she is now ill able to afford,'' said Ceralt, a disturbance in his voice. I had attempted to keep myself from leaning upon him, yet had the drain of my strength been such that I now, albeit reluctantly, rested against his chest. ''That she has so quickly ceased all efforts to struggle takes my thoughts from consideration of what punishment her attack merits.''

''For now, her punishment will be a return to motionlessness,'' said Mehrayn, touching the dampness upon my brow. ''She must remain in the furs, and must be fed what you have prepared for her. Let us see to these things as quickly as may be.''

As Mehrayn and Aysayn rose immediately to their feet, Ceralt turned and lifted me from the furs in his arms before rising. Their bustle and strength dizzied me, so much so that I was little aware of the arms which held me, the shoulder I rested against, wet, dark hair above light eyes which regarded me with too deep a gaze. In a matter of reckid was I once again returned to the furs whose absence was a delight, this time with other sleeping furs and such under the bottom pelt, so that I might lean back in nearly a seated posture rather than lie flat upon it. When Mehrayn placed the second pelt upon me I attempted to refuse it, thereby bringing his arms rather than Ceralt's about me, to prevent the thing. Little need was there for the use of any great portion of the wide-muscled strength in those arms, yet were they kept about me, even with the return of Ceralt and a bowl, that which is called a spoon jutting up from the contents of the bowl. Faintly do I recall attempting to refuse what proved to be well-warmed falum, that thick-grained mixture fed upon by village folk, yet was my need for sustenance too great and the insistences of the males impossible to refuse. The falum slid to the hollow within and soothed it in a manner which the nilno had not, and before the dizziness left me, far more of the grain mixture was gone than remained.

When I at last turned my face from the spoon wielded by Ceralt, able to swallow down not one more mouthful, Mehrayn released me so that I might take the skin of water brought by Aysayn upon his return from seeing to his hand.

"Already do you appear stronger and with some color restored, sister," said he wryly, putting the skin aside so that he might seat himself upon the grass near me. Mehrayn continued to sit on my other side, Ceralt before my bent legs. "Now, perhaps, we might speak further upon the matter of your slave."

"No longer is he a slave, nor was he ever more than merely a captive," said I, looking solely upon Aysayn. "Do you fear so greatly the strength I have recovered, that you continue to refuse to remove the leather upon me? A pity Sigurr's Shadow has not more courage than that."

"Alas, sister, indeed am I sorely afraid," said he, his sigh seeming affected by the grin he wore. "In repayment for a matter of toothmarks, you may now remain hobbled like the wildest of she-gandod, a condition well earned by your precipitant actions. Should one feel insulted, one may offer back insults of one's own; not always is attack called for."

"No others save males are unaware of the fact that the sole reason for insult is to provoke attack," I returned with scorn. "Should the deed be beyond you, I shall do the thing myself."

I then attempted to throw the cover from me so that I might reach the leather upon my ankles, but both Mehrayn and Ceralt immediately prevented me. The two laughed to see themselves in the midst of precisely the same action, caring naught that I had found no amusement whatsoever.

"I see you do indeed know her as I do," said Ceralt to Mehrayn, and both laughed a moment, then stopped. Mehrayn merely nodded in silence, heavily, and each one stared into the eyes of the other.

"So the man is a slave who is no longer a slave who was never a slave," said Aysayn hurriedly, a forced lightness to the words which were addressed to me. "What occurred between you and this slave in Bellinard, and how were you reunited?''

I looked upon him with little of the anger I had felt, naught of the ache which had abruptly blossomed within, then began the tale he had requested. I would not allow Ceralt and Mehrayn to bare blades against one another, and the lie I had chosen to speak as truth would see my will done. I told of the time in Bellinard, of the branch which had felled me, of Relidose and the conveyances, of the city folk and their doings. No trace of amusement was left to Aysayn when I spoke of the manner in which I had been strung by the wrists at the end of each fey's travels to be beaten, then was given to the slave for use. That the beatings and use had been closely and eagerly observed by the city folk angered all three of the males, and Mehrayn struck a large and furious fist into the palm of his other hand.

''If only we had known soon enough that you were gone!'' he growled, his anger echoed on the face of Ceralt. ''We none of us knew you were not somewhere about till darkness fell, and Galiose thought to ask if your kan had been returned to its stabling. We discovered then that it had not been, yet was it necessary to await the new light before we might attempt to follow. S'Heernoh was able to speak of the direction he believed you had ridden off in, and once into the forest we found the track of your kan.''

''Which we followed till we caught it,'' said Ceralt, more bitterness than humor to his laugh. ''Nearly all my life have I hunted and tracked, and not once did it come to me that the beast we followed was unburdened. It then became necessary to retrace our steps, which eventually led us to a place where wagon tracks ran beside your kan's hoofprints. This time did we follow the tracks instead, halting only when darkness forced us to it. Another fey and another darkness, and then the new light brought us to where you lay nearly upon the track we followed.''

''Which you had clearly intended following in the opposite direction,'' said Aysayn , his voice attempting a denial of the bleakness of the others. ''Now, as to the reason why you were allowed to attempt the journey without accompaniment: for what reason *were* you allowed it? Was the man not able to see how clearly you were in need of assistance? Why did he merely go his own way?''

"It was my wish that he do so," I replied, meeting the vast annoyance to be seen in his eyes with calm. "He would have had me travel with him to his home to the west, yet was he aware of the tasks remaining to my hand, the males I must continue dealing with for the time. He was reluctant, but he obeyed my will, for he knew he was my chosen and would be sent for when all battle was done. There is no place at the side of a Midanna war leader for a male before all battle is seen to."

"It was your will that he leave you to your own devices, therefore he did so," said Aysayn, his annoyance somewhat increased. "Clearly your survival mattered little to him, and *this* is the man you would choose for your own? One who would not even accompany you to be sure of your safety?"

"You would have him be as foolish as other males and doubt the ability of a Midanna in the forests which are her home?" I returned with scorn, easing down, somewhat, the fur which covered me. "You would have me choose a male who did not bow to my will above his own? I know of no war leader who would seek to increase her difficulties; only males seek to do such a thing."

"How willing is this—*man* to stand in defense of what is ostensibly his?" asked Mehrayn. "Any man who truly desires a wench will fight for her, against any who seek to take her from him. How willing is *this* man?"

I turned my head to see the green gaze which regarded me, the stubbornness and implacability behind the words which had been spoken. Ceralt, too, looked upon me as though he would stand against any who would take what was his.

"No male I choose need consider the need to stand against others," said I to both, looking from one to the other. "As the choice is mine, so would be what challenges came, for the decision which was opposed would also be mine. Do you think me a city slave-woman, that my possession might be had by any who fought for it?"

"Even a wench who rides for the gods may be possessed by a man strong enough to claim her," said Ceralt. "What eagerness will this man you speak of find to face challenge?"

"I shall not allow my chosen to be challenged," I maintained, deliberately looking away from the two who sat so near. "When battle is done I shall ride to seek him out, and none may deny me. I need not consider the desires of any other."

"What reason, then, need any others consider *your* desires?" asked Aysayn, pointedly. "For what reason, then, should you not merely be taken, no matter your own wishes to the contrary? One who fails to consider others forfeits all rights to *be* considered. I believe the wench should not be allowed further rest, my friends, and also more of the healing salve. We may not ride till she has been restored."

"Indeed," said Ceralt in agreement, Mehrayn also anod and then were all three males rising to their feet. Though I had no true wish for further rest, the props were removed from behind me, the warmed salve was brought, and again it was put to the tracks of beatings. Surprisingly less pain was to be found in the second touching of the thick, brown salve, and quickly was I again set upon my belly amid furs to seek sleep. I had no wish for the furs and no wish for sleep, and certainly no wish for the leather which continued to hold me, yet did the males refuse to hear my protests. Once I had been put so I was not permitted to rise again and, rage though I might, sleep quickly claimed me.

9.

Healing—
and an unexpected journey

I awoke in darkness to find not even Aysayn close beside me,
still gripped in the upset of the nightmare which had robbed
me of even the escape of sleep. I turned to my right side in
the overwarmth of the furs, then resolutely brought my knees
up so that I might reach the leather which held my ankles. A
moment saw my ankles freed, and I put an arm out into the
cool of the darkness, immeasurably relieved to regain that
small sensation of freedom. Dreams, I knew, were very often
sent by the gods, and the one I had just had, surely had been a
sending of the dark god.

I turned to my back then with a sigh, seeing again against
the darkness of the forest, the happenings which had occurred
in my sleep. How strange it is that when within a dream, one
rarely has knowledge that the doing *is* a dream. Rather does it
seem that one walks another land, similar to one's own land
yet in some odd manner different. The land I had discovered
about me had been the forest, yet an indistinct forest peopled
with those more solid and real than it. I sat upon a lenga fur in
the midst of that forest, leather about my ankles, neither
breech nor weapons within sight or reach. Aysayn walked
before me, then, and crouched to send me a look of amusement.

"Now that you are healed, sister, I have come to give the
punishment I promised," he said, locking his fingers between
his knees. "You brought me uncalled for humiliation, and
now I shall do the same for you."

"You may not," I had replied, striving to show naught of
the upset I felt. "I am unarmed, and also am I bound. First
free me, and give me my weapons."

"No need," said Mehrayn, who sat, I then saw, close

upon my right. "My brother was not permitted the use of weapons, therefore neither shall you be."

"Nor shall you be unbound, save with our permission," said Ceralt, as near to me upon the left, beyond my bent legs. "No wench may be unbound, save through the permission of men."

"You will use me unwillingly, then," I had said to Aysayn, of a sudden greatly aware of how large the male was. Wide were his shoulders and deep his chest, full muscled the arms which rested upon his thighs. Large also was his manhood and greatly demanding, more than sufficient to bring mindlessness to a warrior. Great pleasure had he given me the time he had used me, yet had I no wish just then for pleasure from him.

"They will not permit me to use you," said Aysayn with a glance of amusement for both Mehrayn and Ceralt. "No more am I permitted than to punish you, a punishment which they prescribe and approve of. There are matters in which you may not disobey them, woman, for they will not allow it."

"You must learn to be considerate of others, Jalav, else shall you be punished," said Ceralt, a lock of his dark hair reaching for his eyes.

"Should this occur again, it is we who shall punish you," said Mehrayn, his green eyes unrelenting. "We as well as the one you wrong."

"My punishment must be use," I had said to Aysayn, abruptly feeling a great desire for him. "I find much pleasure in use."

"Too much pleasure," said Aysayn with a shake of his head. "Punishment is not meant to bring pleasure. The punishment of men is meant to be more difficult to bear than the punishment of the gods, for a wench must learn to respect men as she does not respect the gods. They are far closer to her, and may do far more. We shall now begin."

"No," I had denied and began to turn from him, yet the leather upon me would not let me rise. Wide hands took my arms, the hands of Aysayn, his strength denying me escape. Though I struggled as I could I was taken across the thighs of the now-seated male, and then was I struck hard with his

open hand. Again and again was I struck so, punished as
though I were a child, given what Ceralt and Mehrayn had so
often given me, with their full permission. Rather than feeling rage, tears quickly came to my eyes, and I looked over
toward the two males who watched as Aysayn continued to
strike me with strength. In place of the satisfaction I had
expected to see, a great disturbance held the males, one
which shifted them in place and brought strangeness to their
eyes. Ceralt ran a broad hand through his dark hair, and
Mehrayn sat with wide fist clenched, and both suddenly
looked up to see the tears running down my cheeks. Abruptly
I knew I had only to speak to have them halt the punishment,
to have them jump to their feet and demand that Aysayn
cease. I loathed that punishment more than the pain of a
wound, more than the feel of a lash, yet did I know as well
that were I to call upon them, they would halt Aysayn and
then turn to face one another. Greater was the flow of tears,
then, from the punishment Aysayn gave and the longing deep
within me, yet was I unable to allow the words they awaited
to pass my lips. Sobbing then took me, of a strength so great
that I awakened to the dark of the true forest, unable at first to
loosen the hold of desolation upon me. When the silent
sobbing at last ended, I had turned to my side and removed
the leather, then had I put myself to my back. I knew not
what meaning such a dream might have, no more than the
clear truth that I must not allow Ceralt and Mehrayn to face
one another. No other thought occurred to me, nor did I seek
others.

When the males discovered that I was awake, a meat broth
was brought me and also more falum. The hollow within had
again grown vocal, and this time was all the falum finished
and the broth as well. After I had eaten my fill the warmed
salve was again applied, the furs were tucked about me, and I
was commanded to sleep. None of the males had attempted
converse with me, a lack I had been grateful for. Sunk in the
pall of the dream I had not refused the commands they gave
and, unbound, again found the release of sleep.

The following fey was worse in that much of my strength
seemed to have returned, yet was I denied permission to leave
the furs. With first light was I given falum, a thick stew,

when the light was highest and nilno when darkness came; between those times were there words of discord and shouting, commands and refusals, struggles and frustration. It was not my intention to obey Mehrayn and Ceralt, nor did I; obedience was forced upon me despite my objections, the strength of the two males too great to overcome. Aysayn did no more than observe their doings with soft laughter and deep amusement, most especially when they held the cover fur down upon me with the weight of their bodies and stroked my hair in an effort to calm my shouting and attempts at struggle. The salve must be kept warm, they continued to maintain, and that till my strength for struggle was gone.

That darkness brought a sleep I had not found for all of the fey, yet was I again awake before it was completely over. The new light would not be long in coming, I knew as I sat upon the pelt, for a moment putting my face in my hands. Ceralt and Mehrayn slept not far distant from where I sat, the dark shapes of their bodies at peace in the darkness which surrounded them, therefore was it necessary that I move with as little sound as possible. I slid from under the hated cover, crawled to the end of the pelt, then at last raised myself to my feet.

Much did it seem as though kalod had passed since last I had stood without pain and without difficulty. A stiffness was upon me by cause of the length of time I had been forced to lie unmoving in the furs, yet had the salve indeed healed nearly all of me, and the provender I had swallowed returned my strength. I stepped from pelt to grass with the silence of a Midanna, delighting in the cool of the darkness as it caressed my flesh, moving toward the still-burning fire and a step or two beyond it before stretching my body all about to remove what aches remained. Soon would the new light make its appearance, and then would I begin the return journey to Bellinard.

"They will be annoyed with you for having left your furs," came a soft voice out of the darkness, from where I knew it would come. "Has the pain gone from you entirely, then?"

"As far as it shall till I have again accustomed myself to moving about," I replied, turning to look upon Aysayn. The male stood his watch of the darkness, a watch earlier shared by Ceralt and Mehrayn.

"You mean to depart before they have awakened," said Aysayn, no questioning in his tone. "You would do such a thing to them when they have toiled so tirelessly to return your health?"

He looked down upon me with sobriety in the depths of his eyes, the flicker of the fire playing across his face. In what manner was I to answer his query, when the only answer lay in discussing the most recent dream visited upon me? In that dream had Ceralt and Mehrayn again been to either side of me, yet not above and upon the covering fur. Without body cloth and breech were the two, beneath the cover and so close about me that there seemed insufficient air to breathe, and then did Mehrayn take me in his arms and press his lips to mine. Ah, Mida! So long had it been since last I called out to the goddess in my heart, yet the feel of those arms about me, the hard strength of his body pressed to mine, the demand and warmth of his lips! Willingly did I give the kiss which was taken, and then was I released so that Ceralt might then pull me to him. He lay upon his back and held me to his chest, and when his lips touched mine I nearly moaned with the pleasure of it. So long a time and so little had I had of him, and so great had my need grown.

So wildly whirling were my thoughts that at first I was unaware of the hands which took my thighs and raised me to my knees. Then did I know I was being entered and I moved in unbearable pleasure, seeking to welcome the presence within, seeking to voice a sound of ecstasy. Ceralt chuckled and his fist came to my hair, and then my lips were again his, to be released only when he willed it. Mehrayn thrust as ever he did, deeply and with strength, my hands and lips held to Ceralt with a kind of abandon, and never had I felt such overwhelming pleasure and release.

When Mehrayn had taken what use he wished, I was released by Ceralt so that I might lie upon the fur and again be held by Mehrayn. His use had brought me so great a pleasure that his arms about me and his lips to mine turned my soul to glowing, and then was I aware of another who sought me. In Mehrayn's place had Ceralt now come, return-

ing the demands of my body and immediately beginning to
see to them. I moaned and moved in the arms which held me,
striving to communicate the inexpressible heights to which I
was being carried, and Mehrayn chuckled as Ceralt had, then
happily continued the touching of lips. When a hand came to
my breast I knew not whose hand it was, nor did I care; when
I awoke to find myself entirely unheld, the moisture flowing
freely from me, surely did I know from whom the dream had
come. Never would the two males I desired above all others
allow another to touch what was theirs. Never would either
of them be yours, had said Mida, and in that instance had she
spoken naught save the truth.

"I may do no other thing than depart before they have
awakened," I replied in what was nearly a whisper, turning
my face from the male who regarded me. "I have chosen
another, and may not dally with these."

"The wounds of your body have been healed, yet the
wounds of your soul remain," said he, gently touching my
shoulder, his voice soft. "Is there no other solution to this
thing, except lies and a rejection of them both? Would not the
presence of one be better than neither?"

"The presence of the one who survives their meeting?" I
asked, looking again upon him to see the pain and desperation he shared. "Should I choose one over the other, you
believe the one not chosen will simply turn and walk from
here? I have known males a shorter time than you, brother. Is
this likely to occur?"

Silence held him briefly, a silence which the darkness
sounds of the forest strove to overcome, and then his head
shook slowly from side to side.

"No, there is little likelihood of such a thing occurring,"
he allowed with defeat heavy upon him. "Under no circumstances would Mehrayn turn and walk from you, nor, I
believe, would Ceralt. Should you not choose one, they will
face one another; should you indeed choose one, they will still
face one another. Is there naught to be done to free us all
from this madness?"

"What more might be done than to choose one above them
both?" I asked, searching anxiously the eyes which held to

me. "You, I know, disbelieved there was another; did they also disbelieve?"

"No, their belief was complete enough," he denied with a frown, rubbing one arm with a hand. "Also was their anger complete, that another would dare to step in the place which belonged to one of them. What will occur after the battle, when such a one must be produced?"

"First must battle be faced and survived," I put him off, thinking of the time of rest I had been promised. "Riding off unnoticed may be done more than once. You have my weapons and breech?"

"And your kan as well, as you may have seen," he said with a nod touched faintly with distraction. "Surely was it Sigurr's will that it survived the forest alone till we found it, therefore did we take it with us when we returned. You will ride directly to Bellinard?"

"Indeed," said I with a nod, reaching my hair to me so that I might unplait it. "There are those awaiting my return, and the strangers. . . ."

"Have taken this long, therefore shall they take a bit longer," said another voice, bringing Aysayn's head up and me about in surprise. Both Mehrayn and Ceralt appeared out of the dark into the circle of light by the fire, and it had been Mehrayn who had spoken. "There is another thing which first must be seen to, before you may return to Bellinard," he said.

"A thing of great importance," agreed Ceralt, his gaze as unwavering as Mehrayn's. "You feel no doubt as to your ability to ride?"

"My ability to ride is as it ever was," I replied, disliking the look the two bent upon me. "Also nothing is important enough to keep me from Bellinard."

"There is one to the west who must first be visited," said Mehrayn, gently stretching the muscles of his right shoulder as he looked about at the dawn sky. "Should we find him unwilling to renounce his place as your chosen, he may have his own choice as to which of us he will face. The results of that choice will make little difference, I think."

"And then we may return to the farther Bellinard," said

Ceralt, fingers to his hips as he also looked about. "With none to distract you from a proper choice. What name is this man of yours called by?"

I looked upon the two with great consternation, a soft hiss of vexation to be heard from Aysayn, who stood behind me. Never had I thought Mehrayn and Ceralt would attempt to seek out the one I had put forward as chosen; S'Heernoh's apprehension upon the point had clearly been correct. These two large, wide, well-muscled males would challenge any they believed about to usurp their place, an arrogance I would not have credited before I had come to know what I then did of males. They had agreed to allow me my choice, yet was that choice to be made solely at their direction and only in accordance with their will and desires. When I had spoken my choice, then would they see to curtailing it yet further.

"Jalav is interested only in the city of Bellinard," said I to the two, with controlled fury. "It is to the city she shall ride, not toward the settlement called the same, for a journey to the west would be an undertaking for fools. Perhaps such is to be expected of males, yet Jalav remains Midanna. Now would I have my breech and weapons, Aysayn."

I had turned toward the third of the males, noting the manner in which he sought to conceal his vexation over the journey the others had proposed, yet was he given no opportunity for reply to my request.

"You will be given what *we* permit you to be given, wench," said Ceralt, something of annoyance to be heard in his voice. "Previously when Jalav was Jalav there was naught to be done with her, yet shall that state of affairs no longer continue. You will ride with us, where we direct you to ride, and will obey what commands you are given. This is a matter between men, and your willfulness shall not be permitted to interfere."

"All females must obey in such a circumstance," said Mehrayn as I turned quickly back in fury toward Ceralt. "The rights of a man may not be denied, and among those rights is the one allowing him the woman of his desire, the woman he will fight to possess and keep. Not even the woman may deny him this, for he is larger and stronger than she and may take her despite her protests. Should another man attempt to deny him, that other must face him with weapons or withdraw his claim. What is the name of the man who accepted your choosing?''

Both had now again regarded me, heedless of my obvious fury. That they would look upon me as a city slave-woman, theirs for the taking, was so greatly enraging that surely did my hand reach for the hilt of the sword not yet returned to me. Had the sword been there, there would likely have been others of our set unable to ride; the males saw the empty reaching gesture, and knew it for what it was.

''You feel insult at being told how desirable you appear in the eyes of men,'' observed Mehryan, with sobriety. ''Did you believe, warrior, that men would find praise for no more than your weapon skill? Have none sought to possess you before this, that you would fall to anger upon being told of *our* intentions?''

''Intentions which we shall no longer allow to go unspoken,'' said Ceralt, folding wide arms across broad chest. ''Presenting our suits in the courteous manner did no more than allow you the belief that you might choose another before us, a belief that we would abide by such a decision. You hold the hearts and souls of two men already, wench; to permit the growth of such a collection would be absurd. We will first face this man you have chosen, and then we will return to the city. You have been asked to speak his name to us; now you must do so.''

I looked first upon Ceralt and then Mehrayn, then did I turn my back upon both, to stand with arms afold and continuing fury in my silence. It mattered not that I had no notion of what the slave-male's name might be; even had I known it, I would not have shared that knowledge as had been demanded. Jalav was free, and a war leader to Midanna, and no male might make demands upon her. This the two behind me would learn, when they found I would not ride with them. It was Bellinard I had come from, and to Bellinard would I return.

''Perhaps it would be best to leave this seeking out of her chosen till after battle with the strangers is done,'' said

Aysayn to the males he rode with, a faint coaxing to be heard in the words. "The girl is barely recovered from the hurt she was given, and cannot be expected to consider your proposals with an unconcerned mind. Should she be left to her own devices for a short while longer, likely she will find that the one she has chosen no longer holds interest for her, and therefore may be put from our minds."

"Yet scarcely is it likely that he will put the wench from his own mind, brother," said Mehrayn with faint reproof. "And would you have us sneak about behind the back of one who considers her his, as though it were our intent to steal what belonged to another? This we cannot and shall not do; therefore must we go and face him. You, of course, may return to the city, should it be your wish to do so."

"No, brother, I shall not return to the city alone," said Aysayn with a sigh, realizing fully the futility of his attempt. "As this was begun together, so shall it end. Best we now break our fast, so that we may ride with the new light."

The skies about us had already begun to lighten very faintly, showing that the birth of a new fey was not many reckid away. The damp of the grass beneath my feet was now more of an annoyance than a freedom, and intensely did I wish there was one I might question concerning the foolishness a warrior was prone to when among males. To believe it might be possible to live with them without strife was witless, yet had I seriously and bitterly resented my not being allowed my choice among them. For what reason would any warrior not bereft wish to choose among them? What was there for her to choose, save commands unending and unreasoning adherence to thoughtless ritual? That males found great pleasure in looking upon Jalav was already known to me; that they found considerably less of pleasure in her doings must again be made known to *them*.

I stood unmoving as the fire was coaxed higher and the males began to bustle about it, then did I begin, without undue fanfare, to take myself slowly toward the still-darkened forests. To survive the forests unarmed was no simple matter, yet would I be unarmed only till I was able to fashion a spear, and then would the danger be behind me. I would return quickly to Bellinard, and then would I . . .

"Where do you think you go, wench?" asked the voice of Ceralt as he abruptly stepped in my path. "One who is unarmed may not wander about as she pleases."

I attempted to move about the male to the right, but he moved as I did, blocking my path, and the anger which had not yet cooled flared again within me. With something of deliberation I reached my left hand out toward his side, hand up and palm forward, not quite touching the ribs there. With curiosity did the male look down understanding naught of my purpose till the heel of my hand caught him hard in the ribs. Ceralt grunted with the force of the blow and doubled over, soon to be upon the ground rather than in the path of a Midanna, and I quickly began to step about him, to reach the screening of the forests before he might recover himself. It had pleased me to do him as I had not been able to during my time of capture to him, yet my pleasure was short in duration; before half a step had been taken, two wide arms circled me from behind and I was borne to the ground just before where Ceralt had knelt.

"Are you bereft, that you would merely stand uncaring before her attack?" demanded Mehrayn of Ceralt, his words somewhat shortened as he fought to keep me beneath him despite my struggles. "Had she reached the deeper forest, we would have been a considerable time finding her again."

"I had not—expected attack," returned Ceralt with effort, seating himself upon the grass so that he might look down upon me where I lay beneath the bulk of Mehrayn, my cheek and body to the damp of the grass, striving uselessly against the strength of the male who held me. "When last we were together, she knew naught of this—outrageousness. How did it come about that she was permitted to learn it?"

"Chaldrin is a master of the art, and is able to deny her nothing," said Mehrayn with something like disgust, taking my wrists behind me as he continued to hold me flat with his body. "It was of great concern to him that she learn to defend herself without weapons, likely forgetting that attack is the far side of the coin of defense. To believe this one would refrain from attack, is to believe that the forests may be ridden without peril."

"Indeed," said Ceralt with a nod, leaning down to me with one hand still pressed to his side, anger in the eyes it was becoming increasingly less difficult to see. "Perhaps a short lesson in the advisability of refraining from attack would now be in order. Merely as an assistance to whichever of us ultimately possess her, of course."

"Sooner shall this Midanna choose the endless dark than one of you," I said amid the panting of struggles, meeting the gaze which looked down upon me. "By all the Midanna who have gone before me do I swear this! Beat me as those others did, and still shall it avail you naught! I shall not choose between you!"

Ceralt's eyes glanced upward to where Mehrayn knelt across me, likely receiving a similar glance from the second male, no words immediately spoken in response to mine. Mehrayn continued to hold my wrists so that I might not free them, yet did one of his hands come to smooth my hair.

"The wench speaks now from anger," said he to Ceralt, who seemed somehow touched with greater pain than that brought by the blow I had given him. "In time will she come to know the depth of the need which holds us, the need which we cannot deny. When anger is gone the need will be hers as well, and then shall she accept what must be done. For now we had best be quickly upon our way."

With a nod filled with weariness Ceralt raised himself from the grass, and then was I, too, pulled to my feet. I immediately attempted to kick my way free of Mehrayn, yet this the male would not allow. His knowledge of the battle method was not as full as Chaldrin's, yet was he knowledgeable enough to keep himself from harm. When I attempted to refuse being returned to the fire, Ceralt, in annoyance, assisted him by striking me with the flat of his hand behind, much as though I were a kan he wished in motion. The sting of the blow caused me to stumble forward, and once before the fire I was thrown to the grass at the feet of Aysayn.

"You will remain there till we have had our provender and are prepared to depart," said Mehrayn as I turned to look furiously up at him. "Should you make another attempt to take yourself off, you will be bound in leather and then given the punishment you have earned by Ceralt. Had you not willfully chosen another before the two who desire you, this journey would not now be necessary, therefore shall you remain silent and obedient. I will not speak of this to you again.''

The green gaze held to me for a brief moment, and then did the male turn with Ceralt to the packs which Aysayn had brought from another part of the camp. I growled low in my throat and began to rise again to my feet, yet the hand of Aysayn came to my shoulder as he crouched at my side.

"They are now alert and you would not escape them," said Aysayn very softly in warning, his hand hard upon my shoulder. "Wait till their eyes are no longer upon you—and without the additional difficulty of being bound. Once you have gone they will surely turn back, and then we may all return to Bellinard."

"Should they show themselves again in the city, I will give them both to the Harra!" I snarled as I pulled my shoulder free of Aysayn's grip, my fury difficult to contain. "Some time has it been since the Harra held male slaves, yet will they want to resume the practice. Had I had the wit of a lellin, surely would I have seen the thing done much the sooner."

"Such a doing would solve your problem without doubt," said Aysayn with a chuckle of great amusement, resting arms upon thighs. "There would, however, be an even greater problem for you if they were to win free of their captivity. Best we think upon this together, and find a solution which will settle the problem in a more peaceful manner. We will find battle aplenty when the strangers honor us with their presence."

"Should we survive to a great enough age to see the thing," I muttered in response, settling myself cross-legged upon the grass. The words Chaldrin had spoken now grew within me, raising doubts I had not earlier felt. What would occur if the strangers did indeed take kalod to appear? Were warriors to sit forever in and about a city, awaiting those who would some fey come? The Sigurri warriors they now waited beside were large and strong and eager to find pleasure with

the Midanna who greeted them; how soon before none save
the war leaders of my warriors were fit to take sword in
hand? Never before had Midanna had males in such numbers
available to them; how soon before the clans were blessed—
and my fighting force undone?

"In some manner do I believe that their arrival is soon to
be," said Aysayn soberly. "Our warriors shall have the time
to do no more than taste of one another before the time for
battle arrives, and perhaps such is for the best. Too long have
ours found it necessary to go without wenches of their own,
and a man with a woman beside him often finds interest in
things other than battle. We shall see to the strangers—and
then shall we see to what problems remain. What will you
have to heal your hunger?"

"I have no hunger to heal," I replied. Those who led
warriors seemed ever possessed of difficulties and problems,
no matter whether the warriors were male or female. Had it
been possible, surely would I have chosen to carry immediate
battle to the strangers and thereby be done with the thing.

The males fed upon provender prepared the previous fey,
and then did they rise to break camp. I remained upon the
grass in the growing light, lost in thoughts of my own, till I
became aware of Ceralt and Mehrayn standing above me. I
raised my eyes to them with little pleasure, and saw that
Ceralt held my breech.

"Woods nymphs are wise to cover themselves in the presence of men," said Mehrayn, his eyes taking me in in a thoughtful manner. "Should they fail to do so, they quickly find
themselves put to use."

Mehrayn stood in black body cloth and swordbelt, Ceralt in
breech and swordbelt, and truly did the two look upon me as
though they contemplated my use. I made a sound of derision
as I rose to my feet, then moved forward till I stood directly
before the Sigurri.

"First would it be necessary to decide in what order that
use was to be taken," I said, looking up into green pools of
calm. "Also would it be necessary to agree that more than
one was to be allowed that use. Surely shall Jalav be well
beyond an age for use before two fools of males are able to

find such agreement. Long before then shall I likely find the
need to take Aysayn for use."

I turned then from Mehrayn and took my breech from the
unresisting hands of Ceralt, who looked toward Sigurr's Sword
with an expression nearly indescribable. Perhaps vexed bewilderment was a description which was best, as though the
male saw the truth in my words yet saw no manner of altering
it. Without interest I walked from them both, then donned my
breech the while Aysayn strove valiantly to hide his laughter.

When at last we all were mounted and the kand were
turned in a westerly direction, Aysayn was no longer amused.
That my weapons would be kept by the males had been clear
to both of us, yet had we not expected that the reins of my
kan would also be denied me. Mehrayn led my kan behind
his own, leaving me naught to do save retain my seat with my
knees and silently curse all males. Softly did Aysayn speak of
the possibility of my later slipping off the kan and away into
the forest, yet was he as aware as I of the presence of Ceralt's
eyes upon me from the left. First was it necessary that the
male look away, and only then would I find it possible to do
what must be done.

The light had not yet reached its highest when we came to
what I had not expected: the end of the forests and the
beginning of a high-grassed plain. The trees had not thinned
sufficiently to give warning of such a thing, and the males
made no attempt to halt before leaving the forests behind.

"The second Bellinard is now not far ahead," said Ceralt,
gesturing in the direction in which we rode. "The wood for
their settlement was brought from here to there, and when the
settlers strove to erect its walls and houses, hunters from the
first Bellinard assisted by keeping them provisioned. It has
been some time since last I visited here."

"And how far beyond the settlement does the city of her
man lie?" asked Mehrayn, his gaze fixed ahead. "You have
knowledge, you said, of the lands to the west."

"Some small knowledge," Ceralt agreed. "Less than five
feyd beyond the settlement is a city I have never visited,
merely have I heard of it from those who have caught sight of
it. Surely is it there that we shall find him."

"Sigurr grant that it be so," said Mehrayn with calm satisfaction, glancing upward toward the fey's light. "We may halt soon for our mid-fey meal, and then we may discuss what number of pelts and such to bring with us into the city of her man. We will require a good supply of the coin they use, for we may not locate him the moment we arrive."

"Should we require a greater number of coins than we possess, there will be little difficulty in obtaining more," replied Ceralt, his light eyes turning full upon me. "Many men would wish the use of a woods nymph, and would pay eagerly for that use. First to use her would be the first to come with the proper coin, and thereafter would be those others with similar coins. Do you agree, Mehrayn?"

"Indeed, Ceralt," said Mehrayn, turning upon his kan to show amusement over the fury I sent to Ceralt with my gaze. "Many would indeed flock about for the use of a woods nymph, and the coins would come more easily than through hunting for pelts to trade. Perhaps we would do well to consider that before any other thing."

The two chuckled well at the great anger they gave me, then did Mehrayn return his attention to where we rode the while Ceralt made certain to watch me carefully. Even so was I nearly of a mind to slide from my kan and return to the forests so close behind us, for the males spoke more with intent to give insult than in truth. Truly close to being brothers had they grown, and although it kept their hands well away from sword hilts, I liked it not. Aysayn, of course, was again amused, and that, too, darkened my humor.

Less than a hin passed in silence, and then did Mehrayn call a halt for the meal the males wished to partake of. A number of paslat had been slain by Aysayn before the forests were left behind, and these did the males mean to feed upon. Ceralt came to put his large hands to my waist and pull me from my kan, the while he and Mehrayn discussed the advisability of having "the wench" see to the preparation of the paslat catch. I spoke no word in refusal concerning their foolishness for I no longer wished to address ones such as they, yet was I prepared to mention the great hunger which would visit them were they to await the accomplishment of that which they discussed. Mehrayn and Aysayn staked the kand where they might feed upon the tall grass, Ceralt watching me closely the while this was done, and then did the two Sigurri return to where we stood.

"Perhaps we would do well to do without a fire," observed Aysayn as he looked toward the west. "As the settlement is not far ahead of us, we would hardly wish to attract their attention. There are those within who would not look kindly upon Jalav."

"They would look even less kindly upon her were we to return her sword and accompany her there," said Mehrayn, left hand resting upon sword hilt as he turned to regard Aysayn. "Would you be averse to a bit of sport, brother?"

"Oh, indeed," grinned Aysayn, suddenly brightening. "It would be the Shining Sands again, a time of brisk pleasure which you were denied, brother. To fully appreciate this wench, one must see the glory of her sword work."

"You would allow her to jeopardize herself in such a manner?" demanded Ceralt as deep pleasure began to touch me at the words of the two Sigurri. "You would permit her to take sword in hand to achieve vengeance which we three might achieve for her?"

"What satisfaction in vengeance achieved by another?" asked Aysayn when Mehrayn stiffened silently at the accusation in Ceralt's voice. "Trespass upon another may be revenged by another, trespass upon oneself only by oneself. What joy and sense of achievement would be yours if I faced Mehrayn in your place and won for you the possession of this wench? Would she then be yours—or in reality mine?"

"But to allow a woman to face such danger!" protested Ceralt, clearly more upset than seeking argument. "A man must protect the woman of his heart, with his own life, if need be!"

"Even when her skill is a full match to his?" asked Mehrayn, his calm returned. "Even when the warrior blood in her is as strong and demanding as that within him? To disallow her battle would be to disallow her life, a doing she would find more painful than to fall in that battle. No man may covet more of a warrior wench than her possession and use."

"To covet her use would be foolishness," denied Ceralt with a gesture of impatience. "The blood runs so hot in these warrior wenches that they are able to give pleasure to many men, and take the same for themselves. Ever are they prepared to greet a man properly—save when they lie sorely wounded from that which others have not denied them. Sooner should a man take the wounds himself, to spare a wench the pain of their presence."

"And bring her the agony of denial in its stead?" demanded Mehrayn, no longer calm. "One does best to stand beside such a wench and give the support of his own blade, and then may he take her joyfully to his furs, knowing her warmth and greeting his alone. As it is his right to stand alone beside her, so is it his right to lie the same."

"So that she will not be too soon used up?" scoffed Ceralt, fists to hips in ridicule. "No man can hope to match the capacity of a woman, for she has merely to receive the while he must be able to give. Sooner would she be used up by wounds, and then her capacity would be nil. What joy in lying beside a wench too badly wounded to be aware of your presence?"

"Wounds most often come to those of little skill, not to warriors born and bred," growled Mehrayn with an icy stare. "A follower of Sigurr knows well of these things, just as he is able to bring full satisfaction to what wench he chooses. No need has he of . . ."

"Brothers, we must not forget the man in the city to the west," said Aysayn with a calm the other males failed to share, stepping quickly between them. My own anger was as great as theirs, and I found myself unable to keep from stepping forward and adding my own voice to the confusion of shout and countershout. Aysayn attempted to soothe me as well, Ceralt and Mehrayn denounced me as I denounced them, arms raised in gestures of anger, and none took note of the strengthening wind which suddenly blew the grass and our hair all about. As I had completely unplaited my hair, Ceralt and Mehrayn found the need to push thick locks of it from their faces, as did I, and only when we were again able to see, did we become aware of the stunned, disbelieving look which had silenced Aysayn. We all of us turned to look

where he did, and were able to see the—*thing* which had
silently appeared upon the grass behind us. As large as a
small city dwelling was it, of metal so bright that it brought
pain to the eye to look upon it, and in no manner had I ever
before seen its like.

"It descended through the air," said Aysayn in a voice so
choked that it was no more than a hoarse whisper. "As a leaf
floats from a tree did it descend, yet so *fast*—!"

No more was he able to say, and no more were we able to
hear; a cloud of vapor shot from the thing, and then was there
darkness all about.

10.

The strangers at last— and truths are discussed

I awoke with great difficulty and filled with anger, for I had dreamed that Ceralt and Mehrayn had indeed sold my use. I pulled myself more firmly from the mists of sleep, and at once became aware of the softness I lay belly down upon, a softness which lacked the smell of a lenga pelt. Indeed was there a strangeness to the odors all about me, a strangeness even greater than that to be found in the cities of males. I forced myself to hands and knees, head hanging down as I strove to open my eyes and regain the aid of sight, and in doing so found that my breech remained upon me, the feel of my leg bands an accompanying presence. My eyes seemed vastly reluctant to open, yet when they did I thought that dreams continued to grip me.

White was the cloth upon which I knelt, a white as pure as the snows to the north, soft and yielding as though there were furs beneath, each yielding place rising again as my weight was removed from it. I had raised one hand from the cloth to learn this, to push back the hair which threatened my vision, and then did I raise my head to look about, and discovered that a vision which was doubted was of little use.

Much did it seem that it was an enclosure in which I knelt, one perhaps three paces by three, seemingly the same in height, clearly an enclosure despite the lack of metal to be seen. In place of metal were there expanses of what almost seemed like maglessa weave, but more easily seen through and without the faint lines of the weave. In the enclosure beside mine, to the left, was Aysayn, sitting with head in hands as though he experienced what difficulty I did in regaining full awareness. The enclosure beyond him held

Ceralt, the next Mehrayn, and both lay upon their white
floors, moving somewhat as they struggled to depart the
darkness. With some little effort I moved to that which
separated me from Aysayn and put one hand upon it, finding
it cool to the touch rather than warm as the air all about. It
was also rigid and unyielding, far from the softness of maglessa
and possessing far greater strength, clearly the reason it was
able to stand unsupported, like the walls of a chamber. Also
clearly would I be unable to pull it down and free myself
from its confinement, yet to what I would have escaped I
knew not. No more was to be seen beyond the forward wall
than an empty chamber, light coming from that which I was
unable to see, walls and floor of a dark orange, the ceiling
white. Perhaps wood or stone lay beneath the brightness of
these colors, yet did it somehow seem more like a strange
metal. If it was there at all and not a dream.

"Are you not able to tear the weave, wench?" came
Aysayn's voice of a sudden, strangely hollow. "Give me
another moment to regain my strength, and we may make the
attempt together."

"The thing is not maglessa weave," I replied, noting the
flatness of my own voice, looking upon him to see that he
now moved his head about to loosen the knots I was able to
feel in my own neck. The male wore his black covering as I
wore my breech, yet were his sword and dagger gone, as
were those of Ceralt and Mehrayn. Coverings, it seemed, had
been left to us, yet not our weapons.

"What else might it be save maglessa weave?" asked the
male, somewhat distressed. "What other thing might appear
so like the weave?"

"I know not," said I, of a sudden noting that the smell of
the air about was not entirely as unknown as I had thought it.
Once before had I smelled something near it, yet had that
been when I had been in Mida's Realm upon this world. Also
had it been the same in Sigurr's Realm, for the short time I
had been able to be aware of it, an odor as though metal
floated unseen in the air. It came to me to wonder, then, how
the two odors might be so near the same—and then was the
answer mine as well, entirely without effort. Those who are

enemies to the gods must surely be gods themselves, had said Ennat, and indeed had the Keeper spoken truth.

"Perhaps this is all unreal and I but dream," said Aysayn, looking about to see what I had seen. "You and I and Ceralt and Mehrayn in a place I have never before come upon—Perhaps they fought, and you as well, and I now seek sleep to deny the loss of all three."

"There was no battle between them, nor did I raise weapon," I corrected the male, seating myself upon the softness so that I might look upon him more easily. "No more occurred than the appearance of a *thing*, and then we slept. Perhaps we should not have so often chided the strangers for failing to arrive."

"I had hoped that that, too, was merely a dream," said he, raising his knees so that he might hang his forearms upon them. "So we have been taken captive by those we were meant to face in battle, and how pleased the gods will be to learn of *that*! Our warriors sit elsewhere, the while *we* walk blindly into their hands!"

"And yet, how might it be so?" I protested, pulling at my hair in annoyance. "Was it not Mida herself who said that the strangers would appear near Bellinard? How might the goddess have been mistaken?"

"Perhaps it was not she who was mistaken," said Aysayn, a thoughtful look to him. "Was it Bellinard the city which was spoken of—or Bellinard the settlement? The settlement, you must recall, was not far from where we were taken."

"It was the city which my Midanna were required to capture," said I, attempting to cast my mind back to the time of discussion with the goddess. "Also was I told of the Sigurri who were held in that city. Mehrayn and the others were indeed found there—yet does it somehow seem that the goddess was unaware of a second Bellinard. How might a goddess be unaware of what occurs in her own world?"

"And how might Sigurr be also unaware?" asked Aysayn, disturbance in the dark of his eyes. "Should your Mida have had the wrong of it, for what reason did he not correct the mistake? Those who were to lead their warriors in battle against their enemies have now been taken captive, and all

through an oversight? Sigurr forgive me the blasphemy, yet I
know of no other way to put the query.''

"Nor I," said I, sharing much of Aysayn's distress. Though
it had been some time since last I had thought of Mida with
reverence, surely did she continue in my eyes to be the
goddess that she was. A goddess may easily be displeased
with one who means to challenge her, and therefore withdraw
her support from that one; yet how might she, through error,
withdraw support from herself? With the Midanna about
Bellinard the city, and Jalav taken near Bellinard the settlement, how were Mida's warriors to stand in defense of their
goddess?

Aysayn and I shared the silence of depression till Mehrayn
and Ceralt had come to themselves, and then did Aysayn
speak to the others of what he and I suspected. Easily was he
able to hear Ceralt, yet I not so easily and Mehrayn not at all.
Mehrayn must speak to Ceralt and Ceralt to Aysayn and then
Aysayn to me if all were to easily hear and be heard, a
cumbersome method of communicating surely meant to disrupt full discussion upon the matter of escape. We none of us
were able to conceive of a manner in which we might depart
that place, for none of us were able to find so much as a hint
of a door leading out. Full solid were the walls of our
enclosures, which neither the strength of the males nor the
most forceful kick taught me by Chaldrin were able to breech.
The others wondered at how we had been placed therein, and
then was it necessary that I speak of the mist used by Mida
and Sigurr to take them about. In no manner had doors been
necessary with the mist, and were our captors not they who
were enemies to the gods? What is possessed by one god may
be possessed by another, and foolish would mortals be to
question that.

Another time of silence passed the while we again examined the enclosure which held us, yet all to no avail. The
walls we had attempted attack upon had scarcely shaken
despite the force of that attack, and Aysayn and I had kicked
together at the wall between us with no more than a handspan
separating the two points of impact. Had the wall been of
wood it would surely have shattered, yet we were merely
bounced away, to sprawl upon the softness we had previously

stood upon. It disturbed me that I had not the skill and strength of Chaldrin, yet was I well pleased that Chaldrin was not with us. Had it been he who failed to breech the wall, surely would the failure have been more keenly felt.

The males had sat themselves upon the white softnesses of their enclosures and I had walked to the far side of mine to look into the nearest empty enclosure, when a section of the far wall beyond our enclosures slid aside to reveal a large number of males and females. These began entering the area at once, their eyes moving from one to the other of us, an air of great excitement clearly upon them. My companions rose to their feet and I moved quickly to the front wall of my enclosure, for never had I seen folk such as these. All were clad alike and in a similar color, yet what that color was was difficult to say. A shimmering, many-hued gray-black did it seem, now a green gray-black, now a blue gray-black, now a red gray-black. The coverings themselves were also odd, fitting to each of those who wore them as the leathers of Ceralt's village folk fit, yet without the separation of chest covering to breech to leg coverings to boots. All of a single piece were they, naught of openings evident, and their boots were of a shiny something, clearly not fur and colored in black.

Beyond their coverings did these folk themselves hold my eye, for even more outlandish than city folk did they appear. Their females—for females they were as their breasts were discernible beneath the tightness of the coverings upon them—wore their hair in many different manners, some so short that even males would not have done the same, some with it about the tops of their shoulders, all seemingly having forced it to stand about in odd postures rather than allowing it to lie flat as hair should. Also were the shades of it rather strange, most especially one of a glaring red. The males, too, seemed to have done the same, and none of them appeared to have ears, though they did. Strangest of all, however, was the size of these strangers, for Mida had been of a size with me, and Sigurr larger yet. They who were enemies to the gods were in no manner the same, for the largest of the males was a good half-head below me, and I a head below the males I journeyed with. Their females were far smaller yet, and much did

I feel as though I stood in capture to no more than warriors-to-be.

"Lord, look at the size of them!" breathed a male who was not among the largest, surely what seemed to be awe in his voice as he looked from one to the other of us. "Even the girl's a giant! And I thought the scout crew had to be exaggerating."

"Probably selective breeding had a lot to do with it," said another male beside the first, mouthing incomprehensibilities the other failed to question. "Take the biggest and the best and mix 'em up, kill off the ones who don't cut it, and that's what you'll get. Pretty damned spectacular, though, and I'll be the first to admit it."

"And I'd be the first to take *that* one aside for a private word or two," said a third male, his eyes moving near to me as though he wished to gaze directly yet dared not. "Everything before her would be nothing but practice, and man, would I like to put that practice to work."

"Who would you borrow the ladder from?" asked the second of the third, he clearly amused. "And what would you do if you got lost?"

"Do you two have to be so vulgar?" asked the red-haired female, turning about to look upon the males with great disapproval. "You're here because you're supposed to be scientists; would you like to be confined to quarters instead, with black marks entered in your records?"

"No, ma'am," replied the second male, considerably crest-fallen, and "Sorry, ma'am," said the third, looking toward the floor, both replies causing the female to nod with satisfaction before turning herself from them again. Though understanding little or naught of what the strangers said, Aysayn and I exchanged looks of surprise. Less than city males did these stranger males seem, for how great a warrior might so small a female be?

Those who stood about and stared were not long left to indulge in their pastime; others appeared in the newly made doorway behind them, paused a moment to look about at those who had come before, then stepped briskly within the chamber. Three females and a hand of males were they, she who led them as large as the largest of all the males, and quickly did those who stood about make way for those newly come.

"What are you all doing here?" demanded the female who led, irritability clear in her voice and manner as she looked about herself. Light of hair and eyes was this female, seemingly well made beneath her covering, her hair no more than twisted about itself rather than forced to stand in some manner like the hair of the others. Her covering was topped by a collar of bright yellow, and then did I see that the collars of the others were of other colors, those of the males most often darker than those of the females.

"With a new ship day about to start, why aren't you people where you're supposed to be?" demanded the female of those about her, causing them all to avoid her gaze. "You'll all get to see these subjects in due time, no need to stand about gawking like tourists."

"You won't be requiring immediate physicals, ma'am?" asked the male who had spoken first, his manner most diffident. Blue was the color of the collar of this roundish male, a blue lighter than that of the other males about him. "We thought you would, so we made certain to. . . ."

"Physicals?" interrupted the female with a laugh of scorn, putting fists to hips as she looked upon the male. "Certainly, Doctor, I'd love to see you conduct a physical. Why don't you just step into the cell with, say, that blond, and start giving him a physical? Take your entire staff if you like."

The male who had spoken moved his eyes to Aysayn, examined the manner in which Sigurr's Shadow stood with arms folded across chest, raised his eyes to look up into the dark gaze which regarded him steadily, then merely stood with widened eyes.

"Exactly," said the female with distant amusement, clearly aware of the discomfort of the male. "You can't expect to work on savages, not until my people and I have tamed them for you. The blood samples we took show them healthy enough and free of infection, and that will have to do for now. Your real work won't start until we have access to the entire population, so you may as well go back to your sick bay. And the rest of you move along, too. We have work to do here, and you're keeping us from it."

Without demurral did those who had come first take themselves off again, she of the strange red hair as well, leaving none save the three females and the hand of males they led, as well as one other. A sixth male had appeared as those who had come first were departing, and once those others were gone, he brought himself into the chamber to join those who remained. Large indeed by stranger standards was this male, nearly of a size with me, the collar of his covering a white such as that which I stood upon. Light of hair was he, with gray eyes set in the squareness of his face, and he halted beside the light-haired female.

"I've sent their belongings to Research and Investigation, so we ought to know the source of that power signal in just a little while," said the male to the female, faint annoyance in the voice of him. "If you weren't such a stickler for Reclamation regs, we would have had it an hour after we had *them*."

"Are you really thinking about trying to steal my thunder, Captain?" the female asked with something of a smile, evidently having comprehended the meaninglessness spoken by the male. "Reclamation is in charge of this project, and I'm in charge of Reclamation. As project Leader all kudos go to me, no matter who discovers what. Waiting to find out about that power source won't matter, not in the long run, and it will probably turn out to be one of the crystals they recently rediscovered. Why waste your time on that when you can be looking at *them*?"

"I'll decide I'm wasting my time when I have that report," returned the male, yet were the words lacking in force for the disagreement they seemed to be. The female had been looking upon Aysayn and Ceralt and Mehrayn, yet the eyes of the male had come to me instead, and examined me with a directness the others had not shown. I returned the light gaze with the little interest I felt, and oddly the male grew amused. "As far as looking at them goes," said he, "that I don't mind in the least."

"Don't be disgusting, Aram," said the female with a glance of disapproval for the male, less than the barest touch of her eyes for me. "I was talking about the unbelievable find they represent, the first in almost a hundred years. Descendants of colonists our own people sent out, retrogressed to the level of utter barbarity, far below any others found in the last two centuries, and I'll be the one remembered as having reclaimed them. I can't wait to get started teaching them.''

"You'd be smarter if you started by finding out if there was anything they can teach *you*," said the male, moving closer to the front wall of my enclosure. "You insisted on playing this according to regulations, Tia, but I don't think you thought the thing all the way through. Can you understand me, girl? What's your name?''

Clearly were the male's last remarks addressed to me, yet had he in some manner increased the annoyance of the female. She left those who had not yet uttered a sound, and moved to the side of the male where he stood before me.

"What do you mean, I didn't think things all the way through?" she demanded, looking up to the male she stood beside. "And stop talking to that female. Don't you realize that barbarian groups like the one these four belong to are male dominated? She's probably their slave, and you'll lose face for all of us by your stupidity."

"Jalav is slave to neither mortal nor god," said I, replying to the sole comment I was able to understand. "Should the stranger female doubt this, she may search for the courage to face her."

"Oh!" exclaimed the female in startlement, raising her eyes to mine with great fluster. The male beside her was deeply amused, a thing which added to the discomfort of the female.

"So much for your slave theory," said the male, sparing the female no more than a glance. "If you'd used your eyes instead of your mouth, you would have noticed that this girl isn't anybody's slave. She meets your eyes too directly, then dismisses you with the arrogance of a Sender. Are you going to accept her offer and face her? You might lose a lot of standing if you don't.''

"Don't be absurd!" snapped the female, a tinge of red continuing to color her cheeks, anger in her eyes. I stood calmly with arms afold as I gazed down upon her, and no more was she able to meet my gaze than a disobedient warrior-to-be. "I'm here to *teach* these barbarians, not get

into fights with them!" said she, now looking solely upon the
male. "Tell me what you meant about my insisting on following regulations."

"It couldn't be simpler," said the male with a shrug,
refusing to move his eyes to the female. "The regulations
you insisted on make you senior to me on this project, but
only as long as you don't make a mistake. If you do make a
mistake, it's to be recorded in the log when you're relieved
by the next highest officer, preferably the captain of this ship,
in other words, me. One slip and you're not only out, Tia,
you're also under. I might even have to put you in the cell
next to hers."

"Why, you miserable, vindictive—*man*!" spluttered the
female, far too outraged to recall my presence, her small fists
clenched as she glared upon the male. "Just because I happened to point out to you last night how little you can expect
to get out of this as opposed to what *I'll* get out of it! You're
jealous, that's what you are, jealous! And you won't get
away with it!"

"The only thing you can do to keep me from getting away
with it is not make any mistakes," said the male, at last
turning his head to look down upon her. "You and the rest of
your bunch insist you can do the job, so get busy and start
doing it. If you're worried about competition, that's just too
bad. In our society competition's the new name of the game,
especially since that's the only way men can get ahead. Prove
you can do the job better than a woman, and they have to
give it to you to keep from starting riots. That's the way I got
to be captain of this ship, and that's the way I'll get everything else I want. Some men don't mind spending their lives
taking orders from women; I do. And I also think I can
handle this better than you will. I don't believe in looking at
people as specimens."

"Well, that happens to be just one of your mistakes,"
returned the female stiffly, greatly affronted by whatever had
been told her. "You can't look at barbarians as anything *but*
specimens, not and keep from sneering at how backward they
are. If you knew anything at all, you'd know that much. As
far as I'm concerned, you can watch me for mistakes all you
like; you won't find any, and you just might learn something.

The procedures I'll be using will be strictly regulation; go ahead and make something out of *that*."

With a final toss of her head the female turned from him, then returned with stiffened back to those who awaited her. The hand of males and two females attended her immediately, and the male before me looked upon me again with a grin.

"If that doesn't make her do something stupid, she really does deserve to have the job," said he in a lowered voice which failed to reach the female. "You seem to follow everything that's being said, but I wonder how much of it makes sense to you. Do you understand what's going on?"

"Jalav understands that she is now in capture to strangers," said I, watching as the female spoke briskly to those about her. "As you are male, perhaps it shall be you who accepts my challenge. Save that you, too, fear to face me."

With the last of my words did I return my gaze to the light-haired male, attempting to bring him sufficient anger through scorn to see myself released from the enclosure. Much was I beginning to believe that never would these strangers stand in answer to a challenge, and indeed did the male's amusement increase rather than decrease.

"Is that the way you always greet strangers?" he asked, raising one arm to rest it upon the maglessa-like material between us. "By challenging them? What if they want to be friends?"

"Those who have no wish to be enemies take care to refrain from taking captives," said I. "Am I to understand that you refuse challenge?"

"For the moment," he agreed with a nod. "Why can't you think of yourself as a guest rather than a captive? Then you'd have no reason to give any challenges."

"Guests are free to come and go as they will," said I, continuing to find difficulty with the outlandish words he spoke. "Allow me to come and go as I please, and then shall challenge perhaps be withdrawn."

"I'll bet you're one hell of a horsetrader," said the male with a laugh of true amusement. "If I give you what *you* want, *maybe* I'll get what I want. I'll have to think about that for a while, but in the meantime I have a question. Tia was

right about the sort of society you have, and I can't help but
wonder who that challenge is coming from. If I decide to
agree to it, who do I have to fight? You or those oversize
boyfriends of yours?''

"For what reason would I give challenge in the name of
another?'' I asked, annoyed that these strangers had no true
concept of honor. "What challenge I give, I alone shall
answer; should Aysayn or Ceralt or Mehrayn wish to face
you, they may give challenge of their own.''

"I see,'' said he, and then did he lower his arm so that he
might turn to look upon Aysayn, who stood so that he might
hear what words were exchanged between the stranger male
and myself. "I take it you're the Aysayn she referred to?'' he
asked. At Aysayn's nod he continued, "Then I'd like to
know what would happen if I agreed to face her. Assuming
you were free at the time, what would you do?''

"I would do naught,'' replied Aysayn, looking upon the
smaller male with faint amusement. "Should it be your wish
to lay down all the burdens of this life, for what reason would
I attempt to dissuade you?''

"Then—you think *she* would win,'' said the stranger male,
grinning at last as though it were Aysayn whose words were
difficult to comprehend. "You think she's better than a man?''

"My sister has taken the lives of many men,'' said Aysayn,
speaking with a quiet pride which warmed me. "To best her
with swords would take a skill few if any possess. Should it
be your decision to face her in such a way, you may judge for
yourself.''

"Swords,'' the stranger male repeated, continuing to look
upon Aysayn. "That wasn't quite what I had in mind. And
you two can't really be sister and brother, so I'm assuming
there's a blood-brother type of relationship between you.
What would happen if. . . .''

"Captain, I thought I made myself clear about not wanting
you to speak to the specimens,'' interrupted the female who
had been named Tia, she and a small number of her followers
approaching. "Since that—female interests you so much,
I've decided to let you do as you please with her, but I
absolutely forbid you to speak to the males. My team and I
don't want our work made any harder. Kira will help you

with the female and make sure you don't blunder too badly, but you're not to go near the others. Do you understand me?''

"Oh, absolutely, ma'am," returned the male in tones most grave, raising one hand strangely to the vicinity of his brow. "Anything you say, Leader.''

"That's something you'd better remember," said the female with a smugness upon her, and then did she turn to look up to Aysayn. "Now, then: How you called, boy? What your name?''

Aysayn looked upon the female and the greater strangeness she now spoke with amusement, yet did he make no effort to reply to her. Little courtesy was there in the manner she had adopted, therefore was there naught of courtesy due in return.

"You not savvy me, boy?" the female then demanded, clearly growing annoyed. "You be plenty scared from what we got, but we not hurt you if you good. You tell me you name and how many boys in you village.''

In no manner did the words of the female convey meaning, and Aysayn quickly lost interest in her mouthings. He and I had both seen that others now attempted speech with Ceralt and Mehrayn, therefore did he take himself off to the far side of his enclosure, to see what they were about. The very last of the female's words were to his departing back, which brought her great indignation.

"Oh! The nerve of that—that—barbarian!" she exclaimed in outrage, then angrily stalked off after one whose patience she would be unwise to try. The male who silently accompanied her followed hurriedly after, however not before casting a final glance toward me.

"And that's the drivel she expects to get somewhere with?" the stranger male before me muttered as he watched her departure, greatly disapproving. "We'll be lucky if she doesn't start a war.''

"Stop being so hard on her, Aram," said the female who had been left behind, her words as soft as the male's had been. Not so large as the other was this female, her pale brown hair worn to her shoulders and bent upwards, her dark eyes large in a slender face. Clearly female was she beneath the covering she wore, and that despite her lack of size.

"It's not her fault if she was born into the wrong family,'' continued the female, looking up toward the male with a calm the first female had lacked. "Her grandmother's a big shot, her mother's a big shot, so *she* has to be one, too. If she'd inherited their Sending talent there would have been no problem, but she didn't so there is. You're just annoyed with her for not being bright enough to keep from bragging to the man she's in bed with."

"A mistake I'm sure you've never made, Kira," returned the male, looking down upon her enigmatically. "Doesn't it bother you that she has the job you should have?"

"In another year or so I'll have my own command," replied the female with a shrug and something of a grin. "My family isn't as important as hers, but then I don't need the help as badly. What I've got I've earned on my own, without the help of anyone, including my mother."

"My mother was usually upset with me," said the male, faint amusement returning to him. "She could never understand why I couldn't settle down the way a man should, but had to have the ambition of a woman. Would you like to meet Jalav?"

"I don't know if I have the nerve," said the female, turning wryly amused eyes upon me. "I know you like them big, Aram, but aren't you overdoing it a little with one like her? She may even have you by an inch or so."

"I thought women were able to appreciate the benefit in size," said the male with a chuckle, then did he, too, turn his eyes to me. "Jalav, this is Kira, a brat of a female who nevertheless knows what she's doing. I'd like you to listen while she explains why we're here."

"I am already aware of the reasons for your presence," I said, looking to both male and female with little warmth. "You think to take us and make us your slaves, yet such a thing shall never be. My Midanna shall not allow it, nor shall the Sigurri."

"But we're not here to make slaves of anyone," protested the female, true upset in the dark of her eyes. "We've come here to help you, to give you the knowledge you would have had if you hadn't gotten cut off from the rest of us so long ago. Your people won't have to suffer and die while they're still young, after a life filled with nothing but privation and the need to fight for what little they have. We've come to make things better for you."

"How shall the lot of Midanna be bettered, should they be deprived of the glory of death in battle?" I asked, disturbed that the stranger female seemed truly sincere. "Without death in battle, the return to life in the Blessed Realm would be pointless, for only those who die in glory may indulge in the pleasure of battle for all eternity. And what of the time we shall spend before death? Is a warrior to spend all of her feyd only hunting, raising weapon in no other way? No warrior would allow such a thing; sooner would she spend her life ending those who would see it so."

The stranger female stood silent before the quiet words I had spoken, large eyes widened even further in upset, and the male, too, appeared disturbed.

"Meaning us," said he, the words quiet as mine and without amusement. "To protect your way of life you'd see us all dead, even if it meant dying yourself. I don't think Tia or anyone else in Reclamation expected such strong objections to our help. You mentioned your Midanna, and something like Sigurri. Who or what are those?"

"The Midanna and the Sigurri are warriors," I said, of a sudden deeming it unwise to mention those in whose names we rode. These stranger folk before me appeared to be naught save pawns to those who were true enemies to the gods, naught save unknowing pets the entity spoken of as Reclamation paraded before us, seeking to put us off our guard. Likely best would be to frighten these pets and send them scurrying for their masters, the sooner to draw them out into facing us in their own selves.

"Jalav is war leader to all the clans of the Midanna," I said, again looking upon both male and female. "Aysayn and Mehrayn lead their Sigurri, male warriors as the Midanna are female, yet greatly skilled nonetheless. Ceralt is High Rider to those village males called Belsayah, scarcely warriors, yet as willing as we to give their lives to cast off the chains of slavery. Should we four be slain, there are others to lead our warriors in our stead."

"Good lord, we picked up the top brass of their armed forces!" said the female, a pained expression clear in the eyes which regarded me, happily not aware of my lie. "If they hadn't gassed them to keep them from panicking, we probably would have lost the entire scout crew."

"That's what happens when you barge in and break up high-level strategy sessions," muttered the male, sending a hand through his hair in vexation. "No wonder your— 'brother' Aysayn has such a high opinion of you. Now what do we do, Kira?"

"We have to make them understand we mean them no harm," said the female, glancing to the male with a look of frustration. "We may have lucked out in picking up the four most influential people in that area, but they'll probably be ten times harder than anyone else to convince. If we do swing them over, though, we can probably avoid a lot of bloodshed. Specifically, ours."

"I'd say that sounds like something worth working for," replied the male, sending a grin to the female who stood beside him. "But how are we supposed to win them over if we keep them locked up in detention cells? Jalav has already told me that in her opinion guests aren't treated like unregenerate criminals."

"Oh, Aram, you can't seriously be talking about letting them out of there," said the female in scoffing, disbelieving disagreement, looking up to meet the eyes of the male. "You heard what the girl said; all they're interested in doing right now is cutting our throats, the sooner the better. If it's all the same to you, I'd like to keep my throat just the way it is."

"And a very pretty throat it is, too," said the male with laughter, putting one finger to the female just above her deep yellow collar. "The only thing wrong with it is the way it tries to avoid admitting what has to be done. How far do you think we'll get convincing them of anything while they believe they're our prisoners? Guests at least pretend to listen to what their hosts are saying; prisoners don't bother."

"Sure they'll listen," nodded the female Kira, folding arms in continuing disagreement. "First they'll listen, and *then* they'll cut our throats. If you think they won't, you're forgetting what sort of culture they come from."

"As a matter of fact, I'm not," said the male Aram, also called Captain, turning his head to regard me. "Jalav, Kira and I can arrange to get you out of that cell, but considering how you feel about us, we aren't sure what you'll do if we let you out. Do your—Midanna—believe in keeping their word once it's given?''

"What warrior of honor would not keep her given word?'' I asked with the great disapproval I felt, yet was I scarcely surprised to be asked such a thing. How might those who serve the enemy be conversant with the demands of honor?

"There you go,'' said the male Aram to the female Kira, an easy grin upon him. "The more primitive the society, the stricter the personal codes of honor. The liar and cheat tends to be wiped out, leaving behind only those who are good to their word. That means we can let her out any time we like.''

"You're overlooking something, Captain Know-It-All,'' returned the female, in some manner less than pleased with the male. "All you've established is that she'll keep her word. Are you forgetting that she hasn't *given* her word?''

"Not at all,'' said the male with a laugh. "She's reasonable enough to make that the easy part. Jalav, if you give us your word not to cause any trouble, we can let you out of there right now. What do you say?''

"You believe I would betray those who follow me and those who ride with me, merely to be freed from captivity?'' I asked with true ridicule, finding no insult in the words of one lacking all concept of honor. "Perhaps the male Aram Captain Know-It-All also believes he speaks with one of the cities.''

"The easy part, huh?'' said the female Kira with a greatly amused laugh to the male who had abruptly lost his own amusement to look pained, then did the female turn to me. "Jalav, we're not asking you to betray anyone,'' said she in an earnestly urging tone. "We would just like an opportunity to show you that we're not as bad as you're all picturing, that we only want to help your people. Can't we call a truce of some sort until we've explained things to you, a temporary peace that won't mean you've made any promises you don't want to make? You'll only have to listen, and if after listening you decide that you still feel the way you do now, we'll simply bring you back here and the truce will be over. Is that something you can accept?''

So small was the female, far smaller than Rogon who was small among the Midanna, yet did she possess something of Rogon's strength and humor. These stranger folk were pawns, I knew, having learned naught of honor from those they served, yet was it possible that they might be made to see what lacks their lives contained, what more might be had from committing themselves to a proper cause. This thought made me pause, and into the breech stepped the female Tia.

"This is absolutely impossible!" she fumed, striding angrily into the midst of the other two stranger folk, failing to see that they were occupied with something other than her distress. "That blond one won't even admit I'm alive, and the other two are worse! That black-haired beast said something about how women need to be taught their place, and the red-head agreed and said the best place was something he called a use-floor for temple slaves! They won't answer any of my questions, and keep asking how many 'warriors' I have! I'm going back to my cabin to check my copy of regulations. If there's anything I can legally use to teach them some manners, I'll do it!"

The female ended her words with a firm nod then took herself off, having given not a single glance to those she supposedly addressed, the third female and hand of males hurrying in her wake. The male Aram and female Kira exchanged a look of mild amusement, then returned their eyes to me.

"I have not the right to speak for any save the Midanna," said I to the questioning in the paired gaze, again folding my arms as I returned their regard. "Should your offer of a truce be accepted, the Sigurri must be allowed to speak for themselves."

"There goes that horsetrading again," sighed the male, yet the meaningless comment did not seem refusal. "I can appreciate your point, Jalav, and that's what's bothering me. We do have to talk to more than just you, but if we try letting all of you out, Tia will throw a fit. How about you and just one of the Sigurri? But we'd have to have the word of both of you."

"Should we agree, you shall have the word of both," said

I with a nod of satisfaction. "I shall discuss the matter with the others, and then inform you of our decision."

" 'Don't call us, we'll call you,' " muttered the female Kira, and then did she smile at a hidden amusement. "Suppose the Captain and I wait on the far side of the room until this discussion is over? I can't say I'm crazy about the idea of including one of those monsters in on this deal, but if Aram gets to have what to look at, I should be entitled to at least as much. Do you mind if we wait?"

"Should that be your wish, you may wait," said I with a shrug, seeing the amusement which had returned to the male beside Kira. "Our decision may perhaps be quickly arrived at."

"I'm beginning to really hate that word 'perhaps,' " said the male, his unexplained amusement increasing. "Every time I hear it I feel like a child being told that 'maybe' he'll get what he wants—if he's good. When the decision gets made, just call us back."

The two stranger folk turned then and walked to the far wall of the chamber, halting beside the place a door had been made to appear, their backs to the enclosures the others and I stood in. I waited no longer than to see that before looking toward Aysayn to find that he had again come to the mageless wall between us, the few words heard by him having put questioning in the dark of his eyes. I gestured to him to accompany me to the rear of our enclosures, then seated myself cross-legged very near to the wall the while he did the same. Had it been possible to speak to Ceralt and Mehrayn as well I would have done so, yet was such a thing then impossible.

"The strangers have requested a truce," said I to Aysayn, attempting to keep my voice from carrying to any save he. "They would speak to us concerning the reason for their being here, seeking to enlist us in the cause they serve for their masters. They wish us to give our word as to their safety during this truce, for they mean to see two of us freed."

"They would enlist *us* in their cause?" asked Aysayn with amusement, his voice now a soft hollowness. "And you believe there are others whom they serve, others we have not as yet seen?"

"Having encountered the foolishness of the female Tia, are you able to doubt it?" I asked with full contempt, again attempting to pull the hair from beneath me. "Those others who have chosen to speak with me are not of the same ilk, therefore has it come to me that they may be persuaded to call forth their masters—or, perhaps, be made to see the greater honor and glory in following another. They have made no mention of those we ride for, therefore have I done the same. Also must it be realized that should the truce produce naught save time gone in useless effort, it will be ended with our return here. Honor demands that we refrain from attack during a period of truce, yet once it has ended . . ."

"Honor no longer binds us," said Aysayn with a slow nod to complete the words I had left unspoken. "Those who were left confined may then be freed, and once reunited all four might then recover their weapons. Have they named the two who are to be released?"

"Myself and one other," I said, "a Sigurri. The strangers fear males, yet do they look upon this Midanna with naught save dismissal despite their words of supposed caution. Both see only a female."

"The blind may not be given blame for their lacks," said Aysayn with deeper amusement, seeing at once that such blindness would be the undoing of the strangers. "Ceralt will not be pleased to be excluded, yet so shall another of us be the same. Am I to accompany you, or Mehrayn?"

"You believe I would have Mehrayn?" I asked with ridicule, annoyed to see Aysayn's continued amusement. "Have I not given my word that I shall not choose between those two? In naught save battle shall I accept one beside me, and the time for battle has not yet come."

"The decision is entirely yours, sister," said Aysayn with a chuckle, preparing himself to rise. "Should it be your wish to be thrown to the shoulder of one of them and carried off despite your protests, none have the right to deny you. I shall inform the others of what we are about."

He rose then and walked to where Ceralt waited within his own enclosure, and the two sat and were quickly in the midst of converse. No single word was I able to hear, but I was able to see Mehrayn in the last of the enclosures, his eyes upon Ceralt and Aysayn, his impatience clear in the presence of his palms to the maglessa wall. The annoyance given me by Aysayn attempted to rise within me to the level of true anger, yet is the warrior who falls to anger amidst enemies, from whatever cause, a fool. I turned upon the white softness beneath me to stretch out upon my right side, legs somewhat bent, elbow supporting weight, hair again draped about me, back to the males. Thrown to the shoulder of one and carried off indeed!

Not long was the time which passed in discussion. The strangers had continued to remain beside the far wall of the outer chamber, doing naught save speaking softly to one another the while the male Aram opened yet another door in the wall, this time a far smaller door. From within the opening did he withdraw a contrivance which appeared to be leather, and then was the opening once again concealed. The contrivance he held was then placed about his middle, as though he donned a swordbelt, yet was the thing thicker and wider than any swordbelt, and also was it constructed in error to be that. Save for those few whose left hands contained more skill than their right, the scabbard for a warrior's sword hung to her left, where she might draw her weapon with ease. The scabbard of this odd swordbelt hung to the male's right, far too short for any sword I had ever seen, longer than the daggers preferred by Midanna. Also was it secured to the male's thigh with a strap, which caused it to be held stiffly in place. Within the short scabbard was there a thing seemingly made of metal, perhaps a metal heavy enough to cause harm if thrown. I snorted softly in contempt as this thought came to me, for if such was the concept of a weapon to these strangers, it would be one with the balance of their thoughts and doings so far shown us. When once the contrivance was in place upon the male, he turned from the wall to look again toward our enclosures, saw the words being exchanged by Aysayn and Ceralt, then brought his gaze to me. His head raised somewhat as he regarded me, and from then on no further words were exchanged between himself and the female Kira.

A short time later a tap sounded upon the maglessa wall behind me, and I sat up and turned about to see that Aysayn crouched beside the wall between us. Ceralt stood to the far wall of his enclosure nearly shoulder to shoulder with Mehrayn, and none save Aysayn appeared in any manner pleased.

"Our brothers have now been informed of our intentions," said Sigurr's Shadow, a look of anticipation to the set of his body. "They would both of them prefer to accompany you, yet am I preferable to one without the other. We must see this matter of the strangers quickly done with, so that all may return to more serious concerns such as courting."

"The male Aysayn finds himself greatly amused," I observed as I took myself to my feet, raising my eyes to his as he straightened as well. "Best would be that he understand that the Harra would find themselves as easily able to make slaves of three as two."

I turned from his soft chuckling to walk to the front wall of my enclosure, and those who awaited a decision straightened where they stood, understanding that the decision they awaited was at hand. When I gestured them to me they came with an odd sort of eager hesitation, and when they stood again before the maglessa wall, the male Aram smiled faintly.

"If the Union ever has royalty, and that royalty ends up in a detention cell, I now know what they'll look like," said he, seemingly indulging an ever-present need for obscurity. "I take it you've made up your minds?"

"We have made the decision to agree to your request for a truce," said I, speaking the thing in words more readily understandable, wondering in passing at the wry amusement to be seen upon the face of the female Kira. "Aysayn and I shall hear your words, yet no more do we pledge than that."

"That's all we want you to do," said the male Aram, pleased satisfaction now upon him. "And your agreeing to the truce means you won't be trying to give your lives for the sake of home and mother? Or taking ours in the same good cause? Both of you?"

"He means he wants to know if we have your words that there won't be any trouble," said the female Kira with a small sigh of exasperation when she saw my frown indicating lack of understanding. "Not being warriors, we'll feel better if we hear you say it."

"We give our word to abide by the truce till the time of

our return to these enclosures," said I, somewhat amused at the need for reassurance shown by these stranger folk. So small were their skills with weapons, then, that they required oaths of peace when in the presence of warriors.

"And you?" said the female to Aysayn, looking up to him where he stood to my left, within his own enclosure. "Just to make us feel better."

"I pledge the same as my sister," returned Aysayn, looking down beyond folded arms upon the small stranger female, his amusement in the brightness of his eyes. "The truce will hold till we are returned to these enclosures."

"That's it, then," said the male Aram, now more eager than hesitant. "Let's get them out of there, Kira."

"Sure, out, but out to where?" asked the female, reaching into the side of her covering by her hip for a flat piece of—something—which seemed neither metal nor cloth. Perhaps the length of a hand was it, red in color, with two small squares of white upon it. "If we give them the Grand Guided Tour half the personnel on this ship will faint, and the other half will run screaming for Tia. I don't know how much time we'll have with them before she finds out anyway, but I'd like it to be as long as possible."

"Don't waste your time worrying about Tia," said the male in answer, lacking the concern of the female. "I've already got her covered, or soon will have. Right now we'll take them to my cabin—unless you'd like to volunteer your own?"

"Yours will do," said the female, her glance at the male of very short duration before she turned to hold the device in her hand somewhat before her. "I'd hate to make you trek all the way to mine when you find you can't hold out any longer. Here goes nothing."

The thumb of the female then touched the lower square of white upon the device, whereupon both she and the male were of a sudden more distinct to the eye than they had been. I knew not the reason behind such a happening till it came to me that the air before me was also cooler, and then did I see that a portion of the front maglessa wall of my enclosure no longer remained where it had been. A doorway had appeared in the wall, without indication of where the section previously there had gone, a doing not far removed from the mist used by both Mida and Sigurr. The male and female retreated a pair of steps as I raised a hand to assure myself that departure was indeed no longer denied me, then did they keep their eyes closely upon me as I emerged into the chamber. Wary was the look they bent upon me, as though doubting their safety despite the assurance given them, a doing fit for those who followed the enemy. Had I not agreed to the truce I might well have allowed the insult I felt free rein, however I had indeed agreed to the truce. I therefore turned from them with deliberate calm, and merely stood awaiting the release of Aysayn.

It was necessary for the female to position herself before Aysayn's enclosure as she had done before mine, in order to see Sigurr's Shadow freed. His doorway appeared as mine had done, without sound and nearly without notice, yet not immediately before him. It was necessary that he walk toward Ceralt's enclosure before he might emerge, and this he did with a caution approaching that of the strangers. Once emerged he looked about himself with faint curiosity and calm, and those who had retreated somewhat before him attempted to recapture the eager satisfaction they had earlier shown.

"Well, it looks like we're all ready to go," said the male Aram, trying to hide the fact that his right hand hung very near to the short scabbard at his side. "Kira, why don't you lead the way, our guests will follow, and I'll bring up the rear."

"That sounds like a good idea," responded the female with an odd smile, her hands held together before her. The device she had used had been returned to her covering, its presence apparently no longer required. "Is it my imagination, or are they bigger now than they were inside the cells?"

"Just remember that everyone in range of a stun charge is exactly the same size," said the male truly amused by the female. "You have their words that there won't be any trouble and now you can add mine to it, so just calm down and start thinking about what to say once we get to my cabin."

"You expect thinking about what to say is going to *calm* me?" the female Kira asked, yet with more amusement than she had previously felt. "The more I understand how important this is, the closer I come to losing the language entirely. Well, nothing ventured, nothing gained. Let's play follow the leader.''

With a gesture to Aysayn and myself the female then moved toward and through the doorway to the chamber, slowly enough so that she might be followed. Aysayn moved after her without hesitation, but I paused to look upon those who remained confined in enclosures, pleased to have them so despite the circumstances. Both stood before the front walls of their enclosures, Ceralt appearing vexed with both hands closed to fists at his sides, Mehrayn with great displeasure in the green of his eyes, arms afold across his chest. I showed the amusement I felt at their continued plight, bringing them true anger, then did I turn and follow leisurely after Aysayn.

''You enjoy living dangerously, don't you?'' remarked the male Aram as he brought himself after me, then moved to walk to my right. The area beyond the chamber was narrow, unadorned, and seemingly all of silvery metal, the feel of it beneath my bare feet odd indeed. ''The rest of your party seemed to be unhappy about more than just being left locked up, and if you didn't give them the horselaugh before walking out, I need to be relieved from my post for hallucinations. If there hadn't been an unbreakable wall between you and them, there's nothing that would have kept them from coming after you. Is there any particular reason why you did that?''

''You ask my reasons for angering Ceralt and Mehrayn, do you not?'' said I, attempting to take meaning from all which had gone before. When the male nodded with rueful understanding that his words had been without full meaning for me, I felt some small sense of satisfaction. ''I gave anger to them for they have earned such anger, attempting to make demands upon me which no Midanna would countenance nor allow. I, who am war leader to all the Midanna, may not be looked upon as no more than city slave-woman.''

The male watched to be sure that we followed along the hall of metal in the wake of the female Kira and Aysayn, yet did he seem as eager to look only upon me.

''You mean they tried to—take advantage of you?'' he asked, an odd look to him. When he saw his words were

again incomprehensible, he groped a moment then added,
"Tried to—you know, force you to have sex with them."

"They attempted to force me to choose between them,"
said I, unsure that this time I answered what he asked. "Both
desire the possession of one who has ever had her own
possession of those males about her, one who has no wish to
choose between them. They believe I might be taken despite
my will to the contrary, in the same manner each of them
have used in the past, and also seek to have me believe they
will not face one another with swords should I obey them and
choose one over the other. They will indeed face one another
in such an event, and all about them know it."

"Wait a minute, I don't think I'm catching all this,"
muttered the male, using one hand to rub at his face. "Are
you saying they're trying to make you accept one of them on
a permanent basis, and don't care that you don't want to?
That if you did choose one of them they would fight anyway,
and if the one you didn't choose won, you'd have to accept
him instead? That he would force you to accept him instead?"

"Indeed," said I, hoping my agreement was to the thoughts
I believed I agreed to. "Each of those males has had me as
captive and each believes it might be done again. City slave-
women obey the commands of those males about them, and
these two believe the same may be done with me."

"I'll be damned," said the male, looking toward the female Kira, who had halted with Aysayn before a wall of
metal somewhat different from those other walls all about.
We had reached them some moments earlier, and the female,
too, had heard the last of my words.

"Stop looking so impressed," said the female to the male
Aram, her amusement evident. "You knew this was a male-
dominated culture, so what did you expect? Jalav sounds like
she has the right attitude for being civilized, though. You're
not going to let them get away with that nonsense, are you,
Jalav?"

"I shall certainly not allow them their will," said I, again
hoping I answered what was asked. "Should the need arise, I
shall myself face them with swords."

"You believe they will agree to face you with weapons?"
asked Aysayn with a sound of ridicule, looking upon me with

something close to annoyance. "They would no more raise weapon to you than I, and sooner would I do such a thing. One of them will have you, wench, and it would be best that you consider how they may be kept from facing one another once you have been claimed."

"She has to do no such thing!" said the female Kira with great indignation before I, myself, might reply, looking up toward Aysayn with fists to hips. "No woman has to accept a man she doesn't want, and that's the law! She doesn't even have to let him make a pass at her if she doesn't want to. Without her permission, all he can do is talk to her! If those two want to beat each other to pulp like idiots, why should *she* care?"

"Kira, what law are you talking about?" asked the male Aram, drawing the angry gaze of the female to him. "These people don't live under Union laws, and probably won't until a full generation grows up under them. The men here take what they want, and the women have no choice but to go along with it. And those two men back there aren't going to fight with their hands, they're going to use swords. If they fight, one of them will die."

"But that's stupid," said the female, her anger lost beneath frowning bewilderment, her eyes on the male Aram. "Why would they want to kill someone else or die themselves for something so unimportant? It doesn't make sense."

"Why do they automatically equate 'stranger' with 'enemy'?" asked the male, his voice gentle yet implacable. "Why would they be in the middle of attacking us if we didn't have a truce arranged? When you get down to the very basics of existence, that's the sort of thought and action you find, something I've read about but wouldn't have believed if I'd never come here. To us it's something we've studied; to them it's the only way of life they know."

"But I still don't understand why they would try to kill each other over a woman," returned the female in exasperation, truly unable to comprehend what she spoke of. "No man as attractive as those two would have to worry about finding *some* woman to accept him, and would probably even have his choice. And why bother in the first place, when

the woman involved has already said she won't· accept either
of them? What can they possibly think they'll get out of it?"

"What they'll get out of it is the woman they want," said
the male, amusement to be seen in his eyes as he looked
down upon the female. "Try to understand, Kira, that the
men of this culture don't wait to be chosen and accepted, they
do the choosing and accepting themselves. You keep talking
about male-dominated cultures; what do you think male-
dominated means?"

"I know what male-dominated means," said the female,
nearly in a growl and nearly returned to her former anger.
"But knowing about it doesn't mean I have to like it. Jalav
won't stand for it, and neither would I."

"But Jalav is a warrior," said the male with a smoothness
which seemed designed to cover the greater amusement he
felt, unseen by the female as she had turned to press impa-
tiently upon a section of the wall we had halted before. "And
according to Aysayn, even she won't get away with it. What
chance do you think *you'd* have?"

"Who says she won't get away with it?" demanded the
female, turning quickly back to glare at the male. "You? You
don't know any more about it than the rest of us. Aysayn?
He's just the least bit prejudiced on the male side, don't you
think? My money is on Jalav—especially if she gets a little
help."

"What do you mean, a little help?" said the male, no
longer amused, taking no note of the small chamber which
had been abruptly brought to view by the sliding back of the
section of the wall we stood before. The female Kira turned
and stepped forward into the small chamber, gestured to
Aysayn and myself to join her, then sent a smile of secret
amusement to the male Aram.

"Well, that's what we're here for, isn't it?" asked Kira,
looking upon the male as he, too, entered the chamber. "To
give the people of this world help? What's wrong with my
doing what we came here to do?"

"We're supposed to be giving *all* the people our help, not
just the women," returned the male, touching a white square
which stood among other colored squares upon the chamber
wall to his right, as he faced us. The wall which had opened

to admit us to the chamber closed once more, confining us all within, yet the stranger folk seemed undisturbed. I sent a glance to Aysayn as he did the same with me, yet neither of us chose to speak upon the matter. Perhaps it was necessary to the customs of the strangers to be confined within a small chamber with those with whom they had executed a truce; should that be so, it would be idle to remark upon the thing. "If you try playing dirty, Kira," said the male Aram, "this isn't going to work out well at all."

"What's the matter, Captain, are you getting worried?" asked the female, smiling upon the male in a very abrasive manner, her hands clasped behind her. "Afraid you'll be losing some vicarious thrills and excitement? Or did you have something else in mind? Just remember: if you can't compete, get out of the game."

"You know, Kira, you're absolutely right," said the male, folding his arms as he looked down upon her, an odd calm having returned to him. "I'd almost forgotten that competition is the name of the game. I appreciate the reminder, and I'll also make sure you don't have to say it again."

He turned then to present his back to the small female, his calm continuing undisturbed, and the female looked upon that back with a frown of great suspicion. Much did it seem that she had garnered as little from the words of the male as had I, and also did it seem that she considered words of her own; before she might speak them, however, the wall which had closed again slid aside, and the male Aram strode forth out of the chamber.

When Aysayn and I were also directed forth by the female Kira, he and I again exchanged looks, this time of greater surprise and deeper lack of understanding. The area of corridor which we had left no more than moments earlier had in some manner been completely changed, so completely that surely did it appear to be another corridor entirely. No longer were the walls of the corridor silver, nor were those walls unbroken. Amid a background of light tan were a number of doors of white to be seen, and also was there a floor covering of tan beneath our feet. Also had the light brightened about us, as though a greater number of candles or torches had been lit, yet were neither candles nor torches evident to the eye.

We followed slowly as the male Aram led us to the left of the small chamber, looking all about us in confusion, and the female Kira brought herself to walk beside me.

"We're not likely to find anyone still hanging around their cabin at this time of the morning," said she, also looking back toward that area from which we'd come. "As soon as we have you two inside, we'll be safe for a while."

The female then looked toward the male Aram where he had paused before the white door at the very end of the corridor, awaiting us expectantly. I, however, was becoming annoyed. So familiar did the words of the stranger folk seem, and yet how difficult they were to make full sense of! What might a "cabin" or a "morning," be, and were we not already within, or, as the female had put it, "inside"? Was the safety they sought a safety from the wrath of their masters, or from those who were personal enemies? So few were those words to raise so large a number of questions, and so difficult was it growing to keep from betraying my foul mood. Aysayn merely looked about himself with calm curiosity, and this, too, I found to be annoying.

When we reached the male Aram he touched a place upon the wall beside the door, then led us within when the door slid aside. I entered behind him, wondering what would have been done to the corridor when we again emerged, and saw a chamber which was well suited to these stranger folk. Smooth were the white walls of the place, smoother even than the stone of the walls in the palace of the High Seat, no silk nor candle sconces to be seen upon them anywhere. Instead were there renderings hung here and there, renderings of a strange city grown many times the size of Bellinard in height, of a small valley as seen from the top of the mountain which overlooked it, of a female who seemed extremely pleased with some matter. Also were there renderings which held as little reason as the speech of the strangers, no more than color and line and shape all intertwined together. About the walls of this chamber were also two small platforms called tables, and a number of odd seats stood about with them upon the dark green of the floor cloth. No leather covered these seats but cloth, a cloth which was white with certain other colors upon it, principally dark green. Perhaps a third of the size of my reception chamber in the palace of the High Seat was it, and the female Kira looked about with as much curiosity as Aysayn and I.

"Not bad, Aram, not bad at all," said Kira, allowing her gaze to fleetingly touch upon those things about her. "I didn't know you had as much room as Tia and myself. I thought men's quarters were smaller."

"You're forgetting that this is the captain's cabin, and that captains are usually women," said the male Aram, looking upon the female as she continued to look about. "If you were curious about it, though, all you had to do was ask. I would have been more than happy to show it to you."

"The way you're currently showing it to Tia?" asked the female, turning to look directly upon the male. "Entertaining the assistant project Leader wouldn't do nearly as much for you as entertaining the project Leader herself, so why would you bother? Mustn't waste all that precious effort, after all."

"She's the one who came to me," returned the male in what was nearly a growl, his skin darkening in apparent discomfort despite the hardened look in his light eyes. "When a project Leader insists, even a captain has to go along with it; ambition isn't involved and never was. If you had been willing to hear more than just conversation from me, you would have found that out a long time ago. And it still isn't too late."

"I don't like crowds, and I don't like standing in line," said the female, continuing to hold the gaze of the male. "Maybe when Tia gets tired of you, I'll think about it—if you haven't been accepted by someone more interesting in the meantime." Briefly did the eyes of the female come to me, and then did she begin taking herself toward the door we had entered by. "I'll make sure the other subjects are fed, and then bring back something for our—guests."

Quickly did the female depart the chamber without a further backward look, and the door closed the opening behind her as though acting of itself. Where the one who opened and closed the doors and walls was I knew not, nor was I able to see a space large enough to hold such a one. I looked more closely upon the walls beside what had been the door, think-

ing to find some small indication of the leather which moved
it, and the male Aram made a sound of deep vexation.

"Damned, illogical females," he growled angrily. "First
they stack the deck against a man, then they blame *him* when
he has no choice but to go along with the deal. What I
wouldn't give for just one hour—!"

"The wench takes your fancy, does she not?" asked Aysayn
of the male Aram, speaking when the other broke off and
failed to resume. "For what reason do you allow her to refuse
you in such a manner? Is she forbidden you by your gods?"

"She's forbidden me by more than gods," said the male
with a snort of something like amusement, yet did he continue vexed. "According to the laws of our culture, I can't
even touch her hand unless she tells me I can, but a woman
of higher rank can drag *me* into bed. I'm free to refuse being
dragged, of course, but only if I'm not interested in seeing
my career move ahead beyond the point it's already reached.
And what do I do with myself once I refuse? Spend all night
and half the day in cold showers? If a man starts refusing
what's offered him, he soon finds it isn't being offered
anymore—by any female. Why don't you two sit down and
help me figure out why I didn't choose piracy as a career?"

The male gestured toward the odd seats which stood about
the chamber, then himself took a narrow, armless seat which
stood behind him. Aysayn chose a seat with arms which
appeared as though it had fed more often and more completely than that which the male Aram had chosen, yet was I
of a mind to see myself with more room about me. Wide was
one of the seats, as though more than one was meant to sit
upon it, and that was what I chose as my own. Softer than
what I had anticipated did it prove to be, taking my bottom
easily and accepting my back in a similar manner, and then
did it come to me to wonder if beneath the seat was where the
one who opened doors might be found. I therefore leaned far
forward to look beneath the thing I sat upon, parting my
knees so that I might do so more easily, yet was able to see
naught save emptiness before my hair fell all about, blocking
the light. A sound of greatly amused laughter came from the
male Aram, and when I raised my head once more, I found
his eyes upon me.

"If you'd like to tell me what you're looking for, maybe I can help you find it," said the male, his light eyes filled with his amusement. "There are no hidden cameras or microphones, if that's what you're worried about."

"I merely seek the place of the one who opens doors," said I, throwing my hair back from about my arms with the annoyance I felt over the obscurity the male continued to indulge in. "And for what reason do those in this place not open doors with the strength of their own arms? Are you so weak, then, that you are unable to do so?"

"You're looking for the one who opens doors," said the male, and although he seemed much at a loss, also did he seem delighted. "No wonder you don't understand half of what I'm saying. I wonder what you would do if I offered to show you my bedroom—you do know what a bedroom is?"

"Should you speak of a bed chamber, I know it for the place those of the cities take their rest," said I, this time finding comprehension in the words of the male, yet none in his intent. "For what reason would a doing be required of me were I to see the place you take your rest?"

"My sister has not truly learned the doings of cities," said Aysayn to the male Aram, his amusement both light and deep. "Nor have you learned what is needful of those wenches called Midanna. Men are most often taken by them for use, a thing known far too well by Ceralt and Mehrayn, and also myself. Is this what you seek? To be used by the one who is war leader to all Midanna?"

"You mean *she* would—take the advantage?" asked the male Aram, incredulous and somewhat indignant. "The women of my own culture may get to decide who shares their beds with them, but at least they don't try taking over once they're in those beds! Doesn't any man ever get the best of these—Midanna?"

"Indeed," said Aysayn, chuckling at the manner in which the other male showed his indignation. "Should a man find himself able to avoid the speed of her blade and withstand the strength of her attacks, he may then take what pleasure he wills. With this wench he would then also need to face Mehrayn and Ceralt, yet would the pleasure he took be adequate recompense for such disaccommodation. The wench is able to give great pleasure."

"Disaccommodation," echoed the male Aram with a short, thin laugh of ridicule. "Massacre would be more like it, and all for the privilege of being—'taken for use'? I think I owe you my thanks for saving what little pride I have left, Aysayn."

"For what reason would you look upon Jalav with thoughts of use, when the one called Kira is your true interest?" asked Aysayn, his dark eyes upon the discomfort of the other male. "My sister is indeed toothsome and luring, yet is one easily able to see that you look upon her to keep from looking upon the other. Your words of explanation concerning the reasons you may not take her meant naught to me."

"I wish they meant the same to me," replied the male Aram with a sigh, leaning forward to rest his arms upon his thighs, hands clasped before him. "She's very independent—very much interested in seeing to her own affairs—and won't even let me tell her how much I want her. If she won't listen, what can I do?"

"The wench has greater strength than you?" asked Aysayn, calm words covering the ridicule he undoubtedly felt. "Her size exceeds your own? Should there be a thing you wish to speak of to her, take her aside and command her to listen. Should she refuse to hear you out, beat her and then begin again."

"In what place might I find my sword?" I interrupted, keeping my eyes upon Sigurr's Shadow. That he would speak so like other males brought me great anger, yet did he bring his eyes to me and gesture aside my insult.

"I speak only of this man and the wench he covets," said Aysayn, unaware of the deep discomfort with which he was then being looked upon by the other male. "The women of this place all seem greatly in need of a beating, to teach them to speak to those about them with courtesy, if naught else. Do you feel the need to take sword in hand to stand in protection of ones such as they?"

It was clear then that the female Tia had brought great annoyance to Aysayn, a male who, in the manner of Midanna, had fought and slain to achieve his place. One may speak any words one wishes to another, yet only if one is willing to defend those words with a sword. These stranger folk were not of that ilk and Aysayn, the Shadow of Sigurr upon this world, was displeased.

"Jalav feels no need to defend ones such as they," I allowed, folding my legs before me upon the seat I had chosen. "The male you address, however, seems of another mind."

"Is this so?" asked Aysayn, looking again upon the male Aram, whose upset had not yet eased. "You would keep these wenches from what their sharp tongues have earned them?"

"It's not as easy as you make it sound," said the male Aram, the complaint in his voice nearly pleading. "I'm not saying I haven't had the same urge myself from time to time, but there's the law to consider, and Kira herself. . . ."

"Then perhaps you are after all meant to go unheeded," said Aysayn, looking upon the male with naught of pity and understanding. "As there are so many excellent reasons between you and your desires, best would be that you leave the wench Kira for another."

The male Aram straightened in what was closely akin to insult, his stumbling words no longer forthcoming, his gaze completely upon Aysayn, yet no further was to be exchanged between the two. Again the door to the chamber slid aside, and the female Kira reappeared carrying a number of things odd in appearance. These she brought to the small platform beside the stranger male, then turned to him once they were upon it.

"I had to tell the galley crew I was entertaining," said she, a look of great amusement to her. "It's a good thing I only needed food for two, or there could have been talk. Did I miss anything while I was gone?"

"Nothing much," replied the male, throwing off the look of anger brought him by the first of the female's words. "Jalav's been looking around, and tells me that what she's looking for is 'the one who opens doors.' I thought I'd leave that one for you to field."

"Thanks, pal," responded the female with a sound much like dismayed amusement, then did she take on a look of vexation. From the large—pouch, it might perhaps be called, though made of something other than leather—she withdrew a small, round thing like the larger round things she had carried in her arm, then two things which seemed similar to goblets, though without their stems, and looked again upon the male Aram. "I'll give these to Jalav and see if I can answer her question, and you give the rest to Aysayn. There's toast and juice and coffee in the bag for him too, which should back up the ham and eggs and home fries on the platter. I have a feeling they're both going to need more than this to stay alive, though."

At the male's nod the female turned to me with her burdens, coming close to seat herself beside me. The large round thing was handed to me with a smile, and I was then able to see that it was of a substance somewhat like leather yet drier and rougher, stiff yet without too great a brittleness. Also was it, like the others of the things she carried, covered over with a skin more like maglessa weave than the walls of my enclosure had been. Soft and yielding was the skin, and easily seen through, and although it clung tightly all about the outer edge of the round thing, there was no doubt it might be broached without undue effort. Beneath the skin, lying upon the round thing, was that which might well have been provender, yet was it scarcely appetizing in appearance, and perhaps enough to fill a very young warrior-to-be.

"First you pull the wrap off, and then you can start eating, Jalav," said Kira, reaching to the skin upon the small round thing she continued to hold, tearing it easily from where it clung. "If you're thirsty, you can start with this juice."

One of the goblet-like holders was then given me, and below the maglessa skin was a dark yellow, cloudy liquid to be seen. Much sooner would I have gone hungry in that place of strangers, yet had I agreed to a truce—and the hospitality which ever accompanies a truce such as that one. One allows one's enemy to be one's host only when that enemy is known to be honorable—or when one is willing to give one's life to prove their dishonor. It was not my life I then sought to give, yet was there no honorable way I might refuse. I sent a glance to Kira, saw her smiling nod, then pulled away the maglessa skin and tasted of the thing called "juice."

"It can't be that bad," said Kira with a laugh, clearly referring to the expression she was able to see upon me. "I had some of that this morning myself, and I thought it was pretty good."

"Perhaps—it was meant for those who are not yet warriors," said I, continuing to taste naught save the very great sweetness of the liquid. To criticize what is given one by one's host is to give insult, yet these stranger folk seemed unprepared to feel insult over such a thing.

"Maybe it was," agreed the female with no more than a small lessening of her amusement, taking the holder and offering the small round thing which had had the skin taken from it in place of the holder. "I hope you like the rest of the meal more than you did the beginning of it."

My hopes joined those of the stranger female, for I would not have appeared dishonorable before those who had no true understanding of honor of their own, yet was it a near thing. That which lay beneath the skin upon the large round thing I held was provender in name alone, tasteless, barely warm, and seemingly prepared many hind, if not feyd, earlier. That which was held by the female was light baked grain, yet had it been burned in some manner and also tasted aged. The second liquid holder contained that which tasted much like the rangi drunk by those of the villages, yet was it lightened in some manner and sweetened as well; in the name of honor did I consume all which had been put before me, yet did I speak silent words in gratitude that there was so little of it. Had there been more, surely would I have shamed myself.

"Well, now that we've got you and Aysayn fed, I think it's time we move on to the reason we brought you here in the first place," said the female Kira as she took the last of the emptied holders from me. Aysayn, I saw, had done the same as I, yet had he been able to finish the liquid called "juice" as well. It came to me then that the male truly had greater strength than I, yet was I not of a mind to envy such strength and wish it for my own. Certain strengths are best left to those who possess them, for I had not again been offered the liquid of over-sweetness, nor had I been asked to finish it.

"Jalav, you asked about 'the one who opens doors,'" said Kira, turning upon the seat beside me so that she might look more fully upon me. "Maybe we can get at a better answer if we start from another point. Do you know what a windmill is? Something that's built to use the power of the wind to perform work that would otherwise have to be done by hand?"

I knew naught of such a device as the female spoke of, yet did Aysayn stir in his seat.

"I am familiar with a device of that sort," said he to the female, his interest clear. "The windturn is used in Sigurr's city to grind wheat for grain, and to bring clear, fresh water to all of the levels. Also is it used upon the outlying farms."

"Good," said the female in great satisfaction, now looking between Aysayn and myself. "The wind turns the—windturn blades, and the movement does the work you want it to. But suppose someone came along on a day when there was no wind, someone who had lived underground all their lives, and wanted to know what turned the blades? How would you explain without having wind there to explain itself? Remember, that particular someone has never experienced wind, and doesn't believe there is such a thing."

"I would wait till the wind returned," said Aysayn with a chuckle, yet did it seem that he was more fully aware of the meaning of the stranger female. "To speak of a thing to one who has never experienced it is more than difficult; sooner would I waste my own breath blowing upon the windturn blades."

"Or to speak of snow to one of the south," said I, of a sudden recalling the derisive thoughts I had had concerning Tarla's description of the thing—till I had seen it for myself.

"What is snow?" asked Aysayn, looking upon me as both stranger folk nodded with smiles. "Never have I heard the term save in reference to Pathfinders."

"Snow falls from the skies as does rain, yet it is white and light and silent," said I, recalling my time in the midst of it with a shudder for the memory of cold. "From low, gray skies does it fall, thickly and at times nearly impossible to see through, mounding upon the ground in deep, soft drifts, colder than one would believe possible. Treacherous is the medium, and best left well behind a warrior of the south."

"And I am to believe in such a thing?" asked Aysayn with

ridicule, shaking his head at my words. "Do you take me for a child, that you offer such ridiculous tales?"

"As you would have me believe that wind might be taught to perform tasks," I returned, attempting to deny the stiffness of insult. "All Midanna know the wind blows where it wills, unchainable and untrainable."

"No, now, you're both right and you've both seen the point," said the female Kira, interrupting before Aysayn might speak further. "Someone who has never seen something will probably never believe in that something until he *has* seen it. If we went to your city, Aysayn, Jalav would be able to see a windturn working, and if we went to cold country, Jalav, Aysayn would be able to see snow. But what would happen if you both had something that *couldn't* be shown to someone else? Would that mean it wasn't real, that it wasn't true? You know it's real, you've used it yourself, but it just isn't something that can be shown to someone else. Does that make it unreal, and a lie?"

"That which is real may be shown to others," said Aysayn with a frown, one hand rubbing at a broad shoulder. "Should it not be possible to show it to others, the thing is likely no more than a dream, without substance save in sleep. To believe a thing real does not make it so."

"What of the Snows of a Pathfinder?" I asked as the stranger folk grew upset and began to deny Aysayn's words. "Rarely are there more than one or two about able to reach them, yet is the truth of them beyond doubting. The Snows may not be shown you, yet they exist in truth."

"That's right, snow and one who finds a path through it," said the female Kira with a smile as Aysayn nodded reluctant agreement. Much did it seem that the female meant the snow of the north rather than the Snows of the White Land, yet did she continue on with haste before I might correct her. "If someone has something that can't be shown to others, that doesn't mean it isn't there—and that doesn't mean what it *does* can't be shown. Our people have found something that can't be seen, and that can't be collected except in very special jars, but once you collect this unseen thing, you can use it. The wind is always there, but without a windturn it can't be used. This unseen force is also always there, in the air all around us, but if it isn't collected, it can't be used. Our people have collected it, and now use it to open doors.''

"Should one be unable to see a thing, how is one to know of its presence so that it might be collected?" asked Aysayn, his suspicion lulled with curiosity. "One need only feel a wind upon one's face and body to know of its presence, and then one may consider how it is to be used. In what manner does one know of the unseen *and* the unfelt?"

"How was it discovered what a windturn might do?" asked the male Aram, drawing Aysayn's eyes. "How many men had to feel wind on their faces and bodies before one of them thought about what could be done with it? I'm not that sort of man, but some men are always asking why, and how, and where, and all sorts of questions that never occur to the rest of us. There's a way to *sometimes* see our unseen thing, in a form as wild and untamed as a wind storm, and a man who asked why saw it. Once he saw it he thought about a way to tame it and use it, and that's why we now can."

"And in a better, more complete way than he ever dreamed was possible," said the female Kira, leaning forward to look soberly upon Sigurr's Shadow. "Are your windturns used only for the original use they were first made, or have you found new uses for them since you've had them? I can see from your smile that you've found new uses above the original one, and I'd like to ask you a question about that: if the man who found a new use had spent all his time simply searching for food and fighting to stay alive, would he still have found that use? Would he have been able to do something like that if others hadn't helped him to live while he thought and planned?"

"No," said Aysayn, a glint to his eyes and a faint smile upon his lips. "Those who thought of the new uses have been men of our city, who found neither the need to hunt nor the need to stand with blade in hand. A new use was also thought of by one of a farm, but he was not alone on the farm. Those who must stand alone have not the time to think such thoughts."

"Exactly," said Kira with satisfaction, leaning back again where she sat. "The ones who think must be protected, otherwise they don't have the time to think. Do you understand what we're talking about, Jalav?"

"Perhaps in a small way," I grudged, thinking upon the doings which had ever been a part of the Midanna. "Each kalod do the sister clans meet in the visiting, and to this visiting each clan must bring two new things which have been learned by them. Save for new forest lore, often are the new things brought to mind by those who have been wounded in battle and must keep to their sleeping leather till they have healed. When one lies upon one's sleeping leather, feeding upon the efforts of one's sisters in the hunt, relying upon the swords of others to see to their safety, what other thing is one to do save think?"

"Then you both understand the point," said the female Kira with a slow nod, looking to both Aysayn and myself. "Those who ask the questions and search for the answers have to have the *time* to do the asking and searching, otherwise nothing new is learned. Now I have another question for you: what would these people learn to do if they never had to do anything but think? And how much new would there be if there were a lot of these thinking people, all thinking about different things?"

"One would be able to find the unseen and tame it for use," said Aysayn with something of a smile, looking upon the stranger female with calm patience. I, too, wondered at the roundabout trail she had chosen to take her through the forest, for the end of the trees was not yet in sight.

"One certainly would," said Kira with a laugh of delight, sharing with Aram the pleasure she felt in the glance she sent to him. "And now I have a story to tell you. A long time ago, a very long time ago, there was a large group of people. These people knew how to do a lot of things, but the one thing they couldn't do was make more living space for themselves in the place they were. The number of their people just kept getting larger and larger, and they didn't have enough room for them all, so one day some of them decided to move to a new place and start their group all over again, where there would be more room.

"Now, these people made their plans and took with them what they could of all the things they knew how to do, but the new place they moved to was very far away and they couldn't go back and forth between the old place and the new. Once they got to the new place they had to stay there, and the new place had nothing that the old one did, nothing but the room to build what was already built in the old place. The first thing they had to build was houses, and they had to hunt and plant to feed themselves, and fight to keep from being killed by the wild beasts in the new place. But these people were very brave, and they knew that it would take time and effort, but they would soon be able to start building all the things the old place had. They knew about all those things, you see, but you can't make wonderful things out of the air around you; to make a windturn, you first have to make the blades, then the tower, then arrange the job you want it to do. If you make the blades but can't find what to make the tower out of, or build the tower and can't make the blades right, you have no windturn. It all has to be put together right, or you have nothing.

"Now, the people in their new place had taken some of their learning with them, but they hadn't had the room to take all of it. What's the sense in knowing exactly how to collect the unseen from the air, if you first have to find a hundred different things before you can do it? Especially if half those things are hidden, and the other half must be made from a different hundred things? The people knew they could never go back to the old place to get the explanations of how to do all the things they wanted to do, but they also knew they didn't have to go back. One of the things they were able to do was talk to the others they had left so far behind, and as long as they could talk to them, they didn't have to go back."

The female now looked upon Aysayn and myself warily, as though unsure as to the belief we felt, yet had Aysayn looked to me at her words, recalling the times I had told him of upon the journey to Bellinard, the times when Mida had spoken to me though her Realm lay an unknowable distance away. The gods were able to do many things, I knew, and were these strangers not servants of gods?

"Now, the people in the new place built their houses and got settled in, and then they were ready to start doing the first of the wonderful things they wanted to do," said the female Kira, pleased that neither Aysayn nor I had protested her tale. "You must remember that when you build a house, knowing how to build a roof or even knowing that there's supposed to be a roof, won't help you if you don't know how to build walls or don't remember that you need walls. Most new things come from old things that are already known, but if you don't know how to do those old things, you certainly can't do the new ones. The people in the new place were ready to put down the floor of their building so that all the rest of it would have a strong foundation to stand on—and then they were cut off from the people in the old place. They knew the people were still there, but suddenly they couldn't talk to them any longer. Do you know what happened then?''

"They likely found the need to begin again," said I with a shrug. "Should Midanna wander very far in the hunt and find a place they would remain in for a while before returning to their home tents, they must make new home tents for the old have been left behind. One merely fashions new home tents from leather and saplings, then looks about as long as one pleases.''

"But what if they didn't know *how* to make those home tents?'' asked the female, her eagerness growing. "What if they knew tents could be made, but didn't know where to get the leather from, and didn't know which trees to look among for saplings? What would they do then?''

"They would live in the forests, without tents, paying for their foolish lack of knowledge with discomfort,'' said I with a snort of disdain. "None save city folk or truly young warriors-to-be would not know so necessary a thing.''

"Well, in a way that's exactly what these people were,'' said the female, now more cautiously eager. "Most of them were certainly young, and had spent their time learning things that were only a small part of all that was known. You seem to know quite a lot about the forest; is it possible to learn that much about it without living in it most if not all of your life?''

"No,'' said I, looking this time upon Aysayn, who rubbed wryly at his face. The Sigurri were warriors in truth, yet had they proven to know less of the forests than had the Midanna, during our journey to Bellinard. Much had Midanna warriors ragged those Sigurri they had come to know, and many a scuffle had developed between female warrior and male. Had swords been drawn by cause of it we would not have felt surprise, yet had naught occurred save scuffling.

"Well, the same is true for all knowledge," said Kira, again pleased with my response. "In order to really know something, you have to study that and very little else. When the people in the new place found they couldn't talk to the old place anymore, they got together and decided to try to do what you suggested, Jalav: they tried to start over. Each person tried to remember as much as he could of the wonderful things they all knew were possible, but a terrible thing happened: they found they didn't have the *time* to think and remember. They didn't have the wonderful knowledge to make their work easier, so the men had to spend their days planting and hunting and building herds of food animals, and the women had to spend their days cooking and taking care of the children, and making clothes for them all to wear. Furniture and places for the animals had to be built, and food had to be prepared and put away for the cold times, and by the time these men and women were able to sit down and rest after that long a day, they were too tired to think.

"But one or two of them made themselves think, and these one or two remembered how to do some of the wonderful things. They were very excited when they called the others together, but their excitement didn't last long. In order to do even one of the wonderful things, a good number of the people had to work together—but everyone they asked to join them had something else to do. That man had to make posts for the fence he wanted to build to keep in his herdbeasts, the fence he needed to make sure his family would be fed for the winter. That woman was too close to having a baby, a baby they could raise and teach to help out around their farm to make life a little easier. All the people had something else to do that they needed to do in order to live, and they didn't have the *time* to think about searching for the wonderful knowledge they knew was there but couldn't reach—or the time to try to get it back.

"And then the first of their children grew old enough to be told about what had been lost," said Kira, her voice now more grim than pleased. "The children listened at night, before they went to bed, and in the morning they got up and worked all day long, the boys in the fields, the girls in the house. They never said so out loud, but they all knew their parents were telling them about things that weren't so. After all, if you knew a wonderful way to plow a field in one day instead of all the days it took to do it by hand, wouldn't you use that wonderful way instead? The children listened and worked, and when they grew old enough they had children of their own, and sometimes smiled when they thought of the stories they had been told, but very few told those stories to their own children. They had never seen these wonderful things, don't forget, and not having seen them meant they didn't believe those things were true. A very few of the things were saved, like reading, or how important it was to search for new things whenever you had the time, but all the rest of it died when the people who had first come to that place died. New children were born, and they grew up to have children of their own, and no one knew or remembered that there were still people left in the old place, people who hadn't forgotten about *them*. Those people were having trouble too, but nothing that cut them off from all the wonderful knowledge they had. It took awhile to get their trouble settled, and then they had to pay attention to what they were doing to keep the trouble from starting again, but eventually they were able to sit down and think about the people who had gone to the new place. They knew they were *their* people even if the children didn't know it, and you don't forget about people who are yours. If they're lost you try to find them, and once you find them you try to help them get back what they've had to do without for so very long.''

"There was more than one group of people who went out looking for new places," said Aram, his voice gentle in the wake of Kira's. "All these groups lost touch with the people they had left, but some for a shorter time than others. Some had built enough of the wonderful things for themselves that they didn't lose the knowledge of the rest of it, and were able to go on alone. Some did lose the wonderful knowledge, but were found soon enough that they still remembered the tales they'd been told about where they came from. The hardest thing for the people in the old place was to find a new place with children who didn't remember them at all. How can you expect children to believe in something they've never seen, something you can't show them? How do you make them know they're *your* people, and all you want to do is help them?"

A silence hung in the air after these final questions were put, a silence thick with confusion and discomfort. Both stranger folk looked to Aysayn and myself, yet Aysayn and I looked to each other. The things told us by Kira and Aram were things they clearly believed, yet were they not the things told us by Mida and Sigurr. Were we to believe the mouthings of those who had taken us captive—or the assurances of the gods we had pledged to follow?

"And yet," said Aysayn at last, his voice calm and sure, "were the enemies of a people to find them, they might well look upon the skill of those people with fear, and conceive of a way to conquer them without the need to face them. To speak of their all being one people would be that way, to keep the swords of those they feared sheathed. In what manner might such a thing be proven or disproven? With two things to be believed, which is to be seen as truth?"

The two stranger folk heard the words spoken by Sigurr's Shadow then turned their eyes to me, to see a calm and sobriety which matched Aysayn's. Indeed the male had spoken my own doubts, and he and I were one in the thing. The male Aram let out a long breath of vexation and slumped low in his seat, and the female Kira shook her head with a sigh.

"I told you it wouldn't be easy," said Kira to the male, putting her head back to rest it upon the wall behind us. "Care to come up with a way to prove we're the good guys and not the bad? I need a short break."

"And I need a long drink," muttered the male, running both hands through his light hair, then did a thought suddenly come to him, causing him to straighten again. "Wait a minute. We didn't find them, they found us. That has to be it."

"What?" asked the female Kira, raising her head again to look upon the male, yet was he too well concerned with looking between Aysayn and myself.

"You wanted to know how we could prove we were all one people, that the tale we told you was a true tale," said

Aram to those he had named guests, the eagerness having
returned to him. "Do you know how we happened to find out
about you? Do you know about the comm call that was
made?"

"I know of the call," said I, reluctant to speak of the
thing, yet in some manner feeling that I must do so. "Aysayn
knows no more of it than what he has been told. Ceralt and I
were present at the sending of the call."

"Jalav, you sound as though you're admitting to a terrible
crime," said Aram in bewilderment, shaking his head somewhat. "I couldn't be happier that you were there when the
call was made. The comm you used must have been very old,
but when the power crystals were properly mounted, it worked.
You called *us*, and *we* answered, proving what Kira said
about the small group being able to talk to the people they
left. If you weren't ours you couldn't have called us, and if
we weren't yours we wouldn't have been there to answer.
Don't you see? That's the proof you wanted!"

Aysayn looked to me for confirmation of what the male
had said, yet was I unwilling to voice such confirmation. It
had been Mida's will that the crystals not be brought together, yet they had been and the call had been made. For
what reason had Mida been so set against the thing, yet had
done naught of her own self to halt it? For what reason had
the Hosta alone been set the task, when surely the goddess
had known that nine clans of our sisterhood would be needed
to take and hold a city of males? For what reason had it been
necessary to raise both Midanna and Sigurri, when no more
than Aysayn and Mehrayn and Ceralt and I were meant to
face the strangers? And should these stranger folk truly be
lost kin to us, as even the voice from out of the comm had
said, for what reason had they been named enemies instead
by Mida and Sigurr? What of the gods the strangers served—
and what of the gods served by Midanna and Sigurri?

"Could—those who received the call not be enemies who
had previously slain or enslaved those we came from?" I
asked, not the male Aram but Aysayn, feeling an illness in
my middle undoubtedly due to the food I was given in place
of true provender. At the look of upset in the eyes of Sigurr's
Shadow I lowered my face to my hands, knowing as well as

he that any powerful enough to slay or enslave those with
things of wonder, would have no need to fear the swords of
Midanna and Sigurri. So easily had we four been taken
captive, by a device which, so Aysayn had said, had fallen
from the skies without damaging itself. The darkness which
my eyes had found was safe and warm, a place of refuge I
was greatly in need of, a place where thought might well not
find me. I had no wish to give thought to that which was
about me, yet the male Aram, as all males, would not be
denied.

"You don't really believe we're not your people, do you,
Jalav," said the male, no question in the gentle manner of his
speech. "You know now that we are what we say we are,
and even suspect that if you don't like something we try to
teach you, you can refuse to learn it. If we were trying to
make slaves of you, we'd insist on everything being done our
way, but we won't be insisting on that. We'll just tell you
what *can* be done, and you'll decide whether you want to
learn how to do it. We're yours and you're ours, and it's time
we got to know each other again."

"Perhaps—it would be best if my sister and I were given
the opportunity to speak between ourselves," said Aysayn,
with distress. "She has seen far more of this difficulty than I,
and I would hear her thoughts upon the matter."

"There shouldn't be any problem in that," said the male
Aram, and I raised my head to see him rise from his seat.
"There's an empty cabin right here on this level, and there's
no reason why you can't. . . ."

"Aram, they're gone!" came a sudden outburst, and the
female Tia nearly ran through the opening door to the male
she called out to. "Two of those savages have gotten out of
their cells, and there's no telling how many people they've
killed by now! You've got to sound a general alarm and help
me find them!"

So odd was the situation that we four were only able to
stare bemusedly upon the female, for she had crossed before
Aysayn to reach Aram, and now stood within reach of his
arm. I, who had taken seat opposite to Aysayn, was perhaps a
bit less than two paces from her, the female Kira beside me,

yet were we also unseen. For none other than Aram had she eyes, and the male before her suddenly grinned.

"Stop worrying, Tia," said he with a drawl, folding his arms with easy unconcern. "I have complete confidence in those people. If they kill anybody, I'm sure they'll take care to make it your project people and not my crew. Why get excited?"

"Aram, this isn't a joke!" insisted the female, reaching a hand to his folded arms, her upset not to be soothed. "It's deadly serious and I'm asking for your help! I need your help. You can't really refuse me—can you?"

The female now looked up to the eyes of the male in a manner most strange, her body having moved nearer his, her voice having abruptly turned low and husky. Surely did she then appear the slave begging use from her master, yet the male failed to find interest in her.

"What's the matter, Tia, are you afraid this is the mistake I was talking about?" he asked, a sharpness now appearing in his eyes beside the amusement, his voice having turned very soft. "Project Leaders are responsible for all subjects brought to the ship, aren't they? If one of them gets loose and runs amok, it's on your head no matter whose fault it is."

"None of that matters if it doesn't get into the log, darling," returned the female, raising her hand to touch the back of it to the face of the male, her voice continuing huskily. "Just because you were lucky enough to have me choose you to relax with doesn't mean you've had it all, you know. I think we can work something out to make you forget about everything but me."

"That seems to be your main problem, Tia," said the male, unfolding his arms to take the hand from his face. "When it comes to thinking, you don't. You consider people so unimportant that you ignore them as you please, then expect them to jump through hoops when you whistle. It's too bad you weren't taught to be considerate instead of important."

"Don't be tiresome, Aram," said the female in annoyance, no longer looking upon the male as she had. "You'll never get anywhere until you learn that other people *are* unimportant. *We're* the only ones who matter, and what matters right now is to find those savages. If I have to go down on this, you have my word I'll be taking you right along with me.''

"This isn't the one you'll be going down on, Tia," said the male, exasperation behind the calm he showed. "The mistake you get caught on will be yours alone, no matter who tries interpreting it differently. And just to set your mind at rest, let's find one of your subjects for you."

The female gasped with indignation as the male's hands came to her arms, then did she cry out with alarm as he thrust her backward and to one side. Surely did the female believe that she would sprawl upon the floor covering, yet had she been thrust, not to the floor covering, but to Aysayn. The hands of Sigurr's Shadow raised to take what the other male had given him, great amusement clear in the dark of his eyes as his fingers closed upon her arms, increasing at the cry of upset torn from her over being drawn into his lap.

"Well, there he is, Tia, and now you've got him," said the male Aram, sharing Aysayn's amusement as he smiled upon a wide-eyed, disbelieving, and fearfully unmoving female. "What did you intend doing with him?"

"Perhaps there is a thing *I* may do with *her*," said Aysayn, looking down to the female he held. Not so small as Kira was this Tia, yet did she seem nearly a child in the massive arms which held her. Well aware was she of whose lap she had been thrust into, yet had she not as yet even turned about to look upon the face of him. This Aysayn saw to by putting a fist in her hair, and turning her head so that she must look up at him. The female drew her breath in sharply in fear at being handled so, and one trembling hand went unwillingly to the wide chest so near to her. "How might this covering be removed?" Aysayn asked the male Aram without moving his gaze from the female.

"Aram, don't tell him!" whispered the female frantically, unable to take her eyes from Aysayn's despite her attempts to back from him. "You can't let him do this to me. I'm the project Leader! You've got to make him let me go!"

"Me?" asked the male Aram with ridiculing amusement, aware that the female was unable to see him. "You expect *me* to be able to make *him* do something he doesn't want to do? If I ever decide on suicide, I might give it a try."

"Aram, please, I'll do anything you say," whimpered the female, continuing to be held by the dark eyes above her. Aysayn's fist was closed upon hair nearly as light as his own, yet was there naught of a feeling of kinship in the slight, trembling body his arm surrounded. It seemed that the female knew what use by him would be for her, for she had tried his patience far too greatly, always unwise with any of the males I called brother. Were Aysayn to use her she would be well punished, and this the female clearly understood.

"Are you sure you don't want to show him some of the great stuff you were telling me about?" asked the male Aram in an easy drawl, that interrupted the high-pitched, incoherent howl of protest immediately begun by the female. "Okay, okay, don't get hysterical. If I get you out of that, you agree to do anything I say? Without argument, without throwing your weight around, without hiding behind regulations?"

"Yes!" The female wept, both hands now to Aysayn's chest, an attempt to keep herself from being drawn close. "I'll do anything, anything!"

"I'll take you at your word, then," said Aram in satisfaction, glancing briefly toward Kira, who sat in silent discomfort beside me. "Aysayn, my friend, will you do me the favor of letting her go? We still have a lot of things to settle between us, and we'll find that easier to do if she's out from under foot."

"Indeed, temple slaves have no place in talks between men," said Aysayn with great insolence, looking upon the female in disapproval before releasing her. Immediately did she take herself from him, her haste so great that she fell to her hands and knees upon the floor cloth, her now-disheveled hair falling about her face. Great indeed was the bravery of the female Tia when a wall stood between her and those she scorned, and her head raised to see the disgust which was surely in my eyes. She stared at me a moment, a frown beginning, and then the male Aram bent to assist her to her feet.

"You're all right, so just go back to your cabin and stay there," said Aram to the female, brushing back the hair which threatened to come entirely loose. "Kira and I will see that your precious project gets off the ground in the right way, and all the credit will be yours without your having to lift a single finger. If I need you for something, I'll send for you.''

The female stared upon him wordlessly, glanced to Kira, looked again at me, then turned and stumbled from the chamber. In no manner had she again looked upon Aysayn, and when the door hid all sight of her, Sigurr's Shadow rose to his feet.

"There are certain females one does best to enslave quickly," said he, sending a brief glance toward the door before giving his full attention to the male Aram. "So that the difficulty they make causes the least amount of harm, you understand. You began to tell of a place my sister and I might speak alone?"

"Yes, the empty cabin," said Aram, seemingly considering Aysayn's suggestion for a very brief time. "If you two will follow me, I'll show you where it is."

"Have you renth or falar?" I asked abruptly as I rose from the seat I had been upon, only slightly concerned over the lack of courtesy shown by my query. "Surely daru is unknown among you, yet would the others do in its stead."

"I don't know what they are," said the male Aram, looking upon me with something of concern. "If you can give me some idea of what you need, I'll be glad to supply it."

"Perhaps when our talk is done," said Aysayn, his gaze upon me as well, his concern deeper than that of the other male. No desire had he to see Jalav with adequate drink in hand, and this I did not understand. "First we must have a place to be alone," said he in a manner which brooked no disagreement.

"This way," said the male Aram, looking between us uneasily as I gazed upon Aysayn with the annoyance I felt. Without further words did the male take himself toward the door of the chamber, halting just beyond it so that he might be more easily followed. Aysayn stood where he had been, clearly demanding that I go before him, and this, too, riled me. With restrained anger I followed the male Aram then, and so great was my distraction that I failed to question him when I saw the corridor unchanged from what it had been when we entered his chamber. Straight ahead were we led, to a door separated from his by two others, and when it had slid aside the male gestured within.

"Take as much time as you need," said he, allowing his eyes alone to follow as I stepped within, Aysayn no more than a pace behind. "Either Kira or I will stop by from time to time to see if there's anything you need. If you want us instead, just come back to my cabin."

"You have our thanks," said Aysayn, clearly dismissing the other, a thing which Aram was swift to understand. The door closed itself as the stranger male took himself back to the place from which he had come, and still I did no more than look about at the chamber we had come into. It was considerably smaller than the other, and also differently filled. Far fewer seats and platforms were to be seen, naught of renderings upon the walls, and also was there a wide square of something upon the floor directly opposite to the door. Perhaps a hand in height was the something, with tan cloth upon it, too low and wide to be comfortably taken as a seat. All about was there the same light to be found in all chambers of that place, without source yet everpresent, and this, too, brought me annoyance.

"I would now hear what disturbs you so greatly over what was said by the strangers," said Aysayn, his voice composed of its usual calm. "Do you find belief in their claims?"

"I feel as though I were again beneath the ground in the Caverns of the Doomed," said I, continuing to look about myself. "No least amount of feylight do these strangers allow within their chambers. Think you we are indeed beneath the ground?"

"I, too, feel the discomfort of confinement," said Aysayn, and then was his great hand upon my shoulder. "To fail to speak of a thing does not make that thing untrue, should it contain truth to begin with, Jalav. The man Aram told of a call having been sent, a call you have previously made mention of. Is this call the proof Aram believes it to be? Has he convinced you that they are indeed lost kin to us?"

"What difference whether they be kin or not?" said I, at last turning to look up into Aysayn's sober gaze. "The Midanna and the Sigurri have been commanded to greet the strangers with naked swords, not as brothers and sisters long lost to us. Are we to deny the commands of the gods we serve, renounce the oaths of fealty and service which were made? The wisdom of Sigurr's Shadow is widely known; speak to me in your wisdom, O Shadow, and tell me in what manner it might be otherwise.''

"Now I understand what twists within you," said Aysayn softly, lifting his hand to this time smooth my hair. "The dishonor of raising weapons to one's kin is great, nearly as great as being forsworn. Your wenches must see the thing the same as we, and indeed are you convinced these folk are kin to us. Is there no least doubt within you, no smallest possibility they do indeed seek to cozen us?''

"There are many doubts within me," said I, turning from him once more to pace about the chamber. "The tale they tell is greatly compelling, yet might it be no more than a child's tale or one to cozen the credulous—were one to discount the call which was sent from the dwelling of Galiose, the call which elicited a similar response from she whose voice came out of the darkness born of the Crystals. At first I thought these strangers moved to the commands of those who were true enemies to the gods, those who were gods themselves, yet do they speak of wonders which any may learn to perform. That their words hold their own personal belief may not be denied; and yet how may mortals be taught what only gods are able to do? One must see from this that the strangers themselves are gods, else have they wonders which are not the doings of gods, merely the doings of mortals. Having seen Mida and Sigurr, I am unable to accept these folk as gods.''

"As am I," said Aysayn in agreement, his voice troubled. "The possibility remains, however, that there are those behind these stranger folk, those who are indeed gods. It would be they we were meant to best, not the ones who hold us captive.''

"Should there be gods behind these stranger folk, we shall not find it possible to best them," said I, turning to look upon him with the bitterness of undeniable truth. "Masters are ever more powerful than their servants, else would they not long remain masters. Were we to face these strangers with swords we would best them, yet are they scarcely likely to don

swords to face us. Sigurr's Shadow, Sigurr's Sword and the
High Rider of the Belsayah all stood armed at the appearance
of these strangers; were they kept from capture by the presence of weapons and the skill to wield them? As easily as
children were we four taken, and just so easily would we fall
in a true battle. What hope would there be for us against any
who might be masters to them?''

"The war leader Jalav now seeks assurances of victory
before considering entering battle?'' demanded Aysayn, angrily. "What of the glory to be found in battle, wench, most
especially in a battle demanded of you by the gods?''

"One finds small glory in slaughter!'' I snapped in return,
raising my head to show my own anger. "Am I to lead my
warriors to battleless, gloryless death which they have no
hope of avoiding? Is this the reason I strove unceasingly to
become war leader to all of the Midanna? To see them fall?
Am I to see them ended as a result of the anger which Mida
feels for their war leader? Sooner would I be forsworn than
allow such a thing.''

"Anger?'' said Aysayn, frowning. "What anger would the
goddess feel toward the one who is her chosen? For what
reason would she feel such anger?''

"Perhaps—perhaps for the reason of my intention to challenge her when the matter of the strangers is done,'' said I,
seeing the frown turn to incredulity upon the broad face of
him. "No longer am I willing to accept what shaming and
pain are given me by her in the name of punishment, no
longer shall I allow her to deny me what males I would take
for my own. Jalav shall stand free, else shall she find the
endless dark.''

"You would refuse to enter battle with mortals possessing
no more than mortal powers, yet seek to give challenge to a
goddess?'' demanded the male, outraged. "Have you lost
what little wit you were possessed of? To even consider
giving challenge to a god—!''

"In battle Jalav must lead the Midanna,'' I returned with
the stiffness of insult, my hand beginning to itch for a hilt.
"To give challenge, only *she* need stand forth, and only *she*
shall do so. Should she be answered with honor rather than

treachery, one to one rather than another standing beside the one she challenges, then shall she pit her skill against . . ."

"Another standing beside the one who is challenged?" said Aysayn with bewildered impatience touched with outrage. "What other is required to stand beside a goddess who faces a mortal? And what other might there be who would add to the presence of a goddess, who would—"

Abruptly were his words ended as he looked upon me, his eyes widening, his light-haired head raising in complete disbelief and the beginnings of great anger. My own anger had caused me to speak the truth to one who would not be able to accept it, yet was I endlessly weary of remaining silent upon the matter of the gods. None knew them as well as I, not Keeper, nor Shadow, nor Sword, nor any who was mortal; to know them as I did, one would need to have felt my shame and pain.

"Many times have the Sigurri asked me of their god, the one who shares the Realm of Mida," said I, not attempting to avoid the wordless outrage leveled at me. "Suffice it to say that they are cut from the same cloth, one no better than the other. The matter is one between Jalav and the gods, and should she be unable to face them separately, they will surely render her incapable of further blasphemies."

With such words did I then begin to turn from him, finding no pleasure in casting doubt upon the beliefs of another. So empty had the life of Jalav become since she was no longer able to call to Mida in need; what glory in bringing such emptiness into the life of another? I began to turn from Aysayn, to leave him as much as I might, yet his hand came to my arm and pulled me back to face him.

"The words you speak are far from sufficient," said he in a growl, his free hand coming to my other arm, the strength of his double grip giving me pain. "Sigurr is the greatest of gods, more powerful than any other, and also more honorable as well! Think you the Sigurri would follow one so low as to interfere in a matter of honor? You dare to defame one who is the very source of honor, the one whom mortals may do no more than attempt to emulate? You would dare to speak ill of him?"

The voice of Aysayn had risen to a shout, his fingers like

metal in my arms, his furious strength shaking me as though I
were made of cloth. No attempt did I make to break the hold
of the male, so clearly did I feel the pain within him, yet was
I unable to keep silent as I had intended.

"At the end of battle, your god fully expects his warriors
to turn upon those Midanna they fought beside and slay
them," I whispered, the breath coming hard to my throat
through the blazing pain of the grip I was held in. "Has he
not yet spoken of it to those who lead his followers?"

"No!" said Aysayn with a shout, throwing me backwards
from him to sprawl upon the low, wide, unexplained square,
his tortured denial a complete and total rejection. So pale had
he grown that surely did I believe him suddenly taken ill, and
then did he fold to the floor cloth and lower his face to
trembling hands. I sat straight where I had been thrown,
pushing the hair from my eyes, never having seen the male as
distraught as he then was, unsure of what might be said or
done. A long moment passed with silence from us both, and
then did Aysayn let his hands fall from a face whose eyes
were closed tight.

"Much have I thought of late upon the wisdom of giving
over my place as Sigurr's Shadow when this matter of the
strangers was done," said he in a lifeless voice. "I thought
myself ill, you see, for thrice have I dreamt that I stood in the
presence of Sigurr, and each time the great god demanded
that at battle's end the wenches we fought beside be taken as
slave or slain out of hand. I found myself unable to believe
that Sigurr would demand a doing so lacking in honor, and
saw the failure as mine instead. Now do you speak of that
which you should not have known, save that you learned of it
from Sigurr himself—and my dreams are truth rather than
illness. Sooner would I have continued thinking myself mad."

He lay upon his back on the floor cloth then, one leg bent
at the knee, the heels of his hands to his still-closed eyes, the
pain emanating from him as thick as early fog in spring. I
saw then that the emptiness had already begun to touch him,
and no longer regretted the words I had spoken.

"You are mistaken," said I in the calm which was no
longer his, sitting cross-legged where I had been thrown. "I
learned the thing not from Sigurr but from Mida, for she

wishes the Midanna to turn upon the Sigurri in a like manner, only first. As I said, the two are cut from the same cloth.''

"The goddess too?" said Aysayn in great surprise, turning his head to look upon me. "And you knew of this even before you came to us, yet spoke not a single word about it?"

"What need had I to speak upon it?" I asked with a shrug, meeting his gaze. "Once the Sigurri were known to me, I determined that never would I see them done in so honorless a manner. This, among other things, was the reason I came to believe there was no other course before me save challenge. My oath of fealty is held by one I have grown to despise above all others, and no longer may I allow such a state to continue.''

"I don't understand," said Aysayn, bewildered and disillusioned. "Ever has the great god been one men emulated willingly, happily, knowing they conducted themselves in all things with honor. For what reason would it not now be the same? Have we lost sight of that which we were truly being taught?"

"I think not," said I with a headshake, nevertheless feeling again the many doubts that continued to plague me. "Ever have Midanna been taught that honor lies above all else, and these latest demands may not be considered honorable. The questions which now remain before us are two: will the Sigurri do as their god demands? And even before that, what is to be done concerning the strangers?"

"You believe our warriors would attack those they stand beside as allies, even should Mehrayn or I command them to it?" he asked with a sound of ridicule, gesturing aside so unacceptable a notion. "Have you learned to know Sigurri so shallowly then?"

"Why do you believe I determined that the Midanna would also not attack?" I asked in turn, equally ridiculing. "It seems we know our warriors far better than those in whose names they ride."

"Indeed," said Aysayn with a frown, clearly disturbed again. "And this, too, do I fail to understand. The great god has ever known well the men who serve him, yet now are we strangers to him."

"Strangers," said I, nodding in agreement. "In some manner like those who now claim to be kin to us, those whom we have no hope of besting. For what reason have we been prepared against their coming, when the skill of our arms has no hope of besting their wonders?''

"In one manner might we best them," said Aysayn slowly, his eyes holding to my face. "Were we to avow belief in their words and intentions, and then invite them to visit with us in the city of Bellinard— The attack which then fell upon them would catch them unawares, and likely be successful. Does the concept not sit well with the other which has been presented us?''

"Indeed is it the very image of the other," said I, meeting his gaze with the bleakness I felt. "This is the manner in which we are viewed by the gods, then; as ones who would greet strangers with smiles, and then bury daggers in their backs the moment they turned their faces from us. I would know what the Midanna have done to earn such an opinion of themselves.''

"They have done no more than the Sigurri," said Aysayn, angry now. "I know not for what reason the gods look upon us so, yet am I aware of the fury such thoughts bring. You asked what is to be done about the strangers; now I ask you the same. What is there which *may* be done?''

"Honorably," said I, knowing the word was meant by him and merely unspoken. "We are pledged to follow the dictates of the gods, yet may we not do so and still retain our honor. Should we inform the strangers with honor that we mean to stand against them, we have no hope of besting them. And even should we have such a hope, they may well be kin of ours, whose deaths would be further dishonor. To fail to act would bring dishonor, to act would do the same; how does one face and best such a trap of contradictions?''

The face of Aysayn was surely as disturbed as mine, yet were there no further words from him. As his lips parted to reply the door of the chamber slid open, though it was not Aram or Kira. Two who seemed male stood there, clad as all the strangers had been clad, their faces covered over with that which allowed no more than their eyes to be seen. As one they raised their arms and threw down a substance that shattered to release a thick, spreading mist, and then was all thought and consciousness stolen from us.

11.

A demand— and a sign of intruders

". . . not at all sure I want to know what she has in mind," said a male voice, coming to me as I struggled to free myself from that which felt as though it stole the very air from my chest. Thick gray fog enfolded my thoughts and desire for movement, and I knew not where I lay nor what went on about me.

"I don't think I've ever before seen her that furiously angry—or that gloatingly happy," said another male voice, one seemingly as familiar as the first. "I don't know what she has in mind either, but I have a feeling we won't be wasting our time if we pity these two."

"The sole benefit here seems to be that we're no longer barred from these subjects," said the first voice, heavier than the second and perhaps somewhat older. "I can scarcely believe the story their bodies tell about the sort of conditions they live under. They actually have unremoved scar tissue."

"Especially the female subject," said the second male, his voice in some manner distracted, and then there came a touch upon my thigh. "She must have had some sort of accident, but just what sort I can't imagine."

"Use your eyes and learning rather than your preconceptions, Doctor," said the first male, his voice gentle despite the air of rebuke about his words. "Her scars were clearly made by edged weapons, not caused by an accident. Just as the back and ribs of the male show he was rather thoroughly whipped."

"Whipped!" echoed the second in great shock. "And weapons? What sort of people are these?"

"Very primitive ones," said the first, a sadness now touching him. "It takes centuries for man to drag himself out of the mud of ignorance and superstition, the wink of an eye for him to slide back again. He won't truly be civilized until he can find a way to permanently keep what his centuries of struggle have brought him. No matter what happens to disrupt continuity."

"They really do need us to help them, don't they?" asked the second, his voice now showing a revelation and odd vulnerability. "We're not here to show them how much better off *we* are, we're here to help them find betterment for themselves. I never really believed that until just this minute."

"You won't have trouble believing it when you see how much hard work we have in front of us," said the first with a chuckle. "Helping people is usually harder than taking advantage of them, especially with people like these. They have your sympathy now because you're picturing them as helpless, but in their own environment they're far from helpless. In their world they're deadly dangerous, and if you forget that even for a minute, you could find yourself facing a lot of time in bio-rehab tanks. Now, now, girl, don't strain like that or you'll hurt yourself. Just relax and don't be frightened."

The second male made a sound of surprise, for clearly only the first had seen that I had returned to myself enough to struggle against what held me. I knew not what it was which closed tight about my wrists, ankles and brow, that which felt like something other than metal, but it was unnecessary to know the makeup of slave chains to wish to be free of them. I knew not what I lay upon nor what held me, yet did I know I wished no part of them.

As the males knew the darkness no longer kept me from the world, I opened my eyes to look upon them; their voices had seemed familiar, and their faces proved the same. Both were stranger males I had seen in the chamber of confinement, those whose coverings had collars of blue. He who had spoken first was the roundish male with a lighter blue upon him than his brothers wore, short, thin hair of brown above dark eyes filled with concern. The second was one who wore deeper blue, and indeed did he appear to have fewer kalod than the first. He, too, was brown of hair and eye, and he regarded me where I lay upon a narrow, raised platform of some sort, wrists held to either side of my body, ankles immovable at the far end of the platform, head able to do no more than turn somewhat from side to side. Much like an alcove in Sigurr's city did it seem, save for the pale blue all about upon walls and ceilings, and also save for the presence of Aysayn to my left, bound as was I upon another narrow platform. Sigurr's Shadow stirred where he lay, in an attempt to break free of the darkness which continued to hold him, as yet unaware of the fact that darkness was not all which held the two of us.

"Is this the manner in which stranger folk observe a truce?" I demanded in a hoarse voice. "Release us at once!"

"What is she talking about?" asked the second male of the first, his expression a frown showing lack of understanding. "What's this about a truce?"

"I have no idea," said the roundish male with a shrug, as perplexed as the other. "Possibly something was said to them that they construed as an offer of peace. Whatever it was, I'm sure it wasn't our project Leader who said it."

"You can bet on that," murmured the second male, his eyes resting thoughtfully upon my face. "Did you hear what she said to me? No? Well, it seems someone told her how hard I was hit when I first laid eyes on this—subject. She told me to be sure to stick around and watch the fun, and afterward I could test how effective the procedure was. I have a feeling that whatever the procedure was that she was talking about, it doesn't come under the heading of truce."

"No, I would tend to agree," said the first male in a similar murmur, his dark eyes watching the other as unblinkingly as the second watched me. "Just a minute ago you were talking about helping these people. Does that by any chance mean you first intend helping yourself, or will you tell the project Leader your interest isn't as sharp as you thought it was?"

The second male stood silent and unmoving in the face of the question put to him, a deep disturbance in the gaze which held to me, and then his head shook slowly from side to side.

"I don't know," said he, the words oddly simple and open. "I really do want to help these people, but when I look at this one—there's nothing humanitarian in the urges which rise. I've never before seen a woman like her in my entire life, and don't ever expect to see another. You like to know what I'll do if I'm given the chance at her? Frankly I'd like to know the same thing."

"The first thing you ought to know is that she probably won't accept you freely," said the first male, the sadness returned to him beneath the gentleness of his voice. "I'm not so old or sedentary that I don't see what you do, Kene—but would you really take a woman against her will, even a primitive one like this? Would you force her to satisfy feelings she hasn't purposely raised in you?"

"That's more than a little primitive itself, isn't it?" asked the second male with a smile lacking all humor and warmth, his arms coming slowly to fold across his chest. "I wonder if anything like that has ever happened to her—but that's foolish; of course it hasn't. These people may be primitive, but they're not animals. And of course I'd never force myself on her, Doctor. I'm just not sure if I would take advantage of whatever Tia has in mind for her."

"That's a considerable relief, Kene," said the first male, putting a hand to the shoulder of the other. "For a moment I thought we might have lost you to the lure of the primitive, a far greater menace than anything bacteriological. I recall an incident on my last project. . . ."

"What occurs here?" demanded the roughened voice of Aysayn, sounding much as I had. I turned my head to see that he, too, strained at that which bound his wrists to the narrow platform, yet he was as unsuccessful as I in finding freedom.

"Please don't upset yourselves," said the roundish male, this time addressing Aysayn as well, his discomfort having increased once again. "The project Leader had you brought here and restrained, but I'm sure she doesn't mean you any true harm. She'll be back in just a short while, and then we'll all find out . . ."

"Truce!" spat Aysayn, looking to me with the great outrage he felt, his eyes speaking silently upon the matter of what was to be done with those possessing so little honor that their words were naught. I, too, recalled the manner in which we had dealt with the followers of the gray Oneness, and let him see that once we had found our way to freedom, we would surely do these strangers the same.

"I would like to know what truce you two keep talking about," said the second male, also looking upon Aysayn. "The only ones authorized to make agreements with natives aboard this ship are Tia and . . ."

"Well, well, I'm right on time, I see," came a voice, and then did the female Tia step forward between the two blue-collared males who immediately gave ground. The stranger female seemed very pleased with matters all about her, and after no more than a glance for me regarded Aysayn. "Now that they've both come out of it, I think we can get started."

"We've—ah—been wondering just what it is you plan to get started with, Leader," said the first male, his voice hesitant as he looked upon the female. She, in turn, looked only upon an icy-eyed Aysayn, and the smile she wore was more than insulting yet less than challenging.

"Regulations state that the project Leader may, if necessary, impress the natives with higher technology if it will convince them to cooperate with us," said she in answer, a reply which surely brought as little to Aysayn as to myself. "Also, Doctor, a native who attacks a member of the project may be taught better, to protect the civilized who work with them and their barbarian ways. This native dared to put his hands on me, and now he will be taught better, at the same time finding himself impressed into cooperating. Oh yes, I think he'll be very impressed, and after him it will be the girl's turn."

"But what do you mean to do?" asked the second male, with veiled impatience.

"I mean to introduce them to electricity," said the female. "They'll be taught to do anything we wish in order to keep themselves from being shocked again, and that will include going to their knees and begging. The female will beg you, Kene, and this male—this, oh so magnificent barbarian—will fall to his knees in front of *me* and kiss my feet, then beg to do anything he can to please me. If he begs nicely enough, I may even let him do it."

"Project Leader, you can't mean that!" said the first male in great shock, his face paling, both males clearly aware of what the female intended. That she somehow meant to have the use of Aysayn was evident, from the manner in which her hand insolently stroked the strength in his uselessly straining arm, if naught else, yet was she far wide of the mark in believing the male would beg. Neither Sigurri nor Midanna would beg, a thing to be known by any who would name themselves enemy to them. I, too, strained against that which held me, finding the same as I had found earlier, unable even to twist the hair which lay beneath me. Anger rose in me nearly as high as it had risen in Aysayn, yet were we unable to free ourselves from the platforms.

"Of course I mean it, Doctor," said the female Tia, laughing lightly at the male behind her as well as the one before her who was unable to keep from the insult of her touch. "Once we have these two obeying us we'll do the same to the others, then set them loose to talk some sense into the rest of those barbarians. Before you know it, we'll have access to the entire population, and then we can do our jobs—which is what we're here for, isn't it, Doctor?"

"Yes, of course," began the roundish male, wringing hands behind the back of the female in agitation. "However, I really must . . ."

"Must get on with it," interrupted the female, at last turning from Aysayn to the male who hovered behind. Her satisfaction had not lessened, yet was she suddenly taken with a small frown. "Now where did Kene disappear to? He was here just a minute ago."

"Kene?" echoed the male, turning with a similar frown to look behind himself. The second, younger male no longer stood in his place nor, apparently, was he to be seen in the chamber. "Why, I don't know where he went. I didn't even hear him leave. Please, Tia, I really must ask you to recon—"

"Now you'll need another assistant," interrupted the female again, annoyance taking her as she paid no mind to the beseeching look of the male. "Well, don't just stand there, Doctor. Get someone else in here, and do it fast. I don't intend spending all day on this."

"Very well, ma'am," replied the male in dejected tones, defeat riding him heavily as he turned away. He passed from view with leaden steps, and the female turned again to Aysayn.

"You think you're so good, don't you?" asked she in tones so soft the words were difficult to hear, her hand reaching forth to stroke the chest of the Sigurri. "You get away with pushing around helpless females like that outrageous strumpet over there, and then get to believing it can be done with any woman. Well, it can't be done with any woman, and that's something you'll be learning very soon now. I think I'm going to enjoy making use of you even more than I enjoyed doing the same thing to Aram."

"Woman, you have long since gone beyond the bounds of my patience," said Aysayn as he looked upon her, the cords in his arms and shoulders and neck standing out clear with the growl in his voice. "Release us at once, else you shall pay dearly for our discomfort when we have seen to our own release."

"You expect to get out of this before I'm ready to let you out?" said the female with great amusement, trailing fingers down the body of the male. "How nice to see real confidence in someone who isn't female. It's a shame that that confidence isn't destined to last very long. But don't spend any time worrying about it, you'll soon have other things to occupy your attention."

The female then turned from a furious Aysayn to the others who stood behind her, clearly having heard their approach. The roundish male had returned accompanied by a second male, one lighter-haired, larger, and less concerned than he who had suddenly taken himself off.

"All right, let's get started immediately," said the female briskly to the two males, who merely stood awaiting her commands. Surely were these slave males, their blue collars perhaps having been placed upon them in lieu of collars of metal. "We'll work on the male subject first, and once he's conditioned we'll do the girl. Get him wired up as fast as you can."

The two males did no more than nod, the first in resignation, the second without concern, and then did they move to the platform upon which Aysayn lay, one to each side of him while the female looked on with bright interest. The males produced lengths of what seemed very thin metal, and after a

number of reckid of toying with the lengths, began to bring
them to the body of Aysayn.

"You must understand, Leader, that this may not do what
you want it to," said the roundish male, his eyes upon the
female. "We've had to adapt this equipment which wasn't,
after all, designed for torture."

"*Teaching*, Doctor, not torture," corrected the female with
a very faint smile, her eyes upon what was then being done to
a struggling Aysayn. "I'm well aware of your disapproval,
but don't let it lead you so far astray that you try disobeying
orders. There are worse things than that to be done to civilized men, as I'm sure you know. If you don't want to see
your entire career go down in flames, you'll make sure I get
exactly what I want."

The male made no rejoinder and his eyes lowered as his
head did, and then had the other male moved so that I was no
longer able to see the first. Indeed were these slave males,
unable to refuse doing what they seemed to have no stomach
for, obeying all commands without strong objection. My
wrists pulled again at what held them, a material far softer
than metal or even leather, yet one which refused to yield to
even the strength of anger and desperation. That harm was to
be given to Aysayn, I had no doubt, yet was I unable to free
myself to aid him.

Too few were the reckid before the slave males completed
their task, and then did they step away from the platform
Aysayn lay upon. Sigurr's Shadow had been draped about
with threads of metal, as though the ones about him had been
maglessa worms rather than males, and the female Tia moved
to take their place.

"I'll make this very simple so that you'll have no trouble
understanding what I want," said she to a thunderously furious Aysayn. "I'm going to ask you questions, and when I
hear answers I like and also believe, I'll have the lesson
stopped. If I don't like what I hear or don't believe it, it will
go on. Is everyone ready?"

Her slender, amused face turned to the slave males who
had done her bidding, they now standing beside a wall which
had had a small door opened in it, and waited no longer than

to see the slow nod of the roundish male before seeking again
the one who lay tightly bound before her.

"Are you ready, too, barbarian?" she inquired with continuing amusement, apparently anticipating the lack of response which she received, other than the cold stare of fury.
"I don't think you'll ever be readier, so here's the first
question: who's the one to be obeyed around here, you or
me? Answer quickly now, we don't want to waste any more
time."

The dark gaze of Aysayn was fully upon the female, yet
did he refuse to respond to so foolish a query. A Midanna
warrior might perhaps stand above a Sigurri, yet not without
the skill of her swordarm. To suggest superiority without a
sword grasped firmly in fist was more than laughable

"If you don't answer, I'll have to assume you're answering
in a way I don't like," said the female, the continuing purr in
her voice untouched by anger. "In that case, you get what a
wrong answer will get you. Give him his first taste of it,
Doctor, about five seconds' worth, I think."

The male at the wall hesitated very briefly as the female
backed a step from the platform Aysayn lay upon, then did he
turn to the opening and put his hand within it. Immediately
there came a sound I had never before heard, a sound somewhat like the crumpling of very thin parchment, and Sigurr's
Shadow writhed upon his platform, his body tightening con-
vulsively, his head thrown back, his teeth and fists clenched
tight against the agony of the unseen. Neither hand nor lash
touched the male where he lay, yet was he taken up, held,
and then released in some manner most painful. Quickly did
the strange sound cease, and when it had done so Aysayn lay
quivering against what had occurred, his breath rasping in his
throat, sweat upon his body, his eyes closed tight to what lay
about him.

"Did you enjoy that?" asked the female as she retook the
step she had earlier given up, her voice a caress of pleasure.
"Do you want more of it? Tell me now who is to be obeyed,
and be sure you speak loudly enough to be heard."

With great effort did Aysayn open his eyes to look upon
the female, yet was there naught of fear to be seen there.

Blood fury flamed in the gaze which held to her, yet was the
female no more than annoyed.

"You are a stubborn one, aren't you?" said she, a muffled
sound to be heard as though she tapped a foot in impatience
upon something other than wood. "I can see being easy on
you is wasted effort, you're much too backward to appreciate
it. Do it again, Doctor, but this time make it ten seconds."

Again the sound of crumpling parchment came, and again
Aysayn was touched with pain, yet was he not released so
soon as he had been the first time. The unseen held him stiff
in silent agony, and when once he was released he gasped as
though the air had been taken from him.

"Are you rethinking your position?" asked the female very
softly, her voice now an even greater insult as she looked
upon one who lay trembling in his bonds. "The next jolt you
get will be fifteen seconds long, half again as long as what
you just had, and the time after it will be twice as long. If
you begin pleasing me you won't be given any more than
one-second reminders, to reinforce what you'll be learning.
You're lucky the current is so low, or you might even be
dead by now. Tell me who is to be obeyed here."

This time the Sigurri made no effort to look upon the
female, and although he maintained his silence behind closed
eyelids, the pain fairly pulsed from his flesh. Madly I struggled against the bonds which held me, the kill-lust rising so
high that my vision swam, my body arching in an effort to
break free. The band about my brow slipped some small
amount, likely due to the moisture which had formed there,
but there was too little resistance in the thing to pull from it
with a single effort. Again I arched upward, using the bonds
about my wrists as a brace, and again the band slipped. A
third time and a fourth did I strain to escape its encircling
clutch, frantic with the need for haste, yet even as I threw it
from me with a toss of my head and raised up as far as I was
able, the female Tia was again looking upon the roundish
male by the wall.

"He's trying to continue disobeying me, Doctor," said
she, the annoyance in her voice having grown stronger. "Show
him again what happens to those who disobey."

The roundish male looked upon the female with the hesita-

tion born of his distress. His palms wiped themselves upon
his covering seemingly without volition, and again his glance
went to the Sigurri.

"If you keep this up, you'll kill him," he said with
pleading in his voice, a slave begging the agreement of his
mistress. "Can't you see he won't give you what you want?
He doesn't have a career you can threaten, and he's no
stranger to pain. You've got to let me *help* him—it's what we
came here for—to *help* them—!"

"No!" denied the female harshly. "He'll do as I say
despite your opinions to the contrary, Doctor, and he'll do it
fast as soon as he learns I'm not bluffing! Now, obey me or
suffer the consequences!"

The mouth of the male opened to speak further, perhaps in
agreement, perhaps in denial, yet was he denied the opportunity to put his thoughts in words. Another voice came first,
one filled with boundless outrage, one which took the attention of all.

"What the hell is going on here?" demanded the male
Aram, having appeared in the opening which was to these
folk a door, the female Kira and the dark-haired male who
had earlier departed hovering just behind. "What do you
think you're doing, Tia?"

"What I'm doing is none of your business, *Captain*,"
returned the female, having whirled to face him at the first of
his words, her chin high in defiance. "I found these two
where you left them, and you're lucky you were gone when I
got back to your cabin, or you'd probably be strapped down
right next to them. I think you ought to know that what you
tried to do to me will be going into the log, *Captain*, so enjoy
the title while you can. Once I'm finished with you, you
won't even be able to get a position as cabin steward aboard a
cruise liner."

"Is that so?" said the male, looking upon the female with
distaste. "Considering the fact that you're already relieved
from your post, just how do you intend to accomplish that?"

"What do you mean, relieved from my post?" said the
female with a snort of ridicule, folding her arms in unconcern. "You have no grounds to relieve me, and you know it.

You'd better get back to wherever you were, Captain; you're in enough trouble already.''

"Where I was was with the people in Research and Investigation," said the male, halting the female as she began to turn from him. "They found the source of that power signal, and were so involved with it they nearly forgot to give me the report I'd been waiting for. Would you like to guess what the source was, Tia?"

"I've already said it was probably one of their comm crystals," returned the female stiffly, yet was there a certain unsteadiness in the manner in which she looked upon the male. "What else could it have been?"

"Well, it *could* have been an everlight cell—but it wasn't," said the male, folding his arms as he met the gaze of the female. "As it turns out, it's a Feridan artifact, and you're the one who kept us from finding out about it immediately. Your order's in the log—right along with my order relieving you of command, something I took care of before coming here. It's too bad you weren't taught how to keep your word any better than you were taught to think, Tia. You could have been relieved without prejudice, merely as a matter of form, but that's not the way it reads now. You won't ever make project Leader again no matter how much influence your family has—the Union doesn't like to be embarrassed."

"You couldn't have done that to me," the female said in denial, shaking her head in disbelieving annoyance, and then her eyes returned to the face of the male. "It couldn't be a Feridan artifact, you're lying if you say it is. You're lying about everything, and it's me you're trying to embarrass, but it won't work. I'm going to be the one to get somewhere with these animals, and there's nothing you can do to stop me. Doctor, you have your orders. Carry them out immediately."

The female had turned again to address the roundish male, yet did he fail to give her the acknowledgment she sought. His eyes remained upon the male Aram, his disturbance clear, and when the female turned again in anger to seek what held him, she suddenly grew very still. Aram and Kira and the dark-haired male had all stepped farther into the chamber, and now was it possible to see two other males as well, those with green collars and white and green cloth about the upper

sleeves of their coverings. Sight of these two males caused
the female Tia to pale and begin trembling, yet the male
Aram looked upon her with little pity.

"I had a feeling I'd need Ship's Security to convince
you," said Aram to the now silent Tia. "They'll take you
back to your cabin and make sure no one gets confused about
whether or not to accept your orders. We're shielding now,
the way we should have been doing right from the start, so
don't bother anyone about getting in touch with headquarters.
They know why we've gone silent, and won't expect to hear
from us until this thing's settled."

"Captain, is it all right now for me to tend that man?"
asked the roundish male when the female Tia merely stood
and stared at the two males with collars of green. "Despite
my orders I made sure to give him no more than absolute
minimum voltage, but he must still be in a good deal of
pain."

"Voltage?" said the male Aram with a frown, looking
immediately toward a still-unmoving Aysayn. "You can't
mean she actually went through with that insanity? Lord,
man, get him out of that fast, and Jalav as well!"

Aram and the roundish male went quickly to Aysayn,
leaving Kira and the dark-haired male to come to where I lay.
I knew not what occurred there among the strangers, yet did I
know that I, too, needed to go to Aysayn—before I saw to
another necessity.

"How do you get these things off?" asked the female Kira
of the dark-haired male as she examined the bonds upon my
left wrist. "Jalav, are you all right? She didn't hurt you, too,
did she?"

"There's a release under the table," replied the dark-
haired male, the words removing the female's gaze of concern from me so that she might seek out whatever device the
male had spoken of. So easily was the thing done, a mere
touch of a hand as small and strengthless as Kira's, and no
longer was I held by unbreakable restraint. I freed my wrists
from the cloth which had grasped them and quickly moved to
sitting, watching with impatience as the two stranger folk
sought for similar release of my ankles. The instant it was
done I kicked free of the bindings, threw myself from the

platform to the accompaniment of gasps of surprise from
those who had freed me, and then was at the other platform.
The male Aram grunted in startlement when I moved him
with the weight of my body from my path, yet had I eyes for
no other than Sigurr's Sword.

Aysayn, too, had been released, but could barely sit up.
The roundish male touched him in some manner, looking
worried though my own concern was considerably lessened.
The dark eyes which came to me showed the pain he had
been given, yet were they also filled with a renewed reassurance which had been lacking since the lashing he had had in
the Caverns of the Doomed. Pain takes the strength from one,
and unendurable pain the spirit as well, yet Aysayn's spirit
was clearly untouched. His body continued to tremble somewhat, yet the flesh will heal when the spirit commands it.

"Don't worry, Jalav, he'll be all right," said the male
Aram, his voice gentle as he touched my arm. "The doctor
wants to make sure his heart wasn't damaged, and then he'll
give him something for the pain. Why don't you wait over
there with Kira, and as soon as we have him on his feet
again, we'll all go back to my cabin."

The male began to urge me away from the platform, and I
looked upon Aysayn a final time before allowing the thing. I
had needed to know whether Aysayn would live, and now
that I knew he would there were other matters to be about.

"So your name is Jalav," said a voice, and I turned my
head to see the dark-haired male who stood beside Kira. The
male looked up to me with eyes alight, and surely did he
appear as one who sought to follow a war leader. "It finally
came to me that the only other one you could have had a
truce with was the Captain," said the male, attempting to
straighten where he stood as I halted before him. "When
truces are made, they shouldn't be broken out of hand,
especially not by those who should know better."

"That's why he came looking for Aram and me," said
Kira, her eyes sober with concern. "I only wish we could
have gotten here sooner, before Aysayn was hurt."

So gentle and disturbed were these stranger folk, as though
naught might be done for the pain and humiliation which had
been given, as though the one who had been halted was now

unreachable. I looked beyond their shoulders to where the female Tia stood, shaking her head as though refusing to hear the soft words spoken to her by the two males with collars of green, they gently insistent despite her refusal. Without undue strength I put my hands to the shoulders of the two folk before me, moved them aside from my path without giving heed to their gasped out protests, then took myself toward she who had caused cowardly pain to be given to my brother.

"... have to come with us, Leader," said one of the males to the female as I reached them, the words sounding as though they had been spoken many times previously. "Technically you're under arrest, but we don't want to have to force you to come with us, and you don't want to make us do it, so why don't you . . ."

"Absolutely not," denied the female with another headshake. "I won't hear of any such thing, and I don't care if . . ."

Her words ended abruptly as I spun her about by the shoulder and took her by the throat, my fingers closing about it as easily as they would about the throat of a child. So small was the suddenly wide-eyed and terrified female, small and seemingly helpless, yet had she dared to challenge those who were in every way her superiors. Her hands rose to claw feebly in an attempt to loosen my grip as she gasped and choked; so ineffectual was the gesture, however, that I was free to ignore it in favor of the attempts of the two green-collared males to assist her. Both came to grasp my arms with shouts of shocked disbelief, striving to force me from the frantically mewling female, yet were they no larger nor more effective than their brothers, neither even so large as the male Aram. A kick to the middle rid me of the one to my right, a kick to the manhood did the same for the other, and then was I able to look down upon the one I held by the throat. Slowly would I tighten my grip till no further air was allowed her, and this was she surely able to see in my eyes. Her hands held to my wrist in strengthless desperation, her widened eyes filled with the knowledge that she looked upon her death— and then was my arm struck in a way which had once been shown me by Chaldrin, a blow which caused the victim to lose all feeling and control. The female Tia was pulled from fingers no longer able to hold her and thrust away, and then was it Aram who stood before me.

"Jalav, you can't kill her!" said he, paling as I growled low in my throat and sought to pass him even before life returned to my arm. "I know what she did was terribly wrong, but can't you see that killing her would also be wrong? She's so much smaller than you, and never bothered to learn the first thing about unarmed combat. Don't you understand that it's wrong?"

"Perhaps the wrong would equal binding those one would not find it possible to best while they were free, and then giving them pain," said I, with a growl, as I flexed my hand to free the numbness. "To do wrong is to invite wrong, and those so invited need not refuse. To overlook a wrong done is to encourage the wrongdoer to do the same again."

"She's absolutely right, Aram," said the female Kira, who also came to stand before me. "You can't let someone get away with hurting you, or you are encouraging them to do it again. But you don't have to worry about her ever getting another chance to do something wrong, Jalav. All her power and authority have been taken away from her, and they'll never be given back. If you let her live she'll have to return home in utter disgrace, a disgrace she'll never be able to overcome. She'll spend the rest of her life remembering what she threw away when she broke her word, and will know that she can never get it back no matter what. That's what will happen to her—if you let her live."

"Should I show her mercy," said I, rubbing at the place where I had been struck but actually seeking to camouflage the shudder which touched me. Well did I know the male concept of mercy, which took the spirit and pride from one without also taking one's life, a cruelty I had known naught of before becoming ensnared in the matters of Mida's Crystals and the coming of strangers. Also did Mida and Sigurr know of the concept, easily finding approval for the soul agony it brought, and now did these strangers show a similar approval. The male Aram nodded anxious agreement with Kira's words, both sets of eyes watching me closely, yet was the deepest and most anxious gaze possessed by Tia, who knelt wheezing, in a heap where she had been thrown, one hand to her throat. Clearly did the female beseech me with her eyes, asking not for the swift death which would end a life fallen to naught, but for the unending horror of a life given over to mercy. To be forced to continue with life under circumstances such as those was nearly inconceivable to me, yet to beg for the thing—! I turned from them all with the deep illness I felt, wishing it were possible to return to the time before the arrival of chaos and remain there, and the male Aram came to put a hand to my shoulder.

"You've made the right decision, Jalav, and by doing that you've also proven yourself to be much more civilized than Tia," said the male, his tone warm as he clasped my shoulder. "She's the real savage around here, and in a little while everyone will know it. Did I hurt your arm very badly?"

I looked down to see that I continued to rub at where I had been struck, feeling an odd amusement touch me. Many times had I been called savage, by the guard males of Bellinard, by the city females who had taunted me, by village dwellers and city dwellers and even by those who rode in the name of the Oneness. Never, however, had I been called civilized till I had committed what was an abomination in my eyes, allowing one to remain among the living when death would have been the far greater kindness. To be civilized, then, was to commit abominations, a revelation which was a good deal less surprising than it should have been. I took my hand from the arm which ached only a bit and shook my head in answer to the question of the male.

"Well, I'd still like the doctor to look at it when he's finished with Aysayn," said Aram, a frown in his tone. "I'll get rid of Tia, and then I'll be back to wait with you."

The dark-haired male who had been with Kira now tended those in green collars, attempting to aid them to a steadier return to their feet, therefore did the small female walk to me alone. A frown rode upon her features, and when she halted beside me, disturbance clouded the gaze which came up to me.

"I wasn't lying when I told you what would happen to Tia, but you don't seem as pleased about it as you should be," said the female, her words slow, her tone puzzled. "Is something bothering you?"

"How is it possible to covet life itself, yet be unconcerned about the quality of that life?" I asked, unsure as to why I put voice to the sudden question. "How is it possible to live on in dishonor when one's soul may be cleansed by death in battle, the dishonor washed away with one's blood? How might one beg such a life from another, and care naught for any other thing than that life?"

"So that's the way you see it," said she, bleakly. "With truth and honor, the brave-hearted way, and you can't understand why Tia would want to do it any differently. I wish I could explain it to you, but I'm afraid I can't—and wouldn't even if I could. I'd like to see you keep your ideals for as long as possible—Jalav, Tia can't help doing what she does, that's what she was taught to do. Try to understand that all of us weren't taught the same thing, and maybe accepting us will be a little easier."

The words of the female merely added to my confusion, therefore did I take my attention from her to see how Aysayn fared. The male now sat upon his platform, slowly stretching arms and shoulders, the roundish male hovering near and watching anxiously. Soon would the Sigurri be as he had been before the difficulty, and I not alone in seeing it so.

"I really do wish I had the nerve to try that friend of yours," muttered the female Kira, her half-lidded eyes moving about the form of the male. "I get all quivery every time those pretty brown eyes brush past me, and I keep wondering what it would be like with him. It would probably kill me, but what a way to go."

"Were he invited in a proper manner, Aysayn would bring no other thing than pleasure to a female," said I, sending a dubious glance down to the tiny Kira. "That is, however, to one who was fully grown. The male is extremely well endowed, and perhaps would be overmuch for one who was—"

"Undersized," finished the female sourly when I did not, her glance to me filled with amusing frustration. "I've never before worried about accommodating a man, but none of them had half what he has—in the way of good looks, that is. Do you really think he'd be too much for me?"

Her wistfulness brought a smile to me, the first I had felt in what surely seemed kalod. The thought came that perhaps the female spoke only to distract me from the upset I had felt, and should that be so, my amusement might only increase.

"There is but a single manner in which the truth of the thing may be determined," said I, looking at the female who now looked up toward me. "I shall speak with him on your behalf."

"Speak to him?" she echoed with something of a squeak, her eyes widening at the thought. "About—what I said? Oh, Jalav, you wouldn't do that to me, would you? He might not wait to make sure he was really invited!"

"He would take you in his arms and determine the truth with full certainty," said I, showing naught of the laughter which wished to bubble from my throat. "The use of one such as he is somewhat vigorous; more so, likely, than the use of one of your own males. He would not, however, intrude were another to be asked before him, one such as the male Aram. He has developed a small fondness for the male Aram, and certainly would not . . ."

"Yes, yes, that's it, Aram," said she with great haste, looking upon me with vast relief. "I've already invited Aram, so I couldn't possibly invite . . ."

"Invited Aram for what?" asked the male Aram as he came up to us, eyeing Kira with curiosity. "What have I done this time?"

"It's what you're about to do," said the female in a mutter, taking the left arm of the male in both of hers. "Since I've already invited *you* to share my bed, Jalav doesn't have to speak to Aysayn about *his* sharing it. *Does* she, Aram?"

"What?" asked the male blankly, for the moment taken aback, and then did the female's meaning come to him as her grip increased quite markedly upon his arm. "Oh, oh, that, sure, of course you don't have to, Jalav. She won't have the time for anyone else. In fact, she's even agreed to stay with me in *my* cabin for a few days. Haven't you, Kira?"

"Sure I have," said the female, forcing the words between clenched teeth as she looked up blackly into the grinning face of the male she held. "Why would I want to see my own cabin's carpeting ruined by spilled blood? You louse."

"Now, now, no personalities," laughed the male, truly pleased as he looked down upon her and covered one of her hands with his own. "I waited to be invited, didn't I? When that was the *last* thing I wanted to do? Now all I have to do is make sure you don't regret the invitation—which is the *first* thing I want to do."

No longer was the male showing amusement, and the female ceased her glare with puzzlement, the two looking upon one another as they had not done before. I knew not why I had put the female Kira into the hands of the male Aram, nor was I aware of where my former amusement had gone; I knew only that the weariness deep within was again attempting to surface, and I had not then the thoughts to give it. I looked instead upon Aysayn and found that he now stood beside his platform, therefore did I take myself over to him.

"The pain has entirely gone from you?" I asked, bringing his eyes from Kira and Aram to me. "You are no longer in difficulty?"

"The lash was harder, yet scarcely so all-pervading," said he with a grimace, still working one shoulder. "It pleases me, however, that the unseen lash leaves no track, for I would not be helpless at such a time and in such a place. What have you done with Aram and the wench?"

"My humor seems to have curdled within me," said I with a grimace much like his. "The stranger female attempted to raise my spirits, and I, in thanks, drove her to the side of a male. It is perhaps all one with my failure to take the life of the female who gave you such pain."

"The matter was not one to be pressed at that time," said he with a headshake, his eyes hard. "These strangers are not the same as we, and little honor or satisfaction would be found in such a slaying. Sooner would I take a swordbelt to the bit for her insolence. In what manner did you drive the wench to where she had no earlier wish to go?"

"The female made pretense of an interest in the one who is my present companion," said I, my amusement returning. "As I knew she had no true wish for your use, I made offer to request that use for her—should there fail to be another whose place you would take. Quickly, then, did she recall that she had already invited the use of the male Aram, and asked the male to verify the invitation. This he did with great speed, and she unable to deny him lest she find herself instead in the arms of one whose use would likely weary her greatly."

"Weary her," said Aysayn with a soft laugh, the foolishness having taken the hardness from his eyes. "In truth I would likely find myself unable to so much as put a hand to her, for I have not a taste for the taking of small girl children. It pleases me, however, that you now think to request my use for another, rather than ordering it taken at dagger point. Is such thoughtfulness to continue?"

"For so long as we remain among these strangers," said I with a shrug, well aware that he ragged me. "Their females do not possess daggers."

"I really do think you should let me give you something for the pain, sir," said the roundish male to Aysayn in a bustle of arrival as the Sigurri chuckled at my sally. "You sustained no permanent damage from what was done to you, but you can't possibly be entirely over the affects as yet. Frankly, I can't see how you're able to stand."

"The lash is harder," said Aysayn to the male as he had said to me, looking down to meet his gaze. "Best you pray to whatever god you follow that you never yourself learn the truth of this."

"Indeed," said I to the wide-eyed male. "To be lashed is to be unable to stand, or breathe, or live in any manner save within a film of glowing red agony. One needs to feel the lash to know the true meaning of pain."

"You can't mean that you've been whipped too?" said the roundish male, his shock quickly replaced by concern. "All that hair must have kept me from seeing—Are you still in pain from it? To be distracted by those wound scars is inexcusable—Will you let me look at it? Perhaps I can help."

"The pain from the lashings has long since passed," said I with a headshake and a small smile for the male's agitation. "It remains only in memory, and cannot easily be dislodged from there. Surely would you be more profitably engaged were you to see to your own wounds."

"I?" said the male, this time in surprise. "I have no wounds. Why would you think I had wounds?"

"You felt the female Tia's actions wrong, and yet you obeyed her," said I, no longer showing a smile. "What other thing might you be than wounded in the soul? Does one who is whole do that which he believes wrong? See to your own wounds, male, and consider the while what your fate would be were you to fall beneath the sway of one like yourself. Such a thing would be truly fitting, would it not?"

The male went silent at my words, his visage paled, and he made no attempt to reply to the questions I had put. His wide, pain-filled eyes clung to my face as his fingers pulled at one another at his rounded middle, and not even the approach of Aram and Kira took him from that.

"Are you all right now, Aysayn?" asked the male Aram, looking upon the Sigurri with critical eyes. "Do you need to do anything else for him, Doctor? And have you checked Jalav's arm?"

The roundish male surely heard the words addressed to him, yet did he remain unspeaking and unmoving another brief moment. Then he turned and stumbled hurriedly away, one hand to his face, shoulders rounded and quivering, the very image of one suffering great pain. Indeed was the male wounded in his soul, yet did it remain to be seen whether healing would prove beyond him.

"Well, he can't say he didn't ask for that," said the male Aram with a sigh, following the other stranger male with his eyes till he was gone. "We heard what you said to him, Jalav, and it was something that had to be said. I suppose he thought he could excuse anything he did by tending it carefully afterward, but I don't think he believes that any longer." Then he looked soberly at Aysayn and myself. "We'd better go back to my cabin now. Something very important has come up, and we've got to get to the bottom of it as fast as possible."

Aysayn and I exchanged looks of puzzlement, yet did we follow as the two stranger folk began to lead us from the chamber. The female Tia and the two males in collars of green were no longer to be seen, yet had the dark-haired male remained, and now stood beside the open doorway. He straightened where he stood when we all of us turned toward him, hesitated very briefly with his eyes upon me, then quickly took himself from the chamber ahead of us. When we, too, had reached the doorway and passed through it into a corridor, the male was no longer to be seen.

"Where did Kene rush off to?" asked Aram of Kira, curiosity causing him to look about. "I thought he'd stick around at least long enough to find out if Jalav wanted to thank him for his help."

"I think that's the trouble," Kira replied. "He may be afraid that's exactly what she would want to do. I had the feeling he didn't really understand what she was like until she pushed us out of her way in order to get to Tia. He looked like he was in shock afterward, especially over the way she—ah—disposed of those two Security men. I'm willing to bet he'll do the rest of his admiring from afar. Very far."

Aram chuckled at the tale he was told, even Aysayn joining him, yet I was impatient. Truly peerless were these stranger males, to look upon one with desire, and then quickly take themselves off through fear. Had it been necessary to face them in battle, their wonders might indeed have been insufficient to protect them.

The corridor we trod was unlike those others we had seen in that the many doors along it were of blue, yet once we had again entered a small, unadorned chamber and waited several moments before emerging, we found the corridor to have again been changed to one of few doors of white. The reason for such a doing continued to escape me, therefore did I come to the decision to speak of it.

"Why may we not remain in the corridor while it is changed?" I asked, looking about myself. "Do you hesitate to show us your wonders? And for what reason need the corridor be changed at all?"

"What?" asked the male Aram, slowing as he turned his head to look upon me with puzzlement. "What do you mean, while the corridor is changed? The corridor isn't changed."

"Most certainly is the corridor changed," I returned, almost scornfully. "Are we to believe this corridor the same as it was before we entered that small chamber? Then the doors were blue, now are they white. Do you think me unable to know one color from the next, unable to see the difference between no doors, and few doors, and many doors?"

"Wait a minute, Aram, I think I know what she's talking

about," said Kira as the male frowned. "Jalav, do you think we keep taking the same corridor, only are changing it from time to time? Where do you think the room is where we left your friends?"

"The chamber is there," said I, pointing in the direction opposite to that in which we walked. "I know not why its appearance has been changed, yet do I know it lies there."

"An inertialess portal system would be somewhat beyond them, wouldn't it?" said the male Aram with a wry look in answer to the one he received from the female. "I could repair one faster than explain it."

"That's because you know too much about it," returned the female, amused. "Jalav, the corridor doesn't change every time we step into that little—chamber; our location changes. The chamber moves us around without our having to walk, and the corridors look different because they are different. The place we left your friends isn't down there, it's a good distance away from this location. Do you understand what I'm saying?"

"Perhaps in part," said I, recalling the mist which was used by the gods to move themselves and others from one place to the next. This, then, was the same without the mist, and I liked not the implications. We had been taken far from those who accompanied us, and would be unable to return to them without the aid of the strangers. A glance to Aysayn showed him far more perplexed than I, for he had never been to the place where Mida and Sigurr dwell, yet was he far from cowed or stricken with awe. As the stranger folk again resumed their walk toward that which was termed the "cabin" of Aram, I knew that Aysayn would not hesitate to assist me, should it become necessary to force the strangers into returning us to those who had been left behind in enclosures.

The chamber we entered was unchanged from when we had last seen it, save for a small box of glaring red, which sat upon one low platform. Aram walked directly to this box as the door behind us saw to its own closing, raised it and put it carefully into the hands of Kira, then turned to regard Aysayn and myself.

"We found this among the belongings of our four—guests," said he, the sobriety returned to his light eyes. "We were able to detect it even before we picked you up, which was the main reason you four were chosen as subjects to begin with. What we'd like to know right now is where you got it.''

I almost said that the red box was no possession of ours, when the male reached to it and opened its top. Kira watched with some concern as Aram reached within, and then was it Aysayn and myself who felt concern. Slowly and with great care did the male withdraw my life sign by its leather, yet even so was I visited with illness to see it so close to another. Great harm was it possible for that life sign to bring to one who was not Jalav, and even seeing it held so carefully, my agitation was not soothed. That I had not realized these stranger folk would have possession of it was inexcusable; had any been harmed by it, the fault would have been mine.

"Best you return that, man, and quickly," said Aysayn to Aram, looking upon the other male angrily. "The thing is unsafe, save in the hands of she to whom it belongs."

"She," echoed Aram, sending his gaze to me instead. "You don't have to worry, Aysayn, I know better than to touch the mechanism itself. This is yours, Jalav?"

"Indeed," said I with a nod, somewhat eased to know that the male would touch no more than the leather of my life sign. His calling of it was unfamiliar, yet did I sense the caution within him.

"If this is yours, then you can tell me where you got it," said he, his light eyes unmoving from my face, his hand continuing to hold forth the life sign. "We both know it isn't something your own culture produced, so where did it come from?"

My lips parted to speak of the manner in which it was given to me by the gods, yet did no sound come forth as the thought struck me that to speak of the gods was perhaps to betray them. The dilemma I had earlier been faced with, concerning how to avoid dishonor in a situation fraught with nothing save dishonorable options, had now expanded in size, and I truly knew not what to do.

"This is one question you can't refuse to answer, Jalav," said the male, seeing my hesitation. "The point is too important to let pass, for all of us."

"There are certain things one does not speak of," said I,

feeling annoyance that the stranger would believe I might be ordered to betrayal. "Should the matter change, the male will then be told."

"Damn it, stop looking at me as if I were a lower life form!" snapped the male, returning my life sign to the red box before putting fists to hips. "I don't like being talked down to, and if you're still thinking I couldn't take you hand to hand, you're quite mistaken. And I can also get what answers I need *without* your cooperation. I asked first to be polite, but good manners go as soon as patience does. Tell me where you got that equiresonator!"

"The male Aram may do as he pleases," said I with a shrug, folding my arms as Aysayn moved to stand more closely beside me. "Pain is no stranger to this Midanna, yet first must the male reach her to give it. No words shall I speak, lest the decision be mine—which it is not."

"Now, just calm down, all of you," said the female Kira, putting one hand to the chest of the angry male beside her as she looked upon Aysayn and myself. "Aram, you can't expect to bully her into answering you any more than you would be able to bully a—a general. From what I saw when she made her move on Tia, she didn't get to be a leader because of her bust measurement. And Jalav, Aram isn't threatening you with pain, he doesn't have to. Getting honest answers out of people isn't hard, and there's no pain involved. We have something called truth drugs, and no one, no matter how strong, can resist them. But instead of arguing and throwing threats back and forth, why don't we all sit down and discuss this calmly? We can start by telling you why we want to know what we do."

"They already must know something," the male Aram declared, glaring at me over the head of the female. "Why else would she refuse to come up with any answers?"

"That's what we have to find out," soothed the female, sending her gaze up to the still-angered male. "Or has your male ego been too badly bruised for you to be sensible? Just because you feel she's challenging you, doesn't mean you have to answer that challenge."

"The hell I don't," muttered the male, his glance to me fierce with anger. "I doubt if the primitive is buried very deep in any of us, and all it needs is the right nudge to bring it to the surface. Every time she straightens up and looks down her nose at me I get nudged, but I can't really argue with you. Let's all sit down and be sensible."

The male turned then to the seat he had taken earlier, with the female perching upon the platform to his left, yet when he had settled himself he saw that Aysayn and I had not stirred from where we stood. The truce earlier made remained between us, yet was there no longer a feeling of kinship.

"Do you intend standing there till you drop?" asked the male with faint annoyance for the coldness I sent to him, then did he turn his gaze to the Sigurri beside me. "Aysayn, my friend, I think you may be able to understand why I lost my temper the way I did. Is she always that arrogant with men?"

"Even after a beating," said the male beside me, faint amusement easing the stiffness of his stance. "Chaldrin speaks of the times he whipped her well, yet did she continue to defy him. Never shall she bow to the will of another, save that that other be—"

Abruptly did Aysayn's words cease, for clearly had he nearly spoken of the gods, and the male Aram smiled without humor.

"You, too, eh?" said he, shaking his head as though in disappointment. "Well, if you two think you know something we don't—aside from where you got that equiresonator—I don't mind proving you wrong. Feel free to sit down any time you get the urge. This is likely to take awhile."

The male settled himself more comfortably in his seat, his head back as he kept his gaze upon Aysayn, and seemed to search within himself for the proper words.

"I really don't know where to begin," said he, the female Kira silent yet attentive beside him. "We've already told you how your people came to this place, as colonists who wanted to open up a new planet. Not long after your colony was established, the word went out to all Senders, who were female, that the power crystals of all comms were to be removed and hidden away. Men ran the Union at that time, but the Senders were more ambitious and better organized than anyone thought. Comms without power crystals can be used for short-distance transmissions but not between stars, and the Senders threatened to isolate every planet in the Union if they weren't given the reins of government. The men in power resisted; there was a long and bitter struggle, but the inevitable winners had to be the Senders. You can't drug a Sender or torture her, otherwise her talent weakens or disappears, and chaining women to comms whose power crystals had been replaced turned out to be highly impractical. Senders have to be conscious and willing, or the whole system breaks down. In order to keep themselves and their planets from absolute breakdown due to the lack of essential interstellar trade, the men in power finally gave in.

"Now, the Senders on the various planets had been ordered not to return their crystals no matter how long it took, until a ship came to their systems announcing success with a prearranged password, so that was the first thing the new Union leaders began doing. They sent out the first few ships—and the third one to go out came back with a startling discovery. One of the planets they had been scheduled to stop at, a planet that hadn't yet been able to develop all of the 'wonders' older settlements had, had been taken over during the years of struggle for leadership by a previously unknown advanced race. The members of the advanced race look like us, but their 'wonders' are even more—wonderful—than ours, proving they were a much older race. Somehow, using their powers, they had started making the entire population of the planet their slaves, and if they hadn't been found out when they were, they would have succeeded."

"The Union suddenly found itself in the middle of a long and totally unexpected war," said the female Kira, her demeanor, too, more sober than it had been. "When it was finally over, everyone found it incredible that there had only been five members of that advanced race directing the battle against them. After that there was a search that went slowly from one less-civilized planet to the next, but only two more very small groups of them were found. They hadn't gotten quite as far as they had on the first planet so the battles against them weren't as bad, but they were bad enough."

"And despite running into them three times, we still know almost nothing about them," said Aram, continuing to look only upon Aysayn. "We know they're from something called the Feridan Complex, but we don't know if that's a single planet, a group of star systems, or an entire galaxy. We know they have high-tech gadgets—sorry, 'wonders,' I mean—that are so far ahead of what we can do that we're lucky we can understand what they're supposed to be for. We can't bring our own knowledge up to that level because there's too much missing in between; it would be like seeing someone very good in hand-to-hand combat without seeing the training he went through to get that good. Seeing the end result doesn't tell you how to get that good yourself, especially if it all happens so fast you barely have the time to see it before it's over. We have 'wonders' that can tell us when Feridan 'wonders' are working, other ones that can keep us from being seen by the Feridan invaders, and 'wonders' that can to some extent stop some of the Feridan 'wonders' from working if we're close enough. We learned how to do those few things from the times we fought them, but that's nothing compared to what we want to learn. Compared to what we *have* to learn.''

"Those Feridans are—*twisted*," said Kira, looking to me with a shudder as she spoke. "They like to hurt the people they take as slaves, hurt them horribly, or else make them as twisted as they are. I've read about some of the things they made people do, and I get sick just thinking about it. We have to find out who and what they are, where they come from—and how we can kill every last one of them before they hurt anyone else, if the rest of them are the same. What we have here in this box is one of their 'wonders,' Jalav, something we've named an equiresonator. We've seen it before, always set to match only one person, and what it seems to do is keep that person's body in the same state it was set for. What I mean by that is, if the person was well rested when the equiresonator was set to him, putting it on him when he's tired will give him back a good deal of the strength he's lost, and even repair damage if it has the chance, using the body's own reserves to do the repairing. How it does this we don't know, but it works faster than anything we have. We found quite a few of them on the slaves of that first planet, and they were the only things keeping those slaves alive. Some had been worked nearly to death, and some had been—used to give pleasure to the Feridans, their own twisted kind of pleasure. That's why we have to know where you got yours, Jalav, to find out if the Feridans are anywhere around here."

Silently I returned the gaze of the stranger female, understanding not half of what had been told me, yet a terrible cold had taken my thoughts in its clutches. I allowed the icy spinning to continue no more than a short while, and then found I could no longer keep from voicing a query.

"For what reason would—that device—do harm to another and not to the one to whom it was—set?" I asked, stumbling upon the words in order to state the question in a manner which would be understandable. The male Aram immediately moved his gaze to me, yet did Kira reply before he might speak.

"As far as we can tell, the equiresonators are an exact match to the people they're set for," said the female, also apparently groping for adequate words. "Even if there was someone on your world who looked just like you, inside their bodies they would be different and the—device would be able to tell. It would then decide that it was your body it was sensing, and that something was wrong, so it would immediately try making what was wrong right. Of course, *we* would know that there was nothing *wrong*, only *different*, but the device wouldn't know it and would try to change what it thought was wrong. If it wasn't taken off the other person immediately it would kill them, and the person the device was set for would suffer, too. There's a—link of some sort between the device and the person who's supposed to wear it, and if the device is activated, the person it belongs to is affected. The device has to be returned to that person, or they could die, too."

Kira ended her words of explanation and merely gazed upon me as Aram did, both silently attempting to sense whether I had garnered what I needed from the reply. Also without words, I sank to the floor cloth and sat cross-legged, so shaken that I knew not whether I could have remained erect had that been my wish. It could not be, it could *not* be, and yet did it seem the answer to many questions.

"Jalav, what disturbs you?" asked Aysayn after a brief

hesitation, crouching to put his hand to my shoulder. "For what reason do you seem so—odd?"

"Aysayn, I greatly fear that Mida and Sigurr have been taken in by these—others," I whispered, noting the concern upon his face. "Have we not remarked how different they have seemed, how unknowing and dishonorable they have become? My life sign— How might I have been given a thing so familiar to these folk, save that its source was not the gods but these others? And my sword, the sword given me by Mida. Into the blade have words been etched, yet words which are unreadable by any of this world. In some manner have Mida and Sigurr been taken captive by those who are capable of wonders even beyond the knowledge of these folk we speak with, perhaps even beyond the wonders of the gods! What are we to do?"

The Sigurri's eyes widened as the shock I myself felt gripped him, and he looked upon me wordlessly. He, it seemed, like myself, was unable to conceive of the manner in which mere mortals might free the very gods themselves from capture. Into the silence stepped the male Aram.

"If you have a particular problem, we might be able to help you with it," said he, an offer as gentle as his previous words had been. "We may not know everything, but what we do know we're willing to share. That's the main reason we've come here—to teach you whatever we can."

"How might you teach true warriors to do battle?" I asked with sudden annoyed impatience. "Have you not said that the battles you fought with these others were won only with difficulty? And what of those who were held hostage to these others? Were you able to free them without causing them great harm? From the manner in which you spoke, I would say not."

"You're right," said he with a nod, leaning forward eagerly. "We did have a hard time winning against the Feridans, and we weren't able to save the people they held the closest. Who are they holding hostage that you're afraid for?"

Again I felt it best that I not speak of the gods, this time to spare them the shame of having others know of their humiliation, yet was I this time alone in my determination.

"These—Feridans—you speak of hold hostage the gods

themselves," said Aysayn, the pain in his eyes an indication
of how deeply touched he was. "Jalav's lady Mida and the
great god Sigurr whom I serve—our confusion was heavy
when we thought they demanded that we do battle with those
who might well be our kin, an action filled with dishonor.
Now are we able to see these others as the source of dishonor, yet we are unable to rescue the gods from them. The
gods hold our oaths of fealty, and we are unable to aid
them!"

So distraught was Aysayn at so great a shame that he hung
his head, yet was the male Aram merely puzzled.

"The Feridans are holding your—*gods?*" he asked, sharing his confusion with the female Kira, their glances to one
another fully eloquent. "How could they be—I mean, what
makes you think they're holding your gods? How would it be
possible for them to do such a thing?"

"We know not how it might be possible, merely that it
is," I grudged, speaking where Aysayn was unable to. "How
else might Mida have given me the device you speak of, the
device you describe as being of those others? Would the
goddess who holds my life vow do such a thing, save that she
moved to the demands of another? Would she have sought so
diligently to take my life, when that life was meant to be
spent in her service? Would both goddess and god have
demanded that Midanna and Sigurri turn upon one another
after they had seen to the common enemy? They would
not—save that they were held by these others."

"What do you mean, your goddess tried to take your
life?" asked Aram with a frown, this time sharing a longer
glance with Kira. "And what's this about people turning on
each other?"

"You must tell them all you know, sister," said Aysayn
when I again showed hesitation, seating himself beside me
upon the floor cloth. "We must learn all we may in order to
defeat these others, and how may our kin be of aid to us
without knowing all we know?"

"Very well," said I with reluctance, unconvinced yet seeing
no other path which might be taken. "I shall speak as you
ask, brother, yet shall I also seek a return for what is given.

Should no aid be forthcoming, there will surely be a reckoning."

The gray eyes of the male Aram touched me then, the thoughts behind them unreflected in their depths, yet was I near to certain what those thoughts must be. The likely displeasure of the male did naught to keep me from beginning my tale, however, therefore I began it with the theft of Mida's Crystal from the Hosta. Strange did it seem to relate happenings which now appeared different than my original view of them, therefore did I speak of them as they had appeared at the time, without the bias of what I had learned. The Hosta rode to retrieve the Crystal held by them as a sacred trust, Bellinard was investigated, endured and survived, three Hosta were taken to Ranistard as slaves, despite all efforts three Crystals were placed within the device of the Ancients, and then were the strangers spoken to. In accordance with the will of Mida was I then brought to her Realm upon this world, told that the coming strangers were enemies, and sent to unite my sister clans of Midanna and raise the Sigurri to stand beside them. With the Sigurri allied to our cause we had to claim the leadership of the enemy Midanna as well, and then did all ride to Bellinard to await the arrival of those who were enemies to the gods. What occurred when once those strangers arrived was already known to Aram and Kira, therefore was there no need to tell it.

So few occurrences, and yet was the relating of them so unbelievably long! At some point did Kira quietly depart the chamber for a brief moment, and two hands of reckid after her return was provender brought to us by a stranger male, who quickly deposited his burden, then as quickly left us once more. Somewhat different was this provender in that it seemed less aged than that offered previously, and also was there a considerably larger quantity of it. With the provender was there drink, somewhat like renth yet with a smoothness not to be found in the drink of villages and cities; that it lacked the presence of brewed daru was not to be mentioned, for even so it was considerably more palatable than that termed juice.

The end of my tale found Aram stretched long in his seat with his head back, half-lidded eyes fully attentive, Kira alone upon the wide seat we had earlier shared, also listening closely. Aysayn had put himself flat upon the floor cloth as he, too, listened to the tale he had not heard before in its entirety. I sat as I had been, cross-legged upon the floor cloth, a cup of the odd renth in my hand, pleased to have found an end to the narrative which had not seemed to wish to end. I allowed a swallow of the drink to slide down my throat, a faint curiosity arising within me amid the silence all about, as to what the cup I held might be made from. Smooth was the thing, as smooth as finished metal, yet was it softer and warmer and clearly not metal. Red was it in color, a red I had never before seen yet undeniably red, shiny and yielding and brightly colored and—

"I think I may finally understand," said the male Aram with a sigh, levering himself up to sit more directly upon his seat. "If I'm right you won't have to worry about your gods being held captive any longer, but I have a question. Even if you don't have those to set free, will you still help us against the Feridans?"

"For what reason do you believe we will have none to free?" asked Aysayn, sitting up so that he might look more easily upon the stranger male. "The gods must be held hostage to these others, else they would not have done as they did."

"There's another explanation you don't seem to be seeing," said Aram with a headshake, dismissing Aysayn's contention with full confidence. "That's probably because you don't know the Feridans, but unfortunately for them, we do. We'll tell you everything we can to help you, but I'd still like an answer to my question."

"You would know of our willingness to end these others no matter the hostages they may or may not hold?" said Aysayn, his voice nearly scornful at the thought of allowing such beings to continue. "To permit an enemy to retain his life, is to give him the gift of your own when once your back has turned. The Sigurri will ride against them no matter what, and also, I think, shall the Midanna."

"I'm really relieved to hear that," said Aram, smiling even more broadly at my nod indicating agreement with Aysayn. The Midanna, too, would ride against those who wished to make slaves of them, as what warrior would not? Those called Feridan would regret having attempted the deed, no matter their wonders, no matter their determination.

"It feels good to finally have us all on the same side," said Aram, looking between Aysayn and myself with what was nearly a grin. "The thing you're not seeing is simply this: why do the Feridans have to have your gods as hostages? Why can't they simply be impersonating them?"

We both of us looked upon Aram with incomprehension, his question in some manner unanswerable, and the female Kira came from her seat to resume her perch upon the platform to the male's left.

"What Aram means is, why couldn't it have been the Feridans you met, Jalav, passing themselves off as gods?" said she, her expression now eager. "They seem to have a device that lets them talk to people over great distances without the need for receivers—ah, something like a comm, I mean—that would seem like god-magic to anyone who didn't know about it. By talking to you almost exclusively in your sleep, the female one made it seem that she could enter your dreams, when all she really did was wake you up part way to talk to you, and then let you go back to sleep."

"And they also have a machine—a device—that moves them around like our portal system," said Aram, nodding in agreement with Kira. "The difference in theirs is, they don't need a car—a chamber—to move in, so they can go anywhere with it. The only thing they have to do is stay in range of the device—damn, how do you explain operating range and field of broadcast, Kira?"

"Operating range is easy," said the female with a grin, again turning her gaze to me. "Jalav, picture yourself with a knife in your hand and your arm able to move, but your feet in a place where you can't free them and your body rigid except for being able to turn in a circle. If Aram comes close enough to you you can stab him, the closer he comes, the better you can stab him. That's because he's in *range* of your knife. If he steps back or stays back, he's out of range no matter how sharp your knife is. That's clear enough, isn't it?"

"Indeed," said I with something of a smile for the amusement I felt, in the main due to the humorous outrage the male attempted to show to the female. "However, it must be recalled that Jalav is also able to cast her dagger, therefore is its range wider than you believe."

"Great," said the male Aram, glancing sourly upon the laughter of the female Kira. "You have her stabbing me, and now she decides to throw the thing at me. While I'm still unperforated, would you like to cover field of broadcast next?"

"I don't think that's necessary," said Kira, looking to me with no more than the end of her amusement. "Do you understand the rest of it too, Jalav? Everything you thought was being done by gods was being done by the Feridans. They're the ones you met, and they're the ones who caused all those 'miracles' to happen."

"Indeed I do not understand," said I, again returned to confusion and lack of humor. "For what reason would these Feridani do me so when I believed I rode in their cause? And for what reason did the gods themselves not intervene? As they have not been bested, their power must surely remain as it has ever been."

"Possibly your—gods were kept from knowing what was happening," suggested the male Aram, again exchanging glances with Kira. "Just the way we can shield—block out—make unnoticeable—our presence to their devices, maybe they can do the same with the sight of gods. And as far as why they tried to kill you, I couldn't even begin to guess. They probably had what they considered a good reason, but that doesn't mean it would look the same to us."

"And your not feeling—ah—interest in men while wearing your life sign may not have been done to you deliberately," said Kira. "The equiresonator is made to keep your body the way it was when the device was set. Passion raises the pulse and increases the rate of breathing, weakens the limbs and causes the body to generally deviate from the norm. The purpose of the device is to stop and change deviations from the norm, so passion would, as a matter of course, be ruled out."

"Passion and deviations from the norm," said the male Aram, grinning upon Kira. "I'll just sit here quietly while you define *those* terms, assistant Leader."

"You have not as yet said what might be done against these Feridani," said Aysayn, impatient with Aram's unexplained amusement with Kira. "Nor have you spoken upon the reason why the Midanna and Sigurri were sent against you. Surely would the Feridani know of your wonders and know, as well, that our weapons were no match."

"Of course they knew," said Aram, once again serious. "The reason they sent you against us is obvious—they didn't want you finding out about them, as you would have if you'd met us as friends. And they didn't want *us* finding out about them. As for why they bothered sending you against superior weaponry, the answer is easy: they expected you to pretend to accept us, and then wipe us out when we weren't expecting it. That's the way *they* would have done it, so why shouldn't they expect the same thing of you?"

The anger in Aysayn's eyes was strong as he looked toward me, outraged that he had been correct in his previous surmise. I, too, felt outraged, to think that these Feridani would see us as honorless as themselves, so twisted as to accept ones in friendship and then attack them in treachery. Indeed did my hand then yearn for the feel of a hilt, and those so-called gods armed as they wished before me.

"And as far as what we can do to help you against the Feridani goes, don't forget we'll be helping ourselves at the same time," said Aram, his discomfort over Aysayn's anger only somewhat apparent. "We can see to it that they don't know we're coming until we're right on top of them, we can send out scramble signals to block the output of most of their gadgets until the signals are neutralized—protect you and your people from their powers for a while, I mean—and can supply transportation to their location for a large number of your followers. We can also supply about a hundred fighters to add to your force."

"We thank you for the offer of fighters, and will consider it," said Aysayn quickly, before I might speak upon the uselessness to be found from those who were not true warriors. "The balance of your assistance we will gladly accept, for these Feridani are indeed enemies to us all. When may we return to our people to discuss the attack we plan?"

"It's too late to get started with it today," said Aram,

glancing to a device with numbers which were ever changing, before stretching hard enough to crack muscles. Then did he rise from his seat to look down upon us. "By the time I arranged for a scout ship to take you back, it would be well after dark on your world. If you'll accept our hospitality for tonight, we can get started first thing in the morning."

"We will accept your hospitality," said Aysayn, again with haste, rising to his feet to forestall my objections. Ever do males find other things to take their attention when no more than battle considerations should concern them, and clearly were stranger males no different than those I was already acquainted with. I, too, stood where I had formerly sat, swallowed the last of the near-renth I had been given, then held out the cup for Aram to take.

"You, young lady, remind me more and more of the higher-ups among the Senders," said he with a sour expression, taking the cup I held out, annoyance behind the sourness. "What's eating you this time?"

"I have no understanding of what eating the male Aram refers to," said I, folding my arms as I looked upon him. "What I know is that when one finds battle necessary, one sees to it at once rather than after all manner of delays. We are now to be returned to our enclosures, I take it."

"Sorry, but you take it wrong," said he, meeting my gaze. "You and Aysayn aren't dangerous strangers any longer, so there's no need to lock you up again. And since all of us can't be great warriors like you, we'll still wait until morning before getting started. Not to change the subject, but are you sure you're old enough to drink that wine you've been putting down? I'd hate to have someone accuse me of letting a kid get blotto."

"You would dare to name the war leader of all Midanna a child?" I demanded, unfolding my arms so that I might straighten in insult. Nothing more was I able to glean from the male's words, for in what manner might the age of a warrior reflect upon what daru she drank? The skill attained by a Midanna determined at what age she was blooded, and once blooded none might halt her in her doings save with a sword. The warrior who swallowed daru too near the time of battle or a hunt did not long survive to do the same again, a thing all those of the clans knew.

"All I can do is tell the truth as I see it," he said with an innocent shrug. "Only children get pouty when they can't get their way on the spot and have to wait for what they want, but adults learn patience. And they also learn good manners. If you were mine, I'd spank you and send you to bed without supper for something like that."

"I would have you recall, friend Aram, that there is truce now between us," said Aysayn with odd amusement in his voice, his wide hand quickly upon my shoulder, his grip hard. "All of us are concerned over what lies before us, therefore is courtesy surely strained. One who feels insult over the doings of a Midanna may challenge her, yet to speak to her as you have done is to give even greater insult, a dishonorable doing when she may not reply by cause of the truce. Was it your intention to give her such insult?"

"No," said Aram with reluctance, glancing to me as he addressed Aysayn. "I was only trying to give back a little of what I was getting. Where I come from, men don't challenge women the way you mean, not even when the women are as arrogant as she is. The most they can do is answer in words—as long as they don't mind losing everything they might have for speaking them. If Jalav feels that insulted, she can use a sword the way Senders in the Union use the power of their positions. If keeping my job—or life—means I can't answer back when I'm insulted, I'd rather lose those commodities and keep my pride."

The male ended with his eyes directly upon mine, the gray gaze steady and unafraid, his shoulders back and head high. To declare one's freedom despite being unable to defend it with a sword is a mark of one who is truly free, one who is warrior in truth if not in deed. Without doubt had I given the male inexcusable insult, seeing him as no more than those of cities and villages, yet had I been mistaken. There was naught to be done save retrieve what had been unintentionally given.

"It was not my desire to give challenge to one who is unable to honorably accept it," said I, returning his look with a matching calm. "Had I known your codes forbade such a doing, I would not have spoken with insult. Despite the insult also given me, I shall not do the same again."

"As long as that also excludes using me for dagger target practice, your apology is accepted," said he, now faintly grinning, hands resting upon hips. "Being killed by a little girl, even one who leads hundreds and hundreds of bloodthirsty warriors into battle, would be somewhat embarrassing. What made you want to challenge me anyway?"

The question put by the male was open and without guile, no more than curiosity vocalized, mild and inoffensive; nevertheless did I find something of difficulty in answering, for at first was I unable to discover within me the true reason for my doing. Then did I see that I had done with the stranger as I had with Mehrayn, seeking one who would best me and thereby rid me of the burden of life, and the weariness deep within nearly rose to cover me. So sweet would be such an ending, were all responsibilities entirely seen to; with duty yet remaining before me, however, no more than a doing of shame was it.

"You are a male, and therefore less than a warrior," said I after a brief pause. "Ever has it been the way of warriors to treat with males as they would, for what male not also a warrior might prevail against her?"

"But what if the—male—*was* a warrior like herself," asked Aram. "What if he did prevail against her?"

"Then she would forfeit her life for the insult she had given," said I with a shrug, wondering at what point the male moved toward. "What more fitting punishment might there be for offering insult to one's superior?"

"I can think of quite a few more fitting," said the male with distaste, yet not in an effort to give further insult. "I may be talking out of turn again, but I can't see murdering a woman just for flapping her tongue too hard. Do you see it differently, Aysayn?"

"Midanna wenches are, of necessity, wenches rather than men," said Aysayn with a shrug much like mine. "A man is more tolerant toward wenches than they are toward him, for he may ever soothe his feelings of insult by tasting deeply of the wench, after having given her a taste of the leather. To slay her would be far less satisfying."

"Now, that I can go along with," said Aram with a grin, deliberately taking no note of the bristling annoyance of the female Kira. "We'll take you two back to that empty cabin, show you how to make yourselves comfortable, then leave you alone for a while. When you're ready for more food, you'll let me know and I'll get it for you."

"I would have what remains of the near renth," said I as the male headed toward the door, the female in his wake. Both halted to turn to look upon me after no more than a pair of steps, and the male seemed faintly disturbed.

"You're talking about the rest of the wine," said he, and then did he look upon Aysayn. "I was only partially joking before, considering how much she's already had of it. Isn't she really too young to be swigging wine the way she's been doing?"

"My sister's capacity for drink is surely sent by the gods," said Aysayn with a touch of amusement and a glance for me. "I have discovered to my chagrin that my own fails to approach hers, most especially with the liquid fire which she and her wenches imbibe from first light to last. In this instance, however, I believe she has had sufficient to last for the time. There remain things which must be discussed between us."

The dark eyes of the Sigurri male moved to rest upon me with calm, a calm which failed to affect me. The male Aram had already turned again toward the door, pleased to deny me further drink at the command of Aysayn. Had we not been in the midst of the strangers I would surely have challenged the male for daring such a thing, yet were we soon to be left with none save each other.

The smaller chamber called cabin was shown to have many things, among them a place where one might relieve oneself without fouling the chamber itself. The use of this place was shown me by Kira, the same shown Aysayn by Aram, and then were we told of the main chamber. All words were accepted by me in silence, Aysayn alone seeing to their acknowledgment, and then were we left to ourselves by the departure of the strangers.

"So, brother, there are things remaining to be discussed between us," I said with a growl, moving to stand perhaps two paces before him, my left palm seeking in vain for a hilt to stroke. "Perhaps you would now care to speak to these things."

"Indeed," said he with a slow nod, seeing clearly how great my annoyance was at the absence of a weapon. "I would speak of the reasons for what is, in truth, an overindulgence on your part which had not been in evidence before our arrival at Bellinard. Also would I know the reason for your giving challenge to one who at first seemed incapable of wielding a weapon, yet who proved to be well-armed with a device unknown to me. In some manner do I believe that you were aware of this device despite being unfamiliar with it, an awareness which led you to seek challenge. What prods you so greatly that you would seek to stand against a well-honed sword with only a thin, useless twig?"

The concern in the eyes which held to me was unanswerable, therefore did I turn from it without reply. I, myself, knew not how it might be answered, save that my time enmeshed by males and gods and strangers had already been far too long, yet promised to continue even longer yet. My suspicion that the male Aram had armed himself in some manner had proven correct. Jalav, who wore no life sign to guard her soul, would truly be gone when once she was bested, yet the attainment of the doing continued to elude her.

"It seems strange that I had not before seen how few kalod are yours, wench," said Aysayn from behind me, his voice soft with concern. "To see the warrior and war leader you are is easiest, for seldom do you appear indecisive or at a loss, and to see a sword in your fist is to see a skill seldom attained even by a man. And yet you are indeed scarcely older than a child, and burdened with the responsibility of the lives of the many who follow you. Would it ease you to have Mehrayn or Ceralt here in my place, or perhaps both?"

"No!" I said at once. In no manner might I choose one over the other, and to have them both would be to have them again at each other's throats, a thing I was just then unable to bear. Indeed would I have joyed in feeling their arms once again about me, and yet— "No," I said again with something of a headshake, and Aysayn came to stand directly before me.

"You will not speak to me of what disturbs you," said he, raising one hand to free my shoulder of the hair which draped it about, no questioning in the words. "You have no need to speak of your reasons for wishing Mehrayn and Ceralt left where they are, for I know them as well as you. In what manner, then, may I indeed be of assistance to you?"

"Go and fetch what drink remains in the chamber of the stranger male," said I, looking up at him directly. "As it was your doing that the near renth remained behind, you may now repair the lack."

"That I shall not do," said he, a shadow of anger forming in the dark of his eyes. "To wallow in drink is the coward's way, and I will not aid a coward to greater avoidance of duty!"

"Duty!" I spat, truly enraged by his insult. "What might one such as you know of duty? Are you not male, and aided, as all males, in seeing to duty? Have you not Mehrayn to direct your legions, and those who send your prayers to your god, and ones to see to your mount and sharpen your sword and oil all your weapons? Even the pain of captivity was yours for no more than feyd, a weapon kept from your hand no longer than the time it took for the ache of the lash to leave you! I am Jalav, war leader of all the Midanna, and these things are mine to do *alone!*"

Again I turned from him, furious that he would dare speak to me so, forcing from me words I would not otherwise have uttered, but I was unable to stride about as I so needed to do. Two wide, strong hands came to my arms to halt me, catching strands of hair beneath them, their grip unbreakable despite the lack of pain.

"I had wondered for some time at the way you tended me when I lay in agony from the lashing," said he, his voice strong yet odd to hear. "Surely did it seem that you knew what I felt, yet such a thought was scarcely possible. None would lash a wench, I knew, and though I tremble yet at memory of the doing, tremble at thought of facing it again, you, I now find, have faced it thrice. Your strength must nearly be spent, girl, to have faced that and recurring captivity, and pain and more pain. Turn not to drink when there are those about you who would share the burden and thereby ease it."

"Sooner would I have the drink," I said. "The drink makes no attempt to pity its drinker, nor does it speak foolishly of those things of which it has no true understanding. Take your pity elsewhere, male; Jalav has no need of it."

"I offer no pity, empty-headed, stubborn, she-lenga!" growled Aysayn, anger tightening the grip of his hands. "No more do I offer than what strength you require, till your own has healed itself and returned. Best you accept the offer, for I shall not allow you further drink. There is battle soon to be before us, and for battle one's head and body must be clear."

"A warrior's doing is the concern of none save herself," I rasped, raising fists before me as I attempted to pull from his hold. "Release me at once, else shall we see how far your learning goes."

"You would know how far my learning goes?" he asked, truly angry. "You mean to obey none save yourself, and attempt to defy one who seeks naught save your well-being? Very well, then, girl child, test my learning; perhaps you will thereby be taught a thing yourself."

Chaldrin had often spoke of Aysayn's skill in weaponless combat. Well did I know that I had no hope of besting the Sigurri who stood behind me, yet shall no true Midanna admit defeat before the final blow is struck. With that in view I twisted between the hands which held me and struck upward with my right forearm, at the same time launching a backward kick, meaning to free my arm and strike the male, both at nearly the same time. The movement had not been taught me by Chaldrin, and quickly did I learn the reason for the lack; my rising arm found naught to halt it, for the male had already moved to grasp the leg which also failed to meet a target. The large male hands which had previously held to my arms were abruptly about ankle and foot instead, twisting with greater skill than I had yet attained, to take my balance and send me flying backward. Much did I expect to land upon the floor covering, as near senseless as I had been when last the male had tripped me so, yet had I forgotten the presence of the low, wide square which the chamber contained. That was the place to which I had been thrown, and when I sprawled upon it Aysayn followed quickly, to see that I was unable to rise again.

"You struggle more now than when last we engaged in such foolery," said he, forcing my wrists beneath me as I fought to free myself from his grip and the too-near presence of his body. "Do you continue to mean to defy me? Shall I show you the folly in such a thought by giving you the hiding Aram would not be displeased to see you receive? As neither Mehrayn nor Ceralt are present in this chamber, I must see properly to their wench for them."

"Jalav is the possession of no male," I grunted, finding yet again how difficult escape from male strength was. The hands about my wrists beneath my back scarcely strained, yet was I unable to free myself no matter the effort I attempted. "Nor shall she abandon a stand even should she be beaten for the lack. Do your worst, male; there shall come a time when I am not held so."

"There shall indeed be such a time," said he, the words soft, his amusement softening as well. "Just as there have been many such times in the recent past. You may not have Mehrayn for Ceralt is there, you may not have Ceralt for Mehrayn is there, and you may not have another for both men would then stand against the third. Their love has taken what little pleasure there was for you in this life, and I much doubt that they have as yet come to be aware of it. You are not made for such denial, sister, no wench is made for such constant strain. Will you not allow me to aid you?"

So soft had his voice grown, as lulling as the nearness of his great body was arousing. I put my head back to the low square beneath me as I closed my eyes, held in his arms and by his strength, the feel of his flesh against my breasts now intruding upon my awareness. So warm was the body pressed to mine, so easily were my lips suddenly taken; a wench who found too great a pleasure with males, had Aysayn called me, and with the emergence of the memory I twisted my face from his.

"The heat rises too rapidly within you to be denied, wench," he murmured, his lips now at my throat, one hand freed so that it might stroke my flesh. "Take what is offered without hesitation, and perhaps a portion of your strength will be returned. As I shall not allow you the drink you demand, I must give you another thing in its place."

"Aysayn, release me," I whispered as his lips and tongue and hand touched me everywhere, yet was there no sound behind the movement of my lips. Soft yet firm was the wide square beneath me, inescapable was the grip of his hand about my wrists, wildly heating was the manner in which the male touched me all about. His warm, gentle breath briefly caressed my face, and then were his lips again upon mine, this time disallowing avoidance. Ah, Mida, how great a pleasure there is indeed in the use of males, nearly as great as once again finding myself able to call to you. My lips met the male's and sought to give what they demanded, and not long was it before one called brother was in full possession of me. So long did it seem since last I had truly joyed in such vigorous thrusting, and long, too, was the time before it was ended. Blessed is she who is brother to a warrior, for in his arms is she able to find pleasure without concern.

12.

Returning— and a difficulty is solved

As those who dwell within the Caverns of the Doomed are able to know the arrival of each new fey without seeing Mida's light, so, too, did the strangers come to the chamber called cabin in which Aysayn and I had slept, to say that they were prepared to return us to our own. Indeed were we prepared to be so returned, therefore did we quickly follow where the male Aram led.

Briefly was it necessary to await the opening of the chamber which traveled about, therefore had I a moment of opportunity to consider what had passed between Aysayn and myself when once we returned to our chamber after having taken provender with Aram and Kira the unseen darkness previous. We had deemed the low square somewhat adequate for seeking our rest upon and had placed ourselves upon it, and then had Aysayn again taken me in his arms. The annoyance I had felt at having been given no more than water with my provender had been heavy, aiding me in resisting the male, yet had Aysayn done no more than chuckle.

"Am I to understand that you find falar-like drink more desirable than my use?" he had asked, holding me firmly to his body despite my attempts to squirm free. "Am I to be thought an inadequate substitute for that which is found in a cup?"

"That which is found in a cup may be put aside when there is no desire for it," I had replied in greater annoyance, looking up to the amusement in his eyes. "Come the fey I am able to do the same with a fool of a Sigurri Keeper, then shall he be deemed equally adequate."

"And yet, blessed Sigurr smiles upon the taking of unwill-

344

ing wenches," said he, a grin now covering his face. "Am I, a devoted follower of the great god, to overlook his teachings merely to soothe the pique of such a female? Sooner would I soothe another part of her."

"No Midanna warrior seeks soothing from the use of a male," said I with a snort of ridicule, seeing that he again attempted to rag me. "Vigorous use brings pleasure and easing, naught which might be considered soothing. Surely will Aysayn soon be offering a gentle caress of concern."

"And yet it is indeed concern which Aysayn feels toward you," said he, his gaze sobered and seeking within me. "Your pleasure from my use was as deep as when I took you in Chaldrin's realm, yet did I feel that you might have had even greater pleasure. Is there a thing you would have me do or fail to do, a thing which would bring you what I wished you to have?"

The arms of the male this time released me when I attempted to move from him, therefore did I lie flat upon my back in the dimness of the chamber, gazing up toward the white of the ceiling. A faint bit of light had been left by the strangers, yet would it have pleased me just then to be in the midst of full darkness. The wide square beneath me gave greater comfort than sleeping furs or leather, yet for some reason I liked it not. Also was the chamber far too close, lacking the sweet cool which often eased the darkness from the warmth of the fey. There would be difficulty in finding sleep in that place, I knew, yet did not know how to change the matter.

"So there is but one thing I must do," said Aysayn, leaning upon an elbow to look down upon me. "I must become either Mehrayn or Ceralt, or perhaps even both. Clearly are you unwilling to discuss the matter, yet must it at some time be discussed. When this battle with the Feridani is done, we shall see to it together."

Then had he lain himself beside me, one arm about my middle, and had composed himself for sleep. As I had earlier surmised, the thing came far more easily to him than to myself.

The chamber which moved about returned us to the corridor which led to the place where Ceralt and Mehrayn were

yet in their enclosures, and then did Aram free the two who
glowered behind the unbreachable walls. The eyes of both
came to me as soon as I entered the chamber, and when once
they emerged they came quickly to stand before Aysayn and
myself.

"What occurs here now, brother?" demanded Mehrayn of
the other Sigurri, his glance to Aram filled with suspicion.
"Ceralt and I thought ourselves forever forgotten."

"Merely were we learning the truth of what we stand in the
midst of, brother," replied Aysayn, and then did he relate
completely our thoughts and surmises, and that which the
strangers had spoken of. Neither male interrupted the telling,
and when the narrative was done, Aysayn added, "The wench
and I have concluded that attack upon Sigurr's Peak will only
allow us to know the final truth. Should those who call
themselves Sigurr and Mida be Feridani, we shall use the
stranger aid to find victory over them. Should they, instead,
truly be the gods we serve, we shall fight to reclaim our oaths
of fealty. Death would be greatly more preferable to living
lives of dishonor."

"Therefore shall we do well to now return to our own,"
said I, filling the silence which Mehrayn and Ceralt seemed
disinclined to break. "Aram and Kira shift with impatience
where they stand, and I, too, feel the same."

Quickly did I receive the agreement of the others, therefore
did we all follow the strangers again, into the chamber which
moved about. Another moment saw us emerging into a wide
area rather than a corridor, clearly made of metal yet so high
and with such distant walls that had there been feylight,
surely would I have thought myself without an enclosure. The
light, however, was no more than that which lit all the
chambers of the place, and many large, oddly made objects
stood all about with strangers scurrying between them. Aram
strode unhesitatingly toward one of the nearer objects, Kira
by his side, therefore did we four also follow, albeit more
slowly. Endless seemed the number of wonders at which one
might look, and yet, they made no sense.

"We'll take you back to your people in this scout ship,"
said Aram when we reached him, gesturing toward the object
which loomed high and large behind him. "And now I think

we'd all better get aboard, before every tech in this shuttle area goes cross-eyed from trying to stare at Jalav."

Aysayn chuckled at the words of the stranger male, yet was it necessary that I glance about before seeing that the males of the place had indeed halted what they were about, to look upon me as males were wont to do. So taken with the wonders had I been, that I had not earlier seen their stares, yet had Aysayn and Aram observed them—and Mehrayn and Ceralt as well—as they also heard the long low two-note whistle which split the air. The two straightened where they stood to look all about, and surely did it seem that had they been armed, they would have brought their anger to the hand upon hand of males who then stood about staring. Without comment, therefore, did I walk after Aram and Kira, and Aysayn followed without the amusement he had earlier shown.

Once within the large object, we were all taken to an area of many seats, seats which were fitted with chains which were not chains. Gray were the walls of the area, and the seats as well, and black were the cloth chains which had strength as great as metal. With the aid of Aram and Kira did we all place the cloth chains upon ourselves across breast and belly and thighs, and also learn how quickly and easily we might free ourselves. Then did Aram and Kira take seats of their own across from where Aysayn and I sat, and enchain themselves as well.

"It won't take long to get down, and once we're there we'll return your weapons," said Aram after putting hand to a small square in the right arm of his seat. "I'm sorry, Jalav, but we'll be keeping your equiresonator, to be turned over to our Union research people. Will not having it make things more difficult for you?"

"The absence of that life sign will be greater relief than difficulty," said I with the faintest of smiles, only then understanding that anticipation of the return of the thing had been an unseen cloud above my head. "To know that it shall not be able to bring harm to another is indeed worth losing what benefits it brought to myself."

"That's an attitude not many people in your place would have," said Kira, looking to me from beyond the male Aram,

an odd glow in her eyes. "If all your people are like you,
Jalav, I think we'll be learning as much as we'll be teaching."

What the female would learn was not completely clear to
me, yet before I might question her upon the point, a faint
vibration began all about the chamber in which we sat.
Perhaps two reckid passed before the vibration ended, and
then did the male Aram look upon us with satisfaction.

"We're now out of the ship and on our way," said he,
making no attempt to free himself of the cloth chains upon
him. "It won't be long now before we have you back where
you belong. Would it be better if we grounded inside the city,
or outside of it?"

Aysayn and I looked upon one another, for surely had we
thought to be returned to the place from which we had been
taken. To arrive in the midst of our warriors in a device of the
strangers might well cause Midanna and Sigurri to attack, an
occurrence which it might prove impossible to avoid. Words
of dismay were immediately exchanged among the three males
who accompanied me, yet did I look upon Aram with a
question.

"This object flies, I take it?" said I in an effort to clarify
what had been asked. "Aysayn had said that what found us to
begin with fell from the skies. This device is the same?"
With Aram's nod, I, too, nodded in decision. "Then we
must—alight—within the gates of the city."

"Why?" asked Mehrayn, his light eyes filled with lack of
understanding. "Sigurri and Midanna are to be found both
without and within the city."

"And yet those within have been cautioned to be alert for
that which may come from the skies," said I, speaking of the
council I had had with my war leaders—and recalling the
later council I had failed to attend. "This were my warriors to
make mention of to yours, therefore are they less likely to
attack without awaiting sight of what emerges from this
object. It would grieve my Midanna to later discover that they
had slain their war leader."

"It would grieve me even more to be slain right along with
you," said the male Aram, looking upon me with wry mis-
givings. "I hope your guess about their not attacking immediately turns out to be good. But whatever made you think of

telling them to watch for something that flies? Your people don't have anything capable of taking to the air."

"A war leader must consider all possibilities," said I with a shrug. "I had thought it was the arrival of gods that we anticipated, and gods are able to do many things mortals may not."

"That's no more than a verbal rationalization for cogitation on the deepest levels," said the male, then grinned at the frowns he received. "What I mean is, you react intuitively in a given situation, acting on a base logic that's essentially non-verbal. Damn. That didn't tell you any more than my first comment did, did it? Let's just say you're a great general, and let it go at that."

The male then sat back in his seat, and I, too, allowed the matter to rest, for there were other things of greater import to consider.

In the following reckid the male Aram left us once, briefly, and then returned to resume his seat. Though naught of provender had been offered us after we had awakened from sleep, I thought it likely that once the reckid became hind, the oversight would be rectified; with this in mind, when faint vibration came briefly and then Aram left his seat to stand beside ours, surely did I believe that he came to anticipate the time of feeding and would question us regarding our desires. In this, however, was I greatly mistaken.

"Well, we're here and down," said he, gesturing to the cloth chains upon us. "You can get out of the safety harness now, and start trying your hands at keeping us from being attacked. I'd try it myself, but I think it would sound better coming from one of you."

"We have already arrived?" asked Aysayn, putting words to the incredulous disbelief I, myself, felt. "Our journey from the city took more than three feyd. How is it possible to have returned there so quickly? Is the place where we were kept truly so close to Bellinard? And for what reason was it necessary that we be bound to our seats so?"

"I think I'm about to need an interpreter again," said Aram, gesturing Kira beside him as the three males with me and I rose from our seats. "Let's start walking as we talk;

even if your people aren't attacking yet, the longer we keep them waiting, the more likely it is that they'll start. The exit hatch we'll be using is this way.''

As quickly as we began to follow in the direction in which the male led, his glance went to Aysayn.

"This scout ship—object—moves so much faster than what you and your party were riding that I couldn't begin to describe it to you—without having you think I was lying. If we had started out from the point you were picked up, we would have been here much sooner. It took as many minutes as it did because we started from much farther away, not because we have a base near the city. As for the reason for the safety harness—Kira, how do you explain what happens if an inertialess ship suddenly loses its drive and is no longer inertialess? I don't know how to say that without the harness we'd splatter.''

"Why don't you try saying that the harness is there in case an emergency comes up, but happily this time it didn't come up?'' suggested the female Kira, faint amusement in the glance she sent to me. "If you try taking it any other way, you have to first explain what inertia is, and I don't think I have enough forward momentum for a job like that.''

"I always knew you were chicken,'' said the male with a grin which the female echoed, and then had we arrived at a place which was wider than the corridor leading from the chamber of seats. Beside one of the dark metal walls were the weapons taken from the others and myself, stacked upon the uneven metal flooring which felt so odd beneath one's feet. Quickly did I move forward to reclaim my sword and dagger, and then stood aside to don them as the males did the same.

"You really do look at home with all that hardware,'' said Aram as his eyes followed the manner in which I placed my dagger in its leg bands, then did they move to observe Aysayn and Mehrayn and Ceralt. "All of you, completely at home, and I think I'm beginning to feel jealous. Are you sure you want us coming with you right now?''

"My brother and I have already explained that we believe your presence vital,'' said I, aware of Aysayn's glance. "Our warriors must see for themselves the strangers who claim kinship with us, else shall we waste precious moments of battle preparation in speaking words of description and reassurance. Where is the door from which we are to emerge?''

"Right here," said Aram, indicating a section of the metal wall we stood beside, his doubts no more than somewhat lessened. "Before we unbutton, though, I think we'd better take a peek."

Once again the words of the male meant naught, yet did the doings of his hands halt what protest I would have made. The male had touched various odd projections upon the wall near to him, and what seemed to be a window appeared immediately beside the projections. We had come to a halt not far from the palace of the High Seat, I saw, and saw as well that many warriors were already about the object in which we stood, with more appearing rapidly each moment. Stares and gestures came from both Midanna and Sigurri, disbelief and outrage amingle upon their faces, yet had none as yet begun to loose arrows or spears at what had appeared before them. For some reason was sound denied entrance through the window, therefore was it possible to hear the sigh of the stranger male.

"Well, here goes nothing," said he in a mutter, and then did a section of the metal wall begin to raise itself. Beyond the bottom of the rising wall was it possible to see the emergence of a flat section of—something—which stretched itself down to the ground, and the entrance of Mida's sweet air, warmed by her light, quickly showed how flat was the air we had breathed during our stay with the strangers.

"All we have to do now is walk down the ramp," said the male Aram, hand resting upon that which I now knew to be a weapon, one which Kira also wore. "Once we're out, the scout crew will close the port behind us, to make sure no one comes souvenir hunting. Are you ready?"

Indeed was I prepared to return to those who were my own, therefore did I move quickly to the place which had now fully opened itself, and looked out. Arrows taut in bows, and arms cocked with spears were to be seen all about among drawn swords held in fists, yet was there no more than the sound of a great gasp at my appearance. Aysayn came behind me, Ceralt and Mehrayn behind him, and as the gasping gained in volume, so, too, did the many demands quickly shouted from many throats.

"As you are able to see, the strangers have arrived," I shouted, my eyes narrowed against the brightness of the light. "Two of them accompany us and we must quickly hold council, for there is battle before us in which they and we shall join against a common enemy. Send without the gates for all war leaders and Princes of the Blood, for there is much to be done and little time to see to it."

"At once, war leader," responded several Midanna, turning and taking themselves off as I and the three males in my wake carefully made our way down the thing Aram had termed ramp. The steepness of its angle of descent was scarcely so extreme that we were unable to remain erect, yet was the thing far less comfortable to walk than would have been a comparable stair. When once we reached the ground I turned to see that Aram and Kira now walked the ramp, a thing I had known of from the increased murmurs of exclamation of those who observed us.

"See to the hastening of all who are to come to council," said Mehrayn to a Sigurri who had approached him in greeting, clapping hand to shoulder in return greeting. "I have not yet sorted the tale completely in my own mind, yet have the Shadow and the Midanna war leader seen the thing clearly."

With a nod the Sigurri warrior made his way among those who surrounded us, allowing his place to be taken by others who clamored to know what we were about. Scarcely was it possible to speak over the growing uproar, therefore did we wait till Aram and Kira had reached us, then began making our way toward the overlarge dwelling called palace.

"Jalav, what occurs here?" demanded Palar, hurrying to remain beside me the while she looked upon the strangers and the odd coverings they wore. "Have we bested them, or they us?"

"Neither, sister," said I with a faint smile for her confusion, knowing full well how she felt. "We have all of us spoken, and have discovered a common enemy. This enemy is greatly powerful, so powerful that neither we nor these strangers would find it possible to best them alone, yet together we shall prevail."

"We, who are warriors, require the aid of the likes of them?" asked Palar with great indignation, again turning her auburn-haired head to inspect those who hurried to match our stride. "They appear to be no more than children, Jalav! In what manner are they to aid us?"

"They possess devices which will best the devices of our enemy," said I, speaking softly so that Aram and Kira might not hear my words. "Also have they beseeched the aid of our warriors, for what being with eyes would not know them for the unskilled folk they are? We would find it possible to defeat the enemy without them, yet they, alone . . . To refuse to share a victory with one who would battle beside her sisters, were she able, is to be filled with a meanness of soul Midanna have never been cursed with. These stranger folk shall be our valued allies."

"Indeed," said Palar with a thoughtful nod, her dark eyes upon mine with a great lessening in confusion. "They shall be our valued allies. And I shall go ahead to be sure you are all properly received. We will speak again in council, sister."

With a brief grin did she then take herself off, trotting through and ahead of those who accompanied us. Surely would my words now be shared with her sister war leaders, and all would know the truth of them when once they looked upon Aram and Kira. Indeed had the presence of the stranger folk been necessary, to take hands from swords and fear from the minds of those who yet thought of the strangers as enemies. None looking upon them could see them so, and quickly would their thoughts turn to the coming battle—as was proper.

With some small difficulty did we gain the palace proper, and from there proceeded to the chambers which were mine. Ceralt departed before then to seek out Galiose and Lialt, and Mehrayn took himself off to confer with those who had been left to command the Sigurri in his absence. Both males had looked upon me briefly before departing, yet had I made it seem that their looks had gone unnoticed. Too many were the matters then before me, to spend thought upon difficulties which seemed without solution.

Fresh provender had already been brought to my audience chamber, and fresh daru and renth as well. I paused only long

enough to ask Aysayn to remain with the nervously silent
Aram and Kira, poured a cup of daru, and then had a Hitta
warrior take me to where Chaldrin had been quartered. It was
necessary that I see with my own eyes that the Sigurri continued to live, and then would I find it possible to consider no
other thing than battle.

The chamber given to Chaldrin was not far from mine, and
indeed did the Hitta know it at once. Much time had Ilvin and
many of her sisters spent there, though the light-haired warrior was then standing watch. I pushed slowly through the
door to find a chamber bright with Mida's early light,
S'Heernoh in a seat to the right feeding upon provender
which seemed just recently brought him, a platform to the left
called bed, in which Chaldrin had been placed. The large,
dark male seemed asleep, and when I halted in uncertainty no
more than three paces beyond the door, S'Heernoh left his
provender and came to stand beside me.

"It pleases me to see you returned unharmed, lady war
leader," said he in a voice of softness, his dark eyes looking
down upon me warmly. "Chaldrin, too, will be pleased, for
he has not ceased to ask of you. We thought it best to tell
him that you rode with certain of your warriors, to be sure
that those who were defeated truly departed these lands. He
grows stronger with each new light, yet shall it be some time
before he is able to stand beside you once again."

"For what reason does he live?" I asked as softly as he
had spoken, my eyes unmoving from the still form upon the
device called bed. "Many times has my sword found what it
sought, and never did the one so found survive. I thank Mida
most fervently that this time it was so, and yet— How might
I have been mistaken over so familiar a doing?"

"Chaldrin has his great size to thank that he continues
among us," said S'Heernoh, smoothly. "The muscle within
him deflected your thrust, else would he surely have died.
The time he must spend unmoving in his bed will be adequate
punishment for the foolishness of his actions, Jalav. He should
not have done as he did."

"You know?" I asked in surprise, at last looking up to the
male. "You know what occurred between us?"

"I know only that the doing was his, that you sought to

call back the slaying thrust even before it reached him," said S'Heernoh, compassion clear in the gaze which came down to me. "For what reason he sought death at your hands, I have not been able to learn."

"I sought death, for I knew that if I lived you would surely watch me starve with complete unconcern," came a whisper of a voice, stronger than I had expected and yet so very, very weak. Quickly did I turn my head to see that Chaldrin was now awake, his dark eyes resting avidly upon me. "Pleased am I to see that you have returned, girl, for this heartless wretch refuses me adequate provender the while he swallows all which ventures past him."

"You are not yet healed far enough to eat as you wish," said S'Heernoh with the severity one would use with a disobedient child, little patience in the tone. "I have told you and told you, and still must I search each Hitta wench entering here, to be sure she does not bring what would surely make you ill. Do you now seek to give me a like chore with the war leader?"

"Few would consider the matter a chore," returned Chaldrin with a shadow of the chuckle usual to him, his eyes more sober than his words. "Have you come to speak with me, Jalav?"

"Indeed," said I, stepping nearer so that I might look down upon him as I sipped from my daru. "Not often does one find so great a fool of a male, therefore have I come to reaffirm your existence. I am told you grow well again, therefore shall I warn you now of the words to be exchanged between us when you are again as you were."

"Words," said he with a look much like that of an erring warrior-to-be, wilting beneath the eye of her war leader. In truth did the male seem far from well, his visage pale, his mighty arms apparently strengthless, his great body swathed in cloth which covered the wound which had downed him. A cover of cloth was upon him from waist to toes, a cover he seemed to require despite the warmth of the chamber. His dark eyes saw the great, seething anger which filled mine to overflowing, and indeed did he seem near to shrinking back against the sight.

"Aye, words," said I, stepping nearer yet. "Words concerning the actions of those who believe they do what is best for another, without first ascertaining the true desires of that other. There shall be no blades between us, for surely there has been enough of that already. Yet shall there be words.''

''I do not believe my strength will be sufficient for such words for quite some time,'' said Chaldrin with an uncomfortable hollowness I had never before heard from him. ''Should the wait prove too lengthy for you, sister, you may certainly begin without me.''

''The wait will likely be unnoticed by me, *brother*,'' I informed him, hearing the chuckling of S'Heernoh where he stood. ''The strangers have arrived, and I have spoken with them. As soon as may be—with the new light at the latest—Midanna and Sigurri ride in war against ones who are enemies to us all. A pity you shall be unable to accompany us, for the wait would then be the same for you.''

''You ride?'' demanded Chaldrin, greater strength appearing within him as though suddenly given by the gods. ''You go to battle when I am unable to stand beside you? I shall not allow it, wench, by my soul I shall not allow it!''

And then did the male begin to struggle as though to rise, truly a foolish act. Quickly did I put aside the cup I held, S'Heernoh coming as quickly to join me, and together were we able to force the large Sigurri back upon the platform. After endless reckid, amid much shouting and struggling, Chaldrin at last lost his battle with consciousness, and then were S'Heernoh and I able to straighten and step back. A trickle of blood had appeared upon the cloth wrapped about Chaldrin's wound, yet were S'Heernoh and I nearly afloat in the moisture of effort.

''Praise all the gods that he is wound-weakened,'' said S'Heernoh, drawing one forearm across his forehead. ''Should he have been in full strength, likely you and I would have found ourselves ignominiously bested.''

''I, most certainly,'' said I, attempting to coax my hair back from about dampened arms and breasts. ''You, however, seemed well able to hold your own against him, despite the need to keep from doing him further harm. Will the struggle do him serious damage?''

''Less, I believe, than allowing him to rise,'' said S'Heernoh, watching as I fought with my misbegotten hair. "Did you speak merely to give him further punishment, or were your words sooth? Have you indeed met with the strangers? Do you truly ride to war?"

"Indeed and truly," I replied, at last able to retrieve my cup of daru. "Perhaps it would be best were Chaldrin bound where he now is, so that he shall not find himself able to add to his foolishness."

"I shall send for servants to do that very thing," said S'Heernoh, nodding firmly with decision. "Also to remain with him and tend him in his weakness. I, of course, shall accompany you to battle."

"You would ride to battle?" I asked, having no wish to give the male insult, yet finding the suggestion more than inappropriate. "You, who bears no more than a dagger as weapon? You, who fears to face no more than the displeasure of Mehrayn and Ceralt? Warriors alone shall ride to this battle, S'Heernoh, for those we face shall be more than cringing city folk. Best would be that you remain where you are truly needed, here, with Chaldrin."

With a final glance for the unconscious Sigurri, I began to turn from S'Heernoh, but the male halted me with a hand upon my arm.

"As you deem it necessary, I, too, shall be a warrior for this battle," said he, striving for calm and certainty above the sudden vexation to be seen in his eyes. "I shall wear a sword as the others do, and shall stand beside you in the place that was Chaldrin's."

"Shall you indeed," said I, sipping again from the daru to cool the words which wished to pour forth from me. "You shall don a blade, and thereby be made a true warrior, one fit to enter battle at the side of a war leader. Just so easily shall the thing be accomplished, in the same manner that we others have achieved our places."

"Lady war leader, I mean no insult against your great skill," he said at once, the words flowing as easily and earnestly as ever they did from him. "Well am I aware of the kalod required to attain even a semblance of such skill, for I have myself spent such kalod in the endeavor. I had chosen to leave my sword behind me for I was displeased with the fruits of my efforts, yet am I far from unskilled. I ask no more than that I be given what the others who wished to join you were allowed: an opportunity to prove myself before you speak a final decision. May I be allowed what others were allowed?''

I stood and considered the male silently for a moment, recalling the aid he had given me in the past, attempting to look beyond the manipulation he strove for. This male S'Heernoh was well-used to receiving all he desired, and perhaps seeing it so again would teach him the folly of his ways.

"Very well," said I at last, giving no indication that I anticipated the outcome of a bout between the male and a warrior. "As the others were allowed their choice, so shall you be: which will you have to face you, Midanna or Sigurri?''

"Forgive me, lady war leader, yet I, too, must choose to face a man like myself," said he, the deep pleasure in his dark eyes betraying the apologetic tone he used. "Were your wenches less skilled, I would not hesitate to face them, knowing I would fail to strike with full strength, and yet they are indeed most skilled. For so desirable an end, I shall not strive with less than my utmost."

"As you wish," said I with a nod. "I shall speak with Aysayn, and the Shadow will find one to face you. Remain here until the meeting has been set, for I would not have Chaldrin left unattended. Also, be sure you set one in your place when you depart."

"Certainly, lady war leader," agreed the male with the short, odd bow he was wont to perform, his hidden pleasure now less noticeable. With the matter seen to my movement was no longer halted, therefore did I take myself from the chamber and return to my own.

Within my meeting chamber were already a large number of war leaders and Princes of the Blood, yet were there clearly many to come. Each war leader attempted to demand an explanation of me as I passed her, yet did I reply that all must be present before the matter might be gone into. Aysayn stood beside Aram and Kira, the stranger folk continuing to appear ill at ease; when once I had worked my way through the throng, the large, light-haired Sigurri left them and stepped out to meet me.

"Our newly made friends seem to anticipate difficulty with our brothers and sisters," said he in a lowered tone, his amusement clear. "Though I have attempted to assure them they have naught to fear, still they persist in looking nervously about themselves and starting in surprise at the arrival of newcomers."

"Clearly, then, are the weapons they wear no match for such large numbers," said I, also keeping my gaze from the stranger folk. "Were they adequately armed, there would be no need for fear."

"One may be adequately armed, and yet be reluctant to use such arms," said he, smiling in an odd fashion. "Either through reluctance of the soul, or hesitation approaching cowardice. One would be wise to ascertain the truth before acting prematurely. How fares our brother Chaldrin?"

"The fool of a male attempted to rise to his feet so that he might join us in battle," said I, disgusted. "With great effort were S'Heernoh and I able to halt him, yet now does S'Heernoh himself seek to join us. I have promised him a Sigurri to face, so that he may prove his worth as a warrior. Will you choose one to stand against him?"

"As that is his wish," agreed Aysayn with a sigh. "One would believe we embarked upon a journey of pleasure, so eager are all those about us to join in. The warrior I choose will be an excellent one; will S'Heernoh be greatly distressed when he is unable to accompany us?"

"Undoubtedly," said I with a nod, "and yet do I prefer the thought of the male distressed to the thought of him slain. Also has it come to me that Chaldrin and any other Midanna or Sigurri who lies ill or wounded, must be removed from this city before our departure. Should there be vengeance sought for the taking of the city after our warriors have been withdrawn, we would not wish our ill and wounded to bear the entirety of it."

"Indeed," said Aysayn, of a sudden seeming more alert and animated than he had been. "Such a circumstance had not occurred to me, yet you are undoubtedly correct. I shall see to both matters now, and then shall return."

With a single swallow did Aysayn take the remainder of what his cup contained, gave me the cup, and then began to depart through the throng. No more than a moment did I watch his departure, and then took myself to those who had named themselves kin to Midanna and Sigurri.

"When last we invited strangers to join us," I remarked to Aram, sending my gaze to his, "they survived the ordeal a hand of feyd or more. Think you those who are the possessors of wonders may do at least as well?"

"First Aysayn, and now you," the male replied, a wryness to his expression and in the manner in which he winced. "I can see I'm not being as nonchalant as I thought I was. Is it likely to insult your people?"

"They would not find insult in the doings of those brought by Aysayn and myself," I reassured the male, also addressing Kira who had stepped nearer to hear our conversation. "Is there some difficulty with which I may aid you? Should you continue to be so ill at ease, the feeling will surely spread and raise suspicions in regard to your intentions."

"Damn it, you're absolutely right," muttered the male, raising one hand to the back of his neck above his white collar. "The only problem is, Jalav, I don't think you *can* help us. Kira and I have both found that to be with you and Aysayn and the other two men, is not the same as being in the middle of dozens of male and female giants, all of them armed with weapons they not only know how to use, but also enjoy using. I don't mean to insult you, but when I think about there being no one but you—and earlier Aysayn— between us and them, and then think about the possibility of having them lose their tempers— It just doesn't do much for our peace of mind."

"You felt my presence inadequate for your safety?" I asked, in some manner more amused than insulted. "You believe that Jalav alone—or Aysayn alone—is insufficient protection?"

"Well—yes," grudged the male, a shame-faced agreement from Kira accompanying the admission. "We appreciate your offer to help, but now you can see there's nothing you can do."

"Perhaps we may find a thing to be done," said I, emptying my cup as Aysayn had done with his, and putting it down. Then did I survey those who stood about as I took two paces forward, and raised one fisted arm for silence and attention.

"Midanna and Sigurri," said I, finding approval in the attention given my words. "Are there any here who are unfamiliar with this warrior who stands before you?"

Surprise greeted my words, and many exchanged looks with those who stood beside them, yet were there none to claim lack of familiarity.

"Very well," said I when none other spoke. "As you all know me, I now ask if there are any who would stand in challenge against me."

Again were there exclamations of surprise, yet were there also none who stepped forth. As I had expected no other response, I shared with them my faint amusement.

"Our guests, those who come from the skies, know naught of what skill I possess with the sword I wear," said I, resting left palm upon hilt as I looked about. "Perhaps there are two here who would care to challenge me in tandem? Should the two be male, they may have the stranger female to taste in the event of victory; should the two be female, they may have the same of the male. Are there two who would face me?"

At these words did those before me begin chuckling, aware, now, that I proposed no serious challenge, though I required serious response from them. Heads shook as they looked about, faintly curious to see whether there were any foolish enough to believe they might do as they willed, yet did there continue to be none with a will to be ended.

"It has come to me that there may be a hand or more of those who are to come who may wish to face me," said I, continuing to look about. "In such an event, are there any here who would stand with me?"

"I!" quickly shouted every Midanna, and "Certainly!" and, "At once!" shouted many of the Sigurri, smiles taking them all at thought of such excellent battle. The smile I wore warmed and my chin rose high with pride, and I turned to look again upon Aram and Kira. The stranger female gazed upon me with great approval, and the male chuckled softly in amusement.

"No wonder Aysayn said calling you a little girl was insulting," said Aram very low, so that only I might hear.

"They're yours, every one of them, but that's not the reason they won't face you. You're better than they are, and they all know it. I didn't ask this question before to keep from sounding nosy and pushy, but I think I can ask it now that you're back among your own people. How many of them are there?"

"Of Midanna war leaders, there are eighteen beside myself," said I, informing the male of naught which he would not soon see of his own self. "The Sigurri Princes of the Blood are four full hands in number."

"That's more than I expected," said the male with a frown. "Aysayn told me that each of his Princes commands approximately one hundred fighters, and I suspect your war leaders do the same. I did some preliminary computer work on moving a fighting force from here to Sigurri's Peak, and the computers tell me we can slip in about two thousand fighters before the Feridans notice what we're doing. After that the risk of landing anyone safely more than triples, which means we'd be throwing away the lives of almost everyone beyond the initial two thousand. You have twice the number we can move."

"Our force must be halved?" I asked with a frown, somewhat unsure of the single thing I had gleaned from the words he had spoken. "We may not all of us invade the domain of these Feridani?"

"I'm sorry," said he, vexed. "We have only six shuttles, and maximum emergency load for each is two hundred. If we're careful with our timing, and the first fighters landed don't show themselves until everyone is moved in, we can get away with ten shuttle loads for certain, twelve if we want to push our luck. After that the safety margin drops to the cellar, and anyone we send out probably won't make it."

"Aram means that our—advisors—tell us that two thousand is the largest number we can expect to get to the place of fighting," said Kira, clearly having noted my confusion over the male's attempt at explanation. "If we try to send in any more, the shuttles will be destroyed and the people in them will die. Won't two thousand be enough to win against whatever forces the Feridans have?"

"Even half the full number of Midanna and Sigurri are

sufficient to best any force sent against them," said I, fists to hips, far more vexed than the male Aram had been. "The entirety of those who serve the Feridani were not shown to me, I know, yet is the size of their force unimportant. We shall best them no matter their number."

"Then what's bothering you?" asked the male, his light eyes filled with perplexity, Kira's look the same. "If you believe you can take them with the two thousand, what's wrong?"

"In what manner am I to choose the ones who shall go?" I demanded. "All here shall demand their share of the glory of the battle; in what manner am I to broach the subject of fully half remaining behind?"

At last did the two stranger folk look upon me with understanding. A long glance was exchanged between them, and then did Aram show something of a smile.

"I can see our cultures are even farther apart than we thought they were," said he, his smile having turned wry. "It never occurred to us that something like that would be the major problem. Will you be able to think of a way around it?"

"I must," said I, turning from him toward the board and the daru it held. But three steps returned me to my cup and a pitcher, but I was scarcely aware of the doings of my feet and hands. Indeed was it necessary that I discover a manner of making the unacceptable acceptable, and that as quickly as I might. Deep in thought, I then took myself to one side of the board and crouched there, seeing naught before my eyes save the whirlings of vexation brought about by idle considerations.

Some uncounted number of reckid passed before I became aware of one who crouched before me. My returning sight found the one to be Aysayn, who looked upon me in an odd manner.

"All those who were to come are now here, wench," said he very softly, yet with fists clenched. "Has it yet come to you what may be done concerning this halving Aram speaks of? I would not have my warriors at each other's throats by cause of it, yet does such a thing now appear inevitable."

"To me as well," I replied, with a sigh, reluctantly straightening from my crouch as Aysayn did the same. "Perhaps we had best begin the tale now, and trust to Mida to provide what is needed when the time comes to speak of it.''

"You may trust to your goddess, sister," said he with a smile of shared pleasure. "I shall trust in Sigurr the while, and surely shall one or the other find what we seek."

"Indeed," said I, as pleased as he that we might consider the gods once again as something other than enemies. I stepped beyond him then to face those who had gathered in that candlelit chamber to await the telling of the tale we had, all conversation suddenly ceasing when they saw me prepared to begin. At my gesture did they all take seat upon the floor cloth, showing me the presence of Rilas and Ennat as well as Galiose and Lialt to the rear of the chamber, and then did I begin speaking of how we had come to find ourselves among the strangers. As the tale was not long, I reached too quickly the summation I had hoped would find me prepared to continue on to that which none of them would wish to hear.

"Therefore are we now aware of the following facts," said I, at the close noting with pride how well those who were leaders among us accepted so incredible a tale. "The ones presented to me beneath Sigurr's Peak as Mida and Sigurr are in truth ones called Feridani, ones who would see both Midanna and Sigurri, not to speak of those of the cities and villages, as slaves to them or slain out of hand. These stranger folk were presented to us as enemies to our gods so that we would slay them, in the process learning naught of those who would take our lives and freedom. In no manner might they truly be Mida and Sigurr, for our gods would not demand the dishonor so often demanded by those who sought to gull us. This warrior before you is not chosen by the gods but by those who are blood enemies to them, yet does she mean to prove their choice a poor one. Aysayn and I shall carry battle to them, battle they had sought to avoid. Are there those here who would ride with us?"

Agreement rose as shouts at us from every throat, leaving no doubt as to the intentions of war leaders and Princes of the Blood. A Sigurri then voiced a question to Aysayn, the first of many which were eagerly put to Sigurr's Shadow. As my cup was drained of daru, with the first question I turned to the board to see to it, my mind still confusedly asearch for that which would avoid battle amongst our own forces. Aram and Kira stood quietly to the side, aware of the stares of curiosity sent toward them, yet no longer disturbed. Galiose and Lialt, to the rear of the chamber, had seemed less believing than Midanna and Sigurri, and when I had turned to the board they had turned to the doors to the corridor, likely departing to seek out Ceralt and a confirmation of what had been said. I reached to a pitcher of daru, annoyed that those who remained upon sufferance would dare to doubt—and then merely held the pitcher without pouring. In the midst of all that had occurred I had forgotten a thing of great importance, a thing which would surely solve the dilemma of numbers for me.

Replacing the pitcher and cup without pouring, I turned again to Aysayn and those who questioned him, striding quickly to where Sigurr's Shadow stood. The male was about to give ear to yet another query, but my abrupt return created a distraction.

"There are a small number of things which have not yet been discussed," said I to the curiosity which touched me from all about, aware of the same even from Aysayn. "There is a greatly difficult decision to be made by those warriors now within this chamber, yet must the decision be made. Honor allows no other course of action."

"What might such a decision be, Jalav?" asked Palar from where she sat, her frown mirrored by most of those about her. I looked from one questioning face to the other, then did I straighten myself where I stood.

"I have been told by the stranger folk with us that the Feridani are possessed of wonders," I said at last, unable to keep the bleakness from my voice. "I, myself, have seen something of these wonders, therefore do I give full credence to the caution which I have had: these folk who are likely kin to us will do all they may to defeat the Feridani wonders with wonders of their own, yet are they considerably weaker than the Feridani. Should they fail, we who ride against the enemy may well fall to wonders even the gods seem unable to overcome. The glory of death in battle is the right of each of us in this chamber, yet shall the glory be tarnished with a matter of honor left unseen to behind us. Those of Ranistard continue to hold captive both Hosta and Silla."

Again were there comments in many voices, shock from the Midanna, lack of understanding from the Sigurri. Quickly did those Midanna near Sigurri explain the meaning of my words, and shortly were all again looking upon me, this time tight-lipped. Sigurri warriors, I knew, greatly disliked the thought of Midanna held captive and their anger was clear.

"All, I believe, are now able to see the dilemma before us," said I, continuing to look about. "Should we most of us fall to the Feridani wonders, who will there be to free Hosta and Silla? Which of us will find it possible to joy in eternity at the side of our gods, when we must recall that there were those abandoned by us for the sake of battle pleasure?"

"Jalav, what are we to do?" blurted Ludir, the Simna war leader putting words to the distress of all. "The Silla—and the Hosta—how might we abandon them? May we free them before we face these Feridani?"

"Should we do such a thing, the Feridani would be warned of our intentions," said I with a headshake, knowing the truth of my words would be quickly seen. "The female, in her guise as Mida, has forbidden the freeing of the Hosta till the strangers have been seen to. Should this command be ignored, surely will she know what we are about. We must strike the Feridani as swiftly as possible—with or without dishonor left behind us."

"We are to abandon those wenches to their fate?" demanded one Sigurri whose name I did not know, the outrage fairly glowing from him. "Should we do such a thing, blessed Sigurr will surely turn his back upon us in disgust!"

"What else can we do?" asked Aysayn, his gaze coming to me with the words, the deep pleasure in the depths of his eyes showing him filled with the knowledge that I spoke to a purpose. "In what manner might such dishonor be kept from us?"

"There is but one thing which might be done," said I, speaking to Aysayn and to the others as well. "Half our number must see to the cleansing of the honor of us all, and must shoulder an additional burden as well: should those of us who face the Feridani fall before the enemy is bested, those who ride to free Hosta and Silla must in some manner

attempt to reverse our failure. To fall in battle may be done
by any; Midanna and Sigurri must gain victory with their
deaths, else shall those who would steal our very gods from
us, end with that which they covet. Can we allow that?"

"No!" came from every voice, male and female alike, and
then did they all, by threes and fours, surge to their feet to
surround Aysayn and myself. With some small difficulty did
I make it known to them that each clan and princely legion
was to be divided in twain, half to attempt the Feridani, half
to free those held captive. Also was half of each group
attempting its own objective to contain a war leader or prince,
half a chosen designate, for there must be experienced leaders
with those who rode to Ranistard, should the need for battle
against the Feridani arise afterward. Those who stood in the
chamber fretted, for each wished to be with both groups. I
left the choice to those who knew their warriors best, and
soon they all began to depart from the chamber. It had
become clear that those who went to Ranistard must arrive
there before the force of so-called warriors already returning
there, therefore would those who rode depart with the new
light and push to reach Ranistard first, to avoid the need for
spilling unskilled blood. Aysayn departed with certain of his
princes, deep in discussion and planning, but I was mistaken
in believing all Midanna had already gone.

"Jalav of the Midanna," came the voice of Ennat, drawing my gaze to her and Rilas, the two Keepers standing side
by side near to the seats of the chamber. Both wore smiles of
great satisfaction, and indeed did Ennat appear filled with
amusement. "I had not thought to say this to you, yet am I,
and Rilas as well, bound to intervene when a Midanna speaks
words which are clearly untrue."

"You both believe I spoke lies?" I asked, more perplexed
than insulted. "How might I have done so, when all I said
may be proven?"

"War leader, you announced yourself as other than chosen
by the goddess," said Rilas, clearly sharing the amusement
of Ennat. "Such a statement is patently not so; are you not to
lead the battle against those who attempted to sully the glory
of Mida? Do you not take vengeance in her name? No other
than one beloved and chosen might do so, a fact most clear to

Ennat and myself. We determined to speak of this to you, so that you would not utter such a falsehood again. Also would we know which set she and I are to accompany. With all warriors riding off to battle, we would not be left behind."

"Rilas, you have spent too long a time with Ennat," said I with a smile, warmed by the words they had spoken. "Those who go to Sigurr's Peak must all be warriors, and those who go to Ranistard will ride hard to arrive before city males already gone on their way. Neither set must be given the added burden of seeing to the safety of Keepers, yet is there a doing which must be seen to despite the certain reluctance of those who will be given the task. In that place shall the presence of Keepers be a blessing, to soothe tempers and pride, and disallow the probable sacrifice of those filled with guilt."

"Of what do you speak, war leader?" asked Ennat, curiosity battling with outrage at the knowledge that she would not be permitted to ride with warriors. Rilas had merely sighed and accepted the limitation, for Rilas had had many kalod more as a Keeper; Ennat, new to the honor, continued to think as a warrior would.

"I refer to those who are ill or wounded or in some other manner incapacitated," said I, speaking gently out of deference to Ennat's hurt. "Already has Aysayn seen to their removal from this city before it is abandoned by us, but those warriors given the task of caring for them are sure to chafe at being left behind, when their brothers and sisters ride off to battle. Those requiring care will likely assure these warriors that they are able to see to themselves, which will surely not be so. I have need of those who will also require the assistance of warriors, but ones who will not feel guilty at keeping them from battle. Will you be able to do such a thing, while you all travel slowly in return to the lands of the Midanna?"

The frown now upon Ennat was one of thought, and Rilas smiled quietly to see the other Keeper's outrage so quickly soothed and silenced. My request had not been idle, she knew, therefore it was likely to be heeded.

"Such a doing does indeed require our presence," allowed Ennat after a moment, the decision reluctant yet firm for all of that. "To permit our warriors to go unattended by cause of

their knowledge of honor would be dishonor in itself, therefore shall Rilas and I accompany them. Also shall I pray to
Mida that she remove some measure of elegance from her
chosen—so that in future her Keepers need not bow so low
and so often to necessity.''

The sourness of Ennat's words and glance brought chuckling to myself and Rilas, and then did the Keepers take their
leave. When the doors swung closed behind their backs, I
turned to find the eyes of Aram and Kira upon me.

"She wasn't joking about your eloquence," said Aram, his
smiling gaze touched in an odd manner with that which
seemed to be desire. "You're also one hell of a leader; one I
wouldn't mind serving under myself. And that's something I
never thought I'd say to a woman.''

"What he means, Jalav, is that he really admires you,"
said Kira with an odd smile of her own, stepping forward to
take one of the male's arms in both of her hands. "He isn't
really volunteering to serve under you in a capacity other than
military, because he already has that sort of commitment with
another female, namely me.''

"Are you serious?" the male asked of the female, looking
down upon her with great surprise. "All we have between us
is last night. You can't mean it was as good for you as it was
for me?"

"Why not?" asked the female belligerently, looking up to
meet the eyes of the male. "I'm old enough to know when
something real comes my way, something I've never had
before. Are you trying to say you're thinking about refusing
me?''

"Refusing you?" echoed the male very softly with a smile
of joy, raising his free hand to touch the face of the female
who was now his. "You'll never live to see the day. And if
you try dumping *me*, I'll hit you with the hardest breech of
promise suit you've ever heard of. Jalav, Kira and I have an
engagement to celebrate. Is there some place private we can
do our celebrating?''

"You may have the use of my inner chamber," I replied to
the sole part of the query I was able to understand, yet pleased
to see that Aram no longer had eyes for any save Kira. I had
no true wish to use the male, yet would it have been neces-

sary that I agreed, had he, an ally, asked it of me. I watched as they walked hand-in-hand through the doorway of my sleeping chamber, then did I look about the now emptied outer chamber, attempting to put my thoughts in order. Surely were there matters of import I had not yet touched upon, matters which would need to be seen to before we faced those called Feridani. . . .

"Jalav."

The single word halted me in the pacing I had begun, for it had come just after the sound of my door being pushed inward. The voice was clearly Mehrayn's, and I found great reluctance in the thought of turning to look upon him. Here, then, was a matter I had not yet attended to, yet was I unable to conceive of a manner in which it might be settled.

"Wench, I have little time to speak with you, yet are there so very many things I wish to say," said he, his voice nearing as his steps did, and then were his hands upon my arms from behind. "With the new light we go to face these Feridani, therefore must I see to my legions, and yet—how may I go to battle without first speaking of what my heart is filled with for you? Should I fall—should I fall, you must know that my love continues on through all eternity, never to be ended, even by death. It is yours no matter your own willingness to accept or refuse it, yours no matter the occurrences which are to come. I have come to hold you one last time in my arms, for the new fey will allow the indulgence in duty alone."

Duty. With the sound of that accursed word I turned beneath his hands to clasp him to me as hard as I might, unable to bear the thought of his loss. So large and strong was that red-haired Sigurri, so broad and attractive to those who were Midanna—and so dear to she who was war leader to warriors. His arms closed about me as mine had done with him, and then were my lips his, his fist in my hair seeing it so. Ruthlessly was I crushed to the warmth and strength of his body, ruthlessly yet so very willingly, and then, far too soon, was I released so that Mehrayn might hurry from the chamber. Perhaps I had seen a glistening in the green of his eyes before he had turned away, perhaps the glistening had been in the vision which was mine. I knew only that I had not wanted him to go, that I had so great a need for his arms about me that I could not bear it, yet had I been unable to speak the words which would have brought him back. Duty had he to see to, and I as well, and nothing would change that.

I stood unthinking and unfeeling for I know not how long, lost to all lucidity and reason, and then, between one breath and the next, became aware of the fact that I was no longer alone. I raised my head in confusion to see who might have entered without speaking and found the light eyes of Ceralt upon me. The male stood no more than two paces away, and when my gaze touched him, he smiled with a good deal of pain.

"I see I intrude at a time when intrusion is unforgivable," he said evenly. "My beloved is needed to assure our victory over those who would enslave us all, therefore am I forbidden to distract her. The lives of so many depend upon what is done with the new light, and Lialt tells me I dare not attempt to keep you from leading those who attack, else shall victory likely not be ours— Woman, how may I consider others, when it is you alone I wish to consider? And how may I not consider others? In what manner have I so displeased the Serene Oneness, that he now demands the risking of *your* life rather than mine? Why am I not allowed to stand in your place?"

The confused, agony-filled demands cut me so deep that I nearly gasped, transfixed by the bewilderment in his gaze, and then were there no longer two paces behind us, not even a finger's width. With arms of metal did Ceralt hold me to him, no more than his breech and mine keeping our bodies from touching at all points, his face buried in my hair.

"Forgive me, satya, yet I may do no other thing than hold you a final time," said he, the words muffled to near incomprehensibility. "I have loved you from the moment I first saw you, and shall love you through all of forever. As I am unable to stand for you, I shall stand with you, and perhaps learn what it is to share pain with one I most wish to keep all pain from. I have no true desire to do this—yet I must—and the pain has already begun. I love you, my Jalav, and shall never cease loving you."

In some manner were my arms as tightly about him as his

about me, the strength in his grip one I longed never to have lessened, and then were our lips upon each other's, frantically taking joys that might never be taken again. I, too, felt the pain he had spoken of, a longing for that which could not be, and again were the arms which held me gone too soon. Ceralt, too, nearly ran from my chamber, and once the doors had ceased their swinging behind him, I slowly folded to the floor cloth and wept as though I were city slave-woman and unashamed.

The strength of the sobs taking me were a storm, one so strong that I lay with cheek to the floor cloth, aware of nothing else, concerned with nothing else. At some time did another enter and pull me from the floor cloth to be held in arms of strength, yet were the arms other than those I longed for so uselessly. Broad was the chest I wept against, attempting to give comfort even in the face of lack of understanding, yet I cared not. The chest was covered with hair of yellow rather than red or black, and naught might be done to change that.

"Sister, why do you weep?" asked Aysayn at last, when the storm subsided. "What has happened?"

I sat upon the floor cloth with my cheek pressed to his chest, his arm tightly about me, my body shuddering still with the echo of desolation. How might I speak of the truth which had been shown me, the truth of that which I now faced? No longer was battle to be between myself and Mida, for she who had caused me such humiliation and pain was less than a god—and considerably more. The battle I would stand in would be shared by those males I could not choose between, those who meant more to me than life itself; what if one or both were to fall? And what if neither fell, what if both were left hale and strong at battle's end, and myself as well? Would they not then face one another, as they had earlier intended to do, and would not one at least fall in that meeting? In Mida's name I could not bear the thought, yet I could not see an alternative. I lay against the warmth of Aysayn, held in his arms, and my tears flowed more freely with the knowledge that never would I find it possible to do the same with those I most desired.

"Perhaps I need not ask why you weep," said Aysayn

with a sigh, the pain of shared understanding in his voice. "Merely shall I marvel that it has not occurred much the sooner. I came with some small amount of news; once I have given it you, I will see that you rest.

"Already are those in need of tending, as well as your Keepers, in the midst of leaving the city," said he, his hand gently stroking my hair. "It was necessary that Chaldrin be given a potion to bring him sleep, yet was the thing done without hesitation. Their set is small, your wenches and my men riding in attendance, yet shall they move no better than slowly. I thought it best to have them as quickly as possible upon their way, so that none will pursue and find them without effort. Should any chance upon them our warriors will see to the matter. Also you must know that another will journey with us to the battle at Sigurr's Peak."

"Another?" I asked, at last finding myself able to push from Aysayn's arms to sit straight upon the floor cloth. I felt as though all strength and will had drained from me, and also did my voice seem hoarse in my own ears.

"Indeed," said Aysayn, attempting a smile as his hand smoothed the moisture from my cheek. "One we had neither of us expected to accompany us. S'Heernoh has faced my Sigurri warrior—and has emerged victorious."

"S'Heernoh?" I echoed in great surprise, indeed, nearly in shock, staring at Aysayn. "I had thought you were to find an excellent warrior to face him, one who would not be easily bested?"

"And so I did," said he, somewhat wryly, a lack of understanding beneath his faint amusement. "The warrior was designated by Mehrayn, who had observed him in battle, and still do I lack comprehension of what occurred. Though I failed to see the thing my own self, I was told that S'Heernoh nevertheless bested him easily and quickly."

"S'Heernoh?" I said again, still unable to accept the truth of the thing, and deeply disturbed. "Had he such skill to call upon, for what reason did he go about bare-waisted? For what reason did he not wear a sword?"

"I know not," returned Aysayn with a shrug, as perplexed as I, yet far less disturbed. "I know only that now he wears the sword he earlier had no wish for, and sends his word to

you that he will be beside you at first light of the new fey.
For the balance of this fey he will accompany the wounded,
primarily Chaldrin, I believe, upon their way, and will return
before darkness has fallen. For the darkness, I am told, there
is one who awaits him.''

"Therefore am I to look elsewhere, should I wish companionship of my own for the darkness," said I with a nod and
something of a smile, then arose from the floor cloth.
"S'Heernoh is more than willing to stand beside me in battle,
yet for the darkness I must seek another.''

"Will you do so?" asked Aysayn gently as I turned from
him, concern behind the words rather than an urge to intrude.
"We will each of us require all the strength we possess, in
the battle to come. Will you use the darkness to restore your
own with pleasure, sister?''

I gazed upon a blue-silk-hung wall without truly seeing it,
feeling from the presence of candles that darkness had already
come, and rubbed upper arms to chase away the chill of the
lightless time.

"Likely I will do that very thing, brother," I replied,
knowing that pleasure would never touch me again, nor did I
wish it to. "There is, however, a battle which we must now
prepare for, therefore must you and I discuss matters other
than pleasure.''

"But what of the rest you were to take?" he asked,
moving to stand before me so that I might see his frown.
"There is indeed much to be done, yet would I first see you
rested.''

"You have my word that I will rest," I assured him,
putting one hand to his arm. "Should there not be opportunity sooner, I will certainly rest once battle is done.''

"Excellent," said he with a smile, well pleased with my
vow, his hand coming to cover mine upon his arm. Though I
had not thought to question Chaldrin upon the oddity of his
appearance before me when I lay in the capture of city folk, I
nevertheless recalled the promise I had been given. One more
task and then I might rest, and soon would that task be behind
me. Once battle with the Feridani was done—then would
Jalav at last find rest.

13.

Battle— and a vow is kept

The new fey began before first light, all being prepared and awake despite the sleep we had forced upon ourselves. The previous fey had been filled with discussions and meetings and questions and demands, so many that our heads all swam from the din of it. Aram and Kira had been as frenzied as we, arranging for the transportation necessary to bring our fighting force to Sigurr's Peak, and then speaking of it in explanation before those who had been chosen to stand against the Feridani. Those who rode to Ranistard had no need to be told of what lay before their brothers and sisters, which was much of a blessing. Had the number of confused questions asked been doubled, likely would we all be there to this very fey in their answering. Much falar and daru flowed down the throats of all, which was a considerable aid when we at last sought out sleeping leather and furs.

Just before the six giant vehicles called shuttles was the smaller vehicle called scout ship to go, a vehicle which was to protect its larger sisters. Upon this ship device were the wonders which would stand our protection, and also those of us who would lead the attack. Aysayn and myself, Mehrayn and Ceralt, Lialt and Galiose and S'Heernoh, Aram and Kira and the roundish male called Doctor. At his own insistence was the roundish male included in our set, to aid us, so he said, should injury befall us. We all allowed his insistence, but I saw to it that he, along with Aram and Kira, would follow far behind those who were to do actual battle. We would likely have need of what healing skill the roundish male possessed, and best was to place him where his skill and life would not be taken by a well-swung weapon.

375

It disturbed me somewhat that we who led would all be within that single vehicle, therefore did I speak with my war leaders and the surrogates who accompanied us, informing them of what they must do should their war leader fail to be there to enter battle with them. Grimly were my words listened to and silently put away against need, yet would none of them consider nor discuss such an eventuality. We would all of us arrive together to face the enemy who challenged us, and together would we find victory. We all of us knew that the protection given us by the stranger folk might prove insufficient against the wonders of the intruders, yet we did not countenance that. We would bring battle to the intruders even were we entirely unprotected from their wonders, therefore was there naught to think upon.

We all stood silently at the edge of the new fey beside our smaller vehicle, watching as those who were to journey with us filed slowly aboard those larger vehicles called shuttles. Four of the six would return for the balance of our fighting force, and bring them after us as quickly as they were able. Thick was the silence surrounding both Midanna and Sigurri, heavier than what might be accounted for by battle-readiness, all likely as wrapped in their own thoughts and concerns as we who watched their boarding. Sooner would I, myself, have seen us upon kand or gandod, yet kand or gandod would not carry us as swiftly as the stranger vehicles, therefore had we had those who rode to Ranistard take our mounts from the city. Those mounts would be loosed a short distance from Bellinard to run where they willed, and upon our return would we seek them out and reclaim them. Those of us who returned. Were any to return.

"I like this not," said Galiose of a sudden in a mutter, looking with displeasure upon the vehicles which were then being boarded by warriors, and also upon that which was ours. "We know naught of these folk, yet do we give our lives and safety into their hands, trusting them to refrain from betrayal. Should we not think this through at greater length?"

"The doing has already been thought upon by those capable of thought," said I, my words and the annoyance of my tone bringing his gaze quickly to me. "Should the strangers have wished our lives, they would not have allowed no more than half our number upon this journey. Those who ride to Ranistard guard us with their very existence, for should we be slain by these folk, it is they who will avenge us. Should Galiose not care to risk himself, he is free to ride elsewhere.''

"Indeed,'' said the dark-haired male, drawing himself up in insult at my words and tone, his half-shadowed form stiffened. "And how are those others to learn of our true fate? Should they be told we were all of us slain by those called Feridani, how are they to know otherwise? Do you mean to have your shade return and inform them?''

"The matter has already been seen to,'' said I, my annoyance with the foolishness of the male growing. "Should Galiose have the stomach to board the vehicle with the balance of us and in such a manner find the end of his feyd, he need have no fear that his betrayal shall go unavenged. Those who ride to Ranistard are Midanna and Sigurri, not village or city folk.''

Galiose stiffened yet further in outrage, though more, I believed, at thought of those who rode toward his city than from the insult I had so deliberately given. The male had not learned of the destination of our other half till they had already departed the city, and wildly had he then shouted and strode about, one moment determined to ride after his returning males to give them warning and hurry them in their return, the next moment realizing that were he to do so, those of us journeying to battle the Feridani would be long gone upon his return to Bellinard. As I had chosen not to speak of the many and detailed instructions given both Midanna and Sigurri concerning what their actions were to be were we others reported slain by the Feridani, the male had grown outraged. Galiose had chosen to remain and enter battle against the enemy rather than ride in the wake of his males, yet was he filled with a great unhappiness which he wished to share with those about him.

"Should we all survive this thing, you will regret having sent fighters against my city, wench,'' he growled low, the heat of the fury within him sufficient to warm the cool of the new fey dimness, his dark eyes looking down upon me. "My men rode here in obedience to my commands, and to know they will return to find their wenches gone is more than I am able to bear. Never shall I countenance betrayal."

"Betrayal such as taking and holding warriors against their will?" I asked, grimly pleased that Galiose knew full well that those I had sent would not fail in their task. "To lose what one never truly possessed is no loss, merely a correcting of previous error. Galiose would do well to be pleased that it is not Jalav who leads the riders against his city. Were it Jalav who led, there would also be no city for his males to return to."

The male fell silent in order to struggle more effectively with his rage, therefore did I turn from him and walk toward where Aram and Kira stood, the words they exchanged low and filled with new-warrior upset. I smiled faintly to see them so, and also at the manner in which their attention came immediately to me.

"Those who accompany us are nearly all within their vehicles," said I, speaking softly so as not to add to their anxiety. "Should we not do the same with ours?"

"That sounds like a good idea to me," said Kira with a shiver, wrapping her arms about herself. "I'm cold even in this uniform. I don't know how you and the others can walk around practically naked and not feel it, Jalav. I'd be frozen stiff and blue from head to toe."

"The air here is no more than somewhat cool," I returned with a widened smile, seeing the manner in which Aram quickly placed an arm about the female. "Sigurr's Peak is truly cold, and we shall none of us be covered during the moments we will require to enter the first of the caverns. Perhaps Kira would do well to remain behind in the vehicle."

"And not be there to help?" demanded the female, nevertheless shuddering faintly at the thought of greater cold. "If the rest of you can stand it, so can I."

"You can be of just as much help from the scout," said Aram, looking down upon her with concern. "That instrumentation needs constant monitoring for the first sign of flux or interference cancellation, and the scout crew will have other things to do beside that. It might be a good idea to make that your post."

"Aram, don't you dare start getting that look!" snapped

Kira at once, bristling at the near-determination in the voice of the male. "If you think I'll let you shut me out of this, you're. . . ."

"Now, now, no one's shutting you out, assistant Leader," returned the male with a smoothness to the words which belied their meaning, turning Kira about to the ramp they stood before. "Let's get aboard the scout, and we'll discuss it. Jalav, why don't you collect your people and get them seated. We'll be back with you in a minute."

The two stranger folk climbed the ramp together, Kira speaking low with great intensity, the male called Doctor following silently, smiling, Aram nodding soberly to the words addressed to him. There was, however, an air about Aram which suggested complete dismissal of all which he heard, truly a doing for one who was male. Had Kira been needed in our number I would have interceded on her behalf; however we did not need the small stranger female, which seemed fortunate indeed. As I turned about to gesture toward those who were to board the small vehicle, I knew without doubt that Kira would be made to do as Aram wished.

No more than a moment saw the balance of us mounting the ramp, and once within did we return to the place of seats. The dimness within was brightened by that stranger light which seemed never to wane, and Lialt and Galiose looked about at the dark metal of walls, floor and ceiling with something akin to awe. Indeed was there greater warmth within—as well as the smell of metal in the air—and truly would I have preferred the cool to be found without.

"Our journey is soon to begin, lady war leader," said S'Heernoh, nearby. "It will be, I am told, of very short duration. Are you as prepared to stand beside me as I am to stand beside you?"

I looked upon the male who paced me along the metal corridor, his usual amusement as clear as the sword he now wore belted about him. In no manner did the weapon which hung between us seem awkward or misplaced, yet was I scarcely pleased to have it so.

"S'Heernoh is not Chaldrin no matter the supposed skill of the Sigurri he bested," I said, the sourness in my tone doing little to dent the amusement of the male. "Perhaps I should have seen to the thing myself."

"To keep me from joining you," said he with a shade less satisfaction, his dark eyes unmoving from my face. "Is my presence so abhorrent to you, then?"

"It is your slaying which I shall find abhorrent," I returned, making no effort to avoid his gaze. "Despite his constant prying—and his lack of willingness to give pleasure to a war leader—the death of the male S'Heernoh would be a loss to this warrior."

"Then I shall not allow myself to be slain," said the male, pleasure filling him full and shining forth from his eyes, his hand coming without thought to gently smooth my hair. "Truly do I have adequate sword skill, lady, although I am indeed not the same as Chaldrin. To face you as he did is a thing I would not find myself able to do."

"There are, in such an event, others who might be faced," came the calm tones of Mehrayn from behind. S'Heernoh and I had halted just before the first of the seats, and at the sound of the words we turned about in surprise. Standing there were Mehrayn and Ceralt, neither male looking well pleased.

"To fall now to the lure of the wench would be ill-advised," said Ceralt to S'Heernoh, his light eyes hard despite the softness of his words. "Your strength so far has been commendable, man; best would be that you continue as you began."

"My debt to you is great, S'Heernoh," said Mehrayn, "yet not so great that I would see the wench by your side rather than mine by cause of it. As Ceralt has said, such commendable wisdom as you have so far shown should wisely be continued."

"The war leader and I discussed survival in the battle before us, my friends," said S'Heernoh with an odd lack of his usual amusement as I stiffened in badly contained fury. "Is this what you would have me keep from? A discussion upon survival?"

Indeed did S'Heernoh look upon the other two males with something like sternness, and unbelievably Mehrayn and Ceralt grew discomforted beneath that dark-eyed gaze. Much did they begin to shift about as a child might beneath the stare of a warrior.

"Should that have been what you discussed, there was little need to touch her," muttered Mehrayn, attempting to recapture calm control. "A man begins by stroking her hair, and then continues on to stroking her in an entirely different manner."

"That she refuses you both brings great pain and uncertainty, does it not?" asked S'Heernoh, his eyes and tone this time filled with quiet compassion, his gaze touching each male in turn. "You must not allow yourselves to see rivals everywhere, my friends, else shall you lose your sanity before the difficulty reaches any sort of settlement. When this battle is done, we will all of us turn our attentions to that settlement."

"Likely *my* sanity will not survive so long a time," said Ceralt, also in a mutter, one hand stroking through the dark of his hair, the look upon Mehrayn saying the same. "I cannot bear the thought of losing her, yet do I see her slipping further from my grasp with each passing reckid. Perhaps the battle itself will end the difficulty—in one manner or another."

The eyes of the two males came to me then, each set filled with yearning, each set bidding me farewell should they not survive what was to come. Much did *I* yearn to go and hold each of them about, to ease some of the pain within me, however I was a war leader with a battle still to fight. Instead of indulging in the behavior of a fool, I quickly turned away from them and sought a seat for the journey soon to be begun, my mind whirling with that which I had no wish to consider. When S'Heernoh quietly took the seat beside mine, I was no more than faintly aware of it.

The male Aram joined us in the place of seats, no other than the roundish male accompanying him, and the two aided us in binding ourselves to the seats we sat in. When they, too, were seated and bound so, the brief vibrating of the vehicle came, and then the silence of a journey begun. I sat in my seat held by chains of cloth, and abruptly knew what I traveled toward. She who had called herself Mida, she who had brought me such pain and humiliation and shaming, would soon be before my blade. The intruder female who had thought to best me would soon have opportunity to see how well her wonders would fare against the edge of a sword—and perhaps would live long enough to regret having challenged me. I put my head back against the softness of the seat and allowed myself a smile in anticipation of the pleasure I would not permit to elude me.

Short indeed was the time before the vibration came again, informing us that we had reached our destination. So difficult was it to believe, that we had traversed many and many feyd of distance in a mere portion of a hin, yet such was the way of wonders. Lialt seemed uncertain and Galiose truculently disbelieving as we freed ourselves and arose, yet were they both distracted by the first words of Aram.

"Please remember that we can't take our time disembarking," said he to all of us, looking from one face to another. "It's going to be really cold out there, and we've got to move as fast as possible to get ourselves into the first of the heated caverns. I still wish we could have taken the time to get you all properly protected, but— Just remember not to stop until you're well inside."

The nods of fervent agreement coming from Ceralt and Lialt matched mine, for surely did we three recall the last occasion of our arrival at Sigurr's Peak. The snow and cold were indeed to be left behind as quickly as possible, a thing the others with us would soon learn.

Aram led us back to the place where we had entered the vehicle, a place which had not yet been opened to the cold without. First was it necessary that we take stranger torches to light our way, torches which glowed without burning, ones which, we had been told, would continue to glow till we had no further need of them. So light and small were these torches that we each were able to carry one with ease, although Aram had another thing to carry in place of a torch. Small was the device, little larger than the torches which had been given us, yet was there a small, calm green light to be seen upon it. As long as the green light continued, had said the male, there was naught to concern us; should the light go to red, however, we were then to prepare ourselves for serious battle indeed.

"We'd better get started," said Aram when we each had

been given a torch, moving through our ranks to the panel beside the door. "Remember now: out and in as fast as you can."

We none of us commented upon the manner in which the male unnecessarily repeated that which had already been said, for his agitation was clear. Though he behaved well for one who was unused to battle, his fretfulness spoke eloquently of the nervousness which held him.

A touch began the opening of the door, and although the thing opened no more slowly than it had upon our arrival in Bellinard, much did it seem that some mishap had occurred with the mechanism. Far too leisurely did the opening before us begin to appear, for the great cold, even worse than I remembered it, sought and found immediate entrance. Soon we were able to see the snowstorm, and no longer did Aram's continued cautioning seem overdone. Much did the stormcold sap the ability for speed from my body and bring my mind the wish to curl up, yet might such a thing not be allowed. Despite vast reluctance I waited no longer than till the ramp was fully extended, then did I plunge down it into the storm and the mounded snow, thinking of nothing to save the caves perhaps three gandod strides before me.

Had the distance been greater, we likely would not have survived to enter the caverns. Beyond imagination and description was the cold of the snow, the storm swirling heavy flakes all about me, the footing treacherous and slowing, even the metal of the torch I held seeking to draw the life from out of me. I ran though I scarcely knew where I ran, and when the dark of the entrance cavern surrounded me, I merely thumbed the switch upon the torch as I had been shown to do, and plunged deeper within with all the speed I possessed. Some of the others ran in my wake and S'Heernoh had continued to pace me, yet were we unable to halt and look upon one another till we had reached that place where the outer cold was negated by inner warmth. As large and dark and brooding as it had first been was that cavern, and my shuddering was only partially from the cold which we had so recently passed through.

"Sigurr protect me from learning any further truths such as that," said Aysayn in a panting gasp, the light-haired male seeming shaken. "That, I take it, wench, was the snow you spoke of, and humbly do I ask your forgiveness for having doubted you. The thing must indeed be seen to be believed."

"Have we all made it through all right?" asked Aram, looking about our group as he came up assisting the roundish male. All of us were wet from the storm and still trembling and gasping from the run through the cold, yet had we all survived and arrived where we were meant to be. Despite their coverings did the two stranger males seem more shaken than we, therefore was it left to me to speak upon what needed to be done.

"There are true torches to be found at the foot of the walls," I said, shaking my head to rid my hair of clinging snow. "Best would be that we light them now, against the arrival of the others."

"Indeed," said Ceralt. "Let those of us with boots see to the task. I remember well the sharpness of the stones upon this floor, therefore shall you and the others walk upon it as little as possible. Lialt, begin at that side if you will, and I shall see to this one."

"And I'll take the wall with the openings," said Aram as Lialt nodded at Ceralt's command, the stranger male glancing briefly upon the device he held. "If we get very, very lucky, I won't have much of anything else to do."

"See that you keep well away from the openings," said I to Aram as the males started off to see to their respective areas. "We would all of us be ill-advised to enter them save with our full force."

"Don't worry, you won't find any heroes in *this* uniform," said Aram over his shoulder with a sound of ridicule, the words clearly meant to reassure me. "When the time comes, one of you others can have the dibs."

"Shall the fey ever come when his words are filled with understanding?" asked Aysayn, looking after Aram with something of amusement. "What are we to do now that the small female is no longer beside him?"

"Perhaps best would be to cease addressing him," said I, sharing Aysayn's amusement. "Then we need no longer spend the effort in attempting to decipher his meaning. One must save one's strength when there is battle in the offing."

Aysayn's chuckle came in agreement, yet did the amusement soon abandon both of us. The cavern pleased me no more than it had when I had first seen it, yet was I this time not alone in feeling so. S'Heernoh stood nearly atop me, not laughing this time, and also did Mehrayn contrive to be within a step of me. Ceralt, when he returned, hovered close as well, and Aysayn looked about with fingertips dancing lightly upon sword hilt. All were in some manner uneasy, and scarcely by cause of what we were about to attempt.

The first of our warriors arrived not long after our own arrival, cold, wet, and panting from the rain, yet were they silent as they had been commanded to be. I forced my way through the males who stood about me, walking carefully to spare my feet, then gave those warriors their next instructions. With the aid of the first did those who followed find their places without difficulty, places which filled the cavern from the side wall across and front outward, a formation which provided the least amount of shifting about. Although Aram's device was meant to take the sound from our presence and warn us against detection, it was necessary to remember that ears were devices in their own right. Should a follower of the intruders hear movement and converse where none was expected, what benefit then in wonders which silenced others?

When all those who had been within the six vehicles were within the cavern, we stood in continued silence awaiting the arrival of the last of our force. As large as the cavern was, it became necessary to begin our movement through the crevasse which led to the chamber of the carving of Sigurr, nearly to that chamber yet short of it. The long, wide corridor beyond the crevasse could hold many warriors, allowing those remaining in the cavern a bit more standing room, yet was I unable to continue on into the chamber to complete the wait. I had deliberately allowed memory of the male intruder to slip from me but it had returned with the return to his realm, and I found myself distracted and nearly distraught. No more was I able to keep from pacing about with left hand to hilt than I was able to halt the pounding of my heart, and all those who looked upon me did so with concern. Ceralt and Lialt were most especially grim, and Mehrayn had taken Ceralt aside to speak with him in whispers. I knew not what they spoke of, yet was my state of mind such that I truly cared not.

No more than a matter of reckid passed before word was given Aram through another device at his left ear, that the first of the vehicles had returned with the balance of our warriors. One after the other did the final three also arrive, therefore was it clearly the time for our advance, before those who came were unable to enter the warmth through lack of room. I turned resolutely toward the chamber of the carving, thinking of how welcome the smoothness of the floor would be to the bottoms of my feet, knowing that the chamber must be traversed before we might press onward, yet was the spittle gone from my mouth and the warmth gone from my flesh. So evil was that place, that surely should it have reeked with putrifaction and screamed with the agony of souls under torment; only silence came from it, however, and only the musty smell of caverns. Calmly quiet did it stand beyond the light of our torches, and the fury which came to me over such a lie at last sent me forward toward it. Behind me came the others of our force, a number of warriors set about Aram and the roundish male to see that no harm came to them, and then were Ceralt and Mehrayn to either side of me.

"There is little need for you to go first again into that place of horrors, Jalav," said Ceralt, attempting to take my arm to halt me. "Mehrayn and I will enter first, and then return to lead you through."

"As though I were aged and infirm?" I asked, pulling my arm from his grip without breaking stride, the anger I felt returning a warmth of sorts to me. "Should the fey come that I am aged and infirm, I shall recall your offer and certainly accept it."

"For what reason must you be so stubborn?" demanded Mehrayn in a low growl, his own anger clear. "Ceralt has told me of what occurred here when last you saw it, and there is little need to face such memories with none to stand beside you. Allow us at least to be with you."

Ceralt began to speak words in objection, attempting to insist again that they two go forward without me, yet had we reached the threshold of the chamber. Without volition I slowed as the light of my torch sped ahead and within, and then did I halt with a chill foreboding. Where the carving had stood was there naught to be seen, as though the chamber had been forever empty, as though naught had ever been within it. Slowly did I pace forward with Ceralt frowning at my side, and Mehrayn seeming confused.

"How might so large a statue as you described be removed, Ceralt?" he asked, looking about with less understanding than those of us who had been there another time. "Might we not have entered the wrong chamber in error?"

"There is no error," said Ceralt, his words coming with effort, his gaze moving slowly about. "What think you, Jalav? Might the presence of the statue have been illusion when first we saw it? At the end the very walls melted from about us— Might we have been made to see a statue which was naught save imagining?"

"The carving was not an illusion," I answered with a great shudder, the light of the torch in my hand bobbing this way and that. "It was scarcely an illusion which took Hannis's female, yet do I now believe that it was also not a carving. It was—"

"The Serene Oneness preserve us," whispered Ceralt as his arm went about me, a paleness to his tone which surely matched the same in mine. "So close to us, and we unknowing, toyed with as though we were children!"

"What do you speak of?" asked Mehrayn as the others of our set came to stand with us, his frown an odd one. "What has disturbed you two so greatly?"

"The carving—was not a carving," said I with effort, seeing Ceralt's face show his distress. "What we thought a carving—what took the small female Deela and gave her such hurt—was the intruder male himself, in the guise of a carving of Sigurr."

"How might such a thing be possible?" demanded Aysayn as Mehrayn merely stared, as taken aback as those of us who relived the time in memory. "In what manner might a living thing pretend to stonehood? What manner of beings are these?"

"Endlessly evil," said S'Heernoh looking grimly about. "Best we continue on, to advance as far as possible before they become aware of us."

Indeed had the male spoken the truth, therefore did we all continue as I had begun, with resolution accompanied by caution. Warriors were placed at each crevasse choice, to be certain none mistook the proper direction, and in such a manner did we continue on as Ceralt and I had once before, save with two great differences. In this instance was my sword readily to hand, and those behind us were warriors all, none to fall shivering and weeping when attack came. I fretted at each of the crevasses we passed, knowing there would be a delay when our warriors found it necessary to pass through only by ones and twos; that such delay was unavoidable I knew as well as any other; the knowing, however, did naught to end the fretting.

One by one did the hind pass beneath our moving feet, the chambers of pressed stone bringing low-voiced, quickly ended mutters from those who accompanied me. So godlike were those chambers, with renderings of Mida and Sigurr pressed into the gray and black of the walls, that most preferred the corridors of true rock despite the sharpness of stones underfoot. Both chambers and corridors lacked sufficient air for those who passed through, and quickly did we come to regret the warmth we had at first craved so greatly. Clearly was the journey through the Peak and downward more easily undertaken by fewer than the number we had brought.

The end of both corridors and chambers came unexpectedly with the rounding of a turn, beyond which we were able to see an opening in the rock leading outward to that vast plain of a cavern where those who inhabited that place had last fallen upon intruders in their domain. Lighted in some manner was that cavern, as though by many unseen torches, and as we made for it Aram pushed through those warriors who surrounded him, and hurried to my side.

"The light just flickered," said he, his tone full of portents of doom, his eyes filled with worry. "We're getting close to the Feridani gadgets, and the closer we are, the stronger *they* are. We're still covered, but that can change at any time."

"Therefore must we now be completely alert," I said, looking about as I spoke, pleased that the male's words had allowed me that much understanding. "Best would be that you return now to those who guard you, for we may be fallen

upon at any time. Once within that cavern we make first for
the chambers of the female, she who presented herself as
Mida. After that shall we discover the place of the male, and
do with him as we have done with her."

"You're going after the Feridans instead of forcing them
to come to you?" demanded Aram with a low yelp, of a
sudden taken by frantic outrage. "What sort of military logic
is that?"

"I don't know what you mean," I said with a sigh, silently
berating myself for having allowed Kira to be left behind. "I
only know than that were we to allow the Feridani to come to
us, surely would they come with all the wonders they were
able to bring. As we go to them, there should be fewer
wonders to battle against."

"Catch them unprepared," muttered the male, seemingly
calmed from his outrage, a glance showing the manner in
which he stared downward without true sight. "Letting them
attack gives them the chance to get ready, attacking them
gives us the chance to rattle them. I guess I can go along with
that."

With such muttering did the male return to those who
would guard him, leaving me to smile faintly as I continued
to look about. We passed through the opening onto the floor
of the vast cavern, then, all of us alert against what defenders
there might be, and suddenly were those defenders very much
in evidence. From all about did they come running and
shouting toward us, males of the cavern, perhaps three clans
or legions in number. Those of us who had passed through
first were perhaps a third to a half of their force, and others
near yet not yet having emerged, and the glee upon the faces
of the attackers showed that they anticipated swift victory. It
clearly had not come to them that they should have known of
our presence much the sooner, and we made no attempt to
speak upon the matter. Merely did we draw our weapons and
meet them with attack rather than despair.

For some few reckid was the battle brisk and most divert-
ing, the greater numbers of the attackers making up for their
lack of true skill, yet were they unable to stand long before
us. The glee they had shown turned quickly to fear, yet were
they far too late in their realization of the truth. By the hand

did they fall before Midanna and Sigurri alike, and when some
threw down their weapons in surrender, they shockingly found
their numbers very few indeed. Bodies lay unmoving everywhere, bodies of attackers rather than warriors, and Mehrayn
and Ceralt made their way to me with redly glistening swords
still held in their fists.

"These are the ones meant to halt us?" Mehrayn asked with
obvious scorn, flicking his blade toward those who lay unmoving. "Barely were they able to raise their weapons to
greet their death."

"The battle went somewhat differently when last I fought
it," said Ceralt, an odd shamefacedness about him. "I now
see the difference in standing with warriors rather than riders
and their trembling women. Your wenches are truly remarkable, Jalav, as are you, yourself. Those men who faced you
had no hope of besting you, a sight which allowed me to face
my own attackers with unburdened mind."

"She is a warrior born and bred," said Mehrayn with a
good deal of pride, the green of his eyes glowing brightly.
Ceralt, too, looked upon me much the same, and abruptly I
found that I had no words to give them. With an unexplained
heat in my cheeks I looked about for what next had to be
done concerning the attackers we had slain, and suddenly
Aram came rushing forward waving the device he held.

"Heads up!" he shouted as he ran, fear in his voice despite
its strength. "They've broken through our cover and know
what's coming off! We're on the red! They know we're
here!"

No more than the last of his words were absolutely clear,
yet were they sufficient to apprise us of our danger. Now
were we able to look about and see the many, many forms
running toward us from all across the cavern, male and
female alike, each holding a bared blade. Our force continued
to come through the opening into the vast cavern, yet were
there many more to come and clearly not sufficient time to
allow their arrival before those of the cavern were upon us.
Ceralt and Mehrayn straightened where they stood, S'Heernoh,
Galiose, Lialt and Aysayn came quickly to join us, and I
tightened my grip upon the hilt in my fist.

"We must hold till our brothers and sisters are able to

stand with us!'' I shouted to those who prepared to meet the
oncoming followers of abomination, all greatly aware of how
truly large a force attacked. ''In the names of Mida and
Sigurr shall we best them, yet must we first hold!''

''We shall hold!'' came from many voices, bloodied swords
raised high in relentless determination, and then did S'Heernoh
speak. At the same time Aysayn turned to look upon me,
approval in his gaze to add to that of Mehrayn and Ceralt, yet
was there an oddness about all of these things. The words of
S'Heernoh failed to reach me, the sight of Aysayn and the
others began to fade, and I became aware of a numbness
which gripped me. Sound of all sort was now disallowed my
ears, those about me faded even further, and amidst the
growing darkness I was able to feel no more than the pounding of my heart. The stone I stood upon, the breech and
swordbelt about my middle, the hilt in my fist—all were no
longer a part of me, no more than I was a part of those who
stood in the cavern. Hands reached for me in the silence
which had wrapped me about, desperate hands which seemed
unable to touch me, and then was there naught save soft
blackness, all sight and sound gone to a nether realm. I know
not how long I stood so; when the time ended and the
blackness cleared, the one who had named himself Sigurr
stood before me.

''So we meet again,'' said the breathy voice of the male,
the words in some manner different from when he had last
addressed me, his gaze unmoving from my face. ''I find it
difficult telling you how delighted I am to see you. Just let
the sword drop to the floor.''

I did not intend to do as he bid, yet did my fingers open of
themselves, allowing the sword to fall from them. Again was
I aware of my entire body, but I was unable to command it to
my will, beyond all save standing where I had appeared. The
breathless laughter of the male came, sending cold all through
me, and then did he turn away toward a magic window which
stood upon a low platform. In the window I saw those who
had accompanied me, now engaged sword to sword with the
defending force, and then a touch of the male's hand ban-
ished all sight of them. No more than blankness was left, a

blankness of dismissal, a thing the male made clear was his exact intention.

"I knew we couldn't afford to have you come in contact with those interfering fools," said he, turning from the window to look upon me again. "That attack won't do you any good, you know; you're too badly outnumbered no matter how good you think you are. Our loyal followers will take care of your savages; Mida and I will see to your long-lost blood relations—and I, personally, will tend to you."

Still breathy was the voice of the male, less dark and remote than he had been, yet remaining for the most part as I remembered him. Dark, unblinking eyes burned into me, and I unable to move no matter how I struggled inwardly. I stood as I had when I had first appeared in that realm of dimness and metal, unchained and untouched yet unable to move save at the command of the male, my sword now upon the flags at my feet, anger beginning in me at such a cowardly stroke. And then the male began to pace slowly toward me, his gaze still unmoving, and into my mind came memory of what had last been done to me. Had I been able, I would have taken a step backward; instead did the thud of my heart increase, and a faint trembling began within.

"I told Mida you would survive," he whispered, truly near now and looking down upon me. "She swore at first that you would die taking that barbaric city, then that my supposed followers would see to you, and then that those other savage females would do what the first groups hadn't been able to. She screamed for hours every time she was proven wrong, but I knew you would survive. I wanted you, and what I want, I get."

His hand raised then to come to my face, and again I would have flinched away had I been able. The touch of the male was the same as the touch of any other, and yet—the gentleness went badly with his cold chuckle of amusement.

"Losing you the way they did will be terribly demoralizing for your people," said he, letting his fingers slide from cheek to throat. "I told Mida she was a fool for letting you leave here again, but she didn't know what she was dealing with. She wanted to see you fail before you died, fail terribly and then die horribly, but you're one of those who succeed in life, almost like me. You fought all those savages into line and then brought them to attack us—and then suddenly disappeared before their very eyes. Without a leader they'll fall apart now, and while they're dying you and I will be together. I'm going to keep you a very long time, my lovely, and do to you things you've never had done before, and I won't even have to work at keeping you alive. You'll survive alone the way you did the first time, and will even live to see every being on this world bow to me in their slavery. All of those savages will belong to *me*, just as you belong to me, but none of them will receive the attention I give to you."

The dark hand went from throat to breast, and then the touch was no longer gentle. Hard fingers closed tighter and tighter upon my flesh, giving me deliberate pain, the laughter coming breathy and whispering from the one who did me so.

"Do you wish you could scream, my beauty?" the whispering voice asked, the chuckling continuing. "But of course you don't. It took quite a lot of effort before you screamed the first time, and I enjoyed that. I knew I *would* make you scream, but not when, and that gave me more pleasure than I've had from any other female of your world. They all begin by screaming, and where's the pleasure in that, after the first few? But you, you resist, and now you're permanently mine. Take off that swordbelt."

My hands went of themselves to my swordbelt, and I knew not whether to fall to anger or fear. No least resistance was I able to make, no least effort to return to those who stood in battle, no least gesture to keep the Feridani male from me. Should this be the manner in which false gods fought, none of us had need of facing those who were gods in truth. Within me I screamed and fought to break free of the thrall in which I was held, yet in fact I opened my swordbelt and simply let it fall.

"I think you have no true idea of how spectacular you are—and how you arouse me," said the male, his whisper having grown heavier, his dark eyes now glinting. "I watched you toward the end of that skirmish you and your savages managed to win, and couldn't take my eyes from you. Your every movement is invitation, most especially with a weapon in your hand. Go to your knees, now, and kiss my feet."

Without hesitation did my body obey, kneeling and bringing my lips to the feet of the male. Over and over did I kiss
them, my knees and palms to the flagstones, my hair falling
over my left shoulder, the fury rising within me frothing with
near-madness.

"So at last you see that no matter how far along the road of
leadership you think you've come, with me you're no more
than another delightful slave," said the male, his amusement
having grown truly great. "You will always obey me completely, my will above yours, no backtalk, no bargaining.
Mida was amused to let you think you had to bargain with
me for something she could have given you just as easily
without your having to pay for it, but she isn't part of this any
longer. Now there's just you and me, and nothing to consider
but my pleasure. Rise to your feet, slave, and follow after
your master."

Again was the male obeyed with speed, and as I rose to
quickly follow in his track, I found that fear had somehow
abandoned me. Well did I know that the male would do me
as he had the instance previous, yet was the terror of the
memory now blunted and buried beneath the fury which
coursed all through me. In no manner would the male face
me in honest challenge, and yet did he attempt to proclaim
his superiority! Many times had Jalav been named slave, yet
had none found it possible to prove the contention. Did Jalav
survive to find release from the power of the male, he, too,
would learn that words easily spoken were not as easily
echoed in actions.

The chamber of the male was large and dim, lit from a
source not easily discerned, the walls and floors stone, the
devices standing all about unobtrusive save for the occasional
glint of metal. To the back of the chamber did the male lead
me, to a place where the stone of the floor was hidden by
black lenga pelts covering all of the area from wall to wall.
Never had I seen a lenga of black, not to speak of the number
which would be required to cover so large an area, yet was I
unable to halt and examine the pelts. The male continued on
across them, to a large, wide platform of black wood covered
over with black silks and further black pelts, and there did he
halt to turn to me once more.

"I find the color scheme tedious after so long a use of it, but the time hasn't yet come when I may abandon it," said he, only his eyes glinting in the dim illumination. "There is, however, one attraction to be currently found in the color black. Approach me more closely."

One step forward brought me nearly upon the male, so close that the scent of him was a lurching deep within. Strong was the odor of desire upon him, yet was he also smothered in what seemed the aroma of flowers, an aroma to be found upon no other male I had ever encountered. The dark chest before me moved as the male raised his arms, and then were his fingers undoing the war leather which bound my hair back. When the leather had come loose the hands then spread my hair all about, just as countless others had done before him, yet far more carefully. The male before me saw to my preparation for his pleasure, a realization which dimmed some part of my fury and revitalized an equal part of the memory of terror.

"So thick and delightful," said he in a whisper of a murmur, drawing one wide strand forward as his hands returned before me, the leather also held. "The sight of you brings me great pleasure, slave. Bare yourself entirely for your master."

So great was my reluctance to do such a thing that surely was my compliance less swift than it had been, yet was I able to do no other thing than comply. With the strings of my breech opened I was able to pull it away, and then was it gone to the black lenga fur beneath my feet.

"Now you may remove your master's body adornment," said he when the breech had slipped from my fingers, the weight of his gaze upon me, his words thickened in their whisper. "How barbaric to adorn one's body, most especially when there are those about one would have appreciate the sight of it."

The black breech about his loins was found first by my eyes and then by my fingers, its strings opening easily despite the stiffened fumbling of my touch. Even more reluctant was I to bare the male than I had been with myself, yet did the thrall I moved under continue to refuse to release me. Beneath the breech the male was eager indeed, his near-silent laughter whispering out at the shudder which touched me as the black leather fell away.

"I see you truly begin to recall our last encounter," he said with a chuckle, continuing to run the strand of my hair through his fingers. "Kneel and greet your master's desire, slave, and then give him pleasure."

Again was I quickly upon my knees, the fur far softer beneath them than the flags had been, yet sooner would I have once more knelt upon the stone, and pressed my lips to it as well. I greeted the male and then pleasured him as he had commanded, nearly retching from the smell of him, yet did the male halt his pleasure before it was entirely done.

"To deny your flesh a short while is to indulge in even greater pleasure," said he, his fist in my hair holding my head from him, his breath coming more heavily than it had. "We'll play another game for a short while, and possibly return to this one later. On your feet now, and raise your chin."

The fist of the male in my hair forced me to rising along with his words, and then was my hair released so that he might take the war leather he had removed and knot it about my throat. Oddly was the thin leather knotted, the end of it no longer than the length of the male's palm, the loop snug about my throat with little loosening even when it was unheld. The male, however, seemed pleased with his doing, and gestured behind me.

"Now you may put yourself in my pleasure place," said he, "on your knees with body straight. Once there you'll discover a great fear of me inside you, just beside the great desire you have for me. Desire will hold you in place until I've touched you, and then fear will send you scrabbling away. You will not be able to leave the bed, and when I command you to halt, you will not be able to move again until you've been touched. If I corner you, you'll need to pay a price before being released to continue your escape. Yes, just so, my lovely slave, just so."

Greatly pleased was the male with the manner in which I knelt upon his platform, in the position I had been commanded to. Also was he surely able to see the tracks of what other things had been commanded of me, the fear and the desire. The fear was a cold knot in my belly, causing my flesh to quiver against the possibility of being touched, the desire causing a burning demand for that which I felt such fear of; the two together twisted me about with dry tongue, pounding heart and trembling limbs. I knelt upon the softness of the furs, my hair draped over my feet, my palms to my thighs, my body straight, gazing unwaveringly upon the one who looked down upon me.

The male looked silently upon me a brief moment, then did he approach the platform and begin to climb upon it, the black of his form nearly humming with his sense of pleasure. The fear he had commanded brought a great wish to back from him, the desire a wish to move forward in greeting, neither intention able to best the forced need to remain where I knelt. Slowly nearer did the male come, his clear intent to bring me greater anguish, and then did his hand reach forth, to stroke between my thighs.

Mida! Never, in all my time among males, had I ever felt such loathing and arousal combined! My time with Ceralt had not been the same, for I had truly desired Ceralt despite my hatred of the capture he had held me in. The Feridani male who now caressed me and brought such heat was true anathema to me, vile beyond imagining no matter that he had commanded feelings other than that from my body. I writhed where I knelt, agonizing over how long he would do me so before allowing me to escape him, aching for the use he would not soon put me to, and breathy chuckling accompanied the stroking.

"I do believe the desire in you is stronger than the fear," said he, greatly amused. "Does the slave burn to please her master? The slave is clearly made to please a master, which is exactly what she'll do—when her master allows it. Now you may try to escape me, hot and squirming slave."

With his words did the male remove his hand, freeing me to quickly crawl from him toward the far side of the platform. Again was the fury ablaze within me, fury at having yet another male speak of me so. Memory of my sword came to me then, scarcely so far away upon the flags that it was beyond consideration, an excellent instrument with which the slave Jalav might serve a male. Upon hands and knees I crawled and stumbled across the furs, a growl rising within me which nearly choked my breath away, the red of kill-lust beginning to tinge the black of evil.

"Stop," said the male with continuing amusement, clearly not yet pursuing. "You move too slowly in your supposed escape, my hot little slave. You're much too anxious to be caught and used, but your master isn't ready for that yet. You'll have to be taught what lack of absolute obedience brings you."

The yielding platform beneath the furs and silks dipped as the male moved toward me, more deliberately than he had earlier, a thing I knew beyond doubt although it was behind me that he moved. I had been halted upon all fours facing away from him, and when he reached me his hand stroked across my bottom.

"This will undoubtedly be somewhat painful as well as frustrating for you, my lovely, but that, after all, is what punishments are supposed to be," the breathy voice murmured with great pleasure, the male bringing himself over me. "We'll have to see if we can force some sound out of you—or if it will be necessary to wait awhile longer. No, don't struggle, I haven't allowed you that."

Immediately did my feeble movements in protest cease, although the doings of the male did not. As the Ranistard male Nolthis had so often used me, now did this Feridani do the same, taking pleasure for himself the while giving none to she whom he used. Pain indeed was there as he entered me, and then did his hands come to the short length of leather which had been knotted about my throat. His pull upon it lacked true strength, yet was the breath taken immediately from my throat, the doing dragging my brow down to touch the fur, where I was at last permitted to breathe. Greater pain caused me to attempt to straighten after a moment, yet the attempt caused the leather whose end continued to be held in the male's fist to tighten once more, which again took the air from my lungs. To continue breathing it was necessary that I remain as I had been bent, I saw, and the male laughed when once this truth was known to me.

"You may now try to escape, child," said he, a panting

behind the words to mark the continuing thrust of his lips. "You'll fail, of course, but now you may try."

Much did I wish that I might at the least gasp with the pain and denial the male gave, yet to know that sound would give him greater pleasure was to vow that none would escape me. His possession of me was nearly complete, and in no manner was I able to deny the leather about my throat, which tightened at my slightest pull against it. Solely was I able to kneel there, brow to the fur, aching from the use the male took, so deeply humiliated by his laughter that I would have screamed with shame-rage, had I not sworn myself to silence. My hands upon the fur beneath the mound of my hair curled to fists, yet did the male take his pleasure in full, finding release only after a good deal of vigorous motion. I then anticipated his lessened withdrawal, yet to my shock was there neither; no lessening and no withdrawal, no more than his laughter in sated understanding.

"Did you believe I would be drained and reduced, child?" he asked, the breathy laughter interrupting his words. "Have you so quickly forgotten my appetites and capacity? You savages discovered what you call the gimba plant, the source of the drug you feed to captive men to make them able to serve many of you; my derivator was able to extract the essence of that plant, which allows me to have pleasure from the female use I take. Aren't you pleased that I'm still able to ease you—when I choose to do so?"

The laughter of another male would surely have roared out to the heights of the chamber; the Feridani's merely whispered and whispered, worse, by far, than any roaring might conceivably have been. His continued presence within me was continued pain, an explanation far clearer than the words he had spoken, and then his free hand came to the place he had scorned for his use. The greater desire he then brought me was even greater pain, and after he had caused me to writhe in need a short while, he laughed again.

"Still no sounds of pain, slave?" he asked, twisting my flesh between his fingers to add to what he gave elsewhere. "Your next punishment will have to be stricter, then, and far longer lasting. Until that time comes, let's continue with the game."

His hand left the leather and he withdrew from me then, and no sooner was I free than I dropped to my left side upon the furs, looking back as I drew up my right leg, then kicked out into the male's desire with all the skill and strength Chaldrin had instilled in me. You may now attempt to escape, the male had said to me, and although the words had not been meant in the manner in which I had taken them, still had they freed me from the thrall I had been under. The Feridani screamed a silent scream as he bent forward, undoubtedly experiencing a great deal of the pain he found such approval of, and I struggled erect despite my own pain then kicked again, this time taking the darkness of his visage for my aim. The male shot sideways and rolled from the platform amid the thrashing of arms and legs; I leaped forward and gained the floor fur running, the place where my sword lay, clear to my sight. Although Chaldrin had not found it possible to stand by my side in that battle, still had his vow been kept through that which he had taught me.

My running steps took me quickly across the floor fur, and as my feet touched the flags I glanced as quickly back, to see that the Feridani male sat upon the fur where he had fallen, hunched over with the remnants of pain, yet watching me carefully and in silence. For what reason he failed to command my return I knew not, and then did I look again and truly see the place where my sword lay. Within a circle of black upon the gray of the flags was it, a circle I had no memory of seeing earlier, a circle I had clearly been standing in when I had arrived in that chamber. My pace slowed as I continued to look upon that circle, and then did a thought come which caused me to halt altogether. Range, had said the stranger female Kira, was that distance at which one might be reached by a device of wonders, a device which might not otherwise reach a warrior. Within that circle had the thralling device of the Feridani been able to reach me, a thing I knew without doubt; were I to return there, even to retrieve my sword, I would indeed be a fool. Once free of the hold of much daru, I also knew, one did not fall again beneath its sway till further daru was swallowed; perhaps, like daru, the thralling device might be bested by its avoidance, its initial effects overcome by my having once been freed. Having halted I then turned to look upon the Feridani, allowing him to know I would not step again within the circle, and the manner in which his chin rose spoke of his snarling displeasure.

"A slave who finds success in life!" he spat, the whisper harsh and penetrating even to where I stood. "Do you now believe you've won something, you mindless savage? Do you even understand why you're avoiding that spot? I very much doubt you understand anything like it, and it won't do you the least good. You'll live a very long time regretting what you did."

Then did the male begin to rise to his feet, just as though I had not twice struck him with kicks of strength. A male of villages and cities would surely be unmoving, likely be senseless, possibly be slain; this Feridani was clearly unlike them, however, and again my thoughts turned toward my sword, the sword I could not reach without entering the circle. Quickly did I throw my hair back over my shoulders with a toss of my head, drew the dagger the male had not removed from its leg bands, and set myself to meet attack.

The Feridani began pacing toward me, chill menace in each step he took, his lack of fear bringing memory to me of how easily he had returned life to those who had been unarguably slain without his aid. Ceralt, and the male I had faced there with swords, and even I had returned to life and health through the doing of that Feridani wonder, a wonder the male surely had the use of for his own self. I tightened my grip upon the hilt of my dagger despite the moisture of my palm, and watched the male slowly closing the distance between us.

And then came an odd, soundless sound, one which was accompanied by a flash of brightness which seemed unconnected with whatever torches or candles illuminated the chamber. Far longer in duration than a flash of lightning was it, and in its glow did both the chamber and the male—change! The chamber itself turned merely dull rather than brooding dark, and the Feridani male—the male was of a sudden no different from any other male, no darker, even, than I! I stared without understanding as the male halted abruptly with a snarl to look about, and then was the darkness returned, to him as well as to the chamber. A moment passed so, during which time the male began to stride toward a device of metal

upon a platform at the wall to my left, and then did the
brightness return, this time apparently to remain a while.

"Those fools!" raged the male, reaching the device of
metal and immediately touching it all about. "They were
supposed to destroy that suppressor when they got their hands
on it! How could it be back in operation? How could it—"

The words of the male ended abruptly as the device he
stood before formed a window of magic, showing him a view
he had clearly not anticipated. The window looked out upon
the vast cavern where the followers of the intruders had been
about to attack Midanna and Sigurri, the place from which I
had been so abruptly taken. Here and there did the fighting
continue, sword to sword with more desperation than eagerness, the unmoving forms upon the stone of the floor so great
in number, that those who continued in battle were scarcely
able to move from where they stood. Those unmoving forms
upon the stone, however, were primarily leather-breeched
followers of abomination, and my spirits rose in triumph even
as the Feridani stared in disbelief. Midanna and Sigurri had
overcome those who had sought their lives, despite the beliefs
of the Feridani male, despite the numbers which they had had
to face, just as I had known they would.

"No," whispered the male, backing slowly from the window in deep shock, his head shaking in an attempt at negation. Brown-haired was that head, the staring eyes having
earlier proved themselves to be as brown, the body beneath
large and fairly wide-shouldered, yet not so large and wide-
shouldered as it had previously appeared. Indeed was the
male no different from others, and he whirled about in alarm
when the door in the wall well to my right flew inward, thrust
aside by Mehrayn and Ceralt, bloody swords bare in their
fists. Behind those two were S'Heernoh and Aram, the latter
glancing repeatedly down to the device in his hand, the eyes
of the former seeking naught save this warrior. Mehrayn and
Ceralt also looked to me briefly, saw the manner in which I
stood, then turned cold, light eyes toward the Feridani upon
whom they now advanced. With a sound of great outrage the
male turned from them, jumped back to the platform which
held the device of metal, reached quickly beneath it, then

turned again to face those who challenged him, now with a sword in his fist.

"Do you savages dare to approach *me* so?" he demanded of Sigurri and Belsayah, glaring upon the two who had not ceased in their stalking of him. "Everyone on my world learns how to use a sword, so if it's swordplay you want, it's swordplay you'll get—and learn just before you die that you can't hope to match me even in that!"

Totally unhearing and unheeding were Ceralt and Mehrayn, the words the Feridani spoke touching them not in the least. With determination did they meet the advance of the furious male, and then were all three blade to blade in battle. The two attempted to down the one quickly, offering naught of honorable battle to one from whom honor was not to be expected; shockingly, however, there occurred another thing which was unexpected. The Feridani male, attacked by two warriors, should surely have fallen, and yet after nearly a dozen strokes had been exchanged, he had not. His blade halted every attempt to reach him despite the speed and strength of the strokes brought to bear, and then did he begin to return a portion of that which he had been receiving. Mehrayn hastily slid one stroke to keep from being sliced and Ceralt staggered backward a step from the weight of the next lightning swing, both males nearly open-mouthed at the manner in which their enemy not only continued to stand, but also now carried the battle to them. I, too, felt so as I watched, yet was there one filled with greater anger than incredulity, greater impatience than awe.

"No," S'Heernoh snapped as he leaped forward to interpose his blade between Ceralt and a backswing sent by the Feridani which would surely have found its target. "You will no longer be allowed to butcher children, monster. As you are so eager to spill blood, you may attempt to spill mine."

"Yours first and then theirs, old man," snarled the Feridani, furious that his kill had been taken from him. "You'll soon find that you would have been wiser to turn and run."

Then did the male begin to advance in attack upon S'Heernoh, his rage adding strength to his arm, insolently ignoring Ceralt and Mehrayn, who had fallen back with S'Heernoh's interception. Oddly enough the gray-haired male seemed to find less difficulty in facing the Feridani than those who had stood before him, yet was I unsure as to how long the thing would continue. S'Heernoh fought with a skill I had rarely, if ever, seen equaled, and yet to consider the Feridani bested by cause of that observation alone would be foolish. I had stood about undoing long enough; there was a sword of mine waiting to be reclaimed.

With the sound of metal striking upon metal ringing sharply, I returned my dagger to its leg bands, turned from the furious exchange of attack and defense, and began looking about. The black circle remained a place I would not and could not enter, therefore did I require a thing which would enter the place for me. Odd was that chamber, filled with furs and silks upon flagstones beside devices of metal and wonder, and at first I was able to see naught which would suit my purpose. Then did my eyes fall upon a strangely even length of wood which had been placed upon a long platform holding devices of metal, as though its use had been about to be begun, yet opportunity for that beginning had not arrived. I quickly approached the platform, took up the squarish length of wood, then turned again toward the circle of black.

The wood was of just sufficient length to reach my sword, but I had to brush and scrape the weapon toward me as the sound of sword battle continued at my back, grunts and muttered curses accompanying the snarl of metal upon metal. After too many moments of frenzied scraping the hilt at last crossed the line of the black circle to where I stood, therefore did I snatch it up and whirl about—to see the final movements of the meeting between brown-haired Feridani and gray-haired Walker.

As my first thoughts were concerned with how S'Heernoh fared against the intruder, the true state of affairs did not immediately come to me; only after having sent my gaze to the Feridani, did I realize that he retained neither fury nor determination. Fear and desperation now rode the features of the male, as closely as the sweat slicking his brow, for the gray-haired male he faced had begun driving him backward, the intention to end him clear in every line of S'Heernoh's body. The teeth of the Feridani were clenched against the strength of the blows falling upon his weapon and then, despite his every effort, his blade was struck aside.

"You!" rasped the male to S'Heernoh, his eyes widened in shock, his tone disbelieving. "You're—"

The following words used by the male were totally incomprehensible, mere gibberish spouted as though they contained meaning, a doing the intruder was not long allowed to continue. S'Heernoh cut through the stream with a lunge impossible to resist, his sword burying itself in the chest of the Feridani, ending words and life alike. Despite my previous doubts upon the point, the eyes of the Feridani dulled, his sword fell from unresisting fingers, and then he crumpled to the stone of the floor.

"Magnificent," breathed Mehrayn from where he stood beside Ceralt, both with weapons still in hand yet points lowered, then did his voice raise to full glee. "Man, you were absolutely magnificent!" he laughed, moving forward with a grinning Ceralt to halt beside S'Heernoh. "Never have I seen a skill to match yours! Why haven't we seen it sooner?"

Ceralt added delighted praise to Mehrayn's, bringing S'Heernoh a much-deserved smile of satisfaction over so glorious an accomplishment; I, too, felt the same, yet was there one final matter which needed to be seen to before we might indulge in leisurely mutual congratulation. I stepped back from those three males who stood happily above the empty husk of he who had been a Feridani, gestured to Aram in a manner indicating that he was to follow me, and stepped silently from the chamber which no longer brooded with dark dread.

"What is it, Jalav?" Aram asked quietly when once he had followed me into the corridor of gray stone, his light eyes concerned. "Is something wrong?"

"Indeed," said I with a nod, working left-hand to pull the knotted leather from about my neck and cast it from me. "Soon, however, all shall be set aright, for you and I and the wonder you bear now go to seek the other of those called Feridani. You are prepared to accompany me?"

"Sure," said the male with surprised yet full agreement, his glance to the device he held reassured by the continuing cast of green. "*I'm* ready to go, but don't you think *you've* forgotten something? I mean, you don't really intend walking around like that, do you? You're not wearing anything at all."

"Coverings, like congratulations, may be left for another time," I replied with a soft sound of ridicule, already having begun leading the way up the corridor. "Should my memory of my previous time here not be amiss, we are not far from the place we seek."

The male seemed less than pleased with my reply, yet did he hasten to lengthen his stride so that he would not be left behind. We strode up the corridor toward the nearest cross corridor, paying no mind to those few unmoving forms upon the stone, and once at the cross corridor I found my suppositions had been correct. The corridor we then emerged from was one I had been forbidden to enter during my previous visit, the rock of the wall beyond it still retaining its lines of black, and from there I had no doubt as to where my destination lay. Without hesitation I turned to the left, stalking the one I had so often thought about in such a manner.

The door to the chamber stood slightly ajar when I reached it, therefore did I ease it farther open and look within before entering, Aram close behind me. The figure I sought stood before a platform which held a device of metal with a magic window, yet was the figure not as it had been when last I had seen it. Tall was that golden-haired figure, yet not so tall as I, and no other thing save its hair was golden. Light was the skin, lighter than mine amidst the clutter of a chamber also stripped of its golden glow, yet had I no doubt that here was the one I sought. The view within the magic window changed rapidly with each frantic touch of the female's hand, yet were my eyes no place other than upon her when I stepped past the threshold.

"Greetings, Mida," said I quite softly, causing the female to gasp and whirl to face me. Blue were her widened eyes rather than golden, and sight of them brought a faint smile to curve my lips.

"You!" said she in a choked voice, and then did she attempt to draw herself up. "How dare you enter these precincts without permission?" she demanded, forcing insult

to bring true outrage. "Sheathe that blade immediately and
go to your belly in apology, else shall your goddess. . . ."

"Do naught save die," I said, treading upon the balance of
her words, the prospect of pleasure rising swiftly within me.
"To battle a goddess has long been my hope and intention,
therefore would you be wise to fetch a blade. To strike you
down where you stand would remove all joy for me, yet am I
prepared to do even that."

"So you do know!" she spat, no beauty remaining in the
face which twisted with spite and hatred, her eyes now
burning with the fury she had earlier sought. "All of our
support equipment is dead, but I don't need it to finish off a
stinking savage like you! If I get nothing else out of this, I'll
at least have the satisfaction of doing that!"

Quickly did she whirl and run to the wall where hung her
golden sword, took it down with a jerk, then turned again to
face me with spiteful anticipation. It was clearly her intention
to see my blood flow to the flags, yet had I the same intention
regarding her, and my intention had surely been first aborning.

With fist tightened about hilt I advanced as she did, then
raised my sword quickly to block the first of her swings.
Great was the strength behind that swing and those which
followed, backed by the rage and spite which filled her, yet
had I expected no other thing. I, too, was filled with rage,
and the strength and speed I had ever found more than
sufficient to best any I faced now became no more than
enough, just sufficient to hold and meet this Feridani female.
So pleasurable was such a state of affairs that the purr of the
hadat rose to my throat, vocal evidence of the truest battle
glory I had ever known. Here, for the first time, was I faced
with true challenge, and to stand victorious at the end of it
would be the sole fitting testimony to true skill.

The female pressed me hard in her initial onslaught, her
golden blade seeking all about for entry to my flesh and
vitals, yet was there ever another golden blade to halt her
thrusts and slashes, the blade in my fist which she, herself,
had provided. I, too, was halted in my attempts to attack;
though while I found such halting no more than a thing to be
overcome, the female I faced looked upon her own frustration
in a different light. At first did her fury grow greater that she

was unable to reach and end me, and then did fear begin its creeping return, the fear she had felt when first she had looked upon me. I was to have fallen before the viciousness of her onslaught, and when I did not she had naught of confidence in her own skill to bolster her.

"How?" she demanded breathlessly after coming near to being spitted, stepping back in an attempt to disengage. "How are you able to stand against me? Why aren't you dead?"

Her voice had risen to a screech of pure frustration, a child being denied what she considered her due, and again a smile of amusement touched me.

"Jalav is able to stand against you, for Jalav is the chosen of Mida," I informed her as I advanced to pursue the battle. "Are you not able to recall that you, yourself, made it so?"

"You're crazy!" she cried, desperately striking my blade from her as she backed yet farther. "You're nothing but a crazy barbarian savage, and you can't. . . ."

Upon hearing the hated word "savage" yet again from the lips of one I loathed so greatly, I rose up with a fury which was impossible to control. Like one taken by a madness did I fall upon the Feridani female, swinging at head, arm, torso, and legs, and then did I strike away her blade and bury mine in her middle, bringing forth a gout of blood from her gaping mouth which her widened eyes no longer seemed aware of. No more than her death was the female aware of, and with such an awareness did she slide to the reddened flagstones, her soul, were one such as she to have a soul, already fled.

"Jalav, you did it!" cried Aram from behind me as I freed my blade from the putrid flesh of she who had dared to face me. "I don't know how you did it, but you sure as hell managed it!"

I turned then to face the wildly elated stranger male, and at that moment did S'Heernoh and Mehrayn and Ceralt make their hasty entrance, all three grim-faced and with swords in their fists. The heaviness of their breathing gave testimony of how hurried they had truly been, and although S'Heernoh carried my breech and swordbelt, he seemed unaware of the fact. All three appeared braced for further battle, and I smiled as I approached them.

"That this one was mine may not be denied," I said, handing my sword to Aram so that I might take breech and swordbelt from S'Heernoh. "You, my fine Walker of the Snows, proved how small a skill you possess by facing that other. Had I not earned the right to do the same with she who had presumed to call herself Mida?"

"Indeed," said S'Heernoh with a grin and laughter, looking down upon me as Ceralt and Mehrayn paced forward to inspect the carcass I had seen to. "Indeed was the right to it yours, lady war leader. You are not harmed in any manner?"

"Had she the heart to match her skill, it would surely have been otherwise," I replied with a headshake, finishing with my breech and beginning to close my swordbelt about me. "Think you there are others of their ilk hereabouts to be seen to, Aram?"

"I seriously doubt it," returned the male, holding my sword gingerly the while I covered myself, and then returning it with the eagerness of one who is unused to the presence of spilled blood and that which spills it. "If there had been any more of them, they would have been set up as gods right along with these two. I'd say that except for whatever mopping up is left, the battle is over—with us as the winners."

The grin of the male matched the pleasure in S'Heernoh and myself, for no longer were there Feridani about who might bring the ills of slavery to our world. Such a doing called for a victory celebration like no other ever indulged in, and surely would I have spoken of the matter had another not spoken before me.

"You heard," said Mehrayn to Ceralt, his voice calm and even as he gazed upon the second male over Mida's remains. "Our duty has been seen to, and all responsibility gone by the boards. We are now no more than two men with none looking to them for leadership."

"Indeed," said Ceralt with a matching calm, returning the gaze being sent to him, his left hand gently arest upon the hilt of his sword. "There is naught now before us of greater import than our own concerns. I regret the need, for I have come to know and respect you, yet does this matter go beyond brotherhood and friendship."

"I, too, feel regret, although you have spoken truly in
regard to our need," said Mehrayn. "To give up all claim to
a woman out of friendship to another man, is to prove that the
woman is not truly the woman of your heart. As I am unable
to withdraw, so do I recognize your inability to do the
same."

"Where shall we see to the matter?" asked Ceralt, looking
about critically at that which surrounded him. "This chamber
seems somewhat limited, and yet might it do should the
need arise."

"I have no true preference," returned Mehrayn with a
shrug, also looking about. "There are surely sufficient chambers in this place that one might be found without the clutter
of this one, and yet shall it certainly do should we find no
other to our liking."

"They can't be talking about what I think they're talking
about," said Aram softly to S'Heernoh, stepping forward to
take the place beside the Walker that I had left. Without being
truly aware of the doing I had backed from where I had
stood, surely an attempt to deny intentions which I could not
bear to accept. "We've got to do something to stop it—if
there *is* any way to stop it."

"I shall find a way," said S'Heernoh grimly, and then did
he and Aram begin walking toward the two who meant to
face one another, no matter the attempts of others. S'Heernoh
might speak and Aram might protest, yet would naught save
the death of one prevent the meeting the two intended. Truly
had I forgotten what victory in the battle might come to
mean: a personal defeat I had not the ability to face. None
might speak upon the doings of warriors, and Ceralt and
Mehrayn were warriors; as I could not speak to halt them,
neither was I able to watch the thing; even before S'Heernoh
and Aram reached the others, I turned and fled the chamber.

Corridor after corridor slipped by beneath my feet, my
surroundings doing naught to bring themselves to my attention, the illness so strong within me that I was aware of
naught else. With one hand to my middle did I stumble from
the unbearable, till at last I found myself emerging into the
vast cavern where battle had taken place. Unmoving forms
lay everywhere, some few of them Midanna and Sigurri, yet

by far the greater number of warriors sat with naught save wounds, being tended by others at the direction of Lialt and the roundish male. Blood spattered the stranger male's covering, the cloth tied about his arm saying some part of it was likely his own, but he was more concerned with those he tended. I turned to my right, away from the sight of healing, knowing full well that even the skills of the roundish male would avail naught were Ceralt and Mehrayn to face one another. One at least would surely fall, never to rise again, and the pain that thought brought me could not be borne. I had faced the one called Mida and stood victorious, and had gained naught from the doing; far better would it have been had I fallen in her stead.

After a number of reckid I halted beside the rough stone wall of the cavern, my thoughts all ajumble, the illness continuing strong within me. I knew not where I might run to escape what would surely be, where I might hide so that word of which of them had fallen might not be brought me. I lifted a trembling hand to brush away the hair which blocked my vision, then raised my head to look about to see in which direction I would next take myself. There were some few warriors about in that part of the cavern, most sitting in sets and speaking softly as they took their rest, and then my gaze fell upon one who of a sudden seemed sent by Mida herself. Galiose sat among the warriors yet was not a part of them, for he who was High Seat of Ranistard sat alone, gazing down to the stone of the cavern floor. Rest had been promised me by the spirit of Chaldrin, and surely had I now earned such a rest; Mida, in her infinite kindness, had provided the means to that rest, and I sent her my heartfelt thanks as I left the wall I had halted beside, and walked slowly toward Galiose. To be the chosen of Mida was not half so fine as to be her beloved daughter, one to whom she gives the aid of her love.

"Galiose," said I when I stood before him, looking down to where he sat. "Galiose, all battle has ended, and we now stand victorious. My warriors no longer have battle thoughts to occupy them, therefore is it necessary that I find other thoughts for them—or other battle."

The male had slowly raised his head to look upward toward me, and unreadable were the shadows darkening his eyes. A faint frown took him at my words, and he shook his head with something like annoyance.

"Should there be a thing you seek to tell me, girl, best would be you speak more plainly," said he, his tone attempting to dismiss my presence. "The battle was long, and now I wish to rest for a while without disturbance."

"Indeed is Galiose wise to rest himself," said I, insolently putting hands to swordbelt as I looked down upon him. "Such rest will stand him in good stead when my warriors and I have reached his city. I have decided that the very existence of Ranistard is offensive to me, and shall see to the offense as I have seen to all others I have come upon: I shall trample it into the ground till it is no longer offensive to any upon this world."

"You cannot mean such words," he said, paling, and then was he rising to his feet to look down at me with great hurt and disbelief. "There are innocents in my city, men and women and children who would be homeless even were they to survive! You cannot mean to attack!"

"For what reason should I not?" I asked, bringing a faint smile to my face. "What are your city folk to me? In what manner did they come to my aid when I required aid? In what manner did they seek to aid my Hosta? They shall be given the consideration given me and mine, no less—and no more."

"I see," he said with a nod, looking down at me with bitterness. "You continue to hold me culpable for that lashing. What is it you truly wish, girl? Do you seek my life in trade for the lives of those of my city? Should that be so, take it and be damned!"

"I have no interest in trading with you, male," I said to the growing fury in his eyes, holding the smile which brought him such anger. "To merely take a life is not to win it, and Midanna have no liking for such city-male doings. Should Galiose wish to aid his city he must face me, and more than that must he stand victorious. Should Galiose triumph, his city shall survive; should Jalav triumph, Ranistard will be no more. Your death will mean the death of your city as well, male, therefore may you banish all thoughts of freeing them from their fate with your lifeblood. Only by besting me shall

you find lasting safety for them, and none yet have ever
bested this warrior.''

"Till now," said he with a growl, straightening where he
stood, his eyes filled with determination. "I have no doubt
you mean what you say, therefore shall I steel myself to the
unpleasant task of butchering a female. To preserve the lives
of many the life of one must be taken, and although I shall
grieve when it is done, the grief of one is far more acceptable
than the grief of many. Where shall our meeting be, and
when?''

"Here," said I, drawing the sword I had not cleaned the
blood from, the sword I had sheathed without thought when I
fled the chamber which had been the Feridani female's.
"And now. Such long awaited pleasure should not be delayed
by even one added hand of reckid.''

"Pleasure," echoed the male with full disgust, also drawing his weapon. "Perhaps this is best after all, for one who
considers killing pleasurable will find no place for herself in
the new world which the strangers will aid us in building. Far
better you find an ending now, and be spared the pain of
knowing yourself a misfit outcast. You have my deep regrets,
wench.''

And then did the male have at me, swinging his sword with
strength and more than a modicum of skill. For one of the
cities he was adequate indeed, yet even as I kept his point and
edge from me, I knew him as less than myself. Had I truly
wished his life I would have had it, and the great startlement
he showed told me he knew it as well. No more than a dozen
strokes had we exchanged before the truth came to the male
and myself, yet are such things quickly known. I immediately
feared that the realization would daunt the male, causing him
to turn and flee from our encounter, yet was Galiose made
from other than that of the Feridani. Rather than run, the
male increased his efforts to down me, an act which pleased
me greatly and brought me respect for the male who was
High Seat of Ranistard. That respect came late was better
than not at all, most especially with so little time left.

More and more frantic grew the efforts of the male, he
barely able to keep my gently questing point from his flesh,
and then came the moment I had awaited, the moment of his

greatest effort. So swift were the movements of the male that
halting himself was no longer possible, and then did I drop
my guard and stand unprotected, welcoming the thrust of his
blade. Oddly slow was the motion of it all, the widening of
Galiose's eyes as he saw his weapon flash unimpeded toward
me, the glint of the blade in the strange light of the cavern,
and then was I struck and pierced through, just as Chaldrin
had been, just as I had wished to be. The blow was more like
that of a fist than of a blade, and as I dropped a sword grown
suddenly too heavy and sank to my knees, I wondered at the
strange lack of pain.

"No, no, what have you done?" Galiose shouted, suddenly beside himself with the upset he had vowed not to feel.
"You have made me slay you, and I cannot bear the pain!"

"You may not take the pain which is mine, male," I
whispered, finding that his sword was gone from between my
breasts, and his arm held me from the stone of the floor. I
had memory of neither thing being done, and knew pleasure
that soon all other memory would be gone as well. I looked
up into eyes from which tears fell freely, and attempted a
smile to soothe away his sadness.

"You have done me a priceless service, brother," I whispered, feeling a great lethargy creeping over me. The wetness
of my strengthless flesh gave me some small discomfort, and
my hair twisted beneath the arm of the male as well, yet did I
smile with gratitude for the gift I had been given. "Jalav is
greatly weary," I said, "and now, through the generosity of
her brother, she will rest. All debts between us are no more,
all guilt and accusations wiped away."

"Why?" asked the male in a tear-choked voice I was
barely able to hear. "You could have bested me easily, and
yet you allowed me to slay you. For what reason have you
done such a thing?"

"I could not choose between them," I said amid the
ringing I now heard in my head, surely the tolling of my
life-bell in Mida's sacred Realm. "In no matter might I
have chosen between them, and now they both shall live.
They will not face one another for there is naught to be won,
therefore shall they both live on. And I—I shall find the rest
promised me by Chaldrin."

The lips of the male parted to add words to the look of devastation he wore, yet were those words not to be uttered. Suddenly before me were Mehrayn and Ceralt, and how pleased I was to see them a final time. My vision had begun blurring with the advance of the lethargy, yet was I still able to see them, although the strength to raise caressing fingers to each of their faces was no longer present. I looked upon them with all the love I felt for them, able to hear no more than a combined mutter made up of the words they spoke, and then were they suddenly gone from before me.

In their place was the visage of S'Heernoh, the gray-haired male I had come to be so fond of. Grief twisted his features till they were nearly unrecognizable, his hands took my arms in a grip which would have been painful had I been able to feel it, and his lips parted to shout the single, strangled word, ''No!''

Yet was it past time for all denial, all hearing and speaking and feeling. The lethargy rose up to cover me with darkness, and Jalav was done with the world.

14.

S'Heernoh—
and a final solution

"Jalav. Hear me. Jalav."

The words, repeated over and over, drew me toward a consciousness I had no desire for. Much of an unreasonable invasion did the words seem, and I felt no hesitation in speaking of it.

"Jalav goes elsewhere, male," I said with words which seemed to have no substance to them. "Leave me be, now, for all my tasks have been seen to and I wish to rest."

"You shall indeed be allowed a time of rest, yet not the one you mistakenly seek, girl," said the voice, drawing me yet farther from the journey I had barely begun. "You must open your eyes and hear me, for there are matters to be settled before you begin your rest."

In growing annoyance I attempted to open my eyes as had been demanded of me, yet found some difficulty in the doing. It came to me then that I had no sense of bodily presence, that spirit alone resided in that place where I was, much as though I had gone to walk the Snows without having been aware of it. With that in mind I ceased attempting to open eyes and merely *intended* their opening, and sight came immediately, accompanied by confusion and a great lack of understanding.

I found I sat in a world all of gray, a world composed solely of mist. Even below my folded legs was there mist of gray, no more solidity in it than to myself. Perhaps a pace before me sat S'Heernoh, the sight of him confirming that it had indeed been his voice which I had heard. To his right and a bit before him sat Ceralt, to his left and also before, Mehrayn, all three entirely without coverings and weapons, as was I.

Somewhat disturbed did the Belsayah and the Sigurri seem, yet did they seem equally determined. I knew not what occurred about me, and the stares of the three males added to my confusion.

"What place is this?" I asked, finding that I spoke with something of a soundless echo, true speech when compared to what was done upon the Snows, more than odd in any other context. "Is this the Gray Place, where souls denied entry to Mida's Realm must wander forever?"

"No, no, nothing like that," S'Heernoh hastened to assure me, his gesture comforting. I saw then a portion of the oddness of speech there, for I heard the male's words with both ears and mind—the echo I had noted. Surely was there a link between that place and the Snows, yet I knew not what it might be.

"This is a place where life has never been, where even the worlds have not yet formed," said S'Heernoh, his gaze unmoving from my face. "Time moves so slowly here that it can't even be measured, so slowly that to spend a lifetime here is to pass a blink of an eye in your own world. When we return there, no time at all will have passed."

I stared upon the male with growing upset, and not for the words he had spoken, which I had scarcely understood. His manner of speech was not what it had been, a thing I had at first failed to note by cause of the strangeness of that place. Much did that manner of speech seem familiar. . . .

"Yes, you're right," said he, the wry look about him greatly aware of the manner in which I had stiffened. "My speech patterns are not what they were, and they sound like those used by the Feridani because—I am one of them."

Ceralt and Mehrayn had turned to stare upon the male as I did, the shock clanging in all of our minds, yet did the male we had known as S'Heernoh wave a hand in impatience.

"I think I should have said, 'we come from the same culture,' " S'Heernoh corrected himself, and then did his face twist in disgust. "I've lived a long time and intend living a considerable time longer, but I'd cut my own throat right now if I ever thought I'd become like those—sickeningly warped pretenders to humanity."

With a headshake and a sigh the male shifted his place upon the gray mist, and then did he return his eyes to me.

"It's painful to admit, but the fault for those—monsters can be lain at the feet of no one but my people," said he, and indeed did the admission seem painful. "We had discovered a brand-new source of energy, trans-continuum in nature— Well, let's just say we found something new, and set up a place to study it called a pilot plant. All of the studying we'd done till then assured us that the new thing we'd found was safe to handle, but what we were doing was groping blindly around the hilt of a sword, finding it easy to hold, and assuming the rest of the weapon would be the same. We were fine as long as the hilt was all we touched—but the pilot plant wrapped a firm hand around the blade we hadn't been able to see.

"There was a minor—explosion," said the male, groping for the words he required. "Even the people right near the explosion weren't seriously hurt, and we laughed with relief and congratulated ourselves, because we'd found such a *safe* source of energy. We didn't know how much of a disaster we'd created until some months later, when crippled and terribly mutated babies started to be born, all within a radius of seventy-five miles of the pilot plant. The energy burst of the explosion had been less than a minute in duration—the storm flowing from our new creation had lasted less than a reckid—and yet people as far away as from Bellinard to half way to Ranistard had been hurt by it. Not so much the people themselves, but their offspring, their babies. Some were so badly twisted by the storm that they were born dead, and they were surely the lucky ones. Some were born to constant, unending agony, some to be violently allergic to the very air they needed to live—and some were born with nothing visibly wrong with them at all.

"Although we didn't know it at first, these were the worst mutants of them all," said the male with a sigh for remembered grief. "They seemed to be fine and they grew up just like any child, but the older they got, the more—different— they became. No very young child has a conscience, that's something that has to be taught them, but these children were impossible to teach. No matter how old they got and what they were taught, they considered no one but themselves. It was always *their* comforts and *their* likes and *their* wishes which concerned them, and causing others pain and difficulty didn't bother them in the least. When their difference was noticed and they were gathered in and studied, it was discovered that they were entirely without social awareness. What benefited them was good, what interfered with their desires wrong, and nothing we were capable of could cause them to change from so socially disastrous an outlook. In our society, just as among the clans, the one who thinks of himself or herself to the exclusion of everyone else around is a danger to that society. If there's a fire and everyone cooperates, everyone gets out alive; if everyone were to try to save themselves alone, most if not all, would die."

"Indeed," said I with a nod, recalling that even children of the wild will not attack if fire roars through the forests. "Those who consider themselves above the good of the clan are quickly ended, so that they shall not give the clan more daughters like themselves."

"We made the mistake of feeling sorry for those children," said S'Heernoh, a weariness now touching him. "They had been given about half the education which they normally would have had, and it was decided not to let them have any more, but also to let them keep what they'd already been given. They were all put in a very large shelter, a place of great beauty where all their needs were taken care of, but where they weren't permitted to come in contact with the rest of society. They stayed in the shelter for many years, so many that most of us forget about them, and then one morning they were gone, they and all their belongings. They had somehow gotten access to a fleet of small ships gathered for a yearly race, had killed the owners and crew of the ships, and then had taken off in different directions. We knew then that we should have killed them before allowing them to run loose among innocent, unsuspecting people, but the realization had come too late."

"And so you now pursue them?" asked Mehrayn, clearly having followed the male's narration. "For what reason do you not ask the aid of others, others such as the stranger folk who have recently come to us? Would their wonders not make your task more easily accomplished?"

"No," returned S'Heernoh, yet gently, for he clearly had no intentions of giving insult. "The last thing we want to do is get involved with the people you come from, and I don't know if I can explain why. First let me say that the biggest problem we face is that you and we seem to share a common beginning; we don't know how that can be or even what that common beginning was, but the fact can't be denied. We all come from the same stock—but our race is many hundreds of years—kalod—older than yours."

We all looked upon the male with lack of comprehension, and this he seemed to expect. Vexation touched him briefly, causing him to run a hand through his hair.

"Picture—picture a full-grown warrior and a child just beginning to learn the skill of a warrior," said he at last, again groping for the proper phrases. "As a full-grown warrior yourself, you know that the child will reach your level of skill, but first it has to grow and learn and practice. But picture that child as one who thinks it's already fully grown, and already has all the skill there is to be had. If it sees you, so much larger and so much more skilled, its first thought might be that it will never grow to match you, no matter how long it tries, so it might as well give up even before trying. Even if the child doesn't think that, it might decide that there's no need for it to work hard acquiring what you already have, and might march up to you and demand to be given your skill without working for it. If you agree, you destroy that child as a warrior; something given is never as precious and meaningful as something gotten by one's own hard work. If you refuse, the child sees nothing but the refusal, nothing but a selfishness trying to keep a skill from others, and grows sullen with resentment. That child is now your enemy, and will never forget its hatred.

"The last thing that might happen is that as soon as the child sees you, it attacks. It knows you're larger and more skilled, and is therefore afraid of you, afraid that you'll attack first and kill it. It doesn't stop to find out how honorable you are, it doesn't ask you whether you would do something that terrible, it merely assumes you would and attacks to save itself. When it finds it can't hurt you no matter how hard it tries, it curls up in shame and total defeat, and eventually dies.''

"So the warrior may not show itself at all to the child,'' said Ceralt, his gaze unmoving from S'Heernoh, his head nodding slowly in understanding. "To protect the child, and allow it to grow to warrior size, it must be kept from knowing of the warrior.''

"Or, should it somehow learn of the warrior, it must be allowed to believe that the warrior is evil,'' said I, also gaining understanding. "To believe that the warrior is evil allows the child to look down upon her, and to strive for her downfall without generating fear or envy.''

"Exactly,'' said S'Heernoh with a smile of approval, looking at each of us in turn. "We can't ask the help of your people without hurting them terribly, and can't even use our wonders ourselves, for fear the child will see the warrior. If we were totally alien to each other we'd have less of a problem; people who don't look like you are different, so if they have more than you do, it's just an accident that you'll either ignore or work hard to match, because people different from you can't possibly be as good. It's a prejudice that helps a race survive.''

Both Ceralt and Mehrayn now nodded with understanding, following the concepts S'Heernoh presented, yet was I aware of distraction. An inner tugging fought for my attention, as though my body sought to draw my spirit back to it from the Snows, and I knew a great desire to obey that tugging. So easily might I just slide from that place, allowing it to blur and fade about me, returning to the thing I had sought so long and eagerly. . . .

"Jalav!'' came S'Heernoh's voice with a snap, returning me to the place of gray mist, in some manner blocking me from the destination I had nearly attained. The anger rose in me at such presumption, an anger which nevertheless brought little strength, and the dark eyes of the male grew soft with pain.

"I know you don't want to be here,'' said he, compassion and hurt clear in the words. "But if you go back to your body now, still feeling the way you do, you'll die no matter what anyone does to try to save you. I can force anyone else on this world to live whether they want to or not, but not you. Your mind is too strong to be forced, and nothing but your wholehearted cooperation will let me save you."

"You must listen and allow it, satya," said Ceralt, his eyes and Mehrayn's again upon me, both echoing the pain S'Heernoh showed. "We—are now aware of the reason for your doing such a thing, and have together vowed to cause you no further grief. We will both of us go our separate ways from you, never to burden you again with our presence."

"We would not have you seek death by cause of our love," said Mehrayn, the green of his eyes glistening somewhat even in that all gray place. "We will not face one another but will instead ride away, so that the woman of our heart may live."

"Won't you two ever learn?" asked S'Heernoh with a sigh as I looked down from Belsayah and Sigurri, feeling yet further of my strength slip away. "You've told her you love her, you've each told her how terrible the other one is, you've demanded that she choose between you, and you've each sworn to fight to the death for her. Now you're telling her that you've both decided to walk out of her life, but you've never once asked her how *she* feels about any of it. Don't either of you care?"

"Most certainly am I concerned over the feelings of my beloved," said Mehrayn, the calm of his voice now tinged faintly with insult. "What man would not be concerned so?"

"Indeed," said Ceralt, a certain stiffness to the agreement. "How is a man to bring his wench happiness, save that he makes himself aware of her feelings?"

"Well, I'm pleased to see that she's so much in your thoughts," said S'Heernoh, a familiar smoothness to his words above the pleasance. "Since you seem to know how important it is for a man to thoroughly understand his woman, I'm sure you both can explain her feelings to me so that I'll understand them as well as you do."

A time of silence went by, while I raised my eyes to see a Mehrayn and a Ceralt who avoided the gaze of the male who looked upon them both. Mehrayn seemed troubled and Ceralt vexed, and S'Heernoh merely sat and smiled pleasantly, patiently awaiting words which were likely never to come. I knew not what foolishness the male played at, yet had I questions which he surely would find it possible to answer.

"This forcing a return to life you spoke of—" said I, drawing S'Heernoh's immediate attention. "It was your efforts which restored Chaldrin, was it not? Never had I seen any survive such a swording, no matter their size and strength. Was it not for you, my brother would long since have fed the children of the wild."

"I knew how much he meant to you, and knew also that part of you would die if he did," said S'Heernoh with a nod, the false smoothness again gone from his voice. "I grabbed his mind and forced it to stay with his body, repaired just enough of the damage so that he could continue living on his own, then released him. Doing something like that takes a lot out of you, or I would have noticed sooner that you were gone."

"Then you did for him what the one who called herself Mida surely did for me," said I, nodding with the very edge of understanding. "When I had walked the lines for the Silla and lay dying, I, too, was given life again."

"She wasn't the one who did it," said the male, his gaze upon me wary, his words painfully slow. "I told you that the twisted children of my people were given no more than half of the education given all the rest. The half they did have covered the use of equipment of all sorts—the use of wonders— but it didn't include the most important part, the full use of the mind. Learning mind control takes a long time and a lot of hard work, and I don't believe the twisted ones would have been able to learn it even if someone had decided to teach it to them. They could operate the mechanical units that required mind control for usage, but anyone can learn that. No, neither one of them could have helped you."

"For what reason, then, did I not find an ending?" I demanded, nearly indignant over the denial the male had spoken. "For what reason was I not slain or terribly crippled?"

"For the reason that I wasn't about to let either of those things happen," said the male, again somewhat shamefaced. "I was much too far away to heal you as quickly or as thoroughly as I would have liked, but I did the best I could

with what I had. You weren't actively seeking death, then, so
I had no trouble pulling you back."

"Even *then* you watched over her?" asked Mehrayn, fully
as surprised as Ceralt and I. "Easily am I now able to see that
your assistance during our journey together was no mere
happenstance, yet am I unable to comprehend the reason for
such doings. For what reason did you give her such aid?"

"One of my reasons was the same reason your two Feridani
wanted her dead," said S'Heernoh as he looked upon me.
"Everyone who read the Snows saw the same thing, and two
of those reading it were the ones who called themselves Mida
and Sigurr. The Snows said that if Jalav didn't make the trip
to Sigurr's Peak, everyone on this planet would be lost. What
that meant was— But maybe it would be better if I started
from the beginning.

"When the twisted ones escaped from the shelter, they
didn't simply run in the first direction they saw. We discovered that they had picked their destinations carefully, from
the records we kept of your people's newest colonies. We
knew about the upheaval taking place in their Union, had
used the opportunity to look in on some of the isolated
colonies, and had found some of them, for the most part the
more primitive ones, of great interest. For their own twisted
reasons, the twisted ones chose the colonies we had been
studying, but the strongest reason was probably the knowledge that we would hesitate before showing ourselves and our
strength in those places, so they were a good deal safer than
anywhere else.

"When the two we just dealt with first came here, they
spent a good deal of time building wonders and studying the
people of this planet. When they felt they were ready they
disguised themselves as Sigurr and Mida, then began kidnap-
ping people to be their slaves and followers. This kept them
busy for an even longer time, but then one day one of their
watching devices gave them warning of a pending disaster:
the power crystals taken so long before from your ancestors'
comm were about to be found and brought together again.

"The twisted ones were absolutely furious," said S'Heernoh
with a shake of his head. "They had already begun spreading
their evil with an eye toward enslaving everyone on the

planet, and they didn't want to be interrupted by the people from the Union. They watched in near helplessness as the Silla simply handed over their crystal, raged when the Hosta's crystal was stolen—and then noticed something that calmed them a good deal. The war leader of the Hosta clan immediately mounted her warriors and rode after the ones who had stolen their clan's crystal, and that gave the two watchers an idea. The Hosta followed their goddess Mida, so why couldn't they use the Hosta to get the crystals away from those who would set them back in a comm? That was when the one calling herself Mida first began appearing to the war leader of the Hosta.''

The male looked upon me with deep compassion, yet did I continue to feel very much the fool. In no manner could I have known of the deception—however, I believed I should have known.

''When the Hosta failed to retrieve the crystals, the twisted ones were furious all over again,'' said S'Heernoh, clearly attempting to draw me from my thoughts by continuing his narrative. ''They could have warned the clan about the men coming to capture and claim them, but they didn't—and ended up paid back for their betrayal. The third crystal was found and placed with the others, and the people of the Union were contacted again after generations and generations of isolation.

''The twisted ones should have properly blamed themselves for the catastrophe, but it was easier to blame a war leader named Jalav. When she escaped over the wall of Ranistard, they made sure to subtly direct her with their long-distance speakers—right into the hands of her enemies, the Silla. As expected she was caught and badly wounded, but I made sure she didn't die the way the twisted ones wanted her to. Again they raged, unable to understand why she survived, unable to detect the efforts of one who had had much more schooling in the use of the mind. They were badly confused, and the main reason for their confusion was what they had seen on the Snows.''

Again S'Heernoh shifted in place with a sigh, and looked about at Ceralt and Mehrayn as well as myself.

''I don't know how well I'm going to do explaining this

next part," said he, looking some small bit vexed. "At this point you have to know just exactly what the Snows are, but I doubt if I can make it clear enough for you. When my people find a planet they want to keep track of, one of the first things they do is tap into a parallel sequence we discovered a very long time ago, and set up a computer watch there. This parallel sequence is a place of no doings of its own—much like the place we're sitting in right now—so the computers aren't distracted. Everything that happens is fed into the computers—computers are wonders that remember everything they're told and can keep track of all that without confusing one bit with another—everything is fed into the computers by spying eyes and ears the computer sends out, and everything learned is displayed for anyone who wants to look at it. The computer uses a special code or language, and shows every possibility it can discover from the information it's been given, as to what will happen next on that particular planet. My people are trained to read and interpret that special language, a language that was developed because of the needs of the computer, not because we didn't want anyone else getting the information. As far as we knew, no one not of our people could reach the parallel sequence *to* get the information."

"But—but that is simply untrue," said Ceralt, his brow creased with the effort to follow the obscurity spoken by S'Heernoh. "The Snows—the 'parallel sequence' has been reached by many of our people, my brother Lialt included among them."

"And the wench," said Mehrayn, nodding toward me where I sat. "She, too, is able to reach the Snows, as you know yourself, S'Heernoh."

"Yes, I do indeed know these things," said S'Heernoh, amused. "That happens to be another reason why your planet is of special concern to us. That drug your Pathfinders use—all by itself it's entirely innocuous—harmless—and can't do a thing to breach the dimensions. Somehow, though, it encourages certain of your minds to do the breaching, something my people can't accomplish until they're taught. We would love to know what your Pathfinders could do if they had the proper training—but we can't interfere to the extent of giving them that training. Your people from the Union, by the way, have never found the same ability, so if you were to mention it to them, they would have no idea what you were talking about.''

"That is truth," said I, recalling the converse with Aram and Kira. "When Aysayn and I spoke of the Snows, the strangers took the word for snow, that which falls from the skies and mounds white upon the ground. I had meant to correct their misconception, yet found no opportunity to do so.''

"It's much better that you didn't try," said S'Heernoh, a sobriety upon him, his hands clasped together before him. "Telling people about something they can't reach or see for themselves just makes trouble for everyone—or causes jealousy if they happen to believe you.

"But to continue with my story. What our twisted children had seen on the Snows was the same seen by all of your Pathfinders: if Jalav didn't make the trip to Sigurr's Peak, everyone on your world was lost. Your Pathfinders took that to be absolute, unbreakable prophecy, but the twisted children knew it for what it was: a prediction handed down by the computer based on available knowledge. It had given the prediction a high probability rating—it was guessing that what it predicted was most likely true—and that was something the children didn't understand, because of their lack of greater learning. The computer had guessed that Jalav would be needed to unite all the warriors required to find victory over the intruders, and without her the intruders would probably win. The children, however, didn't know if they would be lost right along with everyone else, and that was the only thing really concerning them. Since they had failed to kill Jalav through the Silla, they decided to wait and see what happened once she reached Sigurr's Peak. Again the one calling herself Mida pretended to be the prime mover of the entire sequence, just to make sure Jalav stayed in line.

"Once Jalav reached them, the twisted children began thinking about ways to get what they wanted through her. They had joined forces only to make things easier for themselves, not because they liked each other, and began looking for ways to rid themselves of each other, while at the same time preparing for the arrival of the people from the Union.

They made an emergency healer—a device developed for those of my people who often found themselves in dangerous and harmful situations, but who didn't have the strength to heal themselves—and placed it on her. The twisted children had twisted even that useful device, and meant to render it inoperable—turn it off—as soon as they decided they wanted Jalav dead. They expected her to come to rely on it, you see, and start taking foolish chances in the belief that whatever happened to her, it would be healed almost immediately. The one calling herself Mida hated and feared Jalav, but had to use her to get what she wanted. The one called Sigurr had decided he wanted Jalav as his personal slave, so he didn't press the point of killing her when he could have done so. Because of these two reasons, Jalav was allowed to leave Sigurr's Peak alive and unharmed.''

The male's narration had grown grim, his voice turned nearly to a growl, his gaze now inward rather than upon me. We three sat and looked upon him as he spoke, yet were we silent in the face of his anger.

"Jalav joined the nine clans of her sister group, became their leader, then led them against Bellinard," said S'Heernoh with a sigh which returned him to our midst. "Once Bellinard was secure she rode to Sigurr's city with four of the Sigurri, overcame the trouble she found there, and raised the Sigurri the way she thought she was supposed to do. The truth of it was she was never expected to be victorious with the Sigurri, and when she was, the twisted children became frightened. They thought they knew where the people from the Union would land—that's why they ordered the taking of Bellinard—and also considered the nine clans already there wild enough and blood-thirsty enough to destroy the Union people as soon as they appeared. They expected the Sigurri to take Jalav captive and hold her as a slave until the Unioners were killed, and then they would be able to reclaim her at their leisure. When Jalav emerged from it not only free but leading the Sigurri warriors as well, the twisted children decided it was time for her to die.

"The start of their plan for her death was to tell her she had to gain the leadership of the enemy clans," said S'Heernoh, his dark eyes once again resting upon me. "They used their long-speaking device to get Ladayna to steal her life sign, then arranged things so that she would follow the gray-clad, so-called warriors of the Serene Oneness. It was a trap they set and one she fell into—but they weren't including me in their planning. I helped Aysayn find the emergency healer and get it to her in time to save her life, made sure the twisted ones couldn't turn it off, then went forward with my own plans to join her traveling group. The twisted ones were now determined to see her die, and I didn't want to be too far away to prevent that."

"These—followers of the Serene Oneness you speak of—" said Ceralt, a great disturbance holding him close—"From the Sigurri have I heard other references to them, and I find myself unable to understand what occurs. I—I am a follower of the Serene Oneness, and never would I or any I am acquainted with behave as they are reported to have done. For what reason did they do such things?"

"For the reason that they were being influenced by the twisted children," said S'Heernoh, his visage again going grim as he looked upon Ceralt. "In the north there are many people who follow the teachings of the Serene Oneness, but in the south the main deities are Mida and Sigurr. The twisted children sought out every malcontent among the Sigurri, every misfit who thought he should have been chosen to be a warrior, every incompetent who blamed those around him for his own lacks, and gave them the idea of founding a city dedicated to the Serene Oneness. There were a few who tried to imbue the image of the new god with honor and strength of character, but the twisted ones preferred a god of viciousness, deceit and warped self-seeking. Their preferences won out, of course, and would have spread everywhere if the children had been allowed to continue unopposed."

"So those who follow the Serene Oneness in the north are not as those of the south," said Mehrayn, a thoughtfulness to him which seemed to be filled with gladness as well. "I had begun to suspect that that was so, yet am I pleased to have the belief confirmed."

"And I have learned that the Sigurri of the south are not like those called Sigurri beneath Sigurr's Peak," said Ceralt, returning the grin Mehrayn sent to him. "Fully as honorable as followers of the Serene Oneness are they, and this *I* was pleased to have confirmed.''

"There is a thing I fail to understand," said I, looking upon S'Heernoh, who grinned with as much enjoyment as Ceralt and Mehrayn. "As the Feridani had already decided upon death for me—and were clearly the cause of the various mishaps upon that journey—for what reason was I given into the possession of Mehrayn? And for what reason was a pit dug for me, the pit which aided me in avoiding the enemy Midanna who hunted me, and also allowed my healing? Had that pit not been there, I would surely have died.''

"That's the reason I dug it," said S'Heernoh, again somewhat discomforted. "Or, to be more accurate, the reason I had it dug. I wasn't close enough to do it myself, so I had to work through—surrogates. The procedure is prohibited except in extreme emergency, so I won't try to explain it. After you were in the pit I let the emergency healer take care of you, and merely stood guard. And, of course, when it came time to send Aysayn and his warriors after you to that village, I didn't have to check with the computer to know where you were. I was already following your every movement.''

"Then that mist upon the Snows was your doing as well," said I, suddenly seeing the point. "As the device we know as the Snows is a doing of your people, the mist must be the same.''

"No, it so happens it wasn't," said the male, surely aware of my upset upon the point. It had been the mist which had kept me from knowing of the terrible ending which had been Kalir's, due to the wearing of my life sign. "That mist was caused by the children, it being their belief that you had avoided death till then by being able to check the computer probabilities. They misted the sequence to keep you out of it, which also kept them out, but they couldn't use it to keep me out when I wasn't Walking with you. And no, I didn't know what would happen with your life sign. I don't get to check the probabilities for any longer than anyone else—the time flow in that sequence is almost as fast as the flow in this place is slow. We've discovered that having it that way is best—my people are as human as yours, and if humans are given too long a look at the possibilities of the future, they get the urge to tamper. Despite what I told you about certain happenings being so sure to come about that all branchings lead to it, that still refers only to probability. If everything continues on the way it has been going, the computer is saying, the probability of the event is so high that it's a virtual certainty. Even before Jalav was born, the probability of her achieving success in her efforts was so high that she was immediately incorporated into the computations of the computer, setting her presence so clearly into the Snows that any Pathfinder was able to see it. Her abilities plus the certainty of my protection against things she couldn't be expected to cope with did that, but that doesn't mean her success was totally unavoidable. If she had been accidentally killed in battle—highly unlikely because of her skill—or had fallen off her mount and broken her neck—again, highly unlikely—or had been ended by pure chance, the near-certain probability would have immediately been changed to absolute impossibility. *Nothing* is set immovably in the future; that's why the computer deals with certainties only after the event has already happened.''

The male looked closely upon me to be certain I had absorbed his meaning, and indeed did I feel considerably better. It had not been he who had callously contributed to Kalir's sickening ending, and the hand of the Snows was not wrapped about the throats of those who lived upon my world. No more than a mirror was the device called computer, reflecting the doings of those who lived, and then speaking of what likely would occur by cause of their own efforts. This, to me, was far more acceptable than that the Snows ruled us all, and now there was no need to contemplate the invasion of the White Land.

''Still do I fail to understand,'' said Ceralt to S'Heernoh, drawing me back from my thoughts. ''For what reason was this wench chosen to overcome all opposition, so surely that the doing was set even before her birth? That it was so is inarguable, for many Pathfinders have seen and reported the thing. And for what reason was it so certain that you would lend her your aid? Is she truly chosen by the gods, and you the guardian set to her protection?''

"Or perhaps she was meant to be yours, and for this reason you guarded her so carefully," said Mehrayn, something of desperate upset to be heard beneath his calm. "Neither Ceralt nor I were meant to have her, and we the greatest of fools for believing we might."

"No, no, that's not it at all," said S'Heernoh hurriedly, looking from one stricken face to the other. "You're both wrong—and now I'm going to have to tell you certain things I had hoped to be able to gloss over. Ah well, no sense fighting the inevitable. If it hadn't come up now, you would have thought of it sooner or later."

"You must try to understand how really long a time I've been here," said S'Heernoh, once again gazing solely upon me. "A lifetime for my people is much, much longer than a lifetime for yours, even your kin from the Union, because we've learned full mind control. When you can heal injuries and illness in yourself, you can also stop and reverse the clogging of your arteries, the thinning of your blood, the wearing out of your organs. Growing old is a disease we don't let ourselves suffer from—until and unless it's what we really want. I've been here long enough to see your ancestors get cut off from the Union, to see the women who took the power crystals form a protective group that practiced with primitive weapons so that they couldn't be forced to give up what they'd stolen, and then to see them argue and split into two independent groups; to see men leave the rest of the colony in disgust and build their own city, in anger over the colony's refusal to go after the crystal-stealing women and force them to return the crystals. The rest of the colony didn't believe in violence of any sort, and insisted on waiting until the women returned the crystals without being forced to it. By the time others took over who weren't quite so patient, the crystals and the reason for their return were a foolish memory of fairy tales fit only to be laughed at.

"The women grew to be warriors who called themselves Midanna, after the group named Mida their founders were members of. The men who founded their own city also became warriors, calling themselves Sigurri after their first leader, Sig Uris. Those who were the remaining members of the colony, lacking the 'purpose' of the other two groups, merely began spreading out, caring very little about their fellow man. They fought among themselves and cheating became a way of life—and the computer said that if something wasn't done, the probability of their wiping themselves out was so high that it was a virtual certainty.

"You must understand that if not for that, I wouldn't have interfered," said S'Heernoh, now all but begging understanding. "They had to have purpose, something to believe in, something honorable to emulate. I—went down among them, won a wary respect by showing I could be as violent and unethical as they were—then began showing them a better way. It took awhile, but by the time I left there were enough converts to the ethical way of doing things that I knew the concept wouldn't die out—and neither would the people. After a number of years, they even changed my name by spreading it around word-of-mouth. They called their deity . . ."

"The Serene Oneness, for S'Heernoh!" I exclaimed, aware of the manner in which Mehrayn—and certainly Ceralt—now looked upon the third male. "S'Heernoh has no meaning, yet Serene Oneness—"

"Yes, that has meaning," said S'Heernoh with something of a smile, looking toward neither male who looked upon him. "At any rate, once I got myself involved with the people of this world, the computer calculated the possibility of my doing it again, then added me into its calculations. I'd found a great attraction in the women called Midanna, you see, and the computer decided it was only a matter of time before I went to look at them more closely, so to speak. It turned out that the computer was right."

"Wait, wait!" cried Ceralt, his agitation overflowing into words. "We are to believe that *you* are the Serene Oneness? *I* am to believe—Jalav! He has said that your Mida is no goddess! Will you merely sit there and accept such a thing as truth without protest?"

"Perhaps—I have suspected the thing for some time," I informed him with a shrug, looking to the upset in the blue of his eyes. "Often in my kalod have I called to Mida—yet never was I truly answered till the answering came from one of evil, one I would not have had be Mida even if Mida were to be no more. One finds it great comfort to call upon the

goddess, yet did I triumph when the need arose without such
calling. Perhaps Mida is truly a goddess and caused those
before us to name their gathering after herself—and perhaps
she is no more than the yearnings of those who need to follow
one greater than themselves. What matters it, when it is we,
ourselves, who do what must be done? Should the doing be
honorable, what difference if it be done in Mida's name, or
Sigurr's—or in the name of the Serene Oneness?''

Ceralt stared upon me with brow furrowed, Mehrayn did
the same, and S'Heernoh with a smile of great warmth. My
words appeared to have affected all of the males, yet S'Heernoh
seemed affected the least.

"Yes, to behave honorably is the important part," said he,
nodding in agreement. "I hope you understand that that's
exactly what I was trying to do—no matter how upset you get
with me."

I frowned and attempted to question the male, yet did he
wave a hand in dismissal.

"You'll understand what I'm talking about in just a little
while," said he, and the amusement which was so much a
part of him twinkled again in his eyes. "I kept myself out of
the doings of this world for quite a while, indulging in
nothing more than observing and studying, and then one day I
got the urge to walk a planet again for a short while. There
was nothing unusual in the feeling, I'd had it before and had
indulged it before, but this time I suddenly found myself
riding the part of your world that starts south of the Dennin
river. At the time I didn't realize what I was doing, thought I
was just out to stretch some muscles that had gotten rusty
from lack of use—and then I came on a raiding party of men
who had cornered a handful of Midanna and were trying to
capture them. As soon as I saw the Midanna I knew I ought
to get out of there, but they were badly outnumbered, and I
was already there. . . .

"Needless to say, I didn't turn around and ride away. I
joined the fight on the side of the Midanna, and when it was
all over the raiders were either dead or gone, and I had
managed to get myself wounded. Probably by trying to fight
and stare at the women both at the same time. I wasn't so
badly hurt that I couldn't heal myself, but I didn't want to do

it in front of the women and start talk that could end any-where, and the women refused to let me simply ride away. I'd been wounded trying to help *them*, and they were honor-bound to return the favor. We all mounted up, and they took me back to their home tents.

"One of the five warriors took me into her own tent and saw to my wound, then made sure I didn't need anything while I was recovering. She had black hair and green eyes, and was absolutely the most delightful female I'd ever spent any extended time with. At first we just talked, then we went hunting together, cooked together—and finally made love. Not just sex, mind you, but love. I wanted to stay forever, and she wanted me to stay, so we both knew it was time for me to leave. She rode part of the way with me, kept a hand raised in farewell as long as I could see her—and never mentioned that I'd left something behind it had never oc-curred to me I might. Her name was Jadin, and her clan was the Hosta."

With great confusion did I stare upon the male who sat with head bowed, lost in the pain of memory, for Jadin had been the name of she who had borne me. Indeed had she had black hair and green eyes, and yet—

"Your seed!" exclaimed Ceralt, again looking strangely upon S'Heernoh. "It was your seed you left! Then Jalav is—"

"My daughter," said S'Heernoh, raising his head once more to smile despite the glistening in his eyes. "A daughter who was able to take my revenge for me from those who had brutally slain my beloved who was her mother. I watched it all, her birth and growing up, her becoming war leader, the beginning of the search for the crystal— My people have developed a greater strength and speed than yours, and my daughter inherited enough of that to make her a better warrior than anyone else on the planet. Do you wonder now why the computer gave her the probability it did? Or why it was so sure I'd never let her be hurt?"

"I see," said I of a sudden, recalling the words spoken to me by Rilas, when she had first been shown S'Heernoh in Bellinard. "It was for that reason that Rilas recalled you, yet not as one unskilled and swordless. Clearly were you pointed out to her as she was told of what you had done. Yet you assured Rilas that you and she had never met.''

"I wasn't lying,'' said he, a twinkle again in the dark of his eyes. "I told the Keeper that I had never before been introduced to her, which was the literal truth. I saw her once when she visited the clan, obviously the same time she saw me, but we were never introduced.''

"And now do I see a thing as well,'' said Mehrayn, a chuckling beginning in him. "I had thought it fear of myself and Ceralt that had caused you to refuse to attend the wench in Bellinard, yet when I saw your blade skill with the Feridani, it came to me to wonder upon the thing. Now do I understand the doing completely.''

"Indeed,'' said Ceralt with a similar chuckle, S'Heernoh joining them both, yet was I unable to see what amused them.

"As you all are aware of a thing I am not, perhaps you would care to enlighten me,'' I said rather stiffly, disliking such amusement of males even at a time such as that. "I shall undoubtedly find the reason for a male's refusal of a war leader most—enlightening.''

"Satya, he could do no other thing than refuse you,'' said Ceralt with a laugh of disbelief, Mehrayn also mockingly amused. "Have you not heard his words? It was he who fathered you.''

"Well aware am I of the fact that it was he who was the sthuvad who served she who bore me,'' said I with a nod which was also quite stiff. "Am I to believe him so badly overtired from the doing that he is unable to now do the same again? Do you take me for a credulous city female?''

Ceralt and Mehrayn looked upon me gape-mouthed, for some reason unable to find words with which to reply to my queries, yet S'Heernoh was not the same. The gray-haired male threw his head back and laughed so gustily that tears came to his eyes, a doing which occupied some few reckid. When at last the great mirth began to leave him, he looked upon the other two males and shook his head.

"Have you forgotten that the word 'father' means nothing to Midanna?'' he asked the others, bringing wry looks to them. "It isn't surprising her mother told her nothing about me; as a child she wouldn't have understood what her parents had come to mean to each other. As far as she's concerned I'm just someone who happened to know her mother, even if that applies in every sense of the word. Midanna share their men, so why shouldn't she have her share of me? I don't expect her to understand the point, any more than I expect her to listen to what I say without a good deal of struggle.''

"You know she refuses to obey men," said Mehrayn slowly, looking upon S'Heernoh with a stare of thoughtfulness. "Also was there a question of hers which you have not yet answered. I had thought the omission an oversight, yet does it now seem— The time in the caves, the time of the storm, when I addressed her lady and asked to possess her— It was not the Feridani female who caused the life sign to glow. The doing was yours.''

Ceralt joined Mehrayn's stare with a frown and I did the same, only then recalling that S'Heernoh had indeed failed to speak upon the point of my having been given to Mehrayn. The gray-haired male looked up toward me from beneath his brows, his head somewhat lowered.

"I think I'm caught," said he at last, his entire attitude an admission of guilt. "I was hoping none of you would pick up on that, but— The whole affair was so painfully unnecessary that I couldn't stand to let it go on. You were sending Mehrayn away from you to protect him, Jalav, but he wasn't in the danger you thought he was. I kept track of him while we rode through the forest, gently guiding his kan where I wanted it, coaxed those lenga into our path to make us turn aside, then stole that storm from elsewhere and set it over us. Getting you and me into the same cave wasn't hard, nor was bringing Mehrayn in after us. If you had been reasonable about things I never would have played that trick with your life sign, but you weren't being reasonable, and I became annoyed, and then Mehrayn asked his favor—'' The male shrugged, a corner of his grin slipping through, his gaze now directly upon me. "The next time your father suggests something to you, you might recall what happens when he becomes annoyed.''

Great outrage and indignation took me then, the sort which sent my left palm to seek a hilt which was no longer upon me, yet Mehrayn saw none of it. His gaze had remained locked to S'Heernoh, and of a sudden a great happiness took him.

"You are father to her, and you granted her to me!" the Sigurri exclaimed in sudden revelation, straightening where he sat. "Blessed Sigurr sustain me, for I had never thought to see it so."

"Hold, hold," protested Ceralt in distress as S'Heernoh turned to look upon Mehrayn. "I, too, was granted the wench, and that before you. Has he not said that he watched over her? In my village did I draw her from the circle, proclaiming her mine, and naught was done to prevent it. I, too, was granted her, only first!"

There came then a great babble of words as Mehrayn and Ceralt both spoke at once, yet had I already looked down to my hands, so that I need not allow the thing to touch me. No longer did I need to concern myself, for S'Heernoh had said I might not be forced from the path I had chosen. A long moment passed all wrapped in the babble, and then did a silence ensue.

"It seems you two still haven't learned to ask my daughter what *she* wants," came S'Heernoh's voice, far graver than it had been. "Everyone else has had their say, Jalav. Why don't you take your turn?"

"Jalav deserves no other thing than the rest promised her by Chaldrin's spirit," said I, continuing to look down and away from those I had no wish to look upon. "Release her now, male, so that her weariness might at last be seen to."

Again a silence fell, one containing the feel of motion upon the air, and then a sigh came which was clearly S'Heernoh's.

"That wasn't Chaldrin's spirit, daughter mine," said he, the weariness within me apparently having touched him as well. "I needed something to pull you out of that uncaring, horribly wounded and defeated mood you'd fallen into, so I used an image of Chaldrin to reach you. Give me just a little while longer, and maybe we can get this worked out."

The male paused after having spoken softly, yet when his words resumed, even I looked up in surprise.

"I've had more than enough of this childish bickering!" he snapped, his anger unquestionably directed toward Ceralt and Mehrayn, the sternness of his glare bringing a wilting to the two, as though they were possessed of too few kalod to stand their ground against him. "Are you men in name alone, that you act so foolishly? Don't you know what you're doing to the girl you claim to love?"

"I make no claims," said Mehrayn with more than a shade of diffidence, then did he force a partial return of his usual calm. "Merely do I state my love, for the fact that it is. Should you see this as the doing of less than a man, I will face even you in defense of it."

"And I," said Ceralt, as disturbed as Mehrayn, yet also as calm. "There is naught more precious to me than the wench of my heart, and I will face any man who attempts to say other than that."

"Men in love are damned fools," said S'Heernoh bluntly to the two, looking upon each of them in turn, his palms pressed to his knees. It came to me then to wonder for what reason he alone seemed able to move somewhat in the cross-legged seated position we all had been given, yet did his continuing words make the thought a fleeting one.

"Men in love are damned fools," said he, "but that doesn't mean they have to abuse the privilege. If you spent half the effort thinking things through that you put into challenging each other and everyone else in reach, you would have had this all straightened out long ago. You've both been avoiding the most pertinent questions involved here; I can understand why, but that doesn't mean I'm going to let you continue avoiding them. Once they're answered, you should see the truth as easily as I do."

Both Belsayah and Sigurri seemed unsure as to what their response might be, yet were they given no time for a response. S'Heernoh shifted in place yet again, and this time no more than his glance touched me.

"Before we go any further, I think I'd better admit that a good part of the trouble you've had is my fault," said he, the words an admission not easily brought forth, his gaze now avoiding those he addressed. "I've told you that I watched over my daughter, but there were times that was all I *could* do—watch. While she was being put through—things no father should allow to be done to his daughter. If I had been an ordinary man I wouldn't have had to allow them, but because of who and what I am, my daughter had to pay a certain price. It made her stronger, I know, and also know it was necessary, but part of me doesn't want to know those things. Part of me wants to apologize for something that can't ever be excused—in the sort of lame way I'm doing right now—for letting her be hurt so badly that she'll likely see reflections of that pain in every man she looks at for as long as she lives. Some day you may understand, I hope you do, but until then—''

The words of the male ended abruptly, falling into the silence of confusion which we others felt, then did he straighten himself where he sat and turned brisk once again.

''All right, enough of that,'' said he, giving his gaze to the others again. ''No need to go on about what caused the problem; what we need are some answers for it. Now, both of you want my daughter so badly you can't bring yourselves to allow her to have her choice in the matter, isn't that true?''

''Most certainly not,'' said Mehrayn, his sudden stiffness a clear indication of insult. ''The wench has been coaxed and invited any number of times to choose between Ceralt and myself, yet does she continue to refuse.''

''Even has she vowed that she shall speak no choice,'' said Ceralt, somewhat less offended than the Sigurri. ''Were we to accept such a dictum?''

''Perhaps not,'' said S'Heernoh with a faint smile, continuing to look between them. ''But I'd like you both to keep in mind what you just said, while we go on to the next point. When you discussed why she started that fight with Galiose, you both said you were willing to give her up so that she might live. Despite the words exchanged between you just a short while ago, do you still feel the same?''

''For her life, yes,'' said Ceralt heavily, Mehrayn silently anod to show agreement with the words. ''We neither of us would consider turning from her for a lesser reason, yet for her life—yes.''

''Good,'' said S'Heernoh with a nod to match Mehrayn's, his tone now encouraging. ''You don't want to give her up, but you will if that's what's needed to save her life. Now comes an even more important question: would you both *refuse* to give her up, if that was what was needed to save her life?"

"Your words hold no meaning," protested Mehrayn, the bewildered look upon Ceralt saying the same. I, too, felt bewildered, yet was S'Heernoh amused.

"Let me put it another way," said he, again with smoothness. "You said she refused to make a choice. If she makes one now, will you both abide by it?"

Again were the two males silent, this time as they looked upon one another with less full agreement than there had been, yet did they both at last nod their heads.

"Should the wench make a choice, we shall abide by it," allowed Mehrayn for the both, no lightness to be heard in his tone. "It is certain Ceralt feels as I do, yet shall we abide by the decision for her sake."

"Excellent," said S'Heernoh, beaming upon the two as though he saw naught of their grimness. "In that case, as my daughter's father, I'll announce her decision for her."

Perhaps the male believed there would again be silence at his pronouncement; was such the case, he surely felt unexpected disappointment. Both Mehrayn and Ceralt began shouting at once, outrage clearly in the fore, the clamor so great that the words I, myself, meant to speak were buried beneath it. S'Heernoh held up both hands for silence.

"You object?" he asked, looking from one to the other. "Hasn't a father the right to make such a choice for his daughter?"

"When you have already allowed him to claim her in his village?" demanded Mehrayn in a growl, looking coldly upon S'Heernoh.

"When you have already given her to him in a cavern in the woods?" asked Ceralt in the chill, soft way he had.

"Then it seems I've already made a choice," said S'Heernoh, continuing to divide his look between them. "One, I might add, my daughter agrees with. Do we have your agreement as well?"

Mehrayn looked upon S'Heernoh narrow-eyed, Ceralt stared in a manner which suggested S'Heernoh had lost his wits, and I silently watched them all, wondering upon what the gray-haired Walker this time attempted. His dark eyes strove to mask the usual amusement he showed with easy questioning, yet was the amusement still clearly there.

"Well?" said S'Heernoh after a brief time of waiting, his tone indicating expected agreement. "Do you approve of my choice?"

"Perhaps my wits are not quite as swift as I had thought," said Ceralt slowly, leaning somewhat back where he sat. "Although you claim to have chosen, I am able to see naught save that you have indicated . . ."

"The both of us!" said Mehrayn in great upset, also straightening where he sat. "You cannot mean. . . ."

"Why not?" pounced S'Heernoh gently yet implacably, while I merely stared. "My daughter has refused to choose between you because she *cannot* choose; it isn't possible for her to turn her back on either one of you. You both said you would give her up if that would save her life, and I asked if you would refuse to give her up for the same reason. She would rather die than go on without the two of you. Will you let her die?"

The eyes of the two males came to me then, both silently demanding to know what truth had been in S'Heernoh's words. Never would I have found it possible to say the thing of my own self, yet with it already spoken I could not deny it. Indeed did I desire them both, more than life itself, and naught of goddess-demand stood between us. No more than the views of the males themselves stood between us, a far greater barrier than any goddess-made.

"You can see just by looking at her that I've told you the truth," said S'Heernoh, sobriety returned to his voice. "You can also see that she doesn't expect you two to agree. She expects you to hold fast to your prejudices—and let her die."

"No!" said the two males at once, both greatly angered, then did it come to them what they had said. They looked upon each other warily, doubt strong in their eyes, and S'Heernoh voiced a sigh of vexation.

"Stop looking at each other as if you're absolute strangers," he said, annoyance now coloring the words. "You know you've learned to respect each other, that you're both men of honor. Hasn't it occurred to either of you yet that if something happens to one of you, that one can at least be sure he won't be leaving his beloved alone to fend for herself? That she'll still have the other to stand beside her?''

"Indeed is such a thing worth knowing," said Ceralt with a nod, Mehrayn appearing surprised—and unexpectedly pleased in his surprise. "A man need not fear his own fate with the fate of his beloved happily seen to."

"And yet are there other things which might concern a man," said Mehrayn, his pleasure quickly fading. "To be pleased that another sees to his woman after his end, is not to be pleased upon the same point while he lives. To share a slave with others is no more than meet; to do the same with the free woman you have chosen and love—"

"Does having to share her mean your love has to lessen?" S'Heernoh demanded, his voice and eyes sharp. "If it does, it can't have been much of a love to begin with. If it doesn't, then no more than some small part of your pride is hurt, a part that will heal rather quickly. Would you rather lose her entirely than share her? Would you rather see her dead than occasionally in the arms of another man? She's a warrior who would never even consider limiting your needs; will you thank her by trying to limit hers?''

Soberly had Mehrayn listened to the words of S'Heernoh, his eyes troubled, and then did his gaze clear. Slowly and firmly did he shake his head, showing that the decision he had reached had been difficult yet surely *was* his decision, and a warmth and gladness I had not expected filled me. When his green gaze came to me and saw my smile, all doubt vanished from it as though the thing had never been. When we turned then to look upon Ceralt, we found that S'Heernoh already studied his frown.

"Different men, different worries," said the gray-haired Walker, nearly in a murmur. "You have no problem about sharing her with another man, but sharing her life with the life of a warrior is another story, isn't it?''

"Indeed," said Ceralt with a heaviness seemingly demanded of him. "To share her love with another man is still to retain it; to share her with the life of a warrior is far too likely to lose both love and her—in the same swordstroke."

"I can't argue that," said S'Heernoh, his tone filled with compassion. "The life of a warrior is dangerous no matter how skilled you are. The thing that has to be remembered here, though, is that the life of a warrior is what made her what she is, what made her into someone who attracted you in the first place. If you take that away from her, will you still have what you fell in love with? Is it fair to punish her for being the very person you want? If the most important thing in *your* life was taken away, would you want to continue living?''

The blue-eyed gaze of Ceralt had come to me as S'Heernoh spoke, and for a moment after he ceased there was naught save the stare, seeking to read my soul. Then Ceralt heaved a deep sigh, and smiled a smile which warmed as few before had done.

"To keep the thing of greatest importance in my life, then, I must risk it," said he, his gaze unmoving from my face. "Should there need to be the pain of loss, sooner would I have that pain be mine. I will make no effort to keep her from the life of a warrior.''

"Then we are all in accord," said Mehrayn with a grin, looking between Ceralt and myself, yet did S'Heernoh immediately shake his head with the accursed amusement which so often filled him.

"Not quite," said the gray-haired male, this time sending his full attention to me. "When a compromise is necessary, *everyone* has to compromise, otherwise the whole thing falls apart. Well, daughter? Are you ready to do your part?''

"I know not which part you refer to," I replied, disliking the manner in which his demand brought annoyance to the limitless joy which had come to me. Odd had the male S'Heernoh ever been, and odd did he remain.

"I'm referring to your part of the agreement," said he, the words slow and deliberate as he leaned forward to emphasize them. "Mehrayn is giving up his demand to keep you all to himself; in fairness he shouldn't have to share you with anyone but Ceralt. Ceralt is giving up his demand that you leave the life of a warrior behind; in fairness he should have your word to avoid seeking trouble. If trouble comes to you that's a different story, but riding out deliberately to seek battle has to be out.''

"What, then, might be left of the life of a warrior?" I

demanded, dismayed at the instant eagerness to be seen upon
Ceralt and Mehrayn. "You now attempt to take what was
given me by these others!"

"Not without being willing to give something in return,"
said he, his grin in no manner encouraging. "The life you
knew as a warrior has already been doomed, and not only by
the arrival of those from the Union. Do you think many of the
Midanna will find it possible to return to fighting between the
clans, now that they've fought beside one another? How
many of the Midanna and Sigurri will be willing to give each
other up? You three intend forming your own family; do you
expect to do it in Ceralt's village? In Mehrayn's city? In your
home tent? What will happen once those of the cities begin
learning 'civilized' ways from the Union?"

Ceralt, Mehrayn and I exchanged glances, yet were we
unable to answer the queries S'Heernoh had put. What, indeed, would become of us?

"Stop looking so stricken, all of you," said S'Heernoh
with moderate amusement, allowing his eagerness to gleam
forth. "Why do you think I've told you everything I have?
Just to drop you in an unsolvable muddle? Don't you realize I
have a solution?"

"And what shall it be necessary to give up for that solution?" I asked, in no manner willing to tender the male more
than he had already taken. "Should it be our souls, the price
has already been exacted."

"Your souls are yours to keep," said S'Heernoh with a
laugh of greater amusement, truly taking joy from his doing.
"Your bodies and minds are what I want, to train in mind
control—which is the key to reaching and retrieving everything my people have ever learned and developed—and to
explore the newness you've developed. You won't enjoy
what the Union has to teach, and you won't be able to use it.
What I have to teach is something else again, and may even
provide some adventure. Now, let me think. We'll tell Aram
you survived that wound most likely because you were so
near to the emergency healer main console apparatus that it
picked you up without the receptor unit. Once we get back
we'll gather up all the Midanna and Sigurri who want to start a
new life, find our own place in the wilderness, then start

teaching and testing. We'll have to make sure the Unioners don't get curious, of course, but that won't be very. . . ."

The words of the male continued on in thoughtful planning, yet did my eyes go to Ceralt and Mehrayn, whose eyes had already come to me. So eager was I to be with them that even would I allow S'Heernoh his plans—certainly to begin with. Should the time prove uninteresting or too filled with annoyance there would surely be other things to occupy a warrior, and even, perhaps, with the aid of Galiose's male, Phanisar, as I no longer needed to stand as war leader, a daughter. . . .

AN OPEN LETTER
TO THE AMERICAN PEOPLE

Astronauts Francis (Dick) Scobee, Michael Smith, Judy Resnik, Ellison Onizuka, Ronald McNair, Gregory Jarvis, and Christa McAuliffe understood the risk, undertook the challenge, and in so doing embodied the dreams of us all.

Unlike so many of us, they did not take for granted the safety of riding a torch of fire to the stars.

For them the risk was real from the beginning. But some are already seizing upon their deaths as proof that America is unready for the challenge of manned space flight. *This is the last thing the seven would have wanted.*

Originally five orbiters were proposed; only four were built. This tragic reduction of the fleet places an added burden on the remaining three.

But the production facilities still exist. The assembly line can be reactivated. The experiments designed for the orbiter bay are waiting. We can recover a program which is one of our nation's greatest resources and mankind's proudest achievements.

Soon Congress will determine the immediate direction the space program must take. We must place at highest priority the restoration and enhancement of the shuttle fleet and resumption of a full launch schedule.

For the seven.

In keeping with their spirit of dedication to the future of space exploration and with the deepest respect for their memory, we are asking you to join us in urging the President and the Congress to build a new shuttle orbiter to carry on the work of these seven courageous men and women.

As long as their dream lives on, the seven live on in the dream.

SUPPORT SPACE EXPLORATION!

Write to the President at
1600 Pennsylvania Avenue,
Washington, D.C. 20500.